The gray-haired noble reached the top of the tower a few seconds later. The other lords barely noticed as he entered the room. They were too busy overwhelming Cheng Han with contradictory advice. Hsuang slipped to the window, peered out, then swore a vile curse in the name of the Celestial Dragon.

The Tuigan had resorted to magic. A single barbarian stood in front of the two thousand horsemen gathered on top of the smoky knoll. The man was dressed in a long silk robe covered with mystic symbols. In his hand, he held a scepter capped with a human skull. The barbarian's arms were lifted skyward and his eyes were fixed on one of the fires.

The shaman had magically braided the smoke from all fifty cooking fires together. The smoke columns now formed a wide gray ribbon that stretched from the hilltop all the way to Shou Kuan. The smoky bridge crossed the city wall directly over the gate, just a few yards to the right of the bell tower.

As Hsuang watched, the first horsewarriors spurred their mounts toward the hazy bridge. The frightened animals reared and tried to shy away. The determined riders kicked the beasts and lashed them with their reins, guiding the horses onto the gray ribbon as if it were solid rock. When their hooves found solid purchase on the smoke, the horses calmed and began galloping forward. The riders dropped their reins, then pulled their bows from their holsters and began to nock arrows.

Hsuang turned to his fellow nobles. "Get to your armies!" he yelled. "The Tuig

THE EMPIRES TRILOGY

HORSELORDS
David Cook

DRAGONWALL
Troy Denning

CRUSADE
James Lowder

FORGOTTEN REALMS

FANTASY ADVENTURE

Dragonwall

The Empires Trilogy: Book Two

Troy Denning

Cover Art
LARRY ELMORE

DRAGONWALL

Distributed to the book trade in the United States by Random House, Inc., and in Canada by Random House of Canada, Ltd.

Distributed in the United Kingdom by TSR Ltd.

Distributed to the toy and hobby trade by regional distributors.

FORGOTTEN REALMS, PRODUCTS OF YOUR IMAGINATION, and the TSR logo are trademarks owned by TSR, Inc.

First Printing: July, 1990
Printed in the United States of America.
Library of Congress Catalog Card Number: 89-51889

9 8 7 6 5 4 3 2 1

ISBN: 0-88038-919-2

TSR, Inc.
P.O. Box 756
Lake Geneva,
WI 53147 U.S.A.

TSR Ltd.
120 Church End, Cherry Hinton
Cambridge CB1 3LB
United Kingdom

Respectfully dedicated to Mr. Dallas,
and to all educators who care enough
to make a difference.

Acknowledgements

Without the support of many close friends, writing this book might well have proven to be a task beyond me. I would like to thank Jon Pickens and David "Zeb" Cook for granting access to their extensive libraries; Jim Ward for his wonderful suggestions and comments; Jim Lowder for his insight and diligence; Curtis Smith for advice on things oriental; Lloyd Holden of AFK Martial Arts in Janesville, WI for his expertise; and most especially Andria Hayday, for her gentle critiques, constant support, and unending patience.

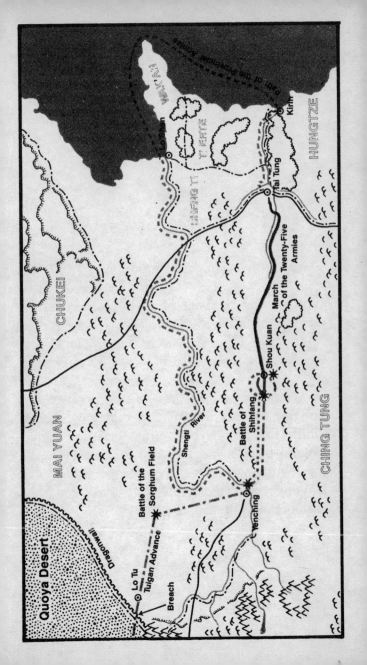

- 1 -

The Minister's Plan

The barbarian stood in his stirrups, nocking an arrow in his horn-and-wood bow. He was husky, with bandy legs well suited to clenching the sides of his horse. For armor, he wore only a greasy hauberk and a conical skullcap trimmed with matted fur. His dark, slitlike eyes sat over broad cheekbones. At the bottom of a flat nose, the rider's black mustache drooped over a frown that was both hungry and brutal. He breathed in shallow hisses timed to match the drumming of his mount's hooves.

As he studied the horsewarrior's visage, a sense of eagerness came over General Batu Min Ho. The general stood in his superior's roomy pavilion, over a mile away from the rider. Along with his commander, a sorcerer, and two of his peers, Batu was studying the enemy in a magic scrying basin. Physically, the barbarian looked no different from the thieving marauders who sporadically raided the general's home province, Chukei. Yet, there was a certain brutal discipline that branded the man a true soldier. At last, after twenty years of chasing down bands of nomad raiders, Batu knew he was about to fight a real war.

Batu forced himself to ignore his growing exhilaration and concentrate on the task at hand. Staring into the scrying basin, he felt as though he were looking into a mirror. Aside from the barbarian's heavy-boned stature and coarse mustache, the general and the rider might have been brothers. Like the horseman, Batu had dark eyes set wide over broad cheeks, a flat nose with flaring nostrils, and a powerful build. The pair was even dressed similarly, save that the general's *chia*, a long coat of rhinoceros-hide armor, was nowhere near as filthy as the rider's hauberk.

"So, our enemies are not blood-drinking devils, as the peasants would have us believe." The speaker was Kwan Chan Sen, Shou Lung's Minister of War, Third-Degree General, and Batu's immediate commander. An ancient man with skin as shriveled as a raisin's, Kwan wore his long white hair gathered into a warrior's topknot. A thin blue film dulled his black eyes, though the haze seemed to cause him no trouble seeing.

By personally taking the field against the barbarians, the old man had astonished his subordinates, including Batu. Kwan was rumored to be one hundred years old, and he looked every bit of his age. Nevertheless, he seemed remarkably robust and showed no sign of fatigue from the hardships of the trail.

Resting his milky eyes on Batu's face, the minister continued. "If we may judge by the enemy's semblance to General Batu, they are nothing but mortal men."

Batu frowned, uncertain as to whether the comment was a slight to his heritage or just an observation. An instant later, he decided the minister's intent did not matter.

Settling back into his chair, Kwan waved a liver-spotted hand at the basin. "We've seen enough of these thieves," he said, addressing his *wu jen*, the arrogant sorcerer who had not even bothered to introduce himself to Batu or the others. "Take it away."

As the *wu jen* reached for the bowl, Batu held out his hand. "Not yet, if it pleases the minister," he said, politely bowing to Kwan.

Batu's fellow commanders gave him a sidelong glance. He knew the other men only by the armies they commanded—Shengti and Ching Tung—but they made it clear that they felt it was not Batu's place to object. They were both first-degree generals, each commanding a full provincial army of ten thousand men. In addition, both Shengti and Ching Tung were close to sixty years old.

On the other hand, Batu was only thirty-eight, and, though he was also a first-degree general, he commanded an army of only five thousand men. In the hierarchy of first-degree generals, the young commander from Chukei clearly occupied the lowest station.

Nevertheless, Batu continued, "If it pleases Minister Kwan, we might benefit from seeing the skirmish line again."

Kwan twisted his wrinkles into a frown and glared at his subordinate. Finally, he pushed himself out of his chair and said, "As you wish, General."

Batu was well aware of the minister's displeasure, but he was determined not to allow an old man's peevishness to drive him into the fight prematurely. The surest way to turn a promising battle into an ignominious defeat was to move into combat poorly prepared.

The *wu jen* circled his bejeweled hand over the basin, muttering a few syllables in the mysterious language of sorcerers. As the barbarian's face faded, a field covered with green-and-yellow sorghum appeared. Along its southern edge, the field was bordered by a long, barren hillock. A small river, its banks covered with tall stands of reeds, bordered the northeastern and eastern edges. Swollen with the spring runoff from far-away mountains, the river was brown and swift.

The only visible Shou troops were Batu's thousand archers, who had formed a line stretching from the river to the opposite side of the field. Each man stood behind a chest-high shield and wore a *lun'kia*, a corselet that guarded his chest and stomach. Made of fifteen layers of paper and glue, the *lun'kia* was inexpensive and remarkably tough armor. The archers' heads were protected by *chous*, plain leather helmets with protective aprons that covered both the front and back of the neck.

Even through the scrying basin, Batu could hear the tension in his officers' voices as they shouted the command to nock arrows. The archers were unaccustomed to being left exposed, for in previous engagements the general had always supported them with infantry and his small contingent of cavalry. This time, the rest of Batu's army was hiding behind the hill, along with twenty thousand men from the armies of the other two provincial generals. These reinforcements were ready to charge over the hill at a moment's notice.

The archers were bait, and they knew it. If the battle proceeded according to Minister Kwan's plan, the barbarian cavalry would sweep down on them. As the horsewarriors massacred the archers, the twenty-four thousand reinforcements would rush over the hill and wipe out the invaders in one swift blow. The plan might have been a good one, had the horsemen been the unsophisticated savages Kwan imagined.

But the enemy showed no sign of taking the bait. So far, all they had done was ride forward and shoot a few arrows. When the archers returned fire, they always turned and fled.

As Batu and the others watched, a subdued and distant thunder rolled out of the scrying basin. A moment later, two thousand horsemen rode into view on the northern edge of the field, five hundred yards from the archers. At first, the dark line advanced at a canter. Then, at some unseen signal, all two thousand men urged their mounts into a full gallop.

The minister and the generals leaned closer to the scrying basin, watching intently. Two hundred and fifty yards out, the barbarians began shooting. Few of the shafts found their marks, for firing from a moving horse was difficult and the range was great. Still, Batu found it disturbing that any of his men fell, for he did not know a single Shou horseman who could boast of hitting such a distant target from a galloping mount.

Although they were equipped with five-foot *t'ai po* bows that could match the barbarians' range, Batu's archers held their fire. They had been trained not to waste arrows on unlikely shots and would not loose their bamboo shafts until the enemy had closed to one hundred yards. The horsemen continued to advance, pouring arrows at the Shou line in a haphazard fashion that, nevertheless, dropped more than a dozen of Batu's men.

Finally, the horsewarriors came into range. The Shou fired, and a gray blur obscured the scene. A thousand arrows sailed over the sorghum, finding their marks in the barbarian line. Riders tumbled from their saddles. Wounded horses stumbled, then crashed end-over-end as momentum carried them forward after their legs had gone limp.

Through the scrying basin, Batu heard the screams of dying men and the terrified shrieks of wounded horses. It was not a sound he enjoyed, but neither did it trouble him. He was a general, and generals could not allow themselves to be distressed by the sounds of death.

The Shou archers fired again. Another gray blur flashed across the field, then more shocked yells and frightened whinnies drifted out of the basin.

"Look!" said Shengti. "They're not breaking off!"

He was right. The barbarians had ridden through two volleys of arrows and were continuing their charge. Batu's stomach knotted just as if he were standing with his men.

"Shall we attack?" asked Ching Tung. He had already turned away from the scrying basin and was moving toward the door.

Noting that none of the riders were drawing their swords or lances, Batu grasped Ching Tung's shoulder. "No!"

As Ching Tung turned to face him, Batu continued, "They're only testing our formation's discipline. If they had intended to finish the charge, they would have drawn their melee weapons by now."

Ching Tung's eyes flashed. He started to say something spiteful, but the thunder in the scrying basin suddenly died. The resulting quiet drew all eyes back to the pool. The generals saw that the enemy horsemen had reigned their mounts to a halt at fifty yards. Batu would have given ten thousand silver coins to know how many more barbarians lurked out of the scrying basin's view. It was a question he knew would not be answered. Kwan's *wu jen* had already explained that his spell had a range of only two miles.

Another gray blur flashed over the field as the barbarian riders fired in unison. The Shou archers, who had been drawing swords and preparing to meet the charge, were not prepared for the attack. Dozens of arrows struck their marks with quiet thuds. Over a hundred men cried out and fell to the flurry.

Batu's troops were well disciplined, however, and a volley of Shou arrows answered a moment later. Another wave of terrible screams and whinnies followed, and the general from Chukei could almost smell the odor of fresh blood.

For several minutes, gray clouds of arrows flew back and forth as the two lines traded volleys. At such close range, arrows penetrated armor as easily as silk. Hundreds of Batu's men fell. Some remained silent and motionless, but most writhed about, screaming in pain and grasping at the feathered shafts lodged in their bodies.

After every volley, a few Shou survivors threw down their weapons and turned to flee. Without exception, they were met by officers who cut them down with *taos*, single-edged, square-tipped swords. Batu disliked seeing his officers dispatch his own men, but he detested watching soldiers under his command turn coward and flee. As far as he was concerned, those who dishonored him by running deserved to perish at the hands of their own officers.

Another Shou volley struck the barbarian line. Hundreds of men fell from their saddles or leaped away as their wounded horses dropped thrashing to the ground. Batu noticed that behind the enemy line, no officers waited to cut down cowards. There was no need. Despite the heavy casualties, not a single barbarian panicked or fled.

"The barbarians outnumber our archers two-to-one," observed Shengti. "Why don't they finish their charge?"

"Because they are unsophisticated savages who have never faced soldiers as disciplined as those in the Army of Chukei. They are frightened," Minister Kwan responded, gracing Batu with a commending smile.

Despite the compliment, the old man's rationalization

alarmed Batu. If Kwan could not see that the enemy was as well disciplined as any Shou army, he was not fit for his position.

"Minister Kwan," Batu asked, "was the Army of Mai Yuan not disciplined?" He inclined his head slightly, trying to make his point seem a genuine question.

"The enemy took Mai Yuan by surprise," Kwan responded, an edge of irritation in his voice. "General Sung could not have known they would breach the Dragonwall."

"If I may," Batu responded, taking pains to keep his face relaxed and to conceal his growing vexation, "I would suggest that if the barbarians surprised Mai Yuan, they can also surprise us. It would be a mistake to underestimate their sophistication or their bravery."

The wrinkles on Kwan's brow gathered into an angry gnarl, and he glared at Batu with his cloudy eyes. "I can assure the young general that I would make no such mistake."

As Kwan spoke, the enemy cavalry wheeled about and rode for the far side of the field. When his officers showed the proper restraint and did not pursue, Batu breathed a sigh of relief. From the behavior of the barbarians, the young general suspected the horsewarriors were trying to lure his men into a trap.

More than three quarters of Batu's archers, over seven hundred and fifty, lay wounded or dead. As military protocol dictated, every third survivor tended to the injured, dragging those who could not walk away from the battle line. The other survivors stood ready, prepared in case the enemy suddenly returned. The number of casualties unsettled Batu, for the heavy losses reflected too well on the accuracy of the enemy bowmen. Nevertheless, he was also proud of his troops' bravery and discipline.

As the barbarian cavalry rode out of the scrying basin's range, Kwan pointed a wrinkled fingertip at the bowl. "Do you see, General Batu?" he asked. "There is no need to worry about the barbarians. They are frightened of your archers, and with good reason." The old man pointed to where the enemy horsewarriors had stopped and traded arrows with the Shou archers.

What Batu saw disappointed him. Dozens of injured barbarians were limping or crawling out of the field. Dazed and wounded horses hobbled about without direction. From beasts and riders too injured to move came a torpid chorus of groans and wails, and nearly two hundred enemy warriors did not move at all. Still, Batu estimated the invaders' casualties at under five hundred, less than two-thirds of his own. His men had not even given as good as they'd received.

"Your archers have been too devastating," Kwan continued, ignoring the scrying basin. "Send a runner. This time, your archers must let the barbarians complete the charge."

Batu's jaw dropped, for the minister was wasting what remained of his limited supply of archers. "Perhaps the minister's eyes are not as sharp as they once were," Batu said, barely able to keep his voice from trembling with anger. "Or he would have noticed that my archers did not stop the last charge, and could not stop the next one if the enemy walked their horses into battle!"

Kwan's response was measured and cool. "My eyes are sharp enough to know when we have the enemy in our grasp. Your *pengs* are a tribute to your discipline," the minister said. The term he used could mean weapon, common soldier, or both, reflecting the opinion that soldiers *were* weapons. "They deserve the empire's praise," Kwan added. "But if we send reinforcements now, my young general, the barbarians will smell our trap and flee. Without horses, we'll never catch them."

"The enemy's nose is sharper than you think," Batu retorted. "He has already smelled the trap, and he is stealing the bait while we watch." Batu looked at his fellow generals. "If the horsewarriors are such fools, wouldn't they have committed themselves by now?"

Neither general answered. They were unwilling to contradict the logic of their young peer, yet unwilling to support him. The Minister of War disagreed with Batu, and the older generals knew it would not be prudent to contradict their superior. As the two men looked away, Batu recognized their caution and realized that he could expect no help from them. He wondered if they would prove as unsupportive on the battlefield.

For a moment, the minister regarded Shengti and Ching Tung thoughtfully. Finally, turning back to Batu, he said, "It is possible that you are correct, General. If there is not enough bait, the rat may smell the trap. So we will increase his temptation."

The concession surprised Batu, and he wondered if it should have. Although it was apparent that the minister lacked battlefield experience, it was equally obvious that only a shrewd politician could have reached such a high post. It seemed to the young general that Kwan had interpreted Shengti's and Ching Tung's silence for what it was. Batu allowed himself the vague hope that Kwan's supervision would not result in a disaster after all.

While the young general considered him, Kwan studied the scrying basin. Finally, the old man pointed a yellow-nailed finger to where the end of the archer's line met the river. "General Batu, take your army and reinforce your archers," the minister said. "Anchor your line here, at the river, and deploy as if expecting a frontal attack. Leave your western flank exposed."

A knot of anger formed in Batu's heart. He openly frowned at the minister, hardly able to believe what he had heard. "If I do that, the barbarian cavalry will ride down the line and drive my army into the river."

"Exactly," Kwan said, pulling his gray lips into a thin smile.

Shengti studied the scrying basin for a moment, then said, "A brilliant plan, Minister! The sloppy deployment will lure the enemy into full commitment. As the barbarians roll up Batu's flank, my army—along with the Army of Ching Tung, of course—will charge over the hill and smash them."

The ancient minister smiled warmly at Shengti. "You are very astute," he said. "Your future will have many bright days."

And my future will be very short, Batu thought. Shengti

had neglected to mention the most clever part of Kwan's plan: a troublesome subordinate would be destroyed. Even if Batu did not perish during the slaughter, the stigma of losing an entire army would destroy his career.

Still, even knowing the consequences, Batu's instinct was to follow the order without question. To his way of thinking, soldiers were dead men. Their commanders simply allowed them to walk the land of the living until their bodies were needed in combat. In that respect, Batu considered himself no different from any other soldier, and if Kwan ordered him to meet the enemy naked and alone, he would be obliged to do so.

Still, a soldier was entitled to the hope of a glorious end. The young general could see no glory in allowing the horse-warriors to slaughter his army like so many swine, especially when Kwan had not taken the time to scout the enemy and could not be certain that anything useful would come of the sacrifice. Hoping to convince the generals from Shengti and Ching Tung to come to his aid, Batu decided to point out Kwan's sloppy preparations.

"While your plan has many things to recommend it, Minister," he began, "I must point out that it may result in the destruction of my army without accomplishing the emperor's will."

Kwan settled back into his chair, placing his elbows on the armrests and lacing his fingers in front of his body. "Please proceed, General," he said, looking Batu in the eye with a milky but steady gaze. "I'm sure we're all interested in your opinion."

The general from Chukei looked at his two peers. They stood well away, their expressionless attention politely fixed on his face. After taking a deep breath, Batu turned back to Kwan. The minister had shifted his gaze to a space just over his subordinate's head.

"You're underestimating the barbarian's strength and sophistication," Batu said. "By exposing my army's flank, you're assuring its pointless destruction."

The minister's expression did not change. He simply sat

quietly, waiting for his subordinate to continue, as if what he had said so far was of no consequence.

Batu pointed toward the battlefield. "You're assuming the barbarians have no plans of their own, and that they'll walk blindly into any trap you lay." The young general waved his hand at his two peers. "If the enemy outnumbers us, its flank guard will engage the armies of Shengti and Ching Tung on the hilltop. They'll never reach the battlefield."

Kwan remained motionless and silent, his attention fixed somewhere behind Batu's head. At first, the young general wondered if the minister had heard a single word. Finally, however, he realized that what Kwan had or had not heard did not matter. Batu had secured his superior's animosity when he had dared to disagree with him. It appeared that Kwan's retaliation would be swift and ruinous.

Realizing that more hasty words would only make the situation worse, the general from Chukei held his tongue and tried to think of a way out of his difficulty. Fortunately, if all Kwan wanted was to be rid of him, Batu thought that he could salvage a respectable death from his predicament.

Bowing very low, Batu said, "Minister, I have asked many impertinent questions, and for that I deserve punishment. But no soldier deserves a worthless death. Allow me to probe the enemy's strength, so that you will know exactly what Shou Lung faces."

For the first time since Batu had begun his protest, Kwan looked directly at him. The minister's expression seemed almost sympathetic. Speaking very slowly and earnestly, the old man began, "General Batu, we have no need to waste time probing that band of thieves. As for any punishment you may deserve, my decision is strictly a military one. It has nothing to do with your imagined rivalries."

Batu could hardly believe what the minister was saying, especially with such an honest expression. If Kwan were lying, he was the best liar the general had ever met. If the old man was sincere, he was the biggest fool Batu had ever encountered.

Before Batu could respond, the minister continued. "Now,

tell me why you believe there are so many sophisticated savages out there."

A lump rose in Batu's throat. The little information he had about the barbarians was far from what could be considered solid or reliable, but he felt confident it surpassed what anyone else in the tent had gathered.

"First," Batu began, "let's consider the enemy's strength. We know that there are at least one hundred thousand barbarians, for it would have required that many to destroy the Army of Mai Yuan. Eyewitness accounts of the battle suggest the actual numbers are far greater."

"An army looks much larger when it's overrunning you," the general from Ching Tung objected. "Those reports are exaggerated."

"Are they?" Batu asked. "For several years now, there have been rumors that Yamun Khahan has been uniting the horse tribes. If this is true, and what we learned at the council in Semphar suggests it is, the barbarians could be fielding close to two hundred thousand troops."

Ching Tung scoffed. "Two hundred thousand! I doubt there are that many men in all the horse tribes together."

"How many miles of horse tribe border do you patrol?" Batu asked, eyeing the other general sharply.

Raising a hand to silence Ching Tung, Kwan intervened. "No one will contest that you patrol more horse tribe border than any of us, General Batu. Please proceed."

"For hundreds of years, tribes of horse barbarians have been crossing the Chukei border to plunder. Their raiding parties have always been small, so we've never had trouble chasing them out. Note that I did not say tracking them down. The barbarians have always been cunning thieves, and more often than not it's all we can do to drive these bands out of the province. When we do catch them, they fight hard and shrewdly, and they never expect or give mercy."

"Yes, we know this. What is your point?" Kwan pressed, shifting in his chair impatiently.

Batu hesitated. This next point was his most critical, and it was the one most likely to bring ridicule down on his head. Nevertheless, if he stood any chance of convincing his peers not to dismiss the barbarians lightly, it was a point he had to make.

After a deep breath, he continued. "You may have noticed the resemblance between the barbarians and myself."

Ching Tung snorted. "How could we miss it?"

Batu suppressed a heated reply. Instead, he said, "My great-grandfather was a Tuigan, as the barbarians call themselves. He settled in the province of Chukei after his clan was destroyed in a tribal war."

"How bold of you to admit it," Shengti said.

The condescension in Shengti's voice was nothing new to the general. Although most Shou prided themselves on lack of prejudice, they made no secret of the fact that they considered all other cultures inferior to their own. As a result, they could not help but look down on those who appeared to be anything less than full-blooded Shou.

The general continued. "While I was growing up, my great-grandfather spent hours telling me stories of life among the nomads. Of course, I can't remember all his tales, but what I do remember is frightening."

"Such as?" Kwan asked. His attention remained fixed on Batu, but it was difficult for the young general to tell whether the minister was genuinely interested or just humoring a condemned man.

"Tuigan tribes are devoted to one thing and one thing only: making war. Their children ride horses before they can walk, and fire bows at full gallop before their beards start to grow. When they're not at war with civilized lands, they're fighting clan feuds so bloody that whole tribes are slaughtered. For fun, they gather hundreds of warriors and massacre every living beast within ten square miles."

"Brawlers and hunters are a poor match for trained soldiers," Ching Tung interrupted.

"You have heard my words, but have you been listening, General?" Batu asked, motioning at Ching Tung sharply. "I am saying that our enemies are born killers with no concept of mercy or surrender. If someone has trained them, given them focus, Shou Lung is in much greater danger than it has ever been in before."

Ching Tung sneered. "Trained armies cannot be made from murdering scum—"

The ancient minister raised his hand for silence, then turned to Batu. "What would you suggest, General?"

"That we proceed with more caution on our first engagement," Batu responded. "Setting traps is fine, provided you know what you are hunting. But the man who sets a fox snare and catches a bear may be the one who gets skinned."

"So what would you suggest?" Kwan asked.

Delighted and surprised by Kwan's unexpected solicitation of his opinion, Batu answered rapidly and enthusiastically, "A series of probing attacks, followed by rapid withdrawals, at least until we know the size and nature of our enemy."

Kwan nodded, then stroked his beard thoughtfully. Finally, he pushed himself out of his chair and squinted into Batu's eyes. "I thought as much," he said. "You speak to us of rumors and hunting parties, then tell us we should withdraw to a safe distance while the enemy burns our fields and sacks our villages. What you propose is not the way of an imperial officer, General Batu. An imperial officer's way is to meet Shou Lung's enemies and crush them in the name of the emperor!"

Batu stared into the minister's eyes for several seconds, but knew he could not make the heat of his anger felt through the milky film that shielded Kwan's eyes from reality. Finally, the general said, "Smashed armies crush no enemies, Minister."

Kwan's face grew red, and his wrinkles squirmed like worms. For an instant, Batu thought the old man would erupt into a fit of screaming, but the minister slowly regained control of himself. After a moment, in a carefully measured voice, Kwan asked, "Will you lead your army into battle, General Batu, or must I find a loyal soldier to take your place?"

Batu answered immediately. "I'll go. If my army is to perish, then I will be the one who leads it to its destruction."

As suddenly as it had contorted, Kwan's face relaxed, and the minister tottered over to the young general's side. He laid a shriveled hand on Batu's shoulder. "Good," he said. "My plan will work. Before you realize what is happening, we'll charge down the hill and this band of thieves will trouble the emperor's sleep no longer. You'll see."

– 2 –

The Sorghum Field

Batu stood, calm and motionless, midway up the hill that marked the trampled field's southern border. The air carried the sweet, grassy smell of young sorghum and the coppery odor of fresh blood. Overhead, the sky spirits were sweeping away the clouds on a cool breeze, and the sun cast a keen light over the field. The general felt lively and limber, his *tao* sword hanging lightly in its scabbard of manta skin. The letter he had written to his wife was in his pocket, ready for the messenger. Today was a fine day to die, the best he had seen in many years.

A young, beardless Shou stepped to Batu's side and bowed. "General, your army is deployed."

The speaker was Batu's adjutant, a junior officer named Pe Nii-Qwoh. The adjutant wore a complete suit of *k'ai*, armor consisting of hundreds of metal plates sewn between two layers of heavy silk. The velvet-trimmed suit had been brocaded with brightly colored serpents, tigers, and phoenixes. His helmet plume consisted of two kingfisher feathers with a pair of fighting dragons carefully embroidered into the feather vanes.

In sharp contrast, Batu's battle dress consisted only of his drab, rhinoceros-hide *chia*. As a general, he rarely engaged in hand-to-hand fighting and had no use for such heavy armor. The weight of a *k'ai* suit would only fatigue him during the battle without providing much benefit.

The general's disdain for heavy armor wasn't uncommon.

Farther down the hill were twenty lean men wearing no armor at all. They stood at attention, their eyes fixed on Pe and Batu. The men were the runners who carried orders from the general to his subordinate commanders.

The messengers reminded Batu of his letter to Wu, and he removed it from his pocket. He started to give it to Pe, then decided to read it one last time.

Wu, it began simply, *We have met the barbarians and are preparing for battle. They promise to be a fine enemy. Although Kwan Chan Sen refuses to admit it, there will certainly be many illustrious battles in this war.*

However, I fear the best of them will be fought without me. My loose tongue has offended the minister, and he has sent my army to perish ignominiously. May he spend eternity lying face down in wet sand. Death is too good for the fool who deprives me of fighting in this magnificent war!

Enough of my troubles. You know where our gold is hidden, so you will not suffer for my absence. Our time together has been blessed, and you have provided me with a beautiful daughter and a strong son. I will miss them both. You have been a good wife, and I depart in comfort, knowing you would never dishonor my memory by taking a lover.

Your worthy husband, Min Ho.

Satisfied that the letter said everything he meant it to, Batu folded it and gave it to his subordinate. "For the messenger," he said.

Pe bowed and accepted the paper. He did not ask where to send it, for the letter was an old ritual. In their marriage vows, Lady Wu had made Batu promise to write her before each battle. So far, it was a promise Batu had kept faithfully, as he had all the other vows he had ever taken.

Pe withdrew a similar paper from his own pocket. The young officer did not usually write his parents before battle. On Batu's suggestion, he had made today an exception.

As his adjutant took the letters down to a runner, the general studied the scene in front of him. From the hillside, he could oversee the entire battle. The field was larger than

Batu had guessed from the scrying basin. It was in a valley located between two small hills. Batu stood on one of them, and the other was six hundred yards to the north. At that moment, the general would have given the lives of a hundred *pengs* to know what was hiding behind the northern hill.

On the east, the field was entirely bordered by the river. One thousand yards from the water, the western edge faded into weeds and wild grasses. Judging by the sorghum field's size, it belonged to some wealthy landlord who employed an entire village to cultivate it.

Pe returned. Glancing down at Batu's army, he asked, "Do you wish to make any adjustments?"

Batu smiled and studied his adjutant's concerned face. "Pe, if you don't speak openly today, you never will."

The adjutant returned Batu's smile with a tense grin. "Please forgive me, my general," he said. "I was wondering how you intend to cover the flank."

Pe pointed at the western edge of the field. Then, as if Batu could have possibly missed the source of his concern, he said, "It remains unguarded."

Batu grinned. Even when ordered to speak frankly, the boy could not help but couch his criticism in the most inoffensive language possible.

"General?" Pe asked anxiously. "Any adjustments?"

Raising a hand to quiet his adjutant, Batu surveyed his army's deployment. He had pulled the surviving archers off the front line and stationed them nearby, where they could tend to their wounds until the battle grew desperate. Below the archers, five hundred cavalrymen stood with their horses, nervously rubbing their mounts' necks or feeding them young blades of trampled sorghum. Batu had often wished for more cavalry, and could certainly have used them today, but Shou Lung's ancient grain fields produced barely enough food to feed the country's human population. A large cavalry was a luxury the army had not enjoyed for nearly a century.

Thirty yards in front of the cavalry was the *feng-li lang*, the ritual supervisor assigned to Batu from the Rites Section of the Ministry of War. The *feng-li lang* was supposedly a shaman who could communicate with the spirit world, but Batu had yet to see the man procure the aid of any spirits.

The *feng-li lang* and his assistant were digging a six-foot-deep hole in the field's sandy, yellow soil. Though Batu did not understand the purpose of the hole, he knew that the pair was preparing a ceremony to ask for the favor of the spirits dwelling in the battlefield. Batu had his doubts about the value of nature magic, but the *pengs* clearly did not share his skepticism. In order to lift the morale of his troops, the general participated in the *feng-li lang*'s pre-battle rites whenever possible.

In the center of the sorghum field were thirty-five hundred infantrymen. They were standing in a double rank along the same line the archers had occupied during the initial skirmish. The common soldiers carried standard imperial-issue crossbows. Straight, double-bladed swords, called *chiens*, hung at their belts. For armor, the *pengs* relied on *lun'kia* corselets and plain leather *chous*. The officers were all attired comparably to Pe, with brightly decorated suits of plated *k'ai* and plumed helmets.

As Pe had observed, the left end of the infantry flank was open to attack. Normally, Batu would take advantage of some terrain feature to protect this vulnerable area, or at least he would cover it with a contingent of archers or cavalry. But Kwan's orders were clear, and the general was too good an officer to disobey. Even a bad plan was better than a broken plan, which was what they would have if Batu did not do as instructed.

Batu ran his eyes down the length of the line, studying the route he expected the enemy cavalry to follow. As the enemy charged, the *pengs* on the left flank would fall, leaving other men exposed. Batu would supply some covering fire with his archers, and his cavalry would mount a counterattack that might slow the charge for a few moments. Still, the Tuigan horsewarriors would smash the line, killing all thirty-five hundred infantrymen.

Batu considered the possibility of issuing an order he had never before given: retreat. If his troops fell back before the charging Tuigan, his army stood a better chance of remaining intact. The reprieve would be a short one, the general knew. As the line curled back on itself, his entire force would be trapped in the reeds along the riverbank.

"And then the slaughter would begin," Batu whispered to himself, picturing the rushing floodwaters red and choked with the bodies of his soldiers.

"Forgive me, General. I didn't hear your order," Pe said.

"It wasn't an order," Batu responded, still eyeing the rushes and the river. "I said, 'And then the slaughter would begin. . . .'" The general stopped, still picturing his army floating down the river—but this time, they were alive. "Unless we can walk on water."

Pe frowned. "Walk on water?"

Batu did not have an opportunity to explain. The *feng-li lang's* assistant arrived, his crimson robe soiled from digging. Bowing to Batu, the boy said, "General, my master requests your presence at the offering."

"Tell the *feng-li lang* that I don't have time," Batu replied tersely, still studying the marsh along the riverbank.

The assistant's jaw dropped. "General, if the earth spirits are not appeased, they will resent having blood spilled on their home."

Pointing at the flooded river, Batu said, "I don't care about earth spirits. Those are the spirits we must appease."

The boy frowned in puzzlement. "But—"

"Don't question me," Batu said. "Just tell your master to make his offering to the river dragon."

When the assistant did not obey immediately, Batu roared, "You have your orders, boy!"

As the youth scrambled down the hill, Batu turned to his adjutant and pointed to the marsh. "Send the cavalry and the archers into those rushes. Until the battle begins, they are to busy themselves cutting man-sized bundles of reeds. Tell them to make certain the bundles are tied together securely."

Pe furrowed his brow, but, after the treatment the *feng-li lang*'s assistant had just received, he did not risk questioning Batu. "Yes, General."

"Next, get out of your *k'ai*. Leave it on the ground. We don't have time to send it to the baggage train."

"This armor has been in my family for three hundred years!" Pe cried.

"I don't care if it's been in your family for three thousand years," Batu snapped. "Do as I order."

"I can't," Pe said, looking away. "It would disgrace my ancestors."

"And execution would not?" Batu retorted, touching the hilt of his sword.

Pe glanced at Batu's hand, then met his commander's gaze squarely. "My honor is more important than my life, General."

"Then do not stain it by disobeying me," Batu replied, moving his hand away from his hilt. As if Pe had never refused the command, he continued. "Send orders to the line officers to remove their *k'ai* as well. They are not to resist a flank attack. When it comes, they are to retreat to the marsh. We will move our command post down there, which is where they will receive their new directives."

Pe looked at the reed bed and frowned. "We'll be trapped against the river!"

Batu smiled. "That is why you and the other officers must remove your *k'ai*."

Pe lifted his brow in sudden comprehension, then grimaced in concern. "General, the river is flooding. You'd be mad to ford it under pursuit!"

"Let us hope the barbarians believe the same thing," Batu replied. "Give the orders to the runners, then wait for me at the marsh."

Pe started to bow, but Batu caught him by the shoulder. "One more thing. In case their *k'ai* has also been in their families for three hundred years, remind the officers that my orders must be followed. Anyone who disobeys will be remembered as a traitor, not as a hero."

"Yes, General," Pe replied, finishing his bow and turning to the messengers. His attitude no longer seemed defiant, but Batu knew his adjutant was far from happy about the commands he had been given.

As six runners relayed the orders to the field officers, Pe headed for the reed bed. The general stayed on the hill a while longer to observe the adjustments. When the archers and cavalry left their positions, hundreds of baffled faces glanced up toward him. Batu thought the cavalry and archers probably realized that they had been assigned to prepare a retreat. What they could not understand, he imagined, was why. In the eight years Batu had commanded the Army of Chukei, it had never retreated. But it had never faced a capable enemy, or been used to bait an ill-prepared trap before either.

The general knew that Kwan might be correct and the Tuigan force might amount to no more than fifteen or twenty thousand untrained men. Still, everything he knew about the enemy, as little as it was, suggested otherwise. Only a leader of considerable intelligence and cunning could have breached the Dragonwall. After that, it would have required a large force to annihilate the Army of Mai Yuan, to say nothing of exploiting the victory by ravaging the countryside for hundreds of miles around. The most convincing evidence of the enemy's competence was the fact that there would be a battle today. Only a well-organized war machine could have been ready to attack less than two weeks after smashing the Dragonwall and the Army of Mai Yuan.

It was the kind of fight Batu had been hoping for all his life, and the prospect of its impending commencement made his stomach flutter with delight. The general from Chukei had always dreamed of winning what he thought of as "the illustrious battle," a desperate engagement against a cunning and powerful enemy. Of course, Batu had not expected his own commander to be the reason his situation was desperate, and he did not think that retreating could be considered illustrious. But if his plan worked, Batu hoped to preserve enough of his army to fulfill his dream another day.

After the archers and cavalry left for the reed bed, the infantry officers began removing their *k'ai* and stacking the various pieces in neat piles. They stared at Batu with expressions he could not see from such a distance, but which he imagined ranged from simple anger to outright hatred. Without exception, he was sure each officer would rather have died than dishonor his family. The general was also sure the officers would do as ordered, for disobeying a direct order would be treason, a stigma far worse than dishonor.

Nevertheless, the general could understand their anger. Like them, he valued his honor more than his life, but he could not allow them the luxury of keeping their heirlooms. Without its officers, an army was no more than a jumble of armed men, and any officer wearing *k'ai* was sure to perish in the retreat Batu was planning.

A dark band appeared atop the opposite hill. From this distance, it was impossible to see individual figures. What Batu could see, however, was that the line consisted of two or three thousand horses. The alarm went up from his lookouts. His troops prepared for combat, making last-minute prayers to Chueh and Hsu, the gods of the constellations governing crossbows and swords.

For his part, Batu merely prayed that Kwan and the others were watching the scrying bowl.

The distant rumble of drums rolled across the field and the line advanced slowly. The drums, Batu realized, were used to coordinate the enemy's maneuvers. He stayed on the hill while the horsemen advanced another hundred yards. The drums boomed again, and the enemy broke into a trot. A ridge of tiny spikes protruded from their line like the spines on a swordfish's dorsal fin. This charge, Batu realized, would be a real one. The spikes could only be lances, and lances meant the Tuigan intended to fight at close range.

What Batu did not understand was why the barbarians

were approaching frontally. No tactician could miss the exposed flank. It was possible, the general realized, that the enemy had guessed that this was a trap. If that were the case, he did not understand why they were attacking at all. Yet, the only other explanation was that the enemy was as foolish as Kwan suggested. That was a possibility Batu preferred to ignore, for it would mean he had sacrificed his career for nothing. More important, it was dangerous to belittle one's adversaries. As the ancient general Sin Kow had written, "The man who does not respect his foe soon feels the heel of the enemy's boot." Batu's own experiences bore out Sin Kow's words.

The drums sounded again and the Tuigan horses broke into a canter. Batu decided to send a message to his officers warning that the frontal attack might be a diversion. Since Pe was already down at the marsh, Batu went to the runners' station. There he sent six runners to issue the warning, cautioning his officers to stay in position until attacked on the exposed flank. After the runners had left, he sent the remainder of the messengers to Pe. He lingered on the hill several moments longer, then followed.

By the time he reached the tall stalks at the edge of the rushes, the barbarians had closed to three hundred yards. The drums broke into a constant roll, and the enemy burst into a gallop. The general remembered that he had not helped to appease the river dragon. He hoped the river spirit, if it really existed, would be satisfied with the *feng-li lang's* ceremony alone.

Pe stepped out of the reeds, a half-dozen messengers at his back. "Every archer and horseman has made three bundles," the adjutant reported. "Their officers wish to know if they should take up their weapons now."

"No," the general replied, his eyes locked on the barbarian charge. "Have them continue making bundles until I give the order to stop."

Pe arched his eyebrows, but immediately turned and relayed the message.

As the enemy charge advanced, Batu watched the wall of

flashing silver and dark flesh with a mixture of awe and horror. The Tuigan rode like spirits, remaining balanced despite bone-jarring jostles and jolts as their mounts leaped across the field. In their left hands, the warriors held iron-tipped lances, and in their right they held curved sabers. The reins hung loose over the necks of their horses. The riders used their knees to direct their beasts and screamed blood-chilling war cries that drowned out even the constant tumult of the drums.

In groups of twenty or forty, Batu's men began firing volleys of crossbow quarrels into the charging enemy. Dozens of the deadly bolts found their marks. Barbarians dropped out of their saddles, and wounded horses stumbled and fell behind their thundering fellows.

After they fired, the crossbowmen did not reload, for the enemy was coming too fast. Instead, they pulled their shields off their backs and drew their *chiens*, then waited in tense silence. Within a few seconds, every Shou had fired. Each man, shield and sword in hand, now awaited the enemy charge.

Batu's crossbowmen had inflicted heavy casualties. Seven hundred barbarians lay in the field, wounded or dying, but the charge continued. The horsewarriors barely seemed to notice their losses.

Batu now regretted placing his archers in the marsh. Had he expected a frontal assault, he would have spread them along the hill. Two hundred and fifty men could hardly have halted the charge, but their rapid fire would have given the horsemen something to think about besides the wretched *pengs* crouching behind their shields.

The cavalry hit the wall of infantry. A sharp, deafening crack echoed off the hills flanking the field. Screams of anger and pain rang out along the line. Agonized whinnies seemed to tremble through the ground. The odor of blood and manure and opened entrails filled the air. Bodies fell.

Through it all, the enemy drums pounded in a crashing, peculiar cadence that filled Batu's head and made it difficult to think. Like the other Tuigan, the thirty drummers were mounted, but they had stopped twenty-five yards from the battle line. Each man had two drums tied together and slung across his horse in front of the saddle. The drummers beat the skins of their instruments with heavy batons in a crazed, irregular rhythm. Unlike the other horsewarriors, the drummers wore heavy armor similar to the suit Pe had abandoned.

Batu grabbed his adjutant's shoulder, then, yelling into Pe's ear, said, "Order our archers to shoot the drummers!"

Pe nodded, then repeated the order to make sure he had understood correctly.

As his adjutant relayed the command, the general glanced at the hilltop behind him. There was no sign of reinforcements. The enemy had not attacked as Kwan had expected, and Batu did not doubt the entire Army of Chukei would perish before the minister admitted his plan needed adjustment.

Still standing at the edge of the marsh, the general returned his gaze to the battle. He was surprised at the number of Shou soldiers who still stood and now fought with their long *chiens*. Holding their shields overhead, they used the ferocious cutting power of their swords to chop barbarians or, when pressed, to lop off horses' legs.

For their part, the Tuigan had discarded their lances. Their horses danced in circles as they slashed at infantrymen with curved blades, meeting with too much success for Batu's liking. From their mounted positions, the barbarians had little trouble beating down, or splintering entirely, the wooden shields of the Shou infantry.

Batu's archers appeared at the edge of the reed bed, twenty yards to the general's right. Two hundred arrows sailed through the air. The closest drummers slid from their saddles, sprouting three or four shafts each. Farther away, beyond the range at which the arrows could penetrate armor, the drummers found themselves struggling with wounded horses. In two cases, they were beating punctured drumheads.

What happened next amazed Batu. As the nearby drums

fell silent, many Tuigan disengaged and turned back the way they had come. Farther away, where the untouched drums were still audible, the Tuigan were confused. Some disengaged and rode away. Others seemed bewildered and met quick deaths as they were overwhelmed by suddenly superior Shou numbers.

Realizing that a pause in the drum clamor was the barbarian signal to break off, Batu made a quick decision. He waved his archers forward, pointing at the far drummers. "After them!" he cried, far from sure that his words could be heard, but confident his gesture's meaning was clear.

The archery officer immediately led his men forward at a sprint. By sending archers into the melee, Batu was placing them in severe danger. Bows could not parry swords, and the archers were not trained in hand-to-hand combat. That was a sacrifice he would have to make. He could not stand by and watch the enemy destroy his entire command, even if that was what Kwan wanted.

As Batu had expected, the archers did not reach the surviving drummers all at once. The nearest drummers fell first, leaving the barbarians even more confused. As some of the horsewarriors retreated, Batu's infantrymen overwhelmed the others. The archers continued forward, pausing to fire at drummers whenever they had a shot. The enemy riders went to extra lengths to attack the Shou bowmen, even at the peril of their own lives. A dozen archers fell for every ten yards the group advanced. Nevertheless, Batu's plan worked. Within minutes, the barbarian cavalry had withdrawn or lay hacked and mutilated along the battle line.

A calm fell over the battlefield. With the air filled by the rank smell of death and the cries of wounded men and horses, the lull was more sickening than peaceful. The Shou infantry stayed on the line, breaking formation only to help the wounded and gather barbarian survivors into groups of prisoners.

Batu looked again toward the hilltop. There was still no sign of reinforcements. The general knew that the Army of

Chukei's role as bait was not yet finished.

He turned to his adjutant and pointed at the body-littered field. "Send a runner down the line. Officers must reform their units, detailing only one man in ten to aid the wounded. Take no prisoners. If a barbarian can lift a sword, slay him."

Pe frowned at the harshness of the command, but simply said, "It will be done." He turned to obey.

Batu caught his adjutant's shoulder. "One more thing: recall what is left of the archers. Remind me to write the emperor commending their courage."

The young man's eyes lit. "Then we are going to survive the battle, my general?"

Batu looked at his army's butchered line. "The rest of this war will be too marvelous to miss, Pe."

As his adjutant passed the orders on, the general contemplated the carnage before him. Considering the small size of the barbarian charge, it had been a bloody battle so far. Judging from what he could see, Batu estimated his casualties at between thirty and fifty percent.

The fight was far from over, the general knew. By disrupting the drummers, the archers had fouled a carefully organized withdrawal. The enemy would not have planned such an operation unless it was timed to coincide with another maneuver, such as an attack on an exposed flank. As much as the general hated to admit it, Kwan had been right not to spring his trap when the barbarians charged. If the minister had sent in the reinforcements, the other Shou armies—not the barbarians—would have been hit in the flank.

While he waited for his adjutant to return, Batu inspected the marsh. Except for a thin screen that remained at the battlefield's edge, the cavalrymen had cut down all the reeds. Bundles lay stacked in great heaps, easily accessible and ready for use.

When Pe returned, the general gave another order. "The cavalry can stop cutting rushes. They are to remove the tack from their horses and fasten it to a reed bundle. Then they must release their mounts."

The general was not issuing the order out of sympathy for the beasts. If events proceeded as he expected, five hundred horses would be an unwelcome hindrance in the reed bed.

Pe balked. "How will we counterattack?"

"If the minister's plan works, there will be no need to counterattack," Batu replied, glancing at the hilltop behind him. "If it doesn't, there will be no opportunity."

Pe nodded and sent a runner with the order.

After the messenger left, Batu said, "Come, Pe. We'll need a better vantage point to see what happens next." He started toward the hill.

The ground began to tremble.

Pe stared at his feet in wide-eyed fear. "What is it?"

Batu frowned, looking first at his own feet, then at the battlefield. The surviving archers, fewer than a hundred men, were hurrying toward the marsh. They stopped and looked at the ground, then turned around. A murmur ran down the battle line. The infantrymen looked west, toward the exposed flank. Those who still had crossbows began reloading them. The others drew their swords.

"War magic?" Pe asked, barely able to keep the terror from his voice.

Batu shook his head. "More cavalry—much more." The general started up the hill at a sprint, Pe and a handful of messengers close behind.

They stopped one hundred feet up the slope. The ground was shaking as if it were in the grip of an earth tremor, and the sound of pounding hooves rolled across the field like thunder. Beyond the exposed flank, a horde of horsemen was charging at full gallop. Their dark figures covered the entire plain. From Batu's perspective, they looked more like a swarm of locust than an invading army. At the least, he estimated their number to be twenty-five thousand.

"Why send so many?" Batu wondered aloud, unable to tear his gaze away from the host. "We could not have hoped to stop a third the number."

Pe was too awe-stricken to respond, but Batu understood the answer to his own question as soon as he had asked it.

The enemy commander knew he was sending his riders into an ambush. He had sent in extra troops to protect himself.

"They know it's a trap," Batu said, turning to his adjutant. "They want to lure our other armies into the open."

Still mesmerized by the charge, Pe did not respond. The barbarians were two hundred yards away from the exposed flank, which was curling back to meet the charge.

The general grabbed his adjutant roughly, shaking the boy out of his trance. "Send runners to Kwan, Shengti, and Ching Tung. The message is: 'The barbarians know our plans. Withdrawal without contact may be wisest course.'"

"We'll be left to face them alone!" Pe stammered.

"We're alone now," Batu growled, noting that the Tuigan swarm would be on them long before reinforcements could arrive. "Send the message!"

As his adjutant obeyed, Batu watched the charge. The cavalry closed to a hundred yards. Determined not to reveal their commander's strategy until the last minute, the officers on the exposed flank did not order the retreat. For the first time in his life, Batu wished his subordinates were not so brave. If they did not withdraw soon, it would be too late. The riders would overrun them and cut them down from behind.

Pe returned to Batu's side. "The message is sent," the adjutant reported. He pointed at the hilltop. "But we're too late."

The general looked up and saw the advance formations of the Shengti and Ching Tung armies cresting the summit. They had brought their bulky artillery with them, and thirty catapults of moderate size lined the hilltop. Behind each catapult were several wagons filled with steaming pitch. The artillerymen carried torches.

"Fools," Batu said, pointing at the sea of Tuigan. "Do they think a brush fire will stop that?"

"Perhaps they intend to burn the artillery and push it down the hill to obstruct the charge," Pe suggested mockingly.

"They'd kill more barbarians," Batu replied, eyeing the

catapults angrily.

An urgent din of voices rose from the western end of the field. At last, with the enemy horses less than fifty yards away, the flank began its retreat. As the line folded, companies along its entire length began to withdraw. Batu cursed. He had intended the line to turn back on itself neatly, not in a mass, but he had not had the opportunity to explain his plan in person. Now, the officers in the middle of the line were giving their orders prematurely, and the general had no doubt the result would be grave.

Within seconds, the Shou lines had become a jumble as retiring units ran headlong into each other. In indignant confusion, the officers began cursing at their men, then at each other. The disarray of the commanders quickly took its toll on the morale of the infantrymen. They began to flee away from the horsewarriors in any available direction. As Batu had ordered, the officers tried to guide their panicked charges toward the marsh, but hundreds of men were instinctively fleeing uphill, toward the reinforcements.

Batu could not save those men. When the armies of Shengti and Ching Tung charged down the hill, the cowards who had disobeyed their officers would be trampled—a fate Batu felt they deserved.

On the other hand, those who had kept their heads would need him when they reached the marsh. Batu sprinted for the reeds, calling for Pe and the runners to follow. As they descended the hill, the ground quaked more violently. Screams of horror and anguish came from the far end of the field. Without looking, the general knew the enemy's first line had caught his men.

As he approached the bottom of the hill, Batu saw a mass of Shou infantrymen gathered in the marsh. The general stopped thirty feet up the hill, directly above the reed bed, and pointed at the bundles of bound rushes.

Addressing the runners himself, he said, "Tell those men to take reed bundles and jump into the river."

The runners glanced at each other, but quickly bowed and rushed to transmit Batu's command to the throng.

Looking at the turbulent waters of the river, Pe asked, "Do you really think the men will follow your order?"

Batu looked west. The horsewarriors were charging down his line almost unimpeded, trampling and slaying every living thing in their path. "Do you think they won't?" he countered.

A series of booms sounded from the hilltop. Batu looked up and saw several catapult-spoons crash against their cross bars. Dozens of flaming pitchballs streaked overhead, landing on the far side of the battlefield and setting fire to the sorghum grass.

A less experienced officer might have thought the catapults had overshot their targets, but the general knew that it would have been impossible to miss the Tuigan horde. The artillerymen had been instructed to aim past the barbarians, trapping the enemy between a wall of fire and the armies of Shengti and Ching Tung.

Though the tactic blatantly sacrificed Batu's army, the plan was a good one—or it would have been, had Kwan taken the time to scout his enemies. As it was, however, the minister had trapped a tiger in a paper cage.

While the artillerymen cranked the catapult spoons down for reloading, four thousand archers rushed over the hilltop. They took a position overlooking the sorghum field and began to fire volleys at the Tuigan riders. The routed soldiers that had been fleeing uphill stopped in their tracks and crouched in grass, fearful of putting themselves between the bowmen and their targets.

The barbarians ignored these developments and continued to charge. Batu's soldiers were dying by the dozens.

"My general!" Pe gasped, staring in open-mouthed horror at the destruction of the Army of Chukei.

Batu laid a hand on his adjutant's shoulder. "Don't despair, Nii Pe. Isn't this what armies are for?"

In the minutes that followed, perhaps two thousand *pengs* reached the marsh and dove into the swollen river, clinging to bundles of reeds. Aside from a steady stream of wounded stragglers, the other three-fifths of the Army of

Chukei lay in the sorghum field. Blood had turned the yellow soil to the color of rust. With his army scattered, Batu had nothing to do except watch the battle. He and Pe remained near the bottom of the hill, thirty feet above the marsh.

The fight began to turn in favor of the Shou. The barbarian charge foundered as horses began to stumble in the mass of dead bodies. The Shou archers fired volley after volley into the churning horde. Small groups of Tuigan tried to mount assaults up the hill. Each time, they met a hail of shafts. The riders in the rear were unhorsed as their dead fellows came tumbling down the slope. The barbarians could not escape the fatal rain across the sorghum field, either, for the valley was engulfed in fire. Nor could they return the way they had come, for their fellows continued to press forward, unaware of the gully of death ahead.

Batu was as amazed at the effectiveness of the minister's plan as he was bitter about the sacrifice of his army. He had never expected the old man's trap to function so efficiently. Though Kwan had sacrificed one small army, it appeared that he would destroy the largest part of the barbarian force without exposing the Armies of Shengti and Ching Tung to a single assault. The battle was an incredible feat of tactics, and the general had to admire his superior's planning.

Batu's thoughts were interrupted by a deafening roar from the hilltop. Again, the ground began to quiver. Fifteen thousand Shou infantrymen rushed over the crest, screaming at the tops of their lungs. As they passed the catapults, they swept the astonished artillerymen along with them and started down the slope. Hundreds of men fell and were trampled by their fellows, but the mass did not slow. When the mob reached the archers, it smashed into the bowmen's line as if crashing a hedge. Batu had never seen such a mad charge.

A moment later, he saw the reason for the crazed rush. All at once, twenty thousand horsewarriors crested the hill. They raced past the catapults and started down the slope, firing as they rode. The horizon turned black with their arrows. Hundreds of Shou fell every moment, and the survivors rushed forward like a herd of panicked horses.

Instantly, Batu realized what had happened. The Tuigan had been playing games with them since the initial skirmishes. The early assaults had been little more than tests of strength and organization. The tentative attacks had been a diversion designed to keep the attention of the Shou commanders focused on the sorghum field.

While Batu and the others concentrated on the skirmishes in the sorghum field, the barbarians had been circling around the Shou armies, probably at a distance of many miles to keep from being observed. When the attack on the Army of Chukei had finally come, it had only been a diversion designed to lull the Shou into thinking their scheme was working. In the meantime, the Tuigan armies had been sneaking forward. After Kwan had finally committed the Armies of Ching Tung and Shengti, the horsewarriors had charged. By the time the minister had realized what was happening, it was too late. The horsewarriors were already in full gallop.

This whole incredible chain of events became clear to Batu as he watched the barbarian riders drive the panicked Shou down the hill. "Magnificent planning," he whispered to himself. "Magnificent execution."

"What did you say, General?" Pe inquired absently, not looking at Batu as he spoke. He was nervously watching the Shou refugees rush down the hill. The fastest runners were less than fifty yards up the slope from their position. Fifty yards beyond that, the first rank of horsewarriors was cutting down stragglers. The riders in the rear ranks were advancing more slowly, pouring a rain of arrows into the fleeing armies.

Batu took a step down the hill. "It's time for us—"

A Tuigan arrow hissed past the general's head, lodging itself in Pe's left shoulder. The adjutant screamed and grasped at the shaft, then his knees buckled. Batu threw out his arms and caught the boy before he hit the ground.

"No, General," Pe gasped, looking up the hill. "There isn't time."

"Be quiet!" Batu ordered. He broke off the shaft, then roughly heaved the youth over his shoulder. "You don't have permission to die. I still have need of an adjutant!"

The steady patter of Tuigan arrows now sounding all around him, Batu rushed down the last ten yards of hill and entered the marsh. He dropped Pe onto a reed bundle at the edge of the river, then hazarded a glance over his shoulder.

The first of the panicked soldiers from Ching Tung and Shengti were almost at the bottom of the hill, less than fifteen yards away. The horsewarriors were only another dozen yards behind them, steadily hacking and slashing their way closer to the front of the fleeing mass.

If he wanted to meet the Tuigan another day, Batu realized, there was no time to fasten Pe to the makeshift raft. He grasped Pe's wrists and guided the boy's hands to the rope securing the reeds together. "Hold on," he ordered.

The general pushed Pe and the bundle into the river, then waded out behind the awkward raft. When his feet began to lose contact with the bottom, he locked his wrists into the rope and kicked with all his might. The swift current grabbed the raft and quickly pulled it farther away from shore.

Behind Batu, a chorus of guttural yells sounded. The general stopped kicking long enough to glance over his shoulder. The barbarians had caught the Shou refugees in the marsh that he and Pe had just escaped. Batu glimpsed one thousand flashing blades and heard one thousand agonized cries. A moment later, the current spun the raft around so that Batu could not see the burning sorghum field, and the river dragon carried him toward safety.

- 3 -

Supreme Harmony

S tate your business in the Hall of Supreme Harmony,"
the chamberlain commanded.

The bureaucrat stood before a set of gilded doors
that opened into the Hall of Supreme Harmony. The
majestic hall stood in the emperor's summer palace, which
was located in the city of Tai Tung, over thirteen hundred
miles southeast of the Dragonwall. The palace had been
converted into a temporary command center for the war
against the barbarians.

Batu Min Ho bowed, scrutinizing the chamberlain with a
single glance. The man had thin lips, narrow eyes, and a dis-
dainful expression. He wore an orange *maitung*—a floor-
length tunic with a high, buttoned collar. On his chest, blue
and white embroidered sparrows soared across the silk sky,
slowly descending around his body in a lazy spiral.

In contrast, Batu wore the same *chia* he had worn during
the battle. It was now cracked and shriveled, with dozens of
stitches popped at the seams. The general himself looked as
worn and as haggard as his armor.

It was no wonder. The two weeks since the battle in the
sorghum field had been the most trying of his life. After escaping the Tuigan massacre on their reed rafts, Batu, Pe,
and less than two thousand Shou soldiers had regrouped
fifty miles downstream. Batu had sent Pe and the rest of the
wounded south with a small escort. The other survivors he
had organized into the semblance of an army.

The general's next move had been to start an orderly retreat. As he moved south, Batu had fanned out his forces, conscripting all able-bodied males from every hamlet his men encountered. The other villagers he had forced to flee, and the makeshift army had burned everything it passed—villages, food stores, grain fields, and even wild grasslands. By seven days after the battle, the wall of smoke had stretched over a front of two hundred miles. Nothing but scorched earth had remained behind.

Batu's strategy had been simple. He had intended to slow the barbarian advance not through combat, but through hunger. Without an ample supply of food, such a large cavalry force would be forced to spend much of its energy foraging. As long as the Tuigan were scavenging, they would not be fighting.

The plan had worked well, and Batu had sent several messengers to Tai Tung reporting his successes. He had been able to slow the enemy's advance to a crawl. At the same time, he had avoided fighting the Tuigan, save for a few minor skirmishes with advance scouts.

So, when he had received an order recalling him to Tai Tung, the general had been surprised. He had also been disappointed. Contrary to what Batu had hoped, Kwan Chan Sen had escaped the slaughter at the sorghum field, probably with his *wu jen*'s help. The recall to Tai Tung had come from the minister. It was in response to that summons that Batu now stood in front of the Hall of Supreme Harmony.

The chamberlain allowed Batu to remain in his bow for a condescending length of time before returning the gesture with a perfunctory head tilt.

Too weary to take offense at the slight, Batu looked up and said, "I am Batu Min Ho, commander of the loyal and worthy Army of Chukei. I have been summoned by Minister Kwan Chan Sen."

The chamberlain studied Batu's ragged *chia* and sneered.

Finally irritated by the man's arrogance, Batu added, "The summons seemed most important."

The bureaucrat nodded. "Yes, it is a matter of great urgency," he said. "The general is to be complimented upon his appreciation of that fact."

The chamberlain turned and whispered to one of the six sentries standing to either side of the entrance. They held themselves at strict attention, their expressionless eyes focused straight ahead. The guards wore the emperor's yellow dragon-scale armor and held broad-bladed polearms called *chiang-chuns*.

After receiving the chamberlain's instructions, a guard bowed and entered the hall, then the bureaucrat turned back to Batu and held out his hands. When the general did not place anything in them, the thin-lipped man said, "May I hold your *tao* and *pi shou?*"

Batu frowned. He felt naked without his weapons and was reluctant to release them. "I am a soldier," he said. "My sword and dagger are the arms with which I serve the emperor."

The chamberlain did not withdraw his hands. "It is a matter of tradition," he explained. "No man may bear weapons in the presence of the Son of Heaven."

Batu swallowed hard. He was relieved that the emperor considered the barbarian threat serious enough to come to Tai Tung personally. At the same time, the general was embarrassed that he had not exchanged his shabby battle clothes for something more splendid. He had never before been in the emperor's presence, and had no wish to insult the Divine One with substandard dress.

The general hurriedly removed his scabbards and gave them to the chamberlain, who passed them to a sentry. Another guard opened the doors, and the chamberlain led the way into a square foyer. As Batu entered the small room, the doors on the opposite side also opened. Minister Kwan, wearing a vermilion *maitung*, came into the room and faced the general.

Batu's stomach felt as though it were filling with hot lead, and he stared at the minister's gnarled face in open spite. Kwan ran his milky eyes over his subordinate's tattered *chia* and barely managed to conceal a grimace. Finally, the old man met the general's glare with a steady gaze, waiting for the ceremonial bow of respect.

Batu tilted his body forward just enough to avoid an open insult. Although he would observe the formalities of station, the general had no intention of treating Kwan with the deference one normally accorded a mandarin.

To Batu's surprise, Kwan smiled warmly and returned the gesture with a deep, courteous bow. "General, how pleasing to see you again."

"Perhaps you mean surprising," Batu said. "I doubt you are pleased." The general's boldness surprised even himself, but he could think of nothing except the old man's folly at the sorghum field.

Though the minister raised an eyebrow, his diplomatic smile did not fade. "To the contrary, General. We military men must stand together. Especially now."

Batu still did not return the smile. "I have not forgotten the battle," he said. "Not any part of it."

The minister's expression grew impatient. "Come now, General. My plan was a sound one—"

"But stood no chance of success," Batu retorted, pointing an accusing finger at the minister's chest, "which you would have realized had you scouted the enemy as I suggested."

The chamberlain gasped, astounded that Batu would dare speak to a mandarin in such a tone. Kwan simply waved the comment aside with a flick of his liver-spotted hand. "There are those who consider your unorthodox retreat less than honorable."

"Saving what remained of my army was not dishonorable," Batu replied evenly.

"We both know what happened at the battle," Kwan said, spreading his palms. "That is no longer of consequence. What is important now is how the emperor perceives the loss. The other mandarins would like nothing better than to use our misfortune to weaken the military. If I am to save your career, we must stand united against their assaults."

Batu could hardly believe Kwan's first concern was political infighting. "Perhaps the minister has not received my reports," the general said. "At this moment, my career—or yours—is of little consequence. There are at least a hundred thousand Tuigan, perhaps twice that number, rampaging through the province of Mai Yuan. Shou Lung itself is in danger of falling."

"Then you must save the empire," Kwan replied. "Stand with me and I will supply the power you need to smash the barbarians."

The general from Chukei sneered. "I doubt you have that power to give."

Batu now realized that though his orders had come from his aged commander, it was not the minister who had called him. The last person Kwan would want near the emperor was the general who had urged him to be more cautious. Batu suspected he had been called by the emperor, probably as part of an inquiry into the disastrous battle.

For several moments, Kwan studied Batu. At last, his true feelings still hidden behind an insincere smile, the minister said, "Your meaning eludes me, General Batu. I am a third-degree general, the Minister of War, a mandarin of the Shou empire, and the Second Left Grand Councilor to the emperor. The limits to my authority are as boundless as the sky."

"Be that as it may," Batu replied coldly, "my duty to the emperor is greater than any loyalty you can buy with empty promises."

The minister's face froze into a mask of anger. "What are you saying, General?" he demanded.

His wide-set eyes fixed evenly on the old man's face, Batu replied, "I must speak the truth before the emperor, if that is why he had me called."

Kwan's thousand wrinkles drooped into a threatening frown. "You are in this with me, you know," he said. "If I fall, so do you."

The minister spoke the truth about that much, at least. If the emperor decided to reorganize the military, Batu did not doubt the changes would be widespread. As the only surviving field general involved in the defeat at the sorghum field, he could very well be relieved of command.

Nevertheless, he said, "My duty is clear, and I will execute it faithfully."

The minister contorted his lips into a knotted snarl. "You will regret your decision, I promise you." That said, the old man turned and left the same way he had entered.

A few moments later, the chamberlain followed Kwan through the doors, motioning for Batu to come behind him.

When the general obeyed, he felt as though he had stepped into a deep, cool well. At ground level, shafts of yellow light spilled into the circular room from nine small windows. The walls, richly painted in vermilion and inlaid with golden dragons, rose seventy feet overhead and disappeared into darkness. Several balconies ringed the chamber, hanging one below another every fifteen feet. Batu could see a pair of imperial guards on the lowest one, though he assumed soldiers patrolled all the walkways.

On the opposite side of the room, forty feet away, a throne of sculpted jade sat upon the marble floor. The chair's crafters had carved it in the semblance of a great dragon, with the beast's head serving as a canopy and its massive legs as armrests. The man sitting in the throne wore a plain yellow *hai-waitao*. Resembling a long robe with billowing sleeves, the garment consisted of a single silk layer.

The man occupying the jade throne could only be Emperor Kai Tsao Shou Chin, Son of Heaven, and Divine Gate to the Celestial Sphere. Like Batu, the emperor had a powerful build, though the Divine One looked much taller. The Son of Heaven's clean-shaven face had strong bones, with the long nose and drooping jaw of the mountain people of Tabot.

Two dozen advisers, all mandarins, sat around the emperor in a large semicircle of heavy wooden chairs. Each mandarin wore a vermilion *hai-waitao* embroidered with gold or silver thread. The sole woman in the court, a lithe beauty with dark eyes and silky hair, wore a *cheosong*. The tight, floor-length dress was embroidered with a golden dragon, which entwined her body from chest to ankle. Long slits ran from hem to hip, allowing freedom of movement and providing an ample view of her slender legs.

Like most educated men of Shou Lung, Batu was familiar with the names, if not the faces, of the emperor's advisers. Since just one female sat on the Mandarinate, the willowy beauty could only be Ting Mei Wan, Minister of State Security. The general recognized only one other person in the room, Kwan Chan Sen, who, as the Second Left Grand Councilor, sat in the second chair to the emperor's left.

The chamberlain signaled Batu to stay where he was, then advanced to the center of the room. After bowing to the emperor, he said, "Divine Son of Heaven and Oracle of the Heavens, General Batu Min Ho seeks an audience in answer to your summons."

The emperor nodded, then the chamberlain motioned for Batu to approach. When he reached the center of the room, the general kneeled and performed the ceremonial kowtow by touching his forehead to the marble floor three times. After he finished, Batu remained motionless, waiting for permission to stand.

The Son of Heaven did not speak for several seconds, and the general noticed that a pool of cold sweat had formed on the floor beneath his brow. His heart was pounding within his rib cage as if he were in a battle, and a queasy feeling tickled his stomach. After what he had faced during the last week, Batu found it amusing that meeting the emperor should make him so nervous.

Finally, in a resonant voice, the emperor spoke. "General Batu, we are pleased you have come to our summer palace. Please rise."

As Batu returned to his feet, the chamberlain bowed and left the room. The general remained in the center of the room, focusing his attention on the Son of Heaven. "Your venerable welcome honors me, Divine One." He waved a hand at his shabby *chia*. "Please excuse the drabness of my appearance. I come directly from the field—"

"That is no excuse for your insult to the emperor," Kwan interrupted, leaning forward in his massive chair and spitting out the words.

A wave of anger rolled over Batu, but he forced himself to relax and keep a calm appearance. Kwan was trying to destroy his credibility. Showing anger would only play into the minister's plan. Instead, the general bowed to his superior and said, "My apologies, Minister. As you must remember, I lost everything but the clothes on my back during our last battle."

Kwan scowled. "My memory serves me well enough to recall your cowardice—"

"General Batu's dress does not offend me," the emperor said, silencing Kwan with a wave of his hand. "I do not expect Shou Lung's soldiers to wear silk armor into combat. However, I do expect to hear their reports without interruption."

Though the emperor's words carried reproach, Kwan's face showed no hint of chagrin. He nodded apologetically and inclined his head, but his confident smile suggested that he had made his point. By publicly chastising Batu and calling him a coward, the minister had cast doubt on any criticisms that the general might in turn level at him.

Batu realized he would have to choose his words carefully, even though he intended to speak only the truth.

After silencing Kwan, the emperor calmly placed his hands on the arms of his throne and turned back to Batu. "Hsuang Yu Po claims you know more about the bloodthirsty barbarians than any living Shou."

Batu frowned in puzzlement. Hsuang Yu Po was his wife's father. As far as the general knew, the lord was in the Hsuang family citadel in southern Chukei, along with Batu's wife and children.

Observing Batu's confusion, the emperor said, "Your battlefield dispatches have not gone unheeded, General. I have asked all nobles to gather here with their private armies. Your father-in-law has been kind enough to respond. He suggested you would have some special insight into the nature of the barbarian menace." As he spoke, the emperor remained upright and motionless, neither gesturing nor shifting in his seat.

Determined to seize every opportunity to discredit Batu, Kwan again risked the emperor's wrath and spoke without permission. "Hsuang is correct. The general is half-barbarian himself!"

The Divine One raised an eyebrow. "Is this true, General?"

"Partially," Batu responded, inclining his head apologetically, though he was not quite sure why. "Before he came to Shou Lung, my great-grandfather was *apa qaghan*—brother to the chief—of the Igidujin tribe. When I was a young boy, he often entertained me with stories of his childhood. I was a good listener, Divine One, but that hardly makes me a Tuigan."

The emperor slid forward to the edge of his throne. "Less than a year ago, my advisers assured me that the Horse Plains contained nothing but small tribes of savage nomads," the Divine One said. "These nomads, my advisers said, would never be more than an irritation on our northern frontier. But in two weeks, this 'irritation' has breached the Dragonwall, captured the garrison city of Lo Tu, utterly destroyed the armies of the Northern Marches, and are driving like an arrow toward the heart of my empire."

Glancing with obvious irritation at Kwan Chan Sen and another mandarin, the emperor continued. "When I ask my advisers how this can be, the answer is always the same. 'The enemy is a nothing more than a disorganized band of barbarians,' they say, or, 'Our mighty armies will crush them in the next battle.' But the only armies that have been crushed are ours. Clearly, my venerable advisers are mistaken."

The Divine One pushed himself back in his throne and locked his gaze on Batu. "Who are they," he demanded. "Who are these savages who have smashed the mightiest armies under the heavens?"

Batu had to fight to keep a grin from creasing his lips. He suspected that the emperor had not summoned him to find a scapegoat, but simply to learn more about the Tuigan. Kwan's fears had been unfounded, and the minister had needlessly lowered himself to asking aid from a subordinate. However, the general realized, the emperor probably had no immediate plan for removing Kwan from his post as Minister of War. This meant that Batu now had an enemy in a very powerful position.

Shoving thoughts of his political troubles aside, Batu closed his eyes and tried to remember all that his great-grandfather had told him about the horsewarriors. He recalled tales of endless lands, countless tribes, dangerous horseback contests, merciless punishments, and battles fought without fear. He also remembered his impression of the Tuigan as they swarmed down on his army in the sorghum field.

Finally, he looked up and said, "Perhaps the barbarians are like locust, Emperor."

The Divine One frowned. "Locust?"

"Yes. Their numbers are countless and their appetite for blood endless. They move like the wind and appear where least expected, but always with terrible results. They kill everything in their path and leave nothing but devastation in their wake."

"I see," said the emperor, pursing his lips thoughtfully.

"Is that why you are burning our fields and chasing our peasants from their homes?" Kwan asked, pointing a gnarled finger at Batu.

Before the general could respond, the emperor turned to Kwan and said, "The only way to stop a locust swarm is to starve it. Let us waste no more time questioning General Batu's competence. So far, his strategies are the only ones that have had any effect on our enemies."

As Kwan heard the words, his wrinkled brow rose in shock.

The emperor continued. "What we must concern ourselves with, Minister Kwan, is what has brought these locust upon us."

The mandarin seated directly to the emperor's left stood and bowed. This man appeared to be in his late fifties, twenty years older than Batu. His eyes were steady and dark, giving him the appearance of a thoughtful and dangerous enemy.

When the Divine One nodded to him, the mandarin said, "The locust have come for the reason they always come: they are hungry. Majestic Shou Lung is a wealthy land, and the uncivilized horse-people are bloodthirsty thieves who envy the harvest of our honest labor."

The emperor shook his head. "No, Ju-Hai."

Batu recognized the mandarin's name. Ju-Hai Chou was the Minister of State and the First Left Grand Councilor. Aside from the emperor himself, he was the most powerful man in the Mandarinate.

"In the two thousand years recorded in the *Histories*, there is only one account of a massed invasion by the horse barbarians," the emperor continued, looking from Ju-Hai to the other mandarins. "It was provoked by a warmonger's attempt to annex part of their lands. Only a fool would believe they have suddenly massed to attack without reason."

"As always, your wisdom outshines the sun, Divine One," Ju-Hai said, folding his hands in front of his body. "But merchants are now afraid to travel the Spice Road, and tax revenue has fallen by twenty percent. In addition, the cost of replacing the northern armies will deplete the treasury. Shou Lung's marvelous economy is facing collapse. Can the reason for the attack matter any longer?"

The emperor nodded. "Oh yes, Ju-Hai. It is written in the *Book of Heaven* that a man cannot harvest rice until he understands the sowing of the seed. Is this not also the way with war? We cannot hope to win until we know what the barbarians seek."

The female mandarin, Ting Mei Wan, stood and spoke. "Perhaps our eyes are turned in the wrong direction. Could the cause of the war lie here, within the Hall of Supreme Harmony?"

"What are you saying?" Ju-Hai snapped angrily.

With the unexpected outburst, a tense silence fell over the room. Ju-Hai glared at Ting with dark, menacing eyes. She returned the stare with a steady gaze and a faint smile. Batu felt sure some unspoken threat was passing between them. Not being privy to the inner workings of the Mandarinate, he could not guess its nature.

The emperor turned to Ju-Hai, his face an inscrutable mask of politeness. "Is something wrong?" he asked, his diplomatic tone disguising any curiosity he felt about the outburst.

The Minister of State flushed. From his embarrassed expression, Batu guessed the mandarin rarely suffered such lapses of control.

"I am unsure of Minister Ting's meaning," Ju-Hai replied, deftly avoiding an explanation for his irrational behavior. "Certainly, no blame can be placed upon the venerable members of this Mandarinate." His face remained tense, and he continued to glare at Ting Mei Wan.

The Son of Heaven turned to the beautiful mandarin and raised an eyebrow to prompt her response. Ting smiled at the Minister of State, then bowed to the emperor and said, "The *Book of Heaven* teaches us that the Divine One rules with the mandate of the heavens. It is written that while the emperor governs with a pure heart and observes the proper ceremonies, Shou Lung will prosper. It is also written that the land will suffer plagues and pestilences when the Nine Immortals revoke their mandate."

Ju-Hai relaxed and took his eyes off the woman. Whatever he had been afraid Ting would say clearly had nothing to do with the *Book of Heaven*. In contrast to Ju-Hai's reaction, the other mandarins muttered in astonishment and stared at Ting in open shock. The emperor's face remained impassive, and Batu could not tell what effect Ting's words were having on him.

The beautiful mandarin continued. "I trust the emperor understands that discussing this matter only demonstrates my absolute loyalty," she said, casting her gaze submissively at his feet. "As we are all confident of the purity of the Divine One's heart, I merely suggest some minor rite may have been overlooked—"

A middle-aged mandarin wearing a purple *hai-waitao* covered with mystic symbols leaped to his feet. "I can assure the Minister of State Security that all ceremonies are being performed properly!" he hissed. From the symbols on his robe, Batu guessed that the man was the High Lord of Imperial Sacrifices.

The Minister of State Security was a dangerous woman, the general decided. After threatening Ju-Hai Chou, she had managed to turn the emperor's scrutiny inward. At the same time, she had portrayed herself as the Divine One's most loyal subject. Then, to protect herself further, she had shifted the focus of blame to the High Lord of Imperial Sacrifices, giving the Son of Heaven an easy target upon which to vent any anger he felt.

The most amazing thing of all, Batu thought, was that the Minister of State Security had managed to keep the motives for her actions completely disguised. The general was more curious than ever about the secret Ju-Hai Chou had been so afraid Ting would reveal.

After a moment of reflection, the Son of Heaven adjusted himself so that he was sitting erect and proud in his throne. "Minister Ting, we thank you for your suggestion," he said, his voice betraying a hint of sarcasm. "We will investigate our rites to be sure they are performed in accordance with the *Book of Heaven*. Until we discover an inconsistency, let us assume the cause of our trouble lies elsewhere. Now—"

A loud scream from the foyer interrupted the emperor's words. Immediately, several guards leaned over the balconies above, training their weapons on the door. Heavy footsteps echoed through the room as other sentries rushed for the stairways. Like the guards, Batu's first thought was of assassins, and he whirled to face the doors.

A moment later, the chamberlain entered the Hall of Supreme Harmony. Behind him, four guards carried the body of a small man dressed in a beggar's robes.

The chamberlain bowed, saying, "A thousand apologies, Son of Heaven. The guards captured this vagabond trying to escape the grounds of the palace. Unfortunately, he threw himself on a sentry's blade as we were bringing him to you." The bureaucrat produced a leaf of folded paper. "He was carrying this."

"Bring it here," the emperor commanded, holding out his hand.

As the chamberlain's footsteps echoed across the marble floor, Batu studied the vagabond's face. It was similar to his own, with broad cheekbones, a flat nose, and wide-set eyes. His head was nicked and cut where it had recently been shaved.

"This man is a spy," Batu declared. "A Tuigan spy."

Resembling a Tuigan as much as he did himself, Batu would have been the last to suggest, based on appearance alone, that the beggar was a barbarian. However, the freshly shaved head was incongruous with the rest of the vagabond's filthy appearance, and it suggested to Batu that the man's hair had been cut as part of a disguise.

"So it seems," the Divine One confirmed, examining the paper that the chamberlain had given to him. "And he is not working alone." The emperor studied Batu thoughtfully, then held the paper out to him. "You may examine this map, General."

Ignoring the scowl on Kwan's face, Batu approached the throne. After a deep bow to acknowledge the great honor that the emperor had bestowed upon him, the general took the paper directly from the Divine One's hand.

A heavy, corrugated line had been drawn across the northwestern corner, where the Dragonwall was located. A lighter line wandered across the middle of the map, showing the location and approximate course of the Shengti River. There was an "X" on the north side of the river, where the city of Yenching was located. Near the bottom and center of the map was another "X," showing the location of the walled city of Shou Kuan. A third mark had been placed in the lower right-hand corner, where Tai Tung and the summer palace were located. Several soldiers had been drawn next to Tai Tung, and the number "13,000" written next to the city. Five infantrymen had been drawn marching toward Tai Tung. Next to each infantryman was a number ranging from "8,000" to "15,000"—the approximate size of one of Shou Lung's provincial armies.

"This is a map of troop movements," Batu remarked, looking up.

The emperor met the general's gaze with an expression that could not be read. "Yes," he said evenly. "The only detail it lacks is the identity of the man I have chosen to lead the war against the barbarians."

The Divine One looked from the general to the dead spy, then to the faces of Ting Mei Wan, Kwan Chan Sen, Ju-Hai Chou, and the other members of the Mandarinate. Finally, he looked back to Batu and said, "Allow me to dismiss my other advisers, General. You and I have much to discuss."

- 4 -

Ju-Hai's Garden

Ju-Hai felt his manservant drape a woolen coat over his shoulders. The meditation, he realized, had come to an end. Without his awareness or control, his mind had retreated from that calm, tenebrous zone within its own depths.

Melancholy, as always, at the necessity of leaving the intangible world, the minister opened his eyes. The sun was about to drop behind the western walls of the summer palace, and he was bathed in the rosy light of late afternoon.

"Has it been that long, Shei Ni?" Ju-Hai asked.

"Yes, Minister," the servant responded.

Ju-Hai was shocked, but not alarmed. He sat in his garden belvedere looking out over his goldfish pond, his legs folded into the blossoming lotus position. Each day, the minister customarily came here to clear his head and order his thoughts. Considering what had happened in the Mandarinate, it did not surprise him that today's session had lasted much longer than usual.

Before him, his jar of trigram sticks rested upon a white lacquered table, next to a hand-lettered copy of the *Book of Change*. When the sticks were spilled on the table, the future could be foretold by comparing the resulting patterns to the diagrams in the book. Though the minister did not advertise the fact to his colleagues, he was a great believer in the trigrams. The rosewood sticks and carved jade jar were two of his most cherished possessions.

After a respectful pause, Shei Ni said, "Minister Ting has

been waiting since midday to see you. I would have announced her earlier, but she did not wish to interrupt your meditation."

Ju-Hai's stomach twisted into a knot. He was still angered by Ting's suggestion that the cause of the Tuigan invasion lay within the Mandarinate. It was true that, after his humiliating outburst, she had deftly altered the emphasis of her suggestion. However, he wished the subject had not been brought up at all. Ju-Hai wondered whether the episode had simply been an unpleasant coincidence, or if Ting had known it would upset him. At the moment, the answer was not important. The minister was still angry with her.

"What is the nature of her business?" he asked. Shei Ni was so practiced in receiving Ting Mei Wan that he could judge the reason for a visit by her manner and dress.

"I believe it is personal," Shei Ni said.

"Then send her away."

"As you wish." Shei Ni bowed, then went into the house.

Ju-Hai rose and began walking along the marble path that circled the goldfish pond. He was disappointed to find himself still angry at Ting, and hoped a tour of his garden might quell his emotions. The tiny park was his taste of paradise, and he went there to escape the strict regimens and orderly thoughts that ruled his public life.

Ju-Hai had taken great care to evoke the spirit of nature in this modest parcel of land. The ground had been modeled into tiny hills and valleys, and anything approximating a straight line had been diligently avoided. The minister had used the influence of his office to fill the garden with exotic specimens from the widest reaches of the empire: camellias, crimson-berried nandins, even a golden larch.

He would have liked to enlarge the garden, but that was impossible. The summer palace was really a miniature city, complete with hundreds of walled houses occupied by status-hungry bureaucrats. To secure even the half-acre plot he now enjoyed, the mandarin had been forced to call upon the emperor for help.

As Ju-Hai studied one of his newest prizes, a peony bush

that would blossom in green, his servant returned. "Excuse me, Master. Lady Ting asks you to reconsider your decision. She points out that she has been waiting many hours to apologize for what happened in the Mandarinate today."

"To apologize?" Ju-Hai repeated, wondering what she really intended. If she had been waiting since the emperor dismissed the Mandarinate, it had to be something important to her. Deciding he could control his anger in order to satisfy his curiosity, the minister said, "Very well, she may join me here."

Shei Ni bowed and went into the house.

In the last six months, Ting had developed an irritating appetite for power. More than once, her hunger had resulted in an embarrassment similar to the one of that day. Ju-Hai had spoken to her about his concerns, but always without apparent effect. He was beginning to fear that it would be necessary to arrange her removal from the Mandarinate.

The prospect did not please the minister, for he was genuinely fond of the female mandarin. Ting had first come to Ju-Hai's attention over fifteen years ago, when she had achieved a perfect score on the civil service examination used to select imperial bureaucrats. Convinced she had cheated, he had summoned her to the Forbidden City and quizzed her personally. By halfway through the session, the girl had convinced the minister that she had earned her perfect score.

During the interview, Ju-Hai had seen the making of a mandarin in the young woman. She had a sharp mind and a dynamic personality, and seemed ruthlessly driven. Afterward, he had investigated her background. Although she had suffered the misfortune of being born into the family of a dishonest rice merchant, the inquiry had uncovered nothing to suggest that she could not be a valuable public servant. From that point onward, Ju-Hai had taken a personal interest in her career. As the minister had expected, she had proven herself more than capable of executing any task assigned to her.

Two years ago, the opportunity to place an ally in the post

of Minister of State Security had arisen. Naturally, Ju-Hai's first choice had been the beautiful young woman he had been developing for thirteen years. Although the minister had expected her to do well, even he had been surprised by the efficiency with which she performed her necessarily merciless duties. In the upper ranks of the bureaucracy, it was well known that revealing even a small weakness to the "Tigress" could prove fatal.

The thought of keeping weaknesses secret reminded Ju-Hai of the trigram sticks he had left on the table. He returned to the pavilion and was just picking up the jar when Ting came out of the house.

"Minister," she said, stopping inside the fan-shaped arbor that served as an entrance to the garden.

The gorgeous mandarin wore an unadorned scarlet *cheosong* that covered her from neck to ankle. The dress was made of gossamer silk that highlighted her voluptuous charms rather than concealed them. In her hands, she held a small potted flower of a type which Ju-Hai had never before seen. Save for its black blossom, the plant resembled a tiny lotus that grew in dirt instead of water. Holding the plant out for Ju-Hai, Ting averted her eyes and bowed as low as her tight clothing would allow.

Ju-Hai put his trigram jar down, then walked over to Ting and accepted the gift. "It's as ravishing as you, my dear," he said, his anger fading as he studied the plant. A few moments later, he asked, "What is it?"

"Cliff blossom. It came from the mountain kingdom of Ra-Khati," she replied, standing upright. "It's a special gift I've been saving. I thought it might express my sorrow for offending you."

Shei Ni appeared at the head of a small procession of servants. Carrying a teapot, cups, and two chairs, they stopped at the arbor and waited behind Ting.

Ju-Hai bowed to show his appreciation. "As always, you must be complimented upon your knowledge of your quarry." The realization that Ting understood him so well made Ju-Hai uneasy. An exotic plant was the only gift that would disarm him so easily. "You are forgiven, my dear. Come over to the belvedere, and we will talk."

"Thank you, Minister." Ting smiled and followed Ju-Hai to the small, open building at the edge of the goldfish pond.

While the servants placed the chairs and poured the tea, Ting picked up the jar Ju-Hai had left on the white table. "Trigrams?" she asked curiously.

"A bauble I sometimes toy with," the minister replied, looking away from the jar with practiced nonchalance.

Smiling playfully, Ting turned the jar over and spilled the sticks. "Tell me what they say."

Ju-Hai gave Ting's gift to Shei Ni for safekeeping. When he looked at the circle of sticks, he half-smiled in amusement. The minister did not need stick magic to tell him what the trigrams had revealed. "The pattern of the sea," he said. "You are always shifting and impossible to predict. This makes you a powerful enemy and a dangerous friend."

Shei Ni and the servants finished their work, bowed, and left the garden quietly.

Ting peered at the sticks, then looked at Ju-Hai flirtatiously. "Is there nothing of love in those patterns?"

The minister chuckled. "Not for me to read."

Ting stepped closer. "Perhaps you should look again."

Ju-Hai backed away and took his seat at the east end of the table. After a long sip of tea, he said, "Surely you did not wait all afternoon simply to dangle your lascivious web before an aging man?"

The beautiful mandarin sighed in exaggerated disappointment. The game between them was an old one. For fifteen years, Ting had been making herself available to Ju-Hai, and for fifteen years the Minister of State had deftly avoided an entanglement with her.

"I have been waiting much longer than one afternoon," Ting replied, taking her seat at the other end of the table. "But you're correct. I have little hope that you'll come to your senses today. I've come to apologize for this morning's mistake."

Ju-Hai nodded, but remained silent. Now that they were

discussing political affairs, his mind had shifted into an orderly, critical thought process. He hoped his silence would force Ting to disclose the true reason for her visit.

Ting lifted her teacup to her lips. After a small swallow, she continued speaking. "Of course, I don't really know what my mistake was."

Ju-Hai smiled, relieved that the Tigress did not know his greatest vulnerability. After a short pause, he answered Ting's half-spoken question. "That should be obvious."

Ting frowned at her mentor. "It isn't."

"It is a foolish wolf that growls at its master," he said. "By suggesting that someone within the Mandarinate brought the barbarians down upon us, you have made many powerful enemies."

Ting's eyes narrowed. "True, but to anger you, my blunder must have threatened you personally."

Ju-Hai smiled at his disciple with as much warmth as he could gather. "I'm disappointed, my dear. Don't you realize how fond of you I am?"

Ting smirked, then her eyes grew soft and she ran a painted nail around the rim of her tea cup. "Why do you never show it?"

"I do," the minister responded. "I have watched over your career very closely."

The seductive mandarin sat up straight. "To what purpose?" she asked. "What have you gotten out of helping me?"

Her soft expression had become as hard as stone, and Ju-Hai knew that this question came from her heart. "What I have gotten," he answered, "is a capable administrator who serves the empire well. That is the only payment I expect or have ever asked."

Ting rolled her eyes in disbelief. Like so many other servants of the state, a lifetime in the imperial bureaucracy had exposed her to such corruption and self-serving incompetence that she automatically discounted such statements. Ju-Hai's answer, however, had been sincere, though he would never convince Ting of that.

"Perhaps you speak the truth," the Tigress said, looking away to show Ju-Hai that she didn't believe he did. "Even so, you would never embarrass yourself before the emperor—not on my behalf, or anyone else's. And considering that someone must have been feeding information to the spy the guards captured, it almost appears that you're a traitor."

The only reason Ju-Hai did not lose his temper was that he had already considered that same point. His outburst had come at the wrong time. Taken by itself, it appeared that the minister was trying to hide something. When he considered the spy and the map, even Ju-Hai could not deny that his behavior cast a pall of suspicion over him.

For several moments, Ting studied her mentor with hard demanding eyes. Finally, her mouth dropped open and she pointed an accusing finger at the minister. "That's it! You *are* a spy."

"Don't be ridiculous," Ju-Hai said evenly. If he thought she were serious, he would not be able to keep from shouting. However, Ju-Hai felt convinced that Ting was merely putting on an act. The accusation had been so dramatic and sudden that it seemed rehearsed.

Besides, if Ting believed him to be a spy, she would not make the mistake of accusing him while alone and inside the walls of his home.

As Ju-Hai expected, the Tigress followed her accusation with a demand. "If you're not the spy, why the outburst? What are you hiding?"

"I am hiding nothing," Ju-Hai lied.

"How can I believe that?" Ting responded angrily. "The evidence is—" She stopped in midsentence and looked around the garden. A moment later, she rose quickly and bowed, saying, "Please forgive me, Minister. I forget myself. Perhaps I should go."

Her voice trembled with a fear Ju-Hai knew she did not feel. If Ting were truly afraid, she would appear angry and dangerous, not timid and apologetic.

"Yes, perhaps you should go," the Minister of State replied. He poured himself some more tea and did not bother to rise.

"If you have that evidence you speak of, take it directly to the emperor."

Ting hesitated, furrowing her smooth brow in confusion. Finally, she said, "But I couldn't. I owe you—"

"If you believe me a traitor," Ju-Hai interrupted, "you owe me nothing. Your duty is to present your evidence to the emperor."

Ting exhaled wearily, then returned to her seat. "I don't believe you're a traitor, Minister, and I never did. But I *am* the Minister of State Security."

Ju-Hai smiled with heartfelt warmth. "Understood, my dear. I expected nothing less."

Ting sighed heavily and turned in her seat to look out over the goldfish pond. "The emperor and the other mandarins are already commenting on your suspicious behavior. What am I to say? That we had tea and that I have your assurance you remain faithful to Shou Lung?"

Ju-Hai shook his head. "No," he admitted. "That won't do."

She looked at him with pleading eyes. "I can't help you unless I know what you are hiding."

"I am hiding nothing," the elder minister responded. It was not difficult for him to lie, even to friends. He did it every day as a normal part of his duties. "You have my word."

"Splendid," she answered, rolling her eyes away from Ju-Hai's. "I'll sleep like the dragons tonight."

For nearly a minute, Ting stared at the pond, watching the fat goldfish swim lazy circles. Finally, she looked back to her mentor. "If you're not the spy, who is?"

"I don't know," Ju-Hai answered, shaking his head sadly. "But if my honor is to be saved, that is the question you must answer."

Ting shifted forward in her chair. "I need some help."

"Perhaps you could compare calligraphy?" Ju-Hai suggested. He lifted his teacup and looked at the table while he drank, as if the matter were of little consequence to him.

Ting shook her head. "I thought of that, but there are only pictures and numbers on the map. Anyone could have drawn it."

Shei Ni entered the garden and approached the belvedere at a brisk pace. He seemed quite flustered, so Ju-Hai did not wait for the customary bow. "What is it, Shei Ni?"

"Minister Kwan," he replied. "He insists upon seeing you right now. I told him you were unavailable, but—"

Ting quickly stood. "If I am to be your defender in the Mandarinate, it might be better if we were not observed having a tryst in your garden."

Ju-Hai nodded, glad that Ting had made the suggestion. He was not anxious for her to hear anything that passed between him and the Minister of War. "Shei Ni will show you out—"

The servant shook his head. "Minister Kwan is already halfway through the house. The guards are stalling him, but they're afraid to manhandle a mandarin."

Eyeing Ting's tight *cheosong*, Ju-Hai said, "I suppose climbing the garden wall is out of the question . . ."

She nodded vigorously.

"Very well," Ju-Hai said, pointing at a hedge on the opposite end of the goldfish pond. It was close enough to the belvedere for Ting to overhear what was said, but Ju-Hai hoped to steer the conversation away from what he did not wish her to know. "Hide behind the shrubbery. I'll deal with this quickly."

No sooner had Shei Ni helped Ting behind the hedge than two of Ju-Hai's household guards appeared at the arbor. They each held gleaming *chiang-chuns*, but were nevertheless backing away from a screaming Kwan Chan Sen. As they moved, they held their polearms in front of the old man and politely tried to explain that he had not yet been announced.

"Minister Kwan!" Ju-Hai called, quickly refilling the teacup that had been Ting's until just a moment ago. "Won't you please join me?"

The guards relaxed, then stepped aside. The ancient mandarin bustled over to the pavilion at such a frantic pace that Ju-Hai feared he would trip and injure himself.

"This is your fault!" the old man stammered, dropping heavily into his seat.

"What?" Ju-Hai asked, topping off his own teacup.

"Batu Min Ho," Kwan replied. "My informants tell me the emperor intends to promote him to General of the Northern Marches!"

"How unfortunate," Ju-Hai replied, feigning sympathy.

"The emperor hasn't consulted me. He hasn't consulted anyone!" the old man hissed.

Though Kwan Chan did not know it, what he said was not true. After hearing about the ingenious manner in which the young general had saved two thousand *pengs*, Ju-Hai had investigated Batu's record.

What he had learned impressed him. Since Batu had been placed in command of the Army of Chukei, the small force had destroyed or chased away more than one thousand barbarian raiding parties, suffering only light casualties itself. Batu had even reclaimed some prime farmland from a tribe of vicious half-humans on the northern frontier. When the general's father-in-law had arrived and described Batu's barbarian heritage, Ju-Hai had suggested the young general as a good choice to lead the war against the Tuigan.

Of course, Ju-Hai had no intention of telling this to Kwan, for he always tried to avoid making enemies needlessly.

After allowing the milky-eyed old man to fume for a few moments, Ju-Hai said, "It's the emperor's will. We can do nothing except live with his decision."

Kwan turned an angry frown on Ju-Hai. "We must make the Divine One change his mind, or that upstart from Chukei will have my seat in the Hall of Supreme Harmony." Kwan paused and shook his wrinkled head sadly. "Imagine, a barbarian in the Mandarinate!"

"Come now, Minister," Ju-Hai objected, frowning at the ancient mandarin. "Batu is hardly a barbarian—"

"How would you know?" Kwan asked, his voice even and reasonable despite his obvious anger. "I've seen our enemy close up. He looks like the barbarians, he smells like them, and he thinks like them!"

"Perhaps that is why the emperor chose him to lead the war," Ju-Hai hazarded. "After all, to hunt a leopard, one must think like—"

"We are not talking about leopard hunts," Kwan snapped. "We are talking about the Mandarinate—*my* seat in the Mandarinate."

Kwan paused, then turned his milky eyes on Ju-Hai. "You are the First Left Grand Councilor," the old man observed. "Use your influence with the emperor to get rid of this Batu Min Ho."

Through Kwan's mask of wrinkles, Ju-Hai could not tell whether the ancient mandarin was threatening him or pleading with him. "I'll do what I can," Ju-Hai lied.

Kwan studied his host for a long moment. Finally, the old man said, "No, you'll *do* it. *You* said we had to crush the enemy quickly, before the emperor started to worry about the barbarians. So I tried, damn you. I'm an old man, too old to be roaming around the empire making war, but I tried."

Kwan paused and pointed a yellow-nailed finger at Ju-Hai's face. "It's your turn. By tomorrow night, Batu Min Ho will be gone. He'll be gone, or I'll tell the emperor why the barbarians attacked Shou Lung."

Ju-Hai ground his teeth, angered by the threat. He was also angry at himself for underestimating the old man's acumen. With Kwan, lies would not work. The Minister of State knew he would have to resort to threats, even if it did mean Ting would overhear the whole sordid business of how this war started. There was nothing to be done about it.

"I'm not going to have Batu Min Ho removed," Ju-Hai began.

Kwan's baggy eyes opened wide in anger. He slammed his ancient fist down on the table so hard the teacups spilled. "Then you're finished!" he spat.

"No," Ju-Hai responded, righting his teacup and speaking in a calm voice. "No, I'm not. What are you going to tell the emperor? That I started this war myself? Don't you think he'll want to know where the assassin came from?"

"It was done at your request!" Kwan pointed out.

"Do you think he'll care?" Ju-Hai demanded, taking pains to keep his voice even and polite. "We started this war together. It's unfortunate that *we* can't finish it. But if we can't do it, we must find someone who can."

Ju-Hai poured more tea for himself, but the pot ran out as he tried to refill Kwan's cup. "We're going to stand aside and let this Batu Min Ho kill barbarians," the Minister of State said. "After he wins the war, *if* he wins the war, we're going to welcome him into the Mandarinate. Undoubtedly, he will have earned the post."

Ju-Hai sipped his tea, evaluating Kwan over the top of his cup. "Until then, instead of two more incompetent, corrupt bureaucrats executed for crimes against their offices, you and I will still be mandarins of the Shou Empire. What could be more fair than that?"

Kwan's face turned from angry red to deep purple. He began to breathe in short puffs. For a moment, Ju-Hai hoped the old man was doing him the consideration of dying out of rage. At length, however, the old mandarin's color returned to normal and he managed to stand.

"This is not over, Ju-Hai," Kwan sputtered. "I do not take kindly to betrayal."

"As long as you take kindly to survival," the Minister of State responded. "My guards will show you out."

After the old man left, Ting returned to the table and sat down. For several minutes, she simply watched Ju-Hai with a patient expression and did not say anything.

Finally, Ju-Hai looked at her. "I may as well tell you," he sighed. "You'll just dig it up on your own, and I'll have an even bigger mess when the emperor wants to know what you're looking for."

"I must know what's happening," she agreed, regarding her mentor with a steady, unreadable eyes.

Ju-Hai rubbed his palms over his brow, then folded his hands on the table. "It's not so complicated," he began. "Over the last two years, a barbarian named Yamun Khahan has united the horse tribes. Recently, he has been wiping out our trade caravans, and tax revenues have been dropping steadily. Several times, we have sent gifts to him, hoping to buy his favor. When that did not work, Minister Kwan and I urged the emperor to send an army west to subdue the horse tribes. But the Divine One refused, not wishing to be the aggressor in a war.

"Minister Kwan and I finally developed a plan to deal with the problem quickly and efficiently. We contacted this khahan's stepmother, a treacherous woman named Bayalun. In return for her promise to leave our caravans alone, we agreed to help her usurp his throne."

"Surely you didn't believe she would keep her word?" Ting asked, raising an eyebrow.

"No," Ju-Hai responded, "but we believed that without Yamun Khahan's leadership, the horse tribes would once again dissolve into the warring clans they have always been. In any case, we sent an assassin to aid Bayalun. Unfortunately, Yamun discovered our plot. In retaliation, he has turned his horde in our direction. I fear we have sadly underestimated both his ingenuity and his strength."

Ting lifted her empty teacup and held it thoughtfully against her lips, considering her mentor's explanation. Several moments later, she asked, "Do you really think this Batu Min Ho can stop the barbarians?"

The minister nodded and met her gaze. "I am convinced that if the Tuigan can be stopped, Batu is the only man who can do it. He knows more about the horse tribes than any of our surviving generals. From what I have seen of our other high officers, he alone possesses the cunning and courage to match Yamun Khahan."

Ting placed her empty cup back on table. "An unfortunate turn of events," she said. "Clearly, you only had Shou Lung's best interests at heart."

Ju-Hai breathed a sigh of relief. "Then you will keep my secret?"

Before answering, Ting studied her lacquered fingernails. "Considering the presence of a spy in our midst," she said, "would it not be wise to place a cadre of guards at the disposal of the Ministry of State Security?"

Ju-Hai closed his tired eyes. It would have been too much to hope that the Tigress would aid him without demanding payment. "What do you intend to do with them?" he asked.

"Use them to keep Tuigan spies out of Tai Tung and the summer palace," she said quickly.

Ju-Hai opened his eyes. Although he did not doubt that she would assign the guards to the duties she mentioned, he also suspected that the force would satisfy her own sense of personal aggrandizement. "How many?" he asked wearily.

"A thousand—no, two thousand," Ting answered. "That is not too much to ask."

The minister shook his head, then prepared an angry stare and met Ting's gaze. "A thousand, and no more. Under no circumstances will I permit anyone to control a force equal to the emperor's personal guard."

Ting smiled to indicate her acceptance of the offer. "Let us wish heaven's favor on General Batu."

- 5 -

The Silent House

After the Mandarinate's dismissal, Batu spent the rest of the day cloistered with the emperor. For many hours, the general stood before the jade throne answering questions about the Tuigan. Though his back and legs grew so weary they fell numb, he did not ask for a chair. Only mandarins were permitted to sit in the Son of Heaven's presence.

The emperor interrogated Batu about every detail of the horsewarriors' lifestyle. He wanted to know about their religion, their marriage customs, even their taste in food and wine. Of course, the general could not answer all the emperor's questions, but he was surprised at how much he could recall under the Divine One's relentless questioning.

Finally, the meager body of knowledge Batu had accrued from his great-grandfather's stories was exhausted. When it became apparent the general could remember no more, the emperor turned the conversation to war strategies.

"General, if these warriors are only a tenth as ferocious and cunning as you say, Shou Lung is indeed in great danger," the Divine One said. "I will assemble a vast army and send it north to meet these barbarians."

Batu found the emperor's plan imprudent, for it ignored the Tuigans' mobility. Fortunately, the general was enough of a politician not to express his reservations bluntly. Instead, he politely nodded, then said, "A courageous decision, Divine One. Yet, such a vast army will need a great many supplies—supplies that must be brought from behind the lines. With the advantage of their horses, will it not be possible for the barbarians to encircle that vast army and cut its supply line?"

The Son of Heaven furrowed his brow and said, "Of course, but the barbarians are the ones who will be trapped. As soon as they appear behind our lines, we'll fall back and smash them. Surely you are familiar with the tactic, General. It is discussed in the *Book of Heaven*."

Batu grimaced inwardly. He had not expected the emperor to be one of those unimaginative Shou who believed the answer to every problem could be found that ancient text. The general did not allow his emotions to show, however. He concentrated upon relaxing his face so his expression would remain unreadable, then said, "Your ruse has much to recommend it—" He paused a moment to allow the emperor to appreciate the compliment "—as did the trap that Minister Kwan laid at our last battle."

The emperor did not miss the implication of Batu's statement. Scowling, the Divine One shifted forward and demanded, "If you do not like this strategy, what plan would you suggest?"

Though confident that there was only one way to defeat the barbarians, Batu hesitated, searching for a diplomatic and inoffensive way to phrase his answer.

"Come now, General," the emperor pressed, pointedly remaining seated at the edge of his throne. "What tactic do you favor?"

Batu saw that he had no choice except to speak his mind candidly. Lifting his chin, he said, "The only way to defeat the Tuigan is to fight as they do—with boldness and imagination, not with standard military tactics."

A brooding frown crossed the Divine One's mouth. "Do you mean to imply that barbarian tactics are superior to those suggested in the *Book of Heaven*?"

At first, the general was inclined to equivocate, to say that the Tuigan strategy was merely more appropriate to circumstances. However, noting that his feeble diplomatic skills had done him little good with the emperor, he decided to leave the flattery to the bureaucrats.

Returning the emperor's gaze, Batu said, "If the barbarians could read the *Book of Heaven*, they might have made the same mistakes that our northern armies did. Unfortunately, the Tuigan are uneducated men. Instead of the advice of venerable ancestors, they rely upon treacherous natures and animal cunning."

The Divine One stared at Batu with emotionless eyes. For several moments, the general stood in silence, hoping he had not angered the emperor too severely. His words had lacked the customary Shou tact, but the general believed what he said.

At length, the emperor calmly pushed himself back into his throne. He studied Batu scornfully, then said, "It disturbs me that you hold the wisdom of our ancestors in such low esteem, General. They have written many pages regarding the art of war, and their wisdom has served us well."

Batu bowed his head. "I agree, Divine One. But to the Tuigan, warfare is no art. It is a way of life. If we are to defeat them, we must understand their natures as well as we understand the *Book of Heaven*."

The emperor's face relaxed, concealing his emotions. "General, how much of the *Book of Heaven* can you recite?"

Batu flushed. "I have read it, of course. But my duties have not allowed much time for study."

The Divine One shook his head in exaggerated disappointment. "There are those who claim that giving you command of the barbarian war is Shou Lung's only hope of victory. Can this be so?"

The emperor's words took Batu by surprise, and his mouth dropped open. The mere idea of being considered for such a promotion stunned him. Yet, as soon as the Divine One had mentioned the possibility, he wanted nothing more.

Finally, Batu nodded. "I *am* the only man that can defeat the barbarians."

The Divine One pursed his lips in cynicism. "I wish you

made me more confident, General, but it doesn't matter. You are the only commander who has led so much as a third of his troops away from a battle against the Tuigan. You are hereby named a general of the second degree and given command of the Northern Marches and the Barbarian War."

Batu bowed very low, elated by the promotion and the prospect of commanding the entire campaign against the barbarians. "I will not fail Shou Lung, Divine One."

The emperor did not respond immediately. Instead, he sent a guard to summon the chamberlain, then finally turned his attention back to Batu. "If you fail, General, you will be failing *me* as well as Shou Lung," he said. "Remember that."

Batu did not understand the distinction. Like all Shou, he considered Shou Lung and the emperor to be one and the same. It was impossible to serve one without serving the other—or to fail one without failing the other. He could not conceive of why the emperor felt the need to point out the unity.

Before the general could puzzle out the question, the chamberlain entered the hall and walked to the center of the floor, next to Batu.

"You wished to see me?" the bureaucrat asked, bowing to the Divine One.

"Yes." The emperor nodded at Batu. "I have promoted Batu Min Ho to second-degree general in command of the Northern Marches. Please find a suitable residence for his family within the summer palace."

The chamberlain's narrow eyes popped wide open. The astonished bureaucrat hazarded a sidelong glance at the shabbily-dressed general, obviously regretting the slights he had given him earlier that day.

"Is there a problem?" the Divine One asked. "Surely, we have plenty of houses left."

The chamberlain looked back to the emperor. "No, there is no problem. I am already thinking of a home that I am sure the general will find most acceptable. I can have it ready within the hour."

"See to it," the emperor said, dismissing the bureaucrat with a flick of his wrist.

After the chamberlain left, the Divine One described in minute detail the forces that he had assembled to battle the Tuigan. Ignoring the pain in his back and legs, Batu listened attentively. He was so invigorated by the promotion that he committed every last detail to memory without effort.

After the emperor dismissed Batu, the chamberlain and a dozen guards escorted the general into the summer palace's maze of streets. As they walked through the stone-paved lanes, the chamberlain kept up a constant patter of explanation. Batu ignored most of the man's narrative. While the general had been sequestered with the emperor, night had fallen and it was now impossible to see even the compound walls of the magnificent houses the chamberlain was describing.

At last, fifteen minutes later, the chamberlain stopped at the south gate of a house. "Does this home meet your approval, General Batu?"

Batu eyed the dark outer wall and gate with a judgmental air. Though smaller than his home in Chukei, this house was constructed of better materials. Where his gate had been made of reinforced oak planks, this one was constructed of solid, black iron. The wall was red brick, instead of tamped earth covered with hardened clay.

Recalling how rude the chamberlain had been when Batu arrived at the Hall of Supreme Harmony earlier that day, the general could not resist making the bureaucrat squirm. "It's not as large as I'm accustomed to," he said softly.

The chamberlain's hopeful smile sagged into a disappointed frown. "But it's one of the largest homes in the summer palace."

The general scoffed, allowing himself to enjoy the bureaucrat's discomfort. Behind the chamberlain's narrow eyes, Batu could almost see the man trying to decide just where a second-degree general fit into the hierarchy of palace life.

Finally, the confused bureaucrat reached an uncertain conclusion. "Perhaps the Chief Secretary of the Bureau of

Bells and Drums could be moved," the chamberlain suggested tentatively. "His house is not nearly as fine as this, but it is a little larger."

Batu grinned at the chamberlain's consternation and decided to continue his game. "How long would that take? I'm very tired and would like to sleep soon."

"But we c-couldn't possibly move him t-tonight!" the bureaucrat stammered. "It wouldn't be civilized!"

Deciding he had more than repaid the chamberlain's rudeness, the general said, "Then I'll make do with this house."

The chamberlain sighed in relief. "A wise choice, General. It is much better appointed than the chief secretary's." He opened the iron gate and bowed. "I took the liberty of having your family brought from Hsuang Yu Po's encampment. They await you inside."

Batu's heart leaped. "Wu and the children? Here?" He had hoped that they had come south with his father-in-law, but he had never dreamed he would see them so soon.

The chamberlain smiled. "It seemed the least I could do."

Regretting the petty vengeance he had taken upon the man, Batu bowed deeply. "May your ancestors dwell in the heavens for eternity."

"Leaving the chief secretary to his home is thanks enough," the chamberlain replied, also bowing.

As Batu walked through the gate, the bittersweet smell of persimmon blossoms greeted him. The slender silhouettes of young persimmon trees lined the walls, making it seem as if the house had been built in a park. The general was more interested in the conspicuous lack of guards than in the foliage. Perhaps the chief secretaries and mandarins did not feel the need for personal guards inside the summer palace, but the general did not share their confidence. He quickly turned back to the chamberlain, saying, "If you please, send me a detail of guards before you retire."

The bureaucrat frowned. "They haven't arrived?"

Batu studied the shadows inside the compound. "No."

As if the general's word were suspect, the chamberlain

stepped through the gate and looked to both sides. "They should have been here. My apologies."

"Think nothing of it," Batu replied. Knowing that he would soon see his family, he was in a generous mood.

Promising to send the guards immediately, the chamberlain bowed and left. Normally, Batu would have had a detail of his own men guard his home, but personal troops were not allowed inside the walls of the summer palace. He had no choice but to use those provided by the emperor.

The general paused at the gate to study his new home and to prepare himself for seeing his family. Like most Shou "houses," this one was actually an arrangement of several one-story buildings inside a walled compound. Twenty feet ahead sat the main hall, a simple rectangular structure with a clay-tile roof. Its exaggerated, upturned eaves were supported by parallel rows of wooden pillars.

Though Batu could not see the building's color in the dim light, he guessed the roof would be traditional green-blue and the pillars would be some earthy red tone. The walls were no more than rice-paper panels that fit between the pillars. Inside the west end of the building, an oil lamp sat on a low table, casting a soft white glow through the translucent walls.

Panels on the southern and northern walls had been moved aside to allow the evening breeze to blow through the building. Through this opening, Batu saw the outer courtyard. It was a small, stone-paved atrium. A large, oddly shaped rock of black pumice sat in the middle of a shallow lotus pool. In Shou homes, it was customary to make the courtyard seem more natural by displaying a strangely shaped boulder.

Buildings identical to the main hall surrounded the courtyard on its other three sides. The room to the west, Batu knew, would be the kitchen, while the children would be sleeping or playing in the one to the east. The building on the other side of the courtyard would be reserved for guests.

Beyond the guest quarters would be a courtyard similar

to the first, also surrounded by one-story buildings. The parents of the household would sleep in the northernmost building. The servants would occupy the halls flanking this second, private courtyard.

The house was silent, so silent that Batu could hear an infant crying down the lane, crickets chirping in the surrounding houses, and the lamp sputtering in the main hall. Listening for the sound of his children's laughter or the shuffle of Wu's slippers, Batu went to the entrance.

Inside, the silhouettes of three elegant couches sat on the eastern end of the room. On the western end, the sputtering oil lamp rested upon the edge of a stone-walled pool. Two marble dolphins rose out of the center of the basin, their mouths upturned and spouting small jets of water. Elaborately sculpted stone benches surrounded the fountain.

The hall's opulence amazed Batu, but not as much as its emptiness concerned him. Someone had occupied the building earlier that evening, or the oil lamp would not still be burning. Yet, there were no cloaks on the benches, no silk slippers left by the doors, no signs of habitation whatsoever.

Of course, there would not be, the general realized. He walked over to the pool and picked up the burning lamp, shining its yellow light into the lavish corners of the room. His family could not have arrived more than half an hour ahead of him. Undoubtedly, the children had been exhausted and Wu had put them straight to bed. She had probably left the lit oil lamp so the general could negotiate his way into their chamber without disturbing the children. The absence of servants was easily explained by the unexpected summons to the new home. No doubt, Batu thought, they would follow tomorrow with the family's personal items.

Then the silence of the house struck the general again. Even if the children and Wu were in bed, he should have heard something—chirping crickets, Wu's rhythmic breathing, his son talking in his sleep. Instead, Batu heard nothing inside the house.

He extinguished the lamp and drew his dagger. If the crickets were quiet, it was because someone was skulking about the compound. He started to call for his wife, but thought better of it and remained silent. Wu was hardly the typical helpless wife of a Shou patrician. If she were in the house with the intruder, it would be the intruder who was in danger.

After allowing his eyes to readjust to the darkness, Batu peered out the door leading into the first courtyard. Again, there was no sign of violence or habitation. The other halls remained dark, and the paving stones of the courtyard looked as cold and as lifeless as the ruins of some long-forgotten citadel.

Batu stayed in the hall for nearly a minute, studying the shadows in the courtyard. The general was doing more than just watching for movement and listening for sound. He was attempting to reach into the dark corners with his *ki*, his life energy, and feel what was there. Wu called this intangible looking *ki*-touch, and she had tried to teach it to Batu many times.

Unfortunately, he had not learned it very well. He was what Wu playfully called a "one way man," a man whose feelings, as well as his thoughts, were ruled by his mind. Even at his best, Batu had barely been able to feel the presence of six servants Wu had sent to hide in a dark room. Right now, he felt nothing save his own nagging fear that something terrible had happened to his family.

Taking care to remain in the shadow of the buildings' eaves, the general circled around the first courtyard. He stopped at the guest hall. When he heard nothing from inside, he slid one of the paper panels aside.

A chill crept down the back of Batu's neck, and he felt with absolute certainty that someone awaited him in the second courtyard. A mixture of emotions—determination, anger, even fear—washed over him. He saw a barely perceptible silhouette standing outlined against the opposite wall, and he wondered if he had finally experienced Wu's *ki*-touch.

Without taking his eyes off the silhouette, Batu silently crawled onto the guest hall's polished wooden floor. Against the dark paper wall, he could barely distinguish the shadow from the darkness surrounding it. He feared that if he turned away, the silhouette would disappear.

It was still there when he reached the other side of the building. Batu curled his knees beneath his body, then reached forward and began to slide the door panel aside. Through the narrow opening, he saw a figure dressed in a dark *maitung*. The man remained motionless.

In the same instant, the general heard a silk slipper whisper across the floor a few feet to his right. Realizing he was about to be ambushed, he rolled left, raising his dagger to defend himself. A sharp pain shot through his forearm, then his fingers went numb and the dagger dropped from his hand. The interior of the hall was so dark that Batu could not see his attacker.

The general rolled toward the assailant, hoping to entangle his adversary's legs. He found nothing but hard empty floor, then two feet settled behind him with feline grace. Something struck him on the shoulderblade with a blow that felt like a hammer strike. His back erupted into agony.

The blow caused terrible pain, but Batu recognized the attack's true intention and knew he had been lucky. His opponent had been trying to drive a toe under his shoulder blade, striking for a vulnerable line of nerves kung-fu artists knew as the bladder meridian. Though the general did not practice the Way of the Empty Hand, he had learned enough of the art to recognize its debilitating techniques.

Ignoring his pain, Batu pushed off the floor and sprang to his feet. His assailant had already struck twice. If the general allowed another blow to land, it might be the last he ever felt.

As Batu stood, the attacker's silhouette withdrew in a twisted, bent-knee stance characteristic of kung fu. The assailant was no taller than Batu, but slight of stature and quite small. To camouflage himself in the night, he wore a set of black pajamalike clothes known as a *samfu*. He had wrapped a black scarf around his head to keep his face hidden as well. So complete was the effect that Batu felt as though he were fighting a shadow.

Unexpectedly, the silhouette relaxed. Realizing this might be his only chance to survive the battle, the general reached for his sword.

With one swift motion, the shadow shifted into the white crane stance and kicked. The sharp clack of teeth cracked through Batu's head, and he felt himself lifted off his feet. His eyes rolled back in their sockets, his vision went white, and he sank into the numb world of emptiness.

Batu plummeted through the black sphere of nothingness for an eternity. I'm dead, he thought. There can be no doubt of that. If the kick didn't smash my skull, the assassin finished the job while I lay unconscious—and even if the assassin didn't kill me, my body has withered and rotted away in all the dark years I've been falling.

Batu was angry and sorrowful. The assassin, undoubtedly sent by Kwan, had robbed him of his chance to fight the illustrious battle.

The fate of his family also pressed on his mind. He feared the assassin had killed them, too. Fortunately, if they had survived, he had no need to worry. Wu knew where the gold was hidden, and she was quite capable of defending the family alone. Batu's confidence in her intelligence and competence was why he had never worried about dying in battle. No matter what happened, Wu would manage.

Batu stopped falling and came to a rest on floating black clouds. How long he lay there, he could not tell. He wondered if this eternal lonely darkness was what every man found in the afterworld, or if it was some special torment reserved for generals who died without fulfilling their destinies.

An eon later, Batu heard a shy titter. Everything remained black, but the familiar smell of a woman's perfume filled his nostrils. Soft hands stroked his chest, and he was cradled in a warm lap. With a deep sense of relief, Batu realized he had at last reached the Land of Extreme Felicity.

He was surprised to find that it was a region of sensual pleasure. Like most Shou, he had imagined it to be a place of strict bureaucratic order, where all beings abided in perfect harmony and every affair proceeded according to the perfect plan of the Celestial Emperor. It was a revelation he did not find at all disagreeable. Somehow, the thought of occupying an obscure post in the infinite bureaucracy paled beside the prospect of spending eternity cradled in the lap of a beautiful woman.

A second titter reached Batu's ears, then he felt himself being dragged across a floor—a solid floor.

"Breathe, my husband." The sultry voice belonged to his wife, Wu. He felt her strong hands massaging his chest.

"Wu?" Batu asked. Her name came out in a strangled gasp, and a wave of agony shot through his jaw. Ignoring the pain and stiffness in his face, he asked, "Are you dead, too?"

A pair of giggles sounded from Batu's feet.

"No, husband. Neither are you."

Batu frowned, then shook his head. The motion caused his face to ache from the nose down, and the general knew that his spirit remained attached to his body. He opened his eyes, then slowly made out his wife's face. She was cradling his head in her lap. Her silky hair hung draped over her shoulder in a long loose tail, and the delicate features of her slender face were tense with apprehension. She wore a black *samfu*, and a black scarf was wrapped around her throat.

"The assassin—you?" he asked.

Before Wu could respond, another pair of giggles came from Batu's feet. The general looked down and saw his two children kneeling there. "How dare you laugh at your father!" he said harshly. "Begone!"

Both Ji and Yo scrambled to their feet, but before they turned to leave, Batu said, "Wait—I guess your father looks silly, doesn't he? Come here and give me my hug."

In the dim light, Batu could see his children's broad grins, but that was all. They rushed to his side—the five-year-old boy, Ji, to the left, and the four-year-old girl, Yo, to the right.

As they embraced him, they were far from careful to avoid the bruises their mother had just inflicted, but Batu did not care. He simply did not feel the pain.

After a moment, the children stood. Wu ordered them to find their grandfather and have him put them to bed. Batu tried to free himself from Wu's grasp, but found his body too sore to move.

"What did you do?" he asked.

"Angry goose nerve kick," she replied. "You were reaching for your sword. My only other choice was to break your arm."

Batu touched his sorest spot, the soft pit just beneath the cleft of his chin. A fresh wave of agony rolled through his entire body. "How long am I going to feel like this?"

"No more than an hour," Wu replied. "I am truly sorry. In the dark, all I could see was your *chia*." She tugged at his tattered armor. "It was so shabby that I thought you were an intruder."

Batu chuckled. "I should have been so lucky. You would have killed an intruder."

At that moment, a tall man carrying a lit lamp entered the hall. "I put the children in the next hall," he said.

The man's long, graying hair was tied in the warrior's top-knot, and he wore the brocaded *hai-waitao* of a Shou nobleman. When the tall man saw that Batu was awake, he stopped and bowed. As always, the nobleman's firm face was unreadable.

Batu tried to stand and found it too difficult. He merely inclined his head for a long moment. "Tzu Hsuang, please forgive me for not rising. I fear your daughter has incapacitated me."

Hsuang acknowledged Batu's apology with a stiff nod, then said, "Yes, so I see. If the damage is permanent, perhaps we should make her the General of the Northern Marches."

His father-in-law's sarcasm was not lost on Batu. Hsuang, the general suspected, had been the silhouette that served to bait Wu's trap. Had Batu fallen for such a textbook ambush on the battlefield, he would have resigned his commission out of shame. "The trap was well laid," Batu acknowledged. "What, besides your modest son-in-law, were you trying to capture?"

"Vagabonds," Wu responded, using the Shou slang for hired assassins.

Placing the lamp on a low table, Tzu Hsuang seated himself on a couch and continued the explanation. "This afternoon, a friend's messenger arrived at my camp to report rumors that you would soon be appointed General of the Northern Marches," Hsuang said. "Needless to say, we were skeptical."

"*You* were skeptical," Wu corrected. "At least until the imperial chamberlain's assistant arrived."

Hsuang ignored his daughter's admonishment. "He offered to escort us to your new home. Before we could leave, however, another messenger arrived. This one was from Ju-Hai," the noblemen said. Using the Minister of State's given name was pretentious, but, when it came to politics, Wu's father was given to affectation. "The minister wished to warn us that Kwan is jealous of your favor with the emperor."

"When we arrived, the house was guarded by Kwan's troops," Wu said, slowly stroking Batu's temples.

"I sent them away immediately," Hsuang recounted, pointing an accusing finger at Batu. "Then you came sneaking in here like a murderer."

"A murderer!" Batu snapped. "This is my house. Where did you expect me to sleep?"

"We did not expect you back so soon, my love," Wu said. She moved her fingers to the sides of Batu's neck and began rubbing it gently. "The messengers said you had been sequestered with the emperor all afternoon, and that you might be with him all night."

Tzu Hsuang regarded Batu with an appraising eye, then asked, "Exactly what passed between you and the Divine One? The last battlefield report said you had lost your army and were retreating before the barbarians."

"Before that, we had already given you up for dead," Wu

added. "Your letter from the sorghum field sounded as though the enemy had his sword to your throat."

"I turned his blade," Batu said, irritated. Tzu Hsuang's observation concerning the loss of his army had pricked the general's ego, as he was sure Hsuang had intended. Though the general and his father-in-law enjoyed cordial relations, Hsuang rarely missed an opportunity to abuse Batu's pride. The aging nobleman would never quite forgive his son-in-law for stealing Wu away from the Hsuang family.

As Tzu Hsuang's only legitimate child, Wu had rarely been refused anything during her early years. Her father had afforded her many privileges usually reserved for noblemen's sons. Sitting at her father's knee, Wu had learned to administer accounts and issue orders with a commanding presence. Fascinated by the military, she had also spent much of her time following the commanders of her father's army. As a result, she had learned the basics of military doctrine, how to handle a variety of weapons, and had begun her study of kung fu.

Unfortunately for Hsuang, his early indulgence resulted in a defiant daughter, at least according to the standards of Shou nobility. By the time a young officer named Batu Min Ho had come to her attention, Wu had become an independent and headstrong young lady. She had also blossomed into a woman of incredible beauty. Despite their great difference in social standing, Batu had set his heart on earning Wu's love.

As it turned out, winning her heart had been the easiest part of the conflict that followed. Batu's rugged features, forthright manner, and determined courtship had appealed to Wu, so she had found many pretexts to enjoy his company. Eventually, she had fallen as deeply in love with the young officer as he had with her.

However, as a man of high standing, Hsuang had possessed no desire to wed his daughter to the son of a minor landowner, especially one only three generations removed from barbarian ancestors. The lord had forbidden his daughter from seeing Batu, then tried to arrange several marriages more appropriate to her station. Each time, Wu had chased away the suitor with her stubborn, disrespectful manners. The animosity between the nobleman and his daughter had eventually become more than Hsuang could bear. The lord had consented to the marriage, but only if Batu Min Ho could elevate himself to the rank of general.

Both Batu and Wu had soon realized that Hsuang was stalling, hoping Wu would outgrow what he considered an infatuation with a low-born soldier. However, the lord had underestimated the young officer's determination and his daughter's love. Batu had left Hsuang's private army and taken a commission in the imperial military. Fifteen years later, he had become one of the empire's youngest generals.

For her part, Wu had resisted her father's repeated attempts to arrange alternative marriages. As a man of his word, Tzu Hsuang had been forced to allow the wedding when Batu returned wearing the armor of a Shou general.

The young general had expected relations with Hsuang to remain cold. To his surprise, the noble had treated him with a grudging respect after the marriage. The lord had made it clear that he would never be happy Wu had married outside of the aristocracy, but Hsuang had also expressed his admiration for the young man's determination in winning her.

Wu stopped stroking Batu's neck. He was surprised to find that the pain had lessened, though he still felt less than steady. "How long before I can return home with the children?" she asked, helping Batu to his feet.

Tzu Hsuang answered for his wobbly-kneed son-in-law, "Your home is now with the emperor's court, Daughter."

Despite the lord's disgust with Batu's present condition, Hsuang's voice was proud.

"My home is in Chukei," Wu answered, guiding her husband toward the couch. "Even my husband's love of war cannot change that."

In any other family, her retort would have been seen as surprisingly disrespectful. Hsuang, however, had long ago stopped trying to impose any sense of propriety upon his stubborn daughter.

Instead, he looked to Batu and asked, "Can't you control your wife's tongue?"

"No better than you can control your daughter's," Batu replied, his lips upturned in a faintly roguish smile.

Wu withdrew her support and dropped the general roughly onto the couch. "You'd both do well to remember that the children and I are not chattel."

The sharpness of his wife's tone surprised Batu, and he realized that she was deeply concerned over something she had not yet discussed. "The barbarians may cut Chukei off from the rest of Shou Lung," he said, trying to find a comfortable position for his sore body. "You'll be more secure with the emperor until the danger passes."

Wu met Batu's gaze with the hard eyes of a dragon. "Then end this war quickly, my husband. Our children will never be safe in the emperor's court, and it is selfish to put them in so much danger."

Tzu Hsuang frowned. "Don't be absurd, Wu. I'll leave my steward to look after your safety, but there is no need to worry. The barbarians will never reach the summer palace."

"I am not concerned about barbarians," she retorted, glancing toward the hall where the children slept.

When her father's and husband's faces remained blank, Wu said, "Don't you see? We are hostages. If Batu fails, or even if he offends the wrong person one time too many, we will certainly die."

– 6 –

The Magnificent Army

The wind came from the west, and it was as arid and as dusty as the barren plains of Chukei. It blew steadily, leaving Batu's face dry and gritty.

He stood in a meadow several miles from Tai Tung. No plaza in the city could hold all the armies the emperor had summoned, so Batu had assembled them here. More than one hundred and fifty thousand soldiers blanketed the hills surrounding the field. Coming from as far south as the cities of Seikung and Sental, the *pengs* were from five provinces and the private armies of twenty-five nobles.

Save for the unit colors on their armor trim, the men of the provincial forces were attired and equipped similarly. Most *pengs* wore leather *chous* on their heads and *lun'kia* corselets, with water-buffalo hide girdles to protect their lower abdomens. They carried crossbows and *chiens* for weapons.

The only variations occurred in the small units of heavy infantry and archers. The heavy infantrymen carried *pao shous*, twelve-foot-long glaives with double-pointed blades, and for close combat, short swords called *pai p'is*. For protection, they wore complete suits of lamellar armor made of hundreds of overlapping steel plates. The archers were equipped like those Batu had commanded in the Army of Chukei, with wooden shields, *lun'kia* armor, double-edged swords, longbows, and forty bamboo arrows each.

Each private army was armored and equipped according to the tastes and wealth of its lord. Some consisted primarily of archers, with small contingents of heavy infantry to protect their flanks. Other armies were organized for versatility and were almost entirely light infantrymen armed with crossbows and *chiens*. One army of five hundred men was even composed entirely of heavy cavalry. Each rider wore a fine suit of lamellar armor and carried a sword and a heavy, two-pronged lance called a *ko*.

Despite their differences in appearance and organization, all the armies exhibited the legendary Shou bearing. So great was their discipline that every soldier stood at strict attention. Batu did not hear a single *peng* talking. As he studied the vast assemblage of soldiers, the second-degree general thought that they did not resemble a gathering of men so much as the bare trunks of a crowded, but silent and stark, forest.

Below the hills, the meadow itself was nearly empty. Batu's new purple pavilion sat in the middle of the dry field. One hundred feet away, the Rites Section of the Palace Bureau had built an earthen pyramid. It was from the top of the pyramid that the Divine One would ask the spirits to bless the army.

Batu's sole companion, a beardless Shou with his right arm bound in a sling, said, "It is a magnificent army, sir."

"Yes, Pe," Batu replied. "It is the most magnificent army Shou Lung has ever seen."

Batu was glad to have his adjutant back, even if the boy's sword arm was all but useless. The day after his promotion to commander of the Northern Marches, the general had sent a chariot officer north to retrieve his wounded aide. Under the care of the emperor's healers, the young adjutant had accomplished a remarkable recovery. Though the general knew Pe was far from fully recovered, the boy did not need to be asked twice to return to battle. There would be little time to train a new adjutant, and the general knew it.

"Perhaps we have a name for your troops now," Pe said. "The Most Magnificent Army."

Batu grinned at the boy's enthusiasm, then cast an eye toward the heavens. The sky was vivid blue and the morning sun brilliant white.

"Don't you think Huan-Ti would take offense at our presumption?" Batu asked, referring to the Shou god of war.

Pe's face grew concerned. The youthful adjutant was an ardent worshiper of all the gods, especially the Divine General. The thought of angering a deity as important as Huan-Ti was enough to make Pe pause. "Of course," he said, casting an apologetic eye skyward, "I meant to say the Most Magnificent Army *of Shou Lung*."

Batu chuckled at the tactful clarification, but did not take his eyes off the clear sky. Like any good commander, he was always concerned with the welfare of those serving him. It had occurred to him earlier that the simple act of standing hour after hour might exhaust such a vast army. He had not yet begun briefing his subordinate commanders, and the emperor had not even arrived from the summer palace. It could easily be six hours before the armies were dismissed.

Using his loudest voice, Batu addressed the thirty armies surrounding the meadow. "Relax. Be seated!" he called. Though he knew his voice would not carry to the edges of the camp, he expected his order to be relayed by the officers.

Tens of thousands of *pengs* began to shift their weight, but a murmur ran round the valley as their superiors quickly recalled them to attention. Even after Batu had issued the command a second time, the entire force remained at attention.

His brow raised in disbelief and shock, Pe suggested, "Perhaps they didn't hear the order clearly."

Batu shook his head. "The wind's not that loud. They heard it," he said. "The order didn't come from their commanders."

"You're the general of the Northern Marches," Pe said scornfully. "You command these armies now."

"Yes, I do," Batu replied, studying the assemblage. "Unfortunately, it appears you and I are the only ones who know that."

"Shall I have their generals send word to be seated?" Pe

asked.

After running his hard eyes over the hills for several moments, Batu said, "No. Let them stand." He turned and entered his campaign tent, where the lord or commanding officer of each of the thirty armies awaited him.

The smell of eel's oil, used to protect metal armor and weapons from rust, permeated the pavilion. Batu's skin prickled with a palpable sense of eagerness, and the room buzzed with conversations conducted in pretentious, subdued tones.

The nobles stood in scattered circles of four or five, grouped according to their shifting alliances. Ranging in age from less than thirty to over sixty, they all wore opulent suits of armor. Each lord was accompanied by an aide whose only function appeared to be holding his master's plumed helmet.

The five generals commanding the provincial armies had gathered in one corner. Uniformly near the age of sixty, the commanders were withdrawn and obviously annoyed by the ostentation and excitement of the nobles. The five men wore the traditional uniforms of first-degree generals: vermilion corselets of *k'ai*, with gilded girdles. Unlike the nobles, they were not accompanied by aides. Beneath their arms, they held their own helmets, simple conical affairs topped by vermilion plumes. Batu recognized only one of the provincial generals, a stocky man named Kei Bot Li. He remembered Kei Bot as an overly ambitious but competent officer.

The scabbards of both generals and nobles were empty. Without exception, the men in the tent were hoping for a few words with the emperor after he blessed the army. Anyone carrying a weapon would not be allowed within a hundred feet of the Divine One, and they all knew it.

In the corner opposite the provincial generals stood Tzu Hsuang and a handful of lesser nobles with whom he had strong political alliances. Hsuang's elaborate plate armor encased his body like an oversized, enamelled tortoise shell.

Aside from Tzu Hsuang and Kei Bot Li, the only other person Batu recognized was Minister Kwan. The minister sat behind the table at the head of the tent, openly asserting his position as commander of all Shou Lung's armies. A dozen frowning nobles surrounded the ancient mandarin, intently listening to the old man pontificate. Kwan wore a suit of battle armor that would have weighed heavily on the brittle bones of any other old man. The suit was similar to that worn by the provincial generals, save that Kwan's corselet and helmet plume were blue, reflecting his exalted rank.

In contrast to the pretentious displays of the other commanders, Batu wore only his new *chia*. His one concession to ostentation was that it was trimmed in purple, the color of a second-degree general. Because of his simple dress, perhaps, Batu's entrance remained largely unacknowledged— save by his father-in-law.

Tzu Hsuang ended his conversation and bowed, and the nobles with whom he had been speaking did likewise. The other lords simply glanced at Batu, then returned to their conversations. The provincial generals regarded him with expressions ranging from open contempt to suspicious scrutiny.

"This is disrespectful!" Pe said, stepping forward and speaking loud enough to be overheard.

"Yes, it is," Batu observed evenly. He was more intrigued by the slights than angered by them. The general from Chukei had not expected his subcommanders to accept his authority with eagerness, but neither had he expected them to treat him with open contempt. Batu suspected that Kwan's presence accounted for their insolence. By attending the war council, the minister was making it clear that he had no confidence in his subordinate.

Batu did not care what Kwan thought of him, but he knew that the rivalry between him and the minister would continue to undermine his authority. It was a problem he would have to address before he could command with full effectiveness. Unfortunately, now was not the time or place. At least in name, Kwan was still his superior. If Batu expected his officers to treat him with respect, he would have to do the same for the Minister of War.

After instructing Pe to stay at the entrance, Batu strode purposefully to the front of the tent. There, he bowed to Kwan and said, "I did not expect to see you here, Minister."

Kwan's shriveled mouth contorted into a malevolent sneer. "Is a third-degree general no longer welcome at his subordinate's war council?"

Behind Batu, a chorus of whispers rustled through the tent. The general wanted to ask if ruining him was worth seeing Shou Lung overrun by barbarians, but he knew the question would accomplish nothing. Instead, after a lengthy pause, he said, "My commander is always welcome in my tent, Minister."

A contrived smile slowly creased Kwan's sagging lips. "I'm glad we agree on that much."

Batu shifted his gaze to the nobles gathered around the old man. "If you will return to your seats, we will begin this meeting."

The nobles glanced at the minister for permission.

"Now!" Batu snapped, exerting his authority over the lords. If he had to honor Kwan's authority, it was equally true that his subordinates had to honor his. The sooner he made that fact clear, the better.

Kwan nodded to the nobles, and they walked around the table. As the general waited for them to take their positions with the other lords, a muffled rattle sounded from the surrounding hills. The lords murmured in concerned tones and looked toward the exit.

Batu nodded at Pe, and the young officer stepped outside. An instant later, he returned and bowed very low. "My lords and generals, the emperor approaches."

Pe quickly retreated out of the doorway as the lords filed toward the exit. Only the five provincial generals waited for the proper dismissal, and then left only after receiving permission from both the general and the minister.

Moments later, Batu found himself alone with Kwan. After staring at the old man for a long moment, the general said, "Isn't defeating the barbarians more important than our political disputes? How far do you intend to carry this?"

Kwan stood and, never taking his eyes off Batu, shuffled around the table. "Carry what?" he asked, turning toward the door. "Come, we mustn't keep the emperor waiting."

The minister's disavowal of their rivalry angered Batu as much as the conflict itself, but the only thing he could do about it was swallow his ire and do as ordered. When he followed Kwan out of the tent, he saw that all thirty armies had fallen to their knees and were pressing their foreheads to the ground in symbolic submission to the emperor. The thirty commanders had gathered in front of the earthen pyramid. They were kneeling, but had not yet touched their foreheads to the ground in a kowtow.

Kwan's aide guided him to the base of the pyramid, where, as a member of the Mandarinate, the minister would kneel during the ceremony. Batu went to his own place, twenty feet away from the earthen mound. He kneeled at the front of the thirty commanders.

One thousand soldiers wearing the yellow dragon-scale armor of the emperor's elite guard marched down the eastern hill. The bodyguard, normally an impressive sight, seemed no more than a few drops in the sea of fighting men assembled in the shallow valley. The mandarins, each riding in a covered sedan chair carried by four bearers, followed the imperial guards. Behind the mandarins came the emperor's palanquin, a huge yellow affair carried by sixteen men. Then, also in sedan chairs, came a series of subministers, high-ranking consorts, imperial relatives, and influential eunuchs. Finally, another thousand guards brought up the procession's rear.

The only sounds in the valley were the rhythmic tramp of the imperial bodyguards and the gasping of the wind. When the first guards reached the center of the meadow, they formed a ring around the kowtowing nobles, Batu's tent, and the pyramid. A few moments later, the first sedans arrived and the mandarins, dressed in white ceremonial robes, climbed out of their chairs. As they went to kneel in their places, two of the ministers, Ju-Hai Chou and Ting Mei Wan, inclined their heads in greeting to Batu.

Next, the emperor's palanquin stopped at the steps, but the Divine One did not show himself. The doors remained shut until the last relative knelt behind the pyramid and the last member of the guard took his place in the defensive ring.

Then, without further ceremony, the Lord of Imperial Sacrifices opened the palanquin door. The Divine One stepped out. He wore a robe of gold cloth and a jade crown carved into a likeness of the sacred sky dragon. Hundreds of mystic symbols, representing all the important nature spirits, had been sewn into his cloak with gold and silver thread.

As the emperor ascended the pyramid, he looked pale and tired. Batu did not find his appearance surprising. To purify himself for this ceremony, the emperor had gone without food or sleep for three days. According to the *Book of Heaven*, the spirits perceived the resulting state of exhaustion as a symbol of submission. Therefore, they were more likely to look favorably upon the Divine One's request. To Batu, who was not a great believer in either the celestial bureaucracy or the mystic spirits, such privations seemed an unnecessary and risky taxation on the Son of Heaven's health.

At the top of the pyramid, the emperor stopped and glanced down at Batu, then at each of the other commanders, and finally at the Mandarinate. At this signal, they all touched their foreheads to the scratchy grass. Batu was unhappy to hear several nobles grunt with the simple effort of lowering their heads to the ground. More often than not, the armies of fat commanders were filled with chubby, unskilled soldiers.

The Divine One did not take time to speak any words of inspiration. Even if the soldiers could have heard him, it was not for him to inspire them. That duty fell solely on the shoulders of their commanders. The emperor was here for one reason only: to ask for supernatural cooperation and aid.

Accordingly, when he raised his arms and looked toward the sky, he spoke in the throaty, mystic language of the ancient shamans. Of all the tens-of-thousands of men assembled in the valley, not more than ten understood his words.

As the Divine One's mystic entreaty droned on, Batu's thoughts turned to his conflict with Kwan. He wondered if all his preparations were for naught. The general felt angry at the thought of the old man interfering with the intricate plan he had developed over the last two weeks. The sound of Batu's grinding teeth was soon louder inside his head than the steady drone of the emperor's voice.

Realizing that where there was one Tuigan spy, there were bound to be more, Batu had gone to great lengths to keep his preparations secret. In fact, only he, Wu, and Tzu Hsuang knew exactly how he intended to defeat the barbarians. Batu had even kept his plans secret from the Divine One, for his father-in-law had hinted that a thousand ears heard what was whispered to the emperor.

It had not been easy to finalize the preparations without revealing his intentions, but Ju-Hai Chou had done a great deal to help. Ju-Hai had convinced the Ministry of Magic to send a hundred wizards to support the armies. The High Minister had even lent Batu the Mirror of Shao, a huge looking glass that allowed men to communicate over great distances. At Batu's request, Ju-Hai had assembled a fleet of five hundred merchant junks. With Ting Mei Wan's help, the minister had also fulfilled another of Batu's requests, arranging the evacuation of an entire riverfront village. In all cases, Ju-Hai had honored Batu's desire to keep the reason for his strange preparations secret.

Now, just a week after being charged with winning the Barbarian War, everything Batu needed was in place—as long as Kwan stayed out of the way, and provided the barbarians did not alter their tactics.

Batu was not confident that he could handle Kwan, but he felt sure the barbarians would not change strategies. According to the field dispatches, his scorched-earth policy had slowed the Tuigan advance to a crawl. Their foraging parties were being forced to search for food hundreds of miles from the front lines.

Despite the general's satisfaction with the course of the war, the week had not been entirely a good one. Batu had spent most of his time making plans, pleading for blind co-operation, and speaking with exhausted riders. There had been little opportunity for leisure. When he did have a moment for his family, Ji and Yo had seemed sad and frightened. His children's misery had almost been enough to make him lament the war.

Batu was so absorbed with his thoughts that he did not realize the emperor had finished the supplication until the mandarins began to rise. He barely managed to return to his feet in time to hide his inattentiveness. His subcommanders stood next, then the thirty armies slowly returned to their feet and waited at strict attention.

The Divine One paused to look over the vast assembly of troops. Then, speaking to the Mandarinate, he said, "I have asked the spirits for their blessing, and here is what they said: 'Emperor Kai Chin, your soldiers have the superior weapons of Shou Lung, the courage of the heavens, and the leadership of a wise general. The barbarians have only the speed of starving horses and boldness born of ignorance. Why do you need our blessing?' "

The Divine One paused and ran his gaze over the commanders of the thirty armies. Finally, he continued. "Here is how I answered: 'Great Ones, we know our armies can defeat the enemy horde. We ask your blessing because no arrow can pierce a spirit's armor, no hero can outrun the wind, and no general can match the wisdom of the universe. What I ask is that you support us with favorable conditions, so that we may catch our enemy and halt his vile invasion.' "

The emperor paused long enough to wet his lips. "Here is what they answered: 'Then you shall have our favor, Kai Chin, for the enemy is an abomination to nature. We would like your armies to destroy this thing, for our sakes as well as yours. If it rains and slows the advance of your armies, do not worry. It will rain on the enemy twice as much. If the sun beats down upon your heads and parches your throats, it will beat down on the enemy twice as hard, driving the moisture from his body. If the winds blow dirt in your faces, then the enemy will lose his way in a whirlwind of dust.' "

The emperor stopped again and looked from the commanders to the soldiers on the hill. Finally, he spoke again, this time addressing the troops. "The spirits have spoken, my *pengs*. We cannot lose!"

The soldiers who could hear, those at the bottom of the hills, raised their weapons and gave a tremendous yell. Then they cheered again, and this time their fellows higher on the hill joined in. By the third cheer, their voices rolled over the meadow like thunderclaps. The emperor turned slowly, studying each of the thirty armies in turn.

With each cheer, Batu felt something stir deep within his chest. He did not know whether it was the vibration of one hundred and fifty thousand voices, his own excitement, or the mystic touch of a nature spirit. He only knew that, for the first time since hearing about the Tuigan invasion, he felt Shou Lung could not lose the war. He turned and raised his right arm, leading the other army commanders as they, too, joined in the cheering.

The roar continued for nearly ten minutes, until Batu's ears rang from the din and his throat ached from yelling. Finally, the emperor descended from the pyramid. The valley immediately fell as silent as it had been when the imperial procession had arrived.

Kwan Chan Sen met the emperor at the base of the steps. "A marvelous address, Divine One," the minister said, bowing low. "General Batu has not yet finished his strategy session. May I invite you and the mandarins to attend?"

The emperor glanced at Batu, who remained standing at strict attention in front of the army commanders. "Yes," the Son of Heaven said, "I think I would like that."

As the Divine One and the mandarins turned toward the command tent, Batu frowned. With spies loose in the summer palace, he had no wish to discuss strategy in front of the mandarins. Besides, he suspected Kwan's invitation was simply another maneuver in the minister's campaign to discredit him.

After the Son of Heaven entered the tent, Batu and the other commanders quickly followed. Kwan had arranged things so the emperor and mandarins were seated at the table in front, leaving no room for Batu. The intention, of course, was to reinforce the young general's position as Kwan's subordinate.

As Batu walked forward to stand at the table, the emperor's face remained impassive, as the general knew it would for the rest of the meeting. During the past week, he had seen enough to know that the Divine One held himself above the petty politics of high bureaucracy.

With the emperor present, the army commanders filed into the tent quickly and silently. It only took a few minutes before the meeting began.

Kwan seized the initiative, placing his arms on the table and saying, "Here we are, General Batu. What do you intend to do with us?"

Batu bit back his anger and turned to address his subordinates, the army commanders. "Our enemies move with the speed of the wind and the precision of the stars," he said. "They are barbarians, but they are cunning and sophisticated barbarians who employ all the war tactics described in the *Book of Heaven*, and many that are not. If we are to defeat these invaders, we must never underestimate them."

Batu paused, and Kwan took the opening to speak again. "Surely your plan consists of more than not underestimating the enemy."

The general from Chukei looked over his shoulder at Kwan. "It does," he confirmed without elaborating. Almost certainly, anything he said with the mandarins present would find its way to the ears of spies.

"Would you be so kind as to explain?" Kwan pressed, a faint sneer on his wrinkled lips.

The young general frowned, trying to think of a way to refuse without insulting the mandarins. He glanced at Ju-

Hai Chou for help. The Minister of State's face betrayed no hint of sympathy, and Batu realized that Ju-Hai expected him to work his own way out of this.

Finally, Batu decided to reveal a partial truth. He said, "The fifty thousand men in the noble armies will ride northwest, toward Yenching, to engage the barbarians."

He purposefully did not mention that Tzu Hsuang would lead that force. The nobles were a proud and contentious lot. They would not accept the command of Batu's father-in-law until the young general had firmly established his own authority.

Fortunately, Kwan pressed along another line. "What is your intention for the provincial armies?" the old man asked, his milky eyes fixed on Batu's face.

"They will go due west to secure Shou Kuan," Batu said. He did not enjoy lying in the Divine One's presence, but he could not reveal his true intention.

As it was, an astonished murmur rustled through the tent. Batu's plan ignored one of the most basic dictums in the *Book of Heaven*: Never split forces in the face of the enemy.

The murmur grew louder, and Kwan could not suppress a grin. The minister's smile gave Batu a clue as to what the old man was doing. The minister had certainly heard about the secrecy with which Batu had gone about his preparations. The old man must have suspected that the younger general would refuse to divulge his entire strategy in front of so many people. Without all the details, any plan could appear poorly conceived.

Batu remembered one of Sin Kow's maxims: "When one discovers a trap, it is not enough to disarm it. One must turn the trap against the man who created it." The young general decided to reverse his strategy and play along with the minister.

After allowing Batu's subcommanders to murmur in astonishment for several seconds, Kwan raised his voice loud enough to be heard. "So, you're splitting the army?"

"Yes," Batu replied, doing his best to feign ignorance.

"What's wrong with that?"

As he had expected, the tent erupted into a chorus of urgent whispers. Kwan's wrinkled face settled into a smirk of satisfaction, but the minister carefully avoided doing anything that the emperor might construe as sowing discontent. If Batu was going to draw the old man into a foolish mistake, he knew he had to provide more bait.

The young general added, "Under Tzu Hsuang's leadership, the noble armies—"

Batu needed to say no more. Twenty nobles jumped to their feet, voicing indignation and outrage. The five provincial generals moved toward Kwan, all expressing reservations about Batu's experience.

Beaming with satisfaction, Kwan allowed the pandemonium to continue for several moments. Feigning a look of confusion and pain, Batu scanned the room as though searching for a friend. His only solid ally, Tzu Hsuang, was frowning, and the emperor's weary face betrayed doubt about choosing Batu to lead the war.

Finally, Kwan moved in for the kill. Rising to his feet, he lifted his hands for silence. The room slowly fell quiet, and, with a triumphant expression, the old man addressed Batu. "General, the plan you have outlined ignores every dictum of basic strategy. Surely, you can't be serious."

Doing his best to appear unsure of himself, Batu glanced from Kwan to his father-in-law to the emperor, then back to the old minister. As if trying to hedge, he said, "Admittedly, I haven't worked out all the details, but this is my general plan. It's the best I can do."

A chorus of angry grumbles ran through the tent. Kwan closed his eyes and shook his head. After a lengthy pause, the minister again motioned the crowd into silence. With an air of extreme reluctance, the old man turned to the emperor. "Divine One, it is with the greatest reluctance that I must insist General Batu be replaced with a more competent officer."

Several nobles voiced their agreement.

The Divine One frowned, then looked at Batu with an expression that seemed half confusion and half anger. The young general returned the appraising look with as steady a gaze as he could summon. His gambit had worked. He had forced Kwan into asking the emperor to choose between them. Now, he could only hope the Son of Heaven would choose correctly.

Help came from an unexpected corner. Ju-Hai Chou turned toward the emperor. "Divine One, if I may speak?"

The Son of Heaven nodded. "We wish you would."

"As you know, I am not a military man. Still, I think there is more to General Batu's plan than is apparent at first glance." He cast an evil eye toward Kwan, who suddenly frowned in concern.

The emperor nodded and turned a thoughtful gaze to Batu, then to Kwan, and finally back to Ju-Hai. "As you say, you are not a military man, First Left Grand Councilor, but we thank you for your opinion."

Kwan smiled at the emperor's words, confident that the Divine One had disregarded Ju-Hai's endorsement.

After another moment's thought, the Divine One addressed Kwan. "Minister, am I to take it that as General Batu's superior, you do not approve of his plan?"

The old man nodded. "It would be a disaster for Shou Lung. The barbarians—"

"If you disapprove of General Batu's plan," the emperor interrupted, his face impassive and his voice even, "then you disapprove of my plan."

Kwan's face withered into a shriveled mask of astonishment. "But—"

The emperor raised his hand up for silence. "We have seen how well you understand the barbarians, Minister Kwan. Let us give General Batu his opportunity. Since you do not approve of my choice in generals, I relieve you of responsibility for it. As General of the Northern Marches, Batu Min Ho now reports directly to me."

Once again, the tent broke into astonished gasps and whispered comments. Kwan rose to his feet. "I beg you to reconsider," he gasped. "This is a grave—"

"That is enough, Kwan Chan!" the emperor said, pointedly turning his head away.

The tent immediately fell silent. The old mandarin closed his mouth and bowed as deeply as his ancient bones would allow. All eyes turned toward Batu, anxiously awaiting the next development.

Sensing that it was time to diffuse the situation, the young general simply bowed to the emperor. "Perhaps that is for the best, Divine One. Minister Kwan is certainly very experienced, but experience will prove of little use against these barbarians."

Kwan stared at Batu with open hatred.

"No doubt," the emperor observed, looking from the young general's face to the other men in tent. "Now, if the mandarins and your officers will excuse us for a few moments, I would like to speak with you privately."

Batu quickly nodded his dismissal to his subordinates, and they filed out of the tent. A few minutes later, he and the Divine One were alone.

The Son of Heaven studied the general for several moments. Finally, he said, "You are a gracious winner, General."

"There seemed no point in pressing the issue."

"A wise decision," the Divine One replied, his eyes suddenly growing cold. "I do not like being manipulated, General. Don't do it again."

Batu kneeled. "I beg your forgiveness," he said. "If I am going to win this war, I must have full command of my troops."

"I hope you are satisfied."

Remembering Kwan's hateful stare of a few minutes earlier, Batu dared to look up. "Not entirely, Son of Heaven."

The Divine One raised an eyebrow. "What else do you wish?"

"At the moment, the only thing that should concern a soldier in my position is his duty," Batu said.

"Yes?"

The general took a deep breath, then said, "I now have a powerful enemy, and I am forced to leave my family alone and unprotected—"

"Do not offend my hospitality by suggesting harm could come to them inside the summer palace." The emperor's reply was controlled and even, but his brow betrayed his irritation. "As you say," the Divine One continued, "the only thing that should concern you is your duty."

Without waiting for a response, the emperor rose. "Now that politics are no longer a consideration, I leave you to the business of war. Do not think of anything else."

Batu touched his forehead to the ground. "I will obey."

"Of course you will," the emperor said. Without giving Batu permission to rise, the Divine One stepped around the table and left the pavilion. The General of the Northern Marches did not move.

Finally, he heard the emperor's procession leave and dared to stand. When he went to the pavilion door, he found Pe and his subordinates waiting.

"What now?" the adjutant asked, bowing.

"We march," Batu replied, scanning the faces of his subordinates.

This time, no one questioned his orders.

- 7 -
The River Fleet

After the emperor left, Batu placed all twenty-five of the noble armies under Tzu Hsuang's command. He also entrusted the Mirror of Shao, along with the wagon required to carry the Ministry of Magic's bulky artifact, to his father-in-law. A few of Kwan's lords grumbled about nepotism, but the general didn't care. His father-in-law was the only noble with whom he had more than a passing acquaintance, and he needed someone he trusted in command of the contentious lords.

Tzu Hsuang took his forces and marched to the river docks in Tai Tung, where he loaded his fifty thousand *pengs* aboard a fleet of barges assembled for that purpose. Hsuang's orders were to sail up the Hungtze as far as the river would carry him, then march west toward the enemy. If the war proceeded according to Batu's plan, Hsuang and the nobles would engage the barbarians just west of Shou Kuan.

Batu took the five provincial armies and went north along the Spice Road. As the general had feared earlier that morning, the afternoon quickly turned hot and dusty. The men, unaccustomed to grueling marches, tired quickly. More than a few fell victim to heat exhaustion.

Nevertheless, Batu did not relax the pace, even when evening fell. Instead, to the unspoken surprise of his stoic subordinates, he continued marching. The general did not call a halt until midnight, when his five armies reached a tiny backwater village that had been mysteriously deserted. It was Chang Tu, the town that he had asked Ju-Hai to evacuate. The hamlet was also where he had ordered his fleet of cargo junks to gather.

As soon as he arrived, Batu ordered the first units onto the junks, issuing strict instructions for all *pengs* to stay in the cargo holds. Under no circumstance was any soldier to appear on deck, where he would be visible to river traffic or bystanders on the shore.

He could have easily loaded the entire army in a day or two. Instead, Batu took his time, allowing only two or three boats to leave the village every hour. The general felt the extra time was well spent. His intention was to camouflage his troop movements as merchant traffic, hoping that any Tuigan spies in the area would lose track of his army.

Eight days later, Batu and Pe boarded the last junk with the last unit. The oarsmen pulled the little ship into the current, and it started down the Ching Tung River. Any doubts that Batu had about this phase of his plan quickly disappeared. On the exterior, even he could not differentiate his troop ships from the thousands of cargo junks already traveling Shou Lung's river systems. More important, he did not think the addition of five hundred ships over the course of a week would seem remarkable to river watchers, especially considering the boost in commercial activity to be expected when a country mobilized for war.

It took four days for the general's junk to reach the mouth of the slow-moving river, only half the time it had taken to load the fleet. The junk slipped past the city of Kirin at dusk, then entered the dark, rolling waters of the Celestial Sea and turned north toward the flotilla's rendezvous point. Batu's stomach grew queasy once they hit the open sea and, within thirty minutes, he wished that he had never set foot on a ship deck.

Six days later, the general finally felt well enough to leave his bunk. He told Pe to summon his subordinates, then dressed and went up on deck. After the rancid smells of the bilges—stale water, moldy ropes, unwashed boatmen—Batu found the sea air invigorating. He leaned on the gunwale and looked out over the Celestial Sea. To the west, a tiny crag of rock floated on the horizon.

Pe joined him and, noticing the direction of Batu's gaze, said, "That's the Horn of Wak'an. According to the sailors, sighting it means we're within four days of Lo'Shan and the Shengti River."

Without taking his eyes off the sea, Batu grunted an acknowledgement. The prospect of another four days of seasickness almost drove him back to his bunk.

However, with his subordinates on their way to meet him, retreat was not an option. Batu stayed at the gunwale, breathing deeply of the salt air and studying the sea. The sky was as blue as the water, with a favorable wind blowing from the east. Between the general's ship and the Horn of Wak'an, the five hundred sails of his motley armada bobbed upon the water like so many prayer flags. The skiffs carrying his five generals were fighting through the white-capped waves toward Batu's pathetic flagship.

"The barbarians will never think to look for us here," Pe said cheerfully. With his good arm, he leaned on the gunwale next to Batu.

Frowning at the boy's jovial manner with jealous contempt, Batu responded, "Of course not."

Sensing his commander's testiness, Pe withdrew his arm and assumed a more formal stance. "I didn't mean to offend—"

"You didn't," the general said, waving off the adjutant's apology. "I'm still ill, and that makes me petulant."

As Batu watched the rowboats approach, he wondered how the first meeting with his subcommanders would go. Today would be the first time he had seen them since loading the fleet, and he still had not informed them of his plan.

A few minutes later, the first boat arrived. The occupant was Kei Bot Li, the only one of his generals Batu knew. Despite his stocky body, Kei Bot climbed out of the boat and scrambled up the rope ladder with the agility of a monkey. As he stepped aboard, Kei Bot greeted Batu by bowing deeply.

"A great pleasure, Commanding General," he said.

Batu returned the bow, his queasy smile a weak imitation of his subordinate's. "The pleasure is mine, General."

Noting Batu's squeamish expression, Kei Bot asked, "The sea does not agree with you, my commander?"

Embarrassed by his inadequacy, the second-degree general reluctantly nodded his head. "I would never have thought lying upon a comfortable bed could be so difficult."

Kei Bot laughed heartily, but before he could respond, the other generals arrived. The four men bustled aboard with an air of impatience. After trading a few perfunctory pleasantries, Batu led the men down to the junk's galley. It was the only compartment on the ship large enough to hold even this small conference. While Pe served tea, the commanding general spread his campaign map on the table, then prepared several writing brushes and bottles of variously colored ink.

The map showed the northern half of Shou Lung. A black line running across the northwest corner marked the location of the Dragonwall. A red arrow showed where the barbarians had breached the wall and were now advancing toward Yenching. Just south of Yenching, a blue line wormed its way horizontally across the paper, dividing the upper third of the map from the lower two-thirds. This was the Shengti River, which crossed the entire breadth of northern Shou Lung, and which was the cornerstone of Batu's plan.

In the center of the map sat Shou Kuan, a black star with a circle around it to show that it was a fortified city. Toward the map's right side, at about the same latitude as Shou Kuan, was Tai Tung. The Hungtze River ran through Tai Tung to a blue area at the eastern edge of the map: the Celestial Sea.

An instant after the commanding general laid out his map, Kei Bot and the other provincial generals leaned over and examined it at length. Batu almost chuckled as he noticed each man, in turn, glance at him in surreptitious puzzlement.

Finally, he said, "It's time I explain what we're doing in the Celestial Sea while the barbarians press the attack a thousand miles away."

Placing a finger on the red arrow marking the path of the Tuigan advance, Batu said, "Despite our efforts to starve them, the barbarians continue to drive southeast at a slow pace."

The young general picked up a brush and dipped it in red ink, then traced a path to Yenching. "Because of the Shengti's usual spring runoff, we know the barbarians cannot ford the river at this time of year. Therefore, they have no choice except to use the Three Camel Bridge in Yenching. Unfortunately, none of our armies can reach Yenching in time to stop them. After crossing the river, they will advance toward the next target of any consequence: Shou Kuan."

Batu extended the red line to within an inch of Shou Kuan, then changed to a green brush. Tracing a line from Tai Tung to just west of the walled city, he said, "This is the route that Tzu Hsuang will march with the noble armies."

The green line advanced and met the red less than a day's march away from Shou Kuan. After drawing an "X", Batu looped the green line back to the walled city. "Following the initial engagement," he said, "the nobles will retreat—"

"Do you have so little confidence in Tzu Hsuang's leadership?" Kei Bot interrupted, pointing at the line of retreat.

Batu lifted the brush, but did not remove his hand from the map. "I have every confidence in Tzu Hsuang and the nobles," he said. "But, as best as I can determine, the barbarians have nearly two hundred thousand mounted men. Their armies maneuver as well as any in Shou Lung, and their officers are bloodthirsty savages.

"At his disposal," Batu continued, "Tzu Hsuang will have fifty thousand exhausted *pengs* commanded by inexperienced and contentious officers."

The first-degree generals all voiced their agreement with Batu's assessment of the noble armies.

Batu looked back to the map. "I think it is safe to assume

the nobles will lose the engagement. Hsuang will lead a controlled retreat to Shou Kuan and take refuge in the fortified city."

The commanding general picked up another brush and dipped it in red ink, then traced a line representing the barbarian pursuit. "The barbarians will follow along this path—"

"How can you be sure?" asked the general from Mai Yuan. "With their horses, the enemy could just as easily outflank Hsuang and wipe out the nobles."

"They might as well outflank the wind," Batu said. "The noble armies will abandon their artillery and flee under cover of darkness. They will be inside Shou Kuan's walls by dawn, long before the Tuigan can pursue safely."

Batu continued the barbarians' red line to Shou Kuan. "The enemy will siege the city."

"They will have no choice," agreed Mai Yuan. "No commander would be fool enough to leave a large enemy force to his rear."

"Precisely," Batu responded, changing brushes again.

"What are we doing out here?" Kei Bot asked, placing a finger on the Celestial Sea.

The commanding general dipped his brush in a fresh pot of ink. He drew a yellow line that ran up the Shengti River clear to Yenching. "We will outflank the enemy and disembark at Yenching," Batu said, drawing an "X" at the city.

"That's more than fifteen hundred miles!" Mai Yuan objected. "It will take weeks to sail up the river."

"Five weeks, more or less," Batu responded. "We should arrive in Yenching at about the same time the barbarians engage Hsuang outside of Shou Kuan."

"Forgive my ignorance," Kei Bot interjected, his cunning eyes betraying no lack of intelligence. "But if the battle is to take place at Shou Kuan, why are we going to Yenching?"

Batu dipped his brush again, then began following the southward paths of both the Tuigan and noble armies. "We will follow the enemy south, cutting its communication routes and destroying its garrisons as we go."

The yellow line reached Shou Kuan. "When we reach Shou Kuan, there will be a second battle," Batu said. "As we approach, Tzu Hsuang's forces will sally from inside the city, holding the enemy's attention. When the barbarians respond, we'll take them from the rear. No matter how the Tuigan react, they'll be caught in a crossfire. Not even their horses will save them."

The five generals remained silent for a very long time. Finally, Kei Bot tapped Shou Kuan with one of his squat fingers. "How will Hsuang know when to feign his attack?"

Detailed comments and questions such as these meant the generals approved of his plan, Batu realized. He smiled, then answered the question. "We have the High Minister of Magic to thank for that," he said. "Tzu Hsuang and I will keep in touch through the Mirror of Shao."

* * * * *

Later that afternoon, just as Batu's ragged fleet skirted the Horn of Wak'an, the general's wife and children stood outside the walls of the Celestial Garden of the Virtuous Consort. The trio was surrounded by eighteen guards, and two more were currently inside, verifying that it was safe to enter.

"Can't we go in?" asked Ji, tugging impatiently at his mother's hand. At five years of age, he looked more like his grandfather than his father. Tzu Hsuang's noble blood showed in the boy's silky hair, refined features, and statuesque proportions.

"We waited long enough!" commented Yo, frowning at the delay. With wide-set eyes, flat high cheekbones, and flaring nostrils, Yo was the child who most resembled her father. Fortunately, Wu thought, she was only four and there was still a good chance the girl would grow out of this particular legacy. On a man, Batu's rugged features were engaging and appealing, but Wu had no doubt they would seem misplaced in the face of a young lady.

Both children were anxious, Wu knew, because it was already approaching dusk. They would have only twenty or thirty minutes to play before darkness settled in and the guards declared it unsafe to remain outdoors.

Nevertheless, the children had to learn to be patient. Wu tugged sternly on each of their hands. "You are the grand-children of a lord and the children of the General of the Northern Marches. Is this how you should behave?"

Reminded of their duty, both Ji and Yo sighed, then fell silent.

The Celestial Garden was the only area in the summer pal-ace where Wu felt secure, for it was the one place where she could go to forget what she viewed as her imprison-ment. It had been just eighteen days since Batu had left, but already the sycophants of the imperial court were maneu-vering to discredit him—in large part, she reflected, be-cause his plan had succeeded too well.

Though reports of her father's progress circulated through the court daily, no one had seen or heard anything of Batu's armies since the emperor's blessing. From what the bureaucrats could tell, the newly appointed General of the Northern Marches had simply taken one hundred thou-sand men and vanished. At first, the bureaucrats had been amazed at such a feat. Their gossip had concerned how he had managed such a thing. As the week had worn on and there was no sign of Batu, however, it had become fashion-able to attribute the disappearance to sinister occurrences.

The desertion theory had begun to circulate two days ago. According to this hypothesis, Batu had rendezvoused with an advanced enemy army and defected with all his sol-diers. The advocates of this notion took great delight in sug-gesting that he would return to Tai Tung at the head of a mixed barbarian and Shou army.

Having helped her husband develop his plan, Wu knew nothing could be farther from the truth. Unfortunately, she was the only person in the summer palace who could say so with absolute certainty. Still, she did not dare speak in her husband's defense for fear that Tuigan spies would uncover Batu's plan.

So, amid the splendor and pageantry of the imperial

court, Wu remained shunned and isolated. For her, it was not a great sacrifice. The ladies of the court, with their plucked and painted eyebrows, seemed universally shallow and dull. Wu had no desire to share in their company.

The children, however, were accustomed to the freedom of immense gardens and a plethora of playmates. In the summer palace, though, room was at a premium and young companions were a rarity. The few children who did live in the court had been forbidden from socializing with "the deserter's progeny." For Ji and Yo, the summer palace had become even more of a jail than it was for Wu.

The one island in this sea of isolation had been the Minister of State, Ju-Hai Chou. Wu suspected that the minister had guessed something of her husband's plan. Several times, he had called to reassure her that Batu had the emperor's complete confidence, no matter what the sycophants whispered. Ju-Hai had also gone out of his way to see that Wu lacked no luxury. He had even convinced the bureaucracy to let Wu and the children use the Celestial Garden.

Of all the things Ju-Hai had done, Wu appreciated this last favor the most. Located in the northwest corner of the palace, the garden was a small retreat no more than two hundred feet on a side. It was a feral place filled with trees of many varieties: plum, small magnolias, white mulberries. There were even two grand willows that, with their puffball shapes and weeping leaves, made the garden seem almost as wild and as marvelous as the parks of Chukei.

From Wu's perspective, however, the best thing about the Celestial Garden was its walls. The ones on the north and east were actually part of the palace fortifications and stood more than thirty feet tall. On the south and west, the walls were twenty feet tall. The garden had only one entrance, the circular "moon gate" on the south wall, before which Wu now stood. Normally, Wu was not such a student of architecture, but the high garden walls meant that she and her children could be alone—providing, of course, the guards did not find any spies or assassins lurking inside.

Wu and her children waited several minutes more before the two guards returned and stepped through the round gate. One wore green lamellar plate and the other an identical set of armor, save that it was blue. The one in green bowed, saying, "The Celestial Garden is vacant, Lady Batu. It is safe to enter."

Wu returned the guard's bow. "The minister shall hear of your vigilance."

As Wu and the children stepped through the gate, her guards snapped to attention and two brief, distinct clatters sounded behind her. There were two clatters because she had two sets of guards under separate commanders and they never did anything together. The ten soldiers in blue came from the Ministry of War. Her husband's enemy, Kwan Chan Sen, had assigned them to watch her at all times. The ten guards in green came from the Ministry of State Security. As a favor to Ju-Hai, Ting Mei Wan had assigned these guards to Wu. The duty of Ting's guards, as far as Wu could tell, was to protect her and the children from Kwan's men.

Neither group made Wu feel secure. She would rather have had a company of her husband's or father's personal guard, but the Grand Master of Protocol had made it clear that he would not permit such troops inside the palace. Wu was left feeling that she could trust only her own skills for the safety of her children and herself.

As she passed through the gate, Wu released the hands of her children. Both bolted for the northwest side of the garden, pausing on their way to roll down a manmade hill and splash through an artificial brook. Wu started to caution them about soiling their clothes, but decided to allow them their fun. With all that Shou Lung was asking of her family, the emperor could give her children new *samfus* if necessary.

In the growing shadows of dusk, Wu could almost forget that she was locked inside the palace. The center of the garden held a fish pond, upon which floated a miniature *sampan* large enough for two people. Though the pond was so small that one could walk around it in less than one hundred steps, a marble bridge spanned its center.

Beyond the pond, the Virtuous Consort's gardeners had formed the terrain into a series of serpentine hills, complete with artificial brooks and miniature cliffs. Along the walls, the trees and shrubbery grew so thick that the stonework behind them was completely hidden, giving the garden the appearance of being an open meadow in a forest. The two weeping willows completed the little park, towering high above the outer wall and draping their shaggy branches upon its crown.

Ji and Yo stopped at the willow closest to the west wall. Ji tugged at his sister's arm and circled the trunk. Yo followed, and they began a merry game of tag, dodging in and out among the long pendant leaves that drooped nearly to the ground. Both giggled wildly and yelled each other's names at the tops of their lungs. Wu did not remind them to keep their voices down. In the Celestial Garden, they could scream as loudly as they wished, for no one could hear them over the high walls.

Suddenly, both children stopped running and peered into the branches.

"What do you see?" Wu called, starting toward the garden corner. "Is it an owl?"

Ji studied the tree thoughtfully, then finally shook his head. "It's too big," he said.

"Well, then," Wu said, stepping across a brook. "It must be a tree troll—"

The pop of a breaking stick came from the willow, then one of its sagging branches rustled.

"It's a man!" Yo screamed, pointing overhead.

Wu broke into a sprint. "Children, get away from there!"

The urgency in her voice stunned the children into inaction. They looked at her with distressed expressions, then both began to cry.

Wu arrived beneath the tree a moment later. Ignoring her children's frightened tears, she shoved them behind her. Automatically, she assumed the stance of the golden crane, her arms raised over her head in a defensive position.

Wu could see a man's silhouette stretched out on a branch, trying to hide in the shadows. He appeared tall and fairly thin, but she could tell little more. The figure wore a black *samfu*, along with a black scarf to camouflage his face.

Wu could think of only one reason he would be in the garden. He was waiting to assassinate her or the Virtuous Consort. In either case, she thought it wisest not to let him escape. Besides, if she captured an assassin, some of the tongues denigrating her husband might be silenced.

In her most commanding voice, she said, "Ji, stop crying and listen to me!"

As she knew he would, her son obeyed immediately.

"This is very important," she continued, not taking her eyes off the figure in the tree. He would hear her instructions, but that could not be helped. "Take your sister and fetch the guards. Tell them to hurry because your mother is in danger. Do you understand?"

"Yes, Mother," he replied.

"Do it right now!" she said. "Run as fast as the wind!"

Ji took his sister's hand, and they sped off toward the gate. Wu continued to watch the silhouette.

As the children crossed the brook, the shadow glanced in their direction. It crawled along the limb toward the western wall. Wu realized that this was no vagabond, for an assassin's first instinct would have been to kill, not to run. The figure had been using the willow trees to climb over the outer wall in secrecy.

It could only be a Tuigan spy, Wu decided quickly.

Almost instantly, she leaped up and grabbed the willow's lowest branch. After the capture of the first infiltrator, the Minister of State Security had instituted stringent security measures to prevent more spies from entering or leaving the summer palace. The guard on the outer wall had been doubled, and even mandarins were thoroughly searched when they entered or left the palace.

Wu suspected that the spy had something important to relay to the barbarians if he was willing to brave the increased security. As far as she was concerned, that information could only decrease Batu's chances of returning alive. She had to capture the infiltrator.

Quickly Wu pulled herself onto the lowest branch, then grabbed the next one and climbed after the spy. As she reached the fifth branch, her hand touched a coil of black rope that the enemy agent had probably intended to use in descending the outer wall. She also discovered a faint, fragrant odor she could not quite identify, but which she had smelled many times before.

The spy had already crawled halfway to the end of the limb, but was moving slowly and carefully. Wu tossed the rope to the ground, then followed the dark figure. She did not bother calling out or ordering her quarry to stop, for he obviously would not obey.

Wu scrambled out on the limb rapidly, relying on her kung fu training for balance and strength. As the spy neared the wall, she caught up to him.

A voice at the gate yelled, "Stop! In the emperor's name, don't go any farther!"

When Wu glanced toward the voice, the spy leveled a vicious kick at her head. She easily ducked away and blocked the foot, then found herself tumbling out of the tree.

Landing head-first, Wu went into a forward roll to absorb the impact. Nevertheless, the fall was a long one and it hurt. The landing knocked the breath out of her lungs and left Wu flat on her back, gasping for breath, the world a white blur before her eyes.

By the time Wu's vision returned, one of Kwan's blue-armored guards stood over her, the tip of his broad-bladed *chiang-chun* held to her throat. The man's sergeant approached, the coil of black rope in his hand.

"When did you sneak this in?" he demanded.

Wu uttered an astonished objection, but her breath had not returned and she managed nothing but a feeble gasp.

The sergeant dropped the rope over Wu's body. "What kind of a mother abandons her children to join her traitorous husband?"

Wu finally drew a breath, then hissed, "How dare you!"

She pointed at the west wall. "The spy is escaping. After him!"

The guard did not bother to look up. "The only spy I see is lying here."

The green-armored sergeant arrived, carrying Yo in his arms. Though the girl had clearly been sobbing a moment ago, she was now too frightened to cry.

"You can't be serious!" said the sergeant in green. "This woman is no spy!"

The soldier in blue, one of Kwan's men, met the eyes of his counterpart. "I suppose Minister Kwan will have to decide that." He did not order his subordinate to move the polearm away from Wu's throat. She realized that only the presence of Ting's guards kept the man from executing her on the spot.

– 8 –

Jasmine

Wu kneeled in a traditional kowtow, her forehead pressed to the floor and her arms stretched out in front of her torso. A tiny pool of perspiration had formed beneath her brow, making the marble feel cold and clammy. Her knees ached horribly and her shoulders were as stiff as those of a statue. At her side, Ji restlessly mimicked his mother's position, his graceful little form folded into an elegant egg-shape. Yo had long since tumbled into a heap and lay asleep on the cold stone. Mercifully, the guards had taken pity on the child and let her rest.

The mother and her children had been awaiting the emperor for over two hours. After allowing the spy in the Celestial Garden to escape unpursued, the two sets of guards had argued about whether Wu should be taken to Minister Kwan or to Minister Ting. They had finally compromised by bringing her to the Hall of Supreme Harmony, where the emperor himself could determine what was to be done with her.

At night, lit only by flickering torches, the Hall of Supreme Harmony seemed more an immense and ominous grotto than an architectural wonder. The incessant click-click-click of boots on stone echoed from the murkiness overhead, where unseen guards were making their rounds on dark balconies. Somewhere in the shadowy perimeter, a lone cricket sang its song. A gentle breeze carried the scent of persimmon blossoms through the room.

Finally, Wu heard the doors open behind her, and someone shuffled across the room. Two more people followed the first, the sounds of their steps echoing off the walls with a purposeful cadence. By tucking her chin against her breastbone and looking beneath her armpits, Wu could increase her field of vision enough to observe the areas to either side of her. She saw Minister Kwan totter into view, followed a short time later by Ting Mei Wan. They both went to take their customary seats, moving out of Wu's narrow range of vision.

The third walker stopped to the kneeling mother's right. Ju-Hai Chou bent down and gently awakened Yo. "Come, my child. You're about to meet the Son of Heaven," he said. "Don't you want to show him your respect?"

At the mention of the emperor, Yo grew alert. "The Divine One?" she asked. "Father's master?"

"Yes," Ju-Hai replied, gently moving her into a kowtow. "Everybody's master."

The minister had barely finished speaking before Wu heard the officious steps of several men directly ahead. It would have been disrespectful to lift her head, but Wu did not need to see the Divine One to know that his entourage had entered the hall. Ju-Hai returned to his feet and executed a deep bow. The guards snapped to attention with a sharp clatter of equipment.

To Wu's surprise, Ju-Hai remained next to Yo.

The emperor took his seat, then said, "What is this all about, Minister Chou?"

"I'm not sure I know, Divine One," Ju-Hai responded. "Minister Kwan sent a messenger to my house claiming to have captured a spy and asking me to arrange a special audience. Naturally, I sent word to you and suggested we meet in the Hall of Supreme Harmony." Ju-Hai waved a hand at Yo, Ji, and Wu. In a voice of exaggerated puzzlement, he said, "When we arrived, all I saw was this woman and her two children."

Wu breathed a silent sigh of relief. At least she had one ally present.

"They are General Batu's wife and children," Ju-Hai continued. "Obviously, there has been some mistake."

"Minister Kwan?" the emperor asked, his silk robe swishing as he shifted in his seat.

"There has been no mistake," the old man replied sharply. "We are all aware of the reports regarding General Batu's desertion—"

"Wild rumors," interrupted Ju-Hai. "Probably started by a jealous rival," he added pointedly.

"We shall see." The emperor's robes hissed as he turned away from Ju-Hai and Kwan. "Minister Ting, can State Security shed any light on this?"

"Perhaps," she replied cautiously. "We have been investigating each rumor, as you instructed."

Wu nearly gasped out loud. The news that the emperor was having her husband's loyalty investigated came as a shock. Until now, she had taken the Divine One's trust in Batu as a given, for the Son of Heaven had extended every courtesy to her and the children. Wu felt angry, dismayed, and betrayed. Only the fact that she was kneeling before the emperor himself prevented her from rising to vent her wrath.

"And what have you found, Minister?" the emperor asked.

"Very little," Ting replied. "Though General Batu's disappearance has made many people suspicious of him, no one can provide the slightest proof of any disloyalty."

"Proof!" Kwan stormed. Though Wu could not see the old minister from her angle, it almost seemed she could feel him pointing an accusing finger at her. "Batu's wife was abandoning her children to join the traitor. What greater proof do you need?"

Ji jumped to his feet. "Liar!" he screamed.

Behind Wu, the guards gasped, but she smiled at her child's boldness. No one had given her permission to rise, so she made no move to silence him.

"Ji," Ju-Hai said, grasping the boy's shoulder. "This is the Hall of Supreme Harmony. You mustn't say such things here."

The boy jerked free of the minister's grip and ignored the reproach. "He's lying! Mama wouldn't leave us."

"I understand that this is difficult for you, my child," Kwan said, his voice dripping with false sympathy. "You mustn't worry. Shou Lung will always care for you, no matter what your mother has done."

"She hasn't done anything!" Ji insisted.

"That isn't for you to say," Kwan replied, his voice growing angry.

Oblivious to the old man's threatening tone, Ji responded. "You weren't even there!"

"That's enough!" Kwan roared, an angry swish of silk indicating that he was rising to his feet. "Remove the children!"

"No," the emperor countered. "The boy is right. Tell me what happened in the Virtuous Consort's garden."

Being addressed by the Divine One himself doused the fire in Ji's heart. He swallowed, looked to his mother's prone form for reassurance, then finally turned back to the emperor.

"We saw something in the tree," he said, looking at the floor. His voice was now quiet and weak.

"What?" asked the emperor. "What did you see?"

"A man."

"Are you sure?" the Divine One asked. "Could it have been something else, like an owl or a cat?"

Ji frowned and looked at his sister uncertainly. She shook her head sternly, and Ji turned back to the Son of Heaven. "No," he said. "We're sure. It was a man."

"Perhaps one of General Batu's spies, come to fetch his wife," Kwan said, the fabric of his *hai-waitao* whispering against the chair arms as the old man finally returned to his seat. "If there was anybody in the tree at all."

"What are you suggesting, Minister?" The emperor asked.

"Nothing that you have not thought of already, Divine One," Kwan replied politely. "Merely that Wu has coached her children in answering our questions."

"That is for me to decide," the Son of Heaven replied. Addressing Ji again, he asked, "And then what happened?"

"We ran to get the guards," the boy replied, pointing a slender finger at the soldiers behind him. "Mother climbed the tree."

"Why do you think she did that?" Minister Kwan asked.

"To catch the man!" Ji replied, frowning at the minister's silly question.

"Wu is not a large woman," Kwan said, addressing the emperor. "Do you really think she would chase a spy alone?"

A long pause followed, and Wu realized Kwan's rhetorical question had made an impression.

Ting Mei Wan came to the kneeling mother's rescue. "In all fairness, Divine One," she said, "General Batu's wife is reputed to have skill in the art of kung fu."

Kwan scoffed, but Wu breathed a sigh of relief. When State Security troops had been assigned to the Batu household, Ju-Hai had made a point of saying that he controlled Ting. Apparently, he had not been lying.

After a moment's pause, the emperor said, "These children must be tired. Perhaps it would be better if they returned to their home."

Ju-Hai signaled to two State Security guards, but Ji stepped boldly forward. "I want to stay," he said.

"Of course you do," the Divine One replied patiently. "But I am the emperor, and you must do what I say. Is that not true?"

Ji looked to his mother's kneeling form, then to Ju-Hai. The minister nodded to indicate that what the emperor said was, indeed, correct. Dropping his gaze to the floor, Ji said simply, "Yes."

"Good," the Divine One replied. "Take your sister and go home with these soldiers. Your mother will be there when you wake in the morning."

The reassurance did nothing to relax Wu. From what she had heard, the emperor often said one thing and did another.

The guards came into Wu's field of vision, and she watched them take her children's hands and turn away. Both Ji and Yo looked after their mother with sad eyes. Wu wanted to kiss and hug them, but she had not yet been given permission to rise and dared not risk offending the emperor.

After the children were gone, the emperor said, "Lady Wu, please stand."

Wu stiffly did as asked. Her body, unaccustomed to the abuse of kneeling for so long, protested with pain. "My gratitude, Divine One," she said, bowing.

"What happened in the Virtuous Consort's garden?" the emperor asked, his enigmatic eyes fixed on her face.

"It was as Ji said," she replied. "He and Yo saw a dark figure. I climbed the willow tree in an attempt to capture him."

"You are an intelligent woman," Kwan said, shaking his white-haired head in skepticism. "Too intelligent to do something so foolish."

"I did not consider it foolish," she countered, purposefully neglecting to address the minister by his proper title. "My husband and father are both away fighting the barbarians, and we all know there are spies in the summer palace. These spies would like nothing better than to see the emperor's armies destroyed, making me both a widow and an orphan in a short period. Given the chance to capture one of those spies, I think it would have been foolish to let the man escape, don't you?"

Kwan looked from Wu toward the emperor. "Perhaps," he said, "if your husband is truly fighting the barbarians, and not rejoining his ancestral relations."

Wu decided to ignore Kwan. As her husband's political enemy, the old man was clearly more interested in discrediting Batu than in finding the spy. Instead, she turned her attention to the emperor himself. "Divine One, while it is true that my husband and his army have disappeared, anyone who claims Batu Min Ho has betrayed Shou Lung is lying."

"Surely, you can prove what you say," Kwan objected, moving to the edge of his chair with a menacing glint in his eye.

"I could," she responded, "but not while there are spies

roaming the summer palace. I will not endanger my husband and the empire so needlessly."

"Lady Wu, Minister Ju-Hai believes in General Batu without reservation, and so do I," said Ting Mei Wan. "Yet, Minister Kwan has met your husband on several occasions, a privilege that few of us have been afforded. His bad opinion carries a great deal of influence within the summer palace. Is there nothing you can say that would prove your husband's loyalty?"

Wu hesitated. By now, it might be safe to disclose that the provincial armies had left disguised as merchant cargo, but Wu doubted that the revelation would quiet the court gossip. Without knowing her husband's entire plan, suspicious minds would simply assume that Batu had sailed away with the army instead of attacking with it. Worse, someone might realize that he was going up the Shengti to cut off the barbarians' advance.

After several moments of consideration, Wu said, "No. I will say nothing."

"You must be able to tell us something," Ju-Hai pressed.

Wu shook her head. "No."

Kwan smiled malevolently. "You are protecting your husband, no doubt?"

Wu nodded, giving the old man an icy stare. "Exactly."

"An admirable reason," Kwan said, turning to the emperor with a smirk on his lips. "From whom are you protecting him?"

"From you," Wu answered angrily. "And from the spy—if you aren't one in the same." As soon as the words left her mouth, Wu chastised herself for letting anger dictate what she said. Her father had often told her that such lapses only demonstrated lack of self-control and betrayed the speaker's weaknesses.

Kwan lifted his wrinkled brow in shock and anger. Ju-Hai and Ting grimaced. Behind Wu, the guards rustled expectantly, ready to take her into custody.

The emperor frowned. "Lady Wu, you cannot say such things."

"Forgive me, Divine One," she answered, barely keeping the anger out of her voice. "But has Minister Kwan not called my husband a traitor, me a child-deserter, and my son a liar? Perhaps it is inappropriate to take offense at an old man's words, but I cannot be blamed for defending my family's honor."

Ju-Hai took her by the arm. "Please, Wu, remember to whom you are speaking."

"I will," she replied, bowing her head to the emperor.

For several moments, the Divine One stared at Wu in open astonishment. Finally, in a carefully controlled voice, he said, "I see where your son comes by his brazenness, Lady Wu. You are lucky that I am fair, for I will not take your outburst into account in making my decision."

The Son of Heaven looked from Wu to Kwan, then back to Wu again, his brow furrowed in deep thought. "You are confident that your husband will defeat these barbarians, Lady Wu?"

"I am," she replied, meeting his gaze.

"Good," the emperor said sharply. "Until that time, you and your family are confined to your house."

Wu did not flinch at the command. The Divine One was simply formalizing what she already knew to be true. She was a hostage guaranteeing her husband's loyalty.

To Wu's surprise, the emperor turned to Kwan next. "Minister Kwan, I am sure Lady Wu finds the constant presence of your *pengs* an insult to her family's dignity. You will remove them."

Kwan's jaw dropped. "How will we guarantee—"

The Divine One raised his hand, and the old man fell silent. "Minister Ting's soldiers will guard the Batu household," the Son of Heaven declared.

Kwan frowned, but did not object.

The emperor was not finished. He turned to Ting Mei Wan. "Perhaps you should turn your efforts toward finding the man Wu saw in the Virtuous Consort's garden."

Ting bowed her head. "Of course, Divine One." Looking at Wu, the minister said, "I shall start immediately, if Lady Wu can describe what she saw."

"With pleasure," Wu replied, happy to have the conversation turned away from Batu and herself. "I didn't see much, just a man wearing a black *samfu*. It looked as if he intended to hide until dusk, then climb out on a limb overhanging the outer wall. When I saw him, he returned the way he had come and climbed over the garden's inner wall."

"Why would he go to the trouble of *climbing* over the outer wall? Why wouldn't he simply leave by one of the gates?" Minister Kwan asked. His voice was devoid of any rancor, but Wu did not doubt the old man was still hoping to cast doubt on her story.

"It is obvious the venerable minister has not left the palace recently," Ting answered, a proud smile on her lips. "My guards are stationed at all exits. They have orders to search everyone who enters or leaves the palace, the mandarins, even myself, included. The spy must have had something he couldn't be caught with." Ting turned her attention back to Wu. "What did this spy look like?"

"His face was wrapped in a black scarf," Wu said, closing her eyes in an attempt to recall every detail. "He was very slender and small, more a woman's size than a man's."

"How do you know it was a man?" the emperor asked.

Wu paused, remembering the fragrant scent she had smelled when she climbed into the tree. It had seemed so familiar, and now she realized why. She had smelled the scent many times before, when visiting the wives and daughters of her father's peers. The smell was jasmine blossom. Vain women enjoyed rubbing the flower over their bodies as a type of perfume.

Finally, Wu answered the emperor's question. "I don't know that it was a man. In fact, now that you mention the possibility, it seems likely the spy was a woman."

Ting frowned and started to say something, but the emperor cut her off. "What else can you tell us?" he demanded. "You must remember everything."

Along with the two sergeants commanding the guards who had been watching her, Wu spent the next twenty minutes answering questions about the incident in the Garden of the Virtuous Consort. At length, it became apparent that nothing more would be learned by continuing the interrogation. The guards had seen nothing but Wu falling out of the tree. The Chief Warder of the Imperial Armory in the Department of Palace Services was summoned and asked to examine the black rope recovered from the scene. He reported that any officer could have taken it out of the armory and no special note would have been taken of the fact. Wu could add little to her description, aside from saying she believed it likely that the figure had been a woman.

The only thing she did not report was the scent of jasmine that had convinced her the spy was female. A whiff of perfume could be interpreted as flimsy evidence for such an assertion, and she did not want to give Kwan another chance to cast doubt on her story.

Finally, the emperor said, "We can't determine the infiltrator's identity from what we have learned tonight. However, with the aid of the heavens, we will soon catch him—or her. Until then, we will refrain from any further political bickering and concentrate our energies upon finding this spy—" The Divine One glanced sternly at Kwan, and then Wu "—and upon teaching our children better manners than our parents taught us."

With that, the emperor rose and walked into the darkness behind the throne. His servants followed with their torches. A few paces later they all disappeared, stepping through a hidden doorway reserved for the Divine One and his attendants.

As soon as the emperor was gone, Minister Kwan furrowed his thousand wrinkles in spite and stared at Wu for several moments. When she did not flinch, the old man rose and briskly left the hall, his guards following close behind.

Ju-Hai was the next to leave. He turned to Wu and clasped her hands. "You are a very lucky woman, my dear," he said. "Your punishment for speaking against Kwan so harshly would have been much greater if the emperor were not so fond of Batu."

"Fond?" Wu said indignantly. "Having him investigated for treason is fondness?"

Ju-Hai nodded. "When the danger is so great, the emperor cannot let his personal feelings interfere with caution. He must be suspicious of everyone and everything."

Wu shook her head sadly. "Thank you for trying to comfort me," she said. "But even I can see that the rumors have had their effect on the Divine One."

Ju-Hai sighed. "As long as I have any influence with the emperor, you need not worry about your husband's reputation."

"You are a true friend, Minister," Wu said, bowing to Ju-Hai. "If there's ever anything I can do for you—"

The minister shook his head. "Think nothing of it. What I do, I do for the good of the empire. Ting will take you home. I'll visit when I can."

After Ju-Hai left, Ting Mei Wan broke into a fit of chuckling. Wu continued to stand in the middle of the floor, frowning in puzzlement. Finally, she asked, "What's so funny?"

Ting stopped laughing. "You and your son," she said. "I've never heard anyone speak to a mandarin like that. I thought you were trying to choke Kwan on his own anger!"

"The thought hadn't occurred to me," Wu said, wishing that she possessed such a cunning mind. "I'll remember it in case the opportunity arises again." She paused to let the subject drop, then bowed to Ting. "I also want to thank you for your support, Minister."

Ting grew appropriately serious, then stood and returned the bow. "Minister Chou has done a great deal for me. When he calls for support, offering it is the least I can do."

The mandarin walked to Wu's side. "Now, tell me how Batu disappeared with five provincial armies! What can he be planning?"

Wu caught the whiff of a familiar scent and was reminded of her father's admonishment to trust no one. Consciously changing the subject, she asked, "How will I ever keep Ji and Yo happy inside that little house?"

Ting chuckled at the obvious tactic and took Wu's arm. "You are careful, aren't you?"

As the mandarin started toward the exit, Wu quietly inhaled. There was no mistaking the fragrance. The Minister of State Security smelled of jasmine blossoms.

– 9 –

Shihfang

A long with his aide and the twenty-four nobles under his command, Tzu Hsuang stood atop a long bluff. The bluff overlooked a shallow valley that, in some primordial time, had once served as the bed of a river nearly a half-mile wide. All that remained of the river now was a deep, slow-moving brook that meandered through three hundred acres of barley fields.

On the opposite side of the valley sat the town of Shihfang. Like all Shou municipalities, Shihfang was enclosed by a defensive barrier. Little more than a ten-foot wall of packed yellow earth, the barrier was broken only where towers flanked the single gate. The town was unusual in that it had been built on high ground, atop a bluff similar to the one upon which Hsuang and his subordinates stood. Wisps of gray smoke drifted out of the few chimneys that rose above the wall. From one bell tower came the steady, measured clanging of the town's single warning bell.

Hsuang did not see a reason for the sounding of the alarm. Shihfang remained untouched and there was no sign of impending attack. Nevertheless, refugees were pouring out of the hamlet as if the place had already fallen. The old noble did not understand why. As far as his scouts could tell, there was not a barbarian within twenty miles. Still, there had to be a reason for what he saw.

Thousands of people choked the narrow road that crossed the valley from Shihfang and turned eastward at the base of Hsuang's hill. On their backs, the peasants balanced long poles from which hung plow shares, effigies of their gods, sacks of grain seed, and a few other meager possessions. Wealthier refugees pulled two-wheeled *rikshas* loaded with bolts of silk, polished wooden tables, ceramic wares, and other household goods. Here and there, servants shouldered the palanquin of some minor bureaucrat or a team of oxen drew the overloaded wagon of a rich landowner. In the midst of the throng was a lone camel with a bulky, box-like seat strapped to its back. Hsuang could just make out a figure sitting beneath the seat's silk canopy.

The old noble pointed at the seat, which was known as a howdah. "That looks like someone important," Hsuang said to his aide. "Perhaps he can tell us what is happening here. Fetch him."

"Yes, my lord," the adjutant answered. He immediately turned and ran down the back of the hill. As Hsuang waited for the man in the howdah, his subordinates quietly stood at his back, adjusting and readjusting their armor, or speaking with each other in tense, subdued tones. They were impatient, and the old noble did not blame them.

It had been nearly seven weeks since the noble armies had left Tai Tung and, as Hsuang knew from a messenger, nearly a month since the emperor had confined his outspoken daughter to her house. In the time it had taken to reach Shihfang, the season had turned from late spring to full summer. Every day, the sun had shone brighter and the weather had grown warmer, baking the men inside their armor during the grueling marches. Even Hsuang had to admit that a battle would be a welcome change from the hot daily trek.

Unfortunately, the lord could not tell whether his men would have their battle today or not, for what he saw at Shihfang did not make sense. While he waited for the man in the howdah, Hsuang continued to study the valley below, trying to make some sense of what he saw.

After descending the opposite bluff, the road ran across the valley. About thirty yards away from Hsuang's hill, it crossed a wooden bridge that spanned the slow-moving brook. A great traffic jam had developed on the bridge as hundreds of refugees tried to squeeze their way across. To make matters worse, a flimsy *riksha* had lost a wheel and was blocking half the lane.

On this side of the brook, the refugees progressed in a more orderly fashion. They followed the road for a mile down the valley, where it became a trail and ascended the bluff. As the fugitives passed below the hill, they invariably stared with dark, curious eyes at the group of lords.

A few minutes later, the camel finally broke free of the bridge and came to the base of the hill. Hsuang's aide helped a corpulent, red-cheeked man climb out of the howdah and struggle up the slope. The man wore the turquoise robes of a prefect, but his expression was dazed and confused. He hardly impressed Hsuang as a man who ran a town, even one as small as Shihfang.

Finally, the man reached the hilltop, gasping and wheezing. Hsuang's subordinates circled around him, anxious to hear any news the man could offer. The chubby bureaucrat eyed the gathering with barely concealed fear.

"Yes, my lords?" the prefect asked, impolitely neglecting to bow or introduce himself.

Hsuang waved his hand at his fellow nobles. "I am Tzu Hsuang Yu Po, and these are the commanders of the Twenty-Five Armies."

"Yes?" the bureaucrat responded, his face betraying his apprehension. "What do the commanders of the Twenty-Five Armies want with me?"

"Why are you abandoning your town, Prefect?" demanded one of Hsuang's subordinates. "You are clogging the road. We cannot reach your town to defend it!"

The prefect blanched, then bowed to the assemblage. "I beg your pardon, lords. Nobody told me you were coming—"

"We are not here to reproach you," Hsuang said, casting an irritated glance at the noble who had spoken without permission. "We only wish to know why you are abandoning Shihfang."

The chubby prefect looked around in confusion. "The rider came and told us to evacuate—"

"Rider?" Hsuang gasped. "What rider?"

"From the retreating army," the bureaucrat explained. "He said the barbarians were coming and that we had to leave at once."

Hsuang frowned. From what Batu had told him of the battle in the sorghum field, he did not think the retreating army should have any riders left. "What did this rider look like?" the old lord asked urgently. "How was his accent?"

The prefect's face fell. "He wore a Shou uniform—"

"Anyone can wear a Shou uniform," Hsuang said, impatiently laying a hand on the bureaucrat's collar. "Describe the man."

The chubby prefect swallowed, then said, "He was short and had a horrendous, guttural accent. I thought he was from Chukei. And the way he smelled! It was like bad wine and sour milk."

"That's no Shou," observed one of the other nobles.

"No," Hsuang agreed, grimacing. "Even in the field, no officer would be shamed by such a disgrace." Addressing the bureaucrat again, he asked, "What else did the rider say?"

The prefect looked away, ashamed that he had allowed the enemy to deceive him. Nevertheless, he answered quickly, "That we are to evacuate the town by nightfall. We aren't to burn the city or the fields because the army needs supplies."

A murmur ran through the crowd of nobles.

"They're out there," said a young lord. He was looking toward the far hills.

Hsuang nodded. "Yes, and General Batu's plan is working. They're resorting to trickery to feed themselves."

"They'll try to sneak in at night, when the stragglers have less opportunity to identify them," said one of the more experienced lords.

This noble was Cheng Han, a broad-shouldered man with a scarred, useless eye and an ugly black stain on his left temple. Like Hsuang, Cheng had a large ducal holding and was entitled to the title of *tzu*. At just seven hundred men, his army was smaller than many of the others in the Twenty-Five, but it was heavily equipped with siegecraft. Tzu Cheng also carried a huge supply of thunder-powder, though the stocky noble's gnarled eye did not make Hsuang anxious to place his trust in the unpredictable stuff.

After a moment's silence, Tzu Cheng continued, "With their horses, our enemies will find it easy to outflank us in the dark. We can't allow that."

Cheng's remark stirred an ember of panic in Hsuang. "I wonder how many other villages these riders have visited?"

Although he did not say so aloud, Hsuang realized that this new trickery stood a chance of defeating Batu's plan. In order to break out of their precarious containment, the Tuigan needed only a few tons of good grain. Shihfang might be the largest town west of Shou Kuan, but it was not the only one. There were hundreds of smaller hamlets within a day's ride, all supported by farming grain.

Hsuang turned to the young noble who had spoken before Tzu Cheng. "Mount your cavalry," he said. "Prepare two hundred for scouting duty. Send the other three hundred out as messengers. They are to spread the word that the barbarians are coming. The peasants must burn everything and flee."

The noble's eyes betrayed his resentment, for the order meant his cavalry would miss the battle. Nevertheless, he bowed stiffly, saying, "As you wish, Tzu."

As the man turned to go, Hsuang caught his shoulder. "I know your riders are good fighters. At the moment, however, they will serve the emperor better as messengers and scouts. They are the only ones who can move quickly enough to spread the alarm, or who can warn us of the enemy's approach before he is upon us."

The youthful noble bowed again, this time more deeply. "I shall lead the scouts personally."

"My thanks," Hsuang said, dismissing the man.

As the young lord left to dispatch his messengers and prepare his scouts for duty, the prefect bowed to Hsuang. "If you won't be needing me any longer, perhaps I could leave?"

"Yes, be on your way," Hsuang answered absently, already turning to an aide. "Have the Mirror of Shao brought up."

As he waited, Hsuang considered his situation. Shihfang lay directly between Yenching and Shou Kuan, so he and Batu had assumed the barbarian army would pass through the village, and that it would be a good place to meet the enemy. It appeared their assumption had been a correct one.

Unfortunately, they had hoped the nobles would beat the barbarians to the town by several days, leaving plenty of time to rest the men and prepare defensive fortifications. It was a hope Hsuang had given up when he saw the fleeing peasants. Even if he could move his *pengs* into position against the tide of refugees, they would never secure their positions before night fell and the Tuigan arrived. The original plan was no longer feasible, so he thought it best to contact Batu and report.

A pair of white oxen drew a small wagon to the top of the hill and stopped. The sideboards had been carefully painted with a hundred coats of red enamel. Dozens of mystic characters had been etched into the lustrous surface. The mirror itself resembled a kettle drum with a three-foot head of smoked glass. Its black shell was covered with yellow symbols telling of all the great feats that had been accomplished in the past with drum's aide.

Ordering his subordinates to wait for him, Hsuang went to the wagon and climbed in. Placing his hands on the edge of the mirror, he looked into the smoky glass and repeated the mysterious phrase that activated the artifact. The glass began to clear and a haze swirled beneath it, making it apparent that the Mirror of Shao was not so much a mirror as a huge bowl with magical gas sealed inside.

Forcing all images except his son-in-law's face from his mind, Hsuang looked into the mist and said, "Mirror of Shao, I am looking for Batu Min Ho, General of the Northern Marches and the one hope of Shou Lung."

Hsuang took great care to address the mirror exactly as the High Minister of Magic had instructed, for he was not

sure how the thing worked and felt uncomfortable using it.
After cautioning him not to use the mirror needlessly, the
High Minister had tried to explain how it worked. When
one used the mirror, the old sorcerer had said, one looked
through the ethereal plane to see and hear whatever he
wished. The explanation had been lost on both Batu and
Hsuang, who could not imagine any kind of plain other than
the type covered with grass and rolling hills.

The mirror's glass became completely transparent, and
Hsuang felt as though he were looking into a pool of clouds.
Several seconds later, his son-in-law appeared in the white
mists. Though the old noble could see only Batu's face, the
young general appeared to be looking at the sky.

"General Batu," Hsuang said.

Batu smiled, but continued staring into the air. According
to the High Minister, only the person looking into the mirror
could see to whom he was speaking. Sound, however, carried in both directions.

"Tzu Hsuang," Batu said. "It's good to hear your voice!"

"And to see your face. How goes the journey?"

"The pilots tell me we are only a few days from Yenching,"
the General of the Northern Marches answered. "We have
lost a few ships to the river, but that is all. The closer we
come to the city, the more my subcommanders believe in
our plan."

"Then you've remained undetected?" Hsuang asked.

Batu nodded. "The men did not believe it was possible.
Now that we have done it, they think nothing is impossible."
The general allowed a proud smile to cross his lips, then
grew more serious. "And you, Tzu Hsuang? Have you met
the enemy?"

Hsuang shook his head. "Not yet, but soon." He described
what he had found in Shihfang, then explained that he
would not be able to secure the town.

"Shihfang is not important," Batu responded. "What is important is that the barbarians follow you to Shou Kuan. Can
you give them a good fight and still have time to retreat?"

"Assuming the barbarians come through the village, yes,"

Hsuang answered. "We can fortify our current position and use the terrain to good advantage. With luck, we might destroy a portion of their army as they cross the valley below."

"Better than we had hoped," Batu observed.

Hsuang bit his lip. "There is a risk. If the enemy is expecting resistance at Shihfang and are as mobile as you say, they might approach along a front of many miles. They could encircle us and cut us off from Shou Kuan. Perhaps I should fall back to Shou Kuan before they attack."

Batu furrowed his brow in thought. Finally, he shook his head. "Don't retreat yet," he said. "If the Tuigan expected resistance, they wouldn't be hoping to trick Shihfang's peasants into leaving grain behind. More important, the Tuigan commander is a shrewd man. If you retreat without a fight, he'll smell our trap. To make our plan work, you must allow the enemy to force you back to Shou Kuan."

"Very well. That is what I shall do," Hsuang answered. It was not the reply he had hoped to hear, but Batu's observations made sense. "I should go now," he said. "We have much to do."

"Just a moment," Batu replied. "What have you heard from Wu?" The young general looked as though he felt guilty for keeping Hsuang from his duties.

"She is, ah, making the most of the comforts in her new home," the old noble answered. He purposely neglected to mention that the emperor had confined her to the house. That fact was not something he felt Batu needed to worry about at the moment.

"Good," Batu replied. "When you send her a message, tell her I am well." He paused a moment, then his expression grew more businesslike. "In case I'm wrong about the Tuigan," he added, "send your scouts out far and wide. Be ready to fall back at the first sign of trouble. Good luck, and let me know how you fare." The general looked away, tactfully indicating that his father-in-law was dismissed.

"Consider it done," Hsuang answered. He took his hands off the mirror. Batu's image faded and the glass became smoky once again. The noble climbed out of the wagon and turned to his aide. "Send the scouts out in a fan pattern. At the first sign of the enemy, they are to report back."

As the adjutant left, Hsuang addressed the cart driver. "When the catapults are moved into position, park the mirror behind them," he said, ordering the man into the most secure position he could think of. "At the first sign that we are losing the battle, take your wagon and ride for Shou Kuan. It is important that you keep the mirror safe."

Next, Hsuang walked a few paces to where his subcommanders were still waiting. Turning to an ancient *nan*, or minor lord, he said, "Take your men into Shihfang and replenish our own stores, then burn the town and the fields." The old *nan* acknowledged the order with a formal bow, then went to obey.

"And us, Tzu Hsuang?" asked Cheng.

Hsuang pointed at the brook in the valley below. "I think that will make an excellent defensive line."

Tzu Cheng nodded. "A wise decision. We can place the artillery up here. With my bombs, we can destroy the enemy as he crosses the valley."

"I was thinking of using flaming pitchballs," Hsuang said, trying to find a diplomatic way to keep Cheng's thunder-powder where it could do no harm. Although gunpowder was not new to Shou Lung, its use in battle was. Hsuang was not sure he wanted to trust it.

"Save the pitch for later," Cheng said enthusiastically. "The thunder-powder will be more effective."

Hsuang saw that he would have to be direct. "Please forgive an old man's superstitions," he said, inclining his head to Tzu Cheng. "I have never seen this thunder-powder used in battle. Lofting it over our own *pengs* makes me nervous."

Cheng's face betrayed his disappointment. "Of course, I understand your concerns, Tzu Hsuang, but I assure you that my artillerists will not make a mistake."

Another noble said, "I have seen this thunder-powder in action. It does little but rumble the ground and create a lot of smoke—"

"You have not seen it used properly, Nan Wang!" Cheng

objected.

Wang bowed to Cheng. "Please forgive me, Tzu Cheng," he said. "I did not finish what I meant to say."

"Which was?" Hsuang asked, raising an eyebrow.

"It strikes me that against charging horses, rumbling ground and thick smoke might be more effective than arrows and flaming pitch," the *nan* finished. He looked toward the fields below.

"If I may speak," offered another minor lord, this one a middle-aged *nan* from Wak'an. "My own troops also use thunder-powder, though not for bombs."

"And how do *you* use this marvelous black sand?" Hsuang asked, turning to face the noble. He had noted earlier that each of this lord's *pengs* carried a large, funnel-shaped kettle, the function of which Hsuang had not been able to guess.

"Rockets, my lord," the *nan* responded. "We pack our kettles with gunpowder and arrows. Place us in front of the lines. When we light our weapons, our arrows will cut the enemy down like a sickle at harvest time."

Hsuang looked doubtful.

"What do we have to lose, Tzu Hsuang?" asked the *nan*. "From all accounts, normal arrows will not stop these barbarians."

"Let us use our thunder-powder," Cheng added, "and I promise we will chase the barbarian horses from the field."

As Hsuang considered the suggestion, he saw the cavalry assigned to scouting duty cross the bridge and ride toward Shihfang. The young noble commanding them had wasted little time doing as ordered, but Hsuang was still impatient for the riders to reach their positions. Until the first scouts reported, he was simply guessing at the barbarian intentions and hoping his son-in-law had judged the Tuigan accurately.

Fortunately, Batu's plan was simple and did not call for an astounding victory on Hsuang's part. In fact, the General of the Northern Marches expected Hsuang and the nobles to be defeated. Considering those expectations, it just might make sense to do as Cheng recommended and experiment with the thunder-powder. If Batu's plan did not work, a new weapon might prove just the advantage the Shou needed to destroy the Tuigan. A battle that the Shou were supposed to lose anyway would be the ideal place to conduct such an experiment.

"Very well, we'll try this thunder-powder," Hsuang said, looking at Cheng. "But not at the expense of tested tactics. Confine the catapults to a line of a hundred yards. If we lose this battle, we will need to retreat past them, and I don't want inadvertent fires or explosions impeding our men." Hsuang turned to the *nan* whose *pengs* carried the bronze kettles. "Your rockets must be separated from the rest of the line. I don't want our secret weapon to route our own troops."

The two nobles smiled broadly and bowed to Hsuang.

With the refugees from Shihfang still fleeing down the road, the battle preparations took until late afternoon. Hsuang put each lord's army where its peculiar composition would be best utilized. In front of the bridge, he placed two thousand seasoned troops from the southern provinces. Three of the noble armies were composed entirely of archers. These he placed at the base of the bluff, where they would be able to fire over the infantry.

The bulk of the armies he arranged in two ranks, one behind barricades on the far side of the brook, and the other behind similar barricades on the close side. His plan was simple: meet the barbarian charge with the first rank. After the enemy broke the line, the second rank would open fire as the barbarians crossed the brook—covering the rest of the army's retreat.

He protected the flanks with pikemen, who could meet and resist an unexpected charge from the sides. The rocketeers he interspersed along the first rank. He even had Tzu Cheng lay several thunder bombs on the bridge, so that it could be destroyed rapidly when the need arose.

By late afternoon, the refugees were gone. Hsuang's armies were in position and prepared for battle. The foragers that the noble had sent into Shihfang earlier started back, bringing with them five tons of dried grain. Pillars of smoke began rising out of the town.

Still, the scouts did not return, and there was no sign of the enemy. Hsuang began to think he had made a mistake, that the barbarians were even now circling around to cut off the Twenty-Five Armies. As the foragers crossed the wide valley below, they paused to set fire to the barley fields.

By early dusk, the fires in the fields had died, leaving only a thick curtain of smoke that hid the opposite side of the valley. Hsuang feared his army would spend the night in the entrenchments.

Finally, horse whinnies began sounding from the opposite side of the smoky dale.

"Are they our scouts?" Hsuang asked of no one in particular. "I can't see anything in this smoke."

A gentle rumble rolled across the burning fields, as if several hundred horses were galloping down the road from Shihfang.

"It can't be the scouts," said one of the nobles. "They wouldn't return all at once."

"It isn't the barbarians," Cheng countered. "There aren't enough of them."

No one took their eyes off the haze-filled valley.

A moment later, a wide line of riders broke out of the smoke and charged toward the brook. Their mounts were small and slender, with graceful forms and fine features. On their chests and flanks, the horses were protected by barding of hardened leather. The men wore long leather hauberks, split front and rear so they could sit in their saddles. Steel skullcaps, shaped in the fashion of a cone and trimmed with fur, protected their heads. Each man carried a short lance and a melon-sized cotton bag. In the fading light, Hsuang could not see the rider's faces, but he did not doubt they had flat noses and broad cheekbones similar to those of his son-in-law.

On the slope below, archers began nocking arrows. Officers looked toward the hilltop expectantly. Hsuang started to give the order to fire, but thought better of it. There were no more than two hundred barbarians. If he attacked, fifty times that number of men would fire. Thousands of arrows would be wasted.

Instead, he remained impassive as the enemy's small line approached. Every archer in the Twenty-five Armies remained stoic and silent, ready to pull his bowstring taut, resisting the temptation to loose an arrow before receiving the order.

Twenty yards on the other side of Hsuang's fortifications, the horsemen hurled the two hundred bags at the Shou line, then wheeled their horses around. The sacks landed among the defenders with dull plops. Small gaps opened in the lines as soldiers, fearing secret weapons or powerful war magic, scurried away from the mysterious bags.

Nothing happened. The riders rode away, disappearing into the smoking fields as if they were phantoms. The bags continued to lie where they had fallen. Eventually, a few soldiers ventured to open the sacks. Some simply stared at the contents in shock, while others closed the bags and looked away in disgust.

The lines began to rustle with murmurs of fear and anger.

"What can be inside those bags?" asked Cheng, frowning at the scene below.

"We shall see soon enough," Hsuang replied, motioning to his aide to fetch a sack.

When the boy returned, his face was pale and distressed. He carried a grimy hemp sack that held something the size of a melon. The youth bowed and presented the bag to his commander.

Hsuang accepted the sack. Noting that every *peng* in the Twenty-Five Armies was watching him, he turned the bag over. The head of a Shou soldier tumbled out. Though Hsuang could not be sure, he assumed the head belonged to one of his scouts.

Aware that any sign of disgust or repulsion would translate into low morale, the lord calmly retrieved the grisly head and returned it to the sack. Before he could think of any encouraging words, however, the ground began to tremble. A distant rumble came from the other side of the valley, and Hsuang's heart suddenly beat harder.

"The barbarians are coming," Cheng said, his mouth open in astonishment. "They intend to fight a night battle!"

Dropping the sack, Hsuang ordered, "Stand ready!"

The order was unnecessary. Like their commander, all forty-five thousand of his soldiers had focused their attention on the field. The dim light and heavy smoke made it impossible to see in any detail what was happening on the opposite side of the valley. To Hsuang, it seemed as though the far hill had come alive and was rolling toward them. His feet began to tingle, and the rumble grew increasingly thunderous. Two hundred yards in front of the first barricade, a teeming mass of galloping horses became visible in the smoldering barley fields.

Hsuang nodded to the noble commanding the rocketeers. "Fire when ready," he said to the *nan*.

The noble lifted his arm to signal, then looked twenty feet down the slope to where his standard-bearer stood. The *nan* did not give the order to fire, however. Though his rockets were more powerful than normal arrows, they were less accurate and had a shorter range.

The barbarians emerged from the smoke completely, riding shoulder to shoulder. They had let their reins fall free and were using both hands to nock arrows in their bows. In the deepening twilight, the riders' bulky silhouettes made them look like no more than shadows. Their line stretched for an entire mile down the valley, and Hsuang thought he could see several more ranks emerging from the smoke. At a minimum, the charge numbered sixty thousand men.

Eyeing the approaching wall of horsemen, Cheng said, "The enemy has committed his entire army. We'll destroy them in a single battle!"

"What makes you think this is the Tuigan's entire army?" Hsuang asked. His eyes remained fixed on the valley below.

Cheng did not answer. Like Hsuang and the others, he

was waiting for the rockets to fire. The rocketeers stood behind the far barricade, separated from the closest conventional troops by gaps of twenty or thirty yards. Each man's kettle held thirty arrows and sat braced atop the barricade. The small end of each kettle was packed with thunderpowder. When the wick was lit, the powder would ignite, shooting the arrows out with incredible force. Or at least that was the theory.

When the barbarians approached to within seventy-five yards of the first barricade, their entire line suddenly reined their horses to a halt.

"What are they doing?" Hsuang demanded, angrily pointing at the enemy. "Why stop a charge in midstride?"

No one could answer.

The air resonated with the twang of sixty thousand Tuigan bowstrings. A black swarm of arrows sailed toward the first barricade. All along the line, men screamed in agony and fell. Hundreds of motionless Shou slipped into the brook and began to drift downstream.

"We cannot wait for the rocketeers any longer!" Hsuang snapped, chastising himself for allowing the barbarians to strike the first blow.

"They're barely within range," the *nan* objected, still holding his signal arm aloft. "If we wait just a little longer—"

"They're as close as they're going to come," Hsuang yelled, pointing at the stationary line. "Give the order!"

Frowning, the noble looked toward his standard-bearer and dropped his arm. An instant later, the turtle and shark crest began swaying from side to side.

The rocketeers touched their torches to the wicks. A series of booms and claps echoed through the valley, and great billows of black smoke rose into the air.

Hsuang could barely believe the results. In ten places, the kettles exploded instantly, flinging chunks of log and stray arrows in all directions. The rocketeers simply disappeared with the rest of the debris, and all that remained where they had stood were gaping holes in the barricade.

When the kettles did not explode, they sprayed their arrows out in an erratic, cone-shaped pattern that usually fell far short of the barbarian lines. The rockets that did reach the enemy, however, were effective. Nearly twenty riders sprouted arrows and flew out of their saddles with such force that there could be no doubt the men's armor had been penetrated. Dozens of horses dropped to the ground and did not move, dead at first impact. Hsuang could see why his subordinate had wanted to wait. At close range, the rockets' impact would have been devastating.

The effect on the Tuigan horses was more impressive than the number of casualties, however. Horrified whinnies and terrified neighs filled the valley. Thousands of mounts threw their riders, and hundreds of riders died beneath their beasts' frightened hooves. Many of the barbarians thrust their bows into their holsters, and used both hands to grab for their reins in a futile attempt to control their mounts. Only a few of the horsewarriors could keep their thoughts on the Shou.

Without looking away from the battle, Hsuang said, "Have the archers open fire."

His aide relayed the message to the appropriate standard-bearers. An instant later, the distinctive bass snaps of ten-thousand bows vibrated up the hill. A flock of shafts sailed over the brook and struck the wall of horsemen. Thousands of riders fell, and more panic spread through the lines as wounded and terrified horses turned to flee.

"Shall I fire the catapults?" Tzu Cheng asked eagerly. "A few more explosions will route the enemy."

"No," Hsuang replied, lifting a restraining hand.

As of yet, the enemy had not regained control of their horses. He saw no use in chasing them away before the archers could take full advantage of the barbarian disarray.

Another flight of arrows struck the enemy line. Several thousand riders fell, but Hsuang could see the horsewarriors calming their mounts. Loud noises might disturb Tuigan horses, but the beasts were accustomed to men dying upon their backs.

The archers fired another volley, killing even more barbarians than they had with the first two. Hsuang nodded to Cheng. "Loose your thunder bombs," he said.

Tzu Cheng relayed the message to his adjutant, and a moment later his standard waved. The artillerists touched their torches to the wicks of the small iron balls resting in their engines' spoons.

The engine commanders released their windlass locks. As the spoon bars slammed against the cross pieces, a series of deep thumps rolled across the hilltop.

One cross piece splintered. The bomb landed in front of the catapult and exploded, spraying hot shrapnel in all directions. Fifty feet away, a ball of flame engulfed four more catapults. A series of lesser explosions followed. An instant later, the splintered remains of four artillery pieces were raining down on the entire line of artillerymen.

Fortunately, that was the only misfire. Most of the bombs hit near the barbarian lines. At least half of the fuses went out before the missiles reached their targets. These powder pods simply burst on impact, spraying black sand everywhere. Of the bombs that did explode, very few landed close enough to inflict any casualties upon the enemy. Some even exploded in the air, over the Tuigan's heads.

The bombs' inaccuracy did not diminish their effect, however. The enemy's horses went wild, throwing their riders. Many thousands bolted, helpless men clinging to their backs. Within seconds, the Tuigan cavalry was fleeing in an uncontrolled panic.

Tzu Cheng smiled triumphantly. "With the miracle of alchemy, we are undefeatable."

"For now," Hsuang said, casting a sidelong glance at the destruction caused by the single misfired bomb. To his dismay, he caught sight of the wagon that carried the Mirror of Shao. The driver was sprawled on the ground next to the seat. The cart sat lopsided where the axle had broken and a wheel had fallen off. The broken end of a catapult spoon lay among the shattered remains of the mirror.

For a long moment, Hsuang could only stare in horror and astonishment at the smashed mirror. To keep from yelling at

Tzu Cheng, he had to remind himself that he was the one who had forgotten to move the mirror when he decided to try the thunder-powder bombs.

A roar of triumph rolled up the hill, bringing the old noble to his senses. He turned back to the battle. Behind the barricades, the soldiers were screaming in jubilation. Over ten thousand barbarians lay dead in the fields, and the Shou casualties had been light. Hsuang could understand their elation, but he knew the victory was only temporary.

In front of the bridge, a handful of men began to run after the barbarians. More followed suit. In seconds, the entire force detailed to defend the bridge was charging after the retreating cavalry.

"I didn't give the order to advance!" Hsuang gasped. "What are they doing?"

"What they're trained to do," said the noble who commanded the bridge guards. "They're destroying a disorganized enemy."

The armies to either side of the bridge also leaped over their barricades to pursue the barbarians.

"No!" Hsuang cried, turning to his subordinates. "Call them back!"

"Why?" asked Cheng.

Hsuang was too astounded to answer. The *Book of Heaven* urged its readers to pursue and destroy a disorganized enemy. Unfortunately, it had not been written with the Tuigan in mind. Against superior numbers of mounted men, pursuit could easily turn into a trap. It had never occurred to Hsuang that he and his nobles might rout the enemy, so he had neglected to discuss this point with his subcommanders. He feared he would pay dearly for the mistake.

Hsuang turned to his adjutant. "Send runners to every commander on the line. They are not to pursue."

"Tzu Hsuang!" Cheng objected, daring to grasp his superior's sleeve. "Now is no time for timidity. We have the enemy in our hands."

Hsuang jerked his sleeve out of the man's grip. "Then we are about to lose our hands," he replied sharply. He looked at his adjutant. "What are you waiting for?"

The aide bowed and went about the task with a vigor appropriate to its importance. Unfortunately, even the most dedicated adjutant could not have prevented what followed. Every army behind the front barricade followed the bridge soldiers. By the time the runners arrived with Hsuang's order, the front barricade was deserted. The second rank of defenders was working its way across the brook to join them.

The messengers managed to recall the second line of *pengs*, but the bridge troops had already led the first rank into the dark, smoking barley fields.

As Hsuang watched fifteen thousand men disappear into the smoky twilight, he said, "Lords, I must regretfully order you to prepare to fall back."

The other nobles stared at him with expressions ranging from astonishment to open fury. "This is madness!" Cheng said. "We're winning this battle."

"No," Hsuang replied. "The battle was lost before we reached Shihfang. Now it is a disaster."

"What do you mean?" asked Cheng. The man's expression was thoughtful and concerned.

Hsuang did not need to answer. The ground began to rumble, as if the spirits had sent a terrible earthquake to shake the nobles to their senses. An instant later, the pained and horrified screams of dying men rolled across the dark fields. The rumble grew more distinct; there could be no doubt that tens of thousands of pounding hooves caused it.

Moments later, dozens of Shou *pengs* appeared out of the smoke. They had thrown down their weapons and were running for the Shou lines, arrows sailing about their heads like a swarm of insects.

Tzu Cheng bowed very low to Hsuang. "I will send the order to destroy the bridge," he said. "Our best chance is to flee under cover of darkness."

- 10 -
The Spy

Qwo, what is troubling you?" Wu asked, her voice a frustrated hiss as she struggled with her *samfu*. Wu's fingers were trembling so much that she could not thread the tog-buttons through their holes.

Without answering the question, Qwo gently pulled Wu's hands aside and began fastening the *samfu*. The gray-haired servant studiously avoided the eyes of her mistress, a sure sign that she disapproved of Wu's intentions.

"It distresses me when you are sullen," Wu continued, letting her hands drop to her sides. "Please say what you are thinking."

Qwo finished closing the *samfu*, then stepped back and studied Wu with watery eyes. Though not yet sixty, the servant appeared much older. Her gray hair was thin and coarse, and her doughy skin was fallen and creased with age. She had the hunched back and stooped shoulders of a woman twenty years her senior.

The two women were in Wu's sleeping hall. The *samfu* Wu had not been able to fasten was her black one, the one she had been wearing when she had surprised Batu and knocked him unconscious.

Qwo reached into the sleeve pockets of her *cheo-sam*, an embroidered robe with huge sleeves and a high collar, and removed Wu's black scarf. "What's the use?" the old woman asked. "You are the mistress. You will do as you please, no matter what I say."

Her tone was more that of a mother than of a servant. In a certain sense, that was appropriate. Born into the Hsuang household only a few years after Wu's father himself, Qwo had spent her entire life serving the family. When Wu's mother had died, it had only been natural for Qwo to assume a maternal role as well as that of nursemaid.

As Qwo unfolded the black scarf, Wu said, "I have no choice—"

"Phaw!" the old woman objected. "Sneaking about in the night, looking for spies. This is man's business!"

"It is my business tonight," Wu replied, taking the scarf and wrapping it around her face.

With no moon out and a low-hanging cloud cover, tonight was truly black. Wu had been waiting for such a night for five weeks, ever since the emperor had confined her to the house. The nobleman's daughter intended to enter the home of Ting Mei Wan, who she believed had betrayed Shou Lung.

Unfortunately, the emperor would never condemn Ting on the basis that had convinced Wu the mandarin was a spy. The only real proof the nobleman's daughter possessed was that Ting perfumed herself with jasmine blossoms, and that the spy in the Virtuous Consort's garden had smelled of the same flower. However, the scent of jasmine was hardly rare inside the summer palace. Ting could easily, and rightfully, claim that hundreds of women scented their bodies with jasmine.

None of those other women had expressed so much interest in Batu's plan, however. After the audience with the emperor, the Minister of State Security had personally accompanied Wu home. Ting had been very friendly and curious about the whereabouts of the provincial armies. When Wu's answers were evasive, the minister had turned the conversation to other things. During the next four weeks, the lady mandarin had visited almost daily under the pretext of bringing gifts for the children. Each time, the minister had gently probed after Batu's whereabouts. Of course, Wu had refused to answer, and the minister had deftly changed the subject.

Wu had not been anxious to believe that Ting was a spy, for the minister treated her and her family with such kindness that the children had begun to refer to the mandarin as their aunt. When Ji had let slip that Ting had asked him if he knew where his father was, however, Wu had finally been forced to accept that her seeming ally was a traitor.

Though Wu had been careful to hide her suspicions, Ting had not visited in the last five days. Wu feared that the mandarin had learned what she wanted to know from some other source. If so, Wu was determined to stop the minister before she could pass the information to the enemy. Being completely convinced that Ting was a spy, Wu felt sure that the female mandarin would take advantage of tonight's unusual darkness to meet a Tuigan messenger. Wu intended to be at that meeting, both to safeguard the secrecy of Batu's plan and to gather the evidence she needed to prove her suspicions.

Qwo shuffled around behind Wu to tie the scarf. "You're disobeying the emperor," she said reproachfully.

"I know," Wu responded. The admission sent cold shivers down her spine.

"And of course you don't care," Qwo said, pulling the scarf uncomfortably tight. "You've always been a disobedient child."

"I haven't been a child for twenty years," Wu said, reaching behind her head to loosen Qwo's knot.

"Well, you've been disobedient much more recently," the servant said, slapping her hands against her thighs. "Why can't you just send a message to the emperor about this spy?"

"Who would the Divine One believe," Wu asked, looking herself over to see if she had forgotten anything, "the daughter of a country noble or a mandarin?"

"You," Qwo said simply, giving Wu a hard look. "Even if he didn't, you would have done your duty."

Wu frowned, though she knew Qwo would not see the expression behind the black scarf. "This is not about duty to the empire," she said. "It's about my father and my husband. If the enemy discovers their plans—"

"The Divine General alone determines the outcome of war. Such matters are not left to the hands of mortals, and no good will come of trying to interfere. Your concern is your household and your children," Qwo lectured. "By risking the emperor's wrath, you are failing in your true duty."

Wu sighed and looked away from the old woman's severe gaze. About that much, at least, Qwo was correct. So far, Wu's boldness had brought her household nothing but embarrassment and inconvenience. If she were caught disobeying the emperor's direct command, however, she would not suffer the consequences alone. In such matters, the entire family carried the burden of dishonor and guilt.

Though Wu was prepared to face any danger for her husband, she could not bear to watch her children pay for her crimes.

A polite cough sounded in the courtyard outside. Qwo's son, who served as Tzu Hsuang's steward, said, "Lady Wu?"

"Come in, Xeng," Wu responded.

A paper wall panel slid aside, revealing a slim man with a hawkish nose and a mild-manner. He was five years younger than Wu, having been born to Qwo in the absence of a husband. Though no one had ever admitted it, Wu suspected that Xeng was her half-brother. He had the same nose and firm expressions that she had seen so often in her father's face. More telling, however, was the jade medallion Xeng wore around his neck. The dragon-shaped pendant could render a man nearly invisible, and had been in Wu's family for hundreds of years. Nevertheless, Tzu Hsuang had given the priceless medallion to Xeng.

After entering the room, Xeng bowed first to his mother, then to Wu. "The Minister of State is here with news of your father," he said. Eyeing Wu's *samfu*, he added, "I'm afraid I implied you had not yet retired for the evening."

"News of my father?" Wu repeated. "I'll see him now."

Qwo grabbed her sleeve. "Like that?"

"Yes," Wu responded, pulling the black scarf off her chin.

"Like this."

She followed Xeng through the rest of the house, then entered the main hall. Ju-Hai Chou sat upon one of the stone benches facing the room's main decoration, the dolphin fountain.

As Wu entered, the minister stood and stared at her black clothing. "I'm sorry," he said, confused. "Did I interrupt your exercises? "

Wu decided to be frank with the minister. "No," she said. "You interrupted my escape."

Xeng gasped, and Ju-Hai frowned. "I don't understand," the minister said.

Wu crossed to Ju-Hai's bench and sat. "There is no need for concern. I intended to return."

"Return!" Xeng exclaimed, taking a single step toward the bench. "The emperor himself has forbidden you to leave. What can you be thinking?"

Wu glared at Xeng, but he remained oblivious to the anger in her eyes.

Ju-Hai sat next to Wu, laying his hands in his lap and locking his fingers together. "I'm curious, too. What *are* you thinking?"

Wu looked back to minister. "I'll explain in a few minutes," she replied. "First, tell me of Father."

The minister looked away uncomfortably. Wu began to fear her father had been killed.

"We don't have all the details," Ju-Hai began, taking Wu's hand. "This is what we do know: six days ago, the nobles met the barbarians outside the town of Shihfang. They lost over half their number."

A knot formed in Wu's stomach. Batu's plan had called for casualties, but she had not expected the toll to be so high.

"The messenger said they were falling back to Shou Kuan," the minister continued.

"And what of Tzu Hsuang?" Xeng inquired urgently, moving to Ju-Hai's side.

The mandarin frowned at being addressed so directly by another person's domestic. "Tzu Hsuang is organizing the retreat," the minister said. "He wasn't injured, as far as we know."

Both Wu and Xeng breathed sighs of relief.

The minister turned his back on the steward and looked Wu in the eye. "I'm afraid I must ask you to tell me where Batu went with the provincial armies," he said. "The news of the nobles' loss has upset the Divine One. He's beginning to voice doubts about your husband's loyalty. It's time to reassure him."

Ju-Hai's admission did not upset Wu, for her current confinement was evidence enough that the emperor had little faith in her husband. Before answering the minister, however, she looked at Xeng. "Perhaps you should inform your mother of the news."

Xeng acknowledged the order with a bow, then turned and left the room. He took care to close the wall behind him.

After the rice-paper panel slid into place, Wu turned back to Ju-Hai. "Tell the emperor not to be concerned," she said. "Batu did not expect the Twenty-Five Armies to win at Shihfang."

"That won't satisfy the Divine One," Ju-Hai responded, shaking his head. "Kwan is taking advantage of the loss to turn the emperor against us."

"I won't say where Batu is," Wu said stubbornly.

Ju-Hai stood and half turned away. "The time for mysteries is past," he snapped. "You must tell me something that will reassure the Divine One."

"If I do as you ask," Wu insisted, retaining her seat on the bench, "the Tuigan will learn my husband's plan."

"Don't be foolish," the minister answered, scowling. "Shou Lung's secrets are safe with the emperor."

"Are you sure?" Wu asked, meeting Ju-Hai's angry glare with a steady gaze.

Her question caused the mandarin to pause and suppress his anger. "What do you mean?" he asked warily.

"There's a spy in the Mandarinate," Wu answered quickly.

Ju-Hai showed no surprise at the accusation. Instead, he simply narrowed his eyes and demanded, "Who?"

Knowing how much her revelation would hurt the minister, Wu took a deep breath. "Minister Ting Mei Wan," she said at last.

For several moments, Ju-Hai stared at the nobleman's daughter with an incredulous look. Finally, he asked, "What makes you think Ting has betrayed the emperor?"

His voice was calm and curious. It was impossible to tell whether he was more interested in the issue of Ting's betrayal or the reason for Wu's accusation.

"Jasmine."

"Flowers?"

"Blossoms," Wu responded. "I smelled them on the spy in the Garden of the Virtuous Consort."

"And Ting Mei Wan perfumes herself with jasmine," Ju-Hai finished, shaking his head almost imperceptibly. "Is that the basis of your suspicion?"

Wu shook her head. "She has been asking about Batu's plans."

"So have I," Ju-Hai responded. "Does that make me a spy?" Before Wu could answer, the minister raised his hand. "Don't answer. You might lose the only friend you have left."

Wu stood and took Ju-Hai's arm. Despite the affection she felt for the minister, it was the first time she had touched him. "Ju-Hai," she said, "I could never doubt you, but Ting is different. She even asked Ji—"

He freed his arm. "Do you have proof?"

Hurt by the rejection, Wu backed away and sat on the bench. "Not really," she responded. "When you arrived, I was just leaving to find some."

"Why?" Ju-Hai asked, studying her with the sharp eyes of an interrogator. "Do you know something more?"

"No," Wu admitted, looking away. "But if Ting has something to tell her masters, a dark night like tonight would be the time to go to a messenger."

"Then you are proceeding on no more than suspicion?"

Wu nodded.

The minister's face became less stern. "I suppose that is all you can do," he allowed. "Ting is a smart woman. She would not be exposed any other way."

"So you believe me?" Wu asked, brightening.

"No," the mandarin answered bluntly. "I've known Ting Mei Wan for many years, much longer than I've known you."

Wu turned away from the minister. If Ju-Hai would not help her, it would be impossible to expose Ting's treachery.

A moment later, however, Ju-Hai said, "Still, I cannot dismiss such an accusation lightly."

Wu turned to face the minister again. "Then you'll investigate?"

Ju-Hai shook his head. "Even if you're right, Ting is far too clever to give herself away to me."

Wu frowned, sensing that the minister was leaving something unsaid. "So you want me to go ahead and follow her?"

"I'm not saying that," the minister replied cautiously.

"You're not saying I should leave the matter to you or the emperor," Wu observed.

"What you suggest is very dangerous," Ju-Hai said, fixing his eyes firmly on hers. "If you are caught outside your house, I will be powerless to help you. The emperor may conclude that Kwan is correct, and that both you and your husband are traitors. I assume you have already thought about these consequences."

Wu nodded. "I would be beheaded."

"Your servants and children as well," Ju-Hai added. "Where treason is involved, even the Son of Heaven must be ruthless."

"I realize that." As Wu spoke the words, a wave of weakness rolled over her body.

The minister stared at her with a demanding, merciless expression. "On the other hand, if Batu does not defeat the barbarians soon, the emperor will still conclude that you are traitors. It is a difficult choice. I would not wish to make it."

"What are you saying?" Wu demanded, rising.

"I am saying nothing," Ju-Hai answered. He stared at her with cold, dispassionate eyes. Suddenly, he bowed. "I only called to relay the news of your father. If you'll excuse me, it's late and I should be going."

The minister turned and showed himself out of the main hall, leaving Wu alone to puzzle over his words.

When Ju-Hai stepped out of the Batu compound, two different sets of guards snapped to attention. One set was his personal bodyguard of six men, which he had left outside Wu's home. The other set belonged to Ting. Until tonight, he had assumed that they were protecting the Batu family from Kwan's assassins. Now, he wondered if they were more dangerous than the servants of the Minister of War.

He paused in the gate and looked down the street. The night was close, and the air felt heavy with moisture. Overhead, the sky was moonless and black. Beneath the walls of the Batu compound, the darkness was as absolute. The minister could not see even the silhouettes of the guards that he knew would be standing there. It seemed a fitting night for accusations of treachery and betrayal.

Ju-Hai was not anxious to believe Wu, and he could find plenty of reason to doubt her suspicions. Certainly, it was not unusual to smell jasmine in the Virtuous Consort's garden. Though he had never been inside, he did not doubt that the small park contained at least a few of the climbing shrubs. Even if that was not the case, Ting was far from alone in using jasmine blossoms as perfume.

As for asking about Batu's plan, the female mandarin could hardly be blamed for her inquisitiveness. For nearly two months now, the general's disappearance had been the primary source of court gossip. Even the emperor had occasionally voiced his curiosity about what had happened to the General of the Northern Marches and his hundred thousand *pengs*.

Still, Ju-Hai could not dismiss Wu's accusation out-of-hand. For several months now, Ting had seemed more independent and power-hungry than usual. He had taken this as a sign that she was growing more secure in her position as a mandarin. He also saw that it could be a result of a secret allegiance to a new master.

Ju-Hai was deeply fond of Ting. In a world of double deceits and elaborate subterfuges, her undisguised mercenary streak seemed almost honest. Though he had never trusted her completely, Ju-Hai had always felt that if he knew what she wanted, he could work with her to achieve what he desired.

It had never occurred to the Minister of State that his protege might want something badly enough to betray Shou Lung. Even by the most ruthless standards of court conduct, such behavior was unthinkable. He could not believe that Ting would resort to such treachery.

Ju-Hai was far from confident in his opinion, however, and knew that he could not expect to discover the truth through direct questioning. Opening an official inquiry was also out of the question. If it proved nothing, it would needlessly damage Ting's reputation, making the Tigress an enemy for life.

Wu was the only tool Ju-Hai had available to discover the truth. He did not doubt that Hsuang's daughter would do as he wanted, for he had carefully guided the conversation to make her feel that she had no choice except to expose the spy herself. Ju-Hai did not enjoy such callous manipulation, but he was willing to do it for the good of the emperor.

At the same time, the minister also felt obliged to provide what assistance he could. His agents had been quite impressed with Wu's kung fu, and Ju-Hai knew the general's wife would have no trouble getting into Ting's house. However, leaving her own home, which was tightly ringed with guards, might prove more difficult.

Ju-Hai started away from the compound, surrounded by his bodyguard. Fifty yards later, he looked down an alley and, feigning surprise, asked his guards, "What's happening there?"

His bodyguard peered into the alley. "Where, Minister?" asked one.

"There—a figure. Don't you see it?" Ju-Hai pointed at the right side of the darkened lane. "Stop in the name of the emperor!" he yelled.

No one answered, but he had not expected a response. As far as he knew, the alley was empty. He was simply trying to lure the guards away from Wu's house.

When he looked back toward the Batu compound, he was pleased to note that his plan was working. In the light of gate lamps, he saw Ting's guards looking in his direction.

"Guards!" he called. "Come quickly—it's a spy!"

As he had hoped, the mere mention of a spy was enough to lure the guards away from their posts. The tramp of heavy boots echoed down the street, and a moment later twelve sentries rushed into view. Ju-Hai's own bodyguard closed ranks around him. If there was danger nearby, the last thing they would do was leave their master alone.

Ju-Hai pointed down the alley. "There!" he said, speaking to Ting's guards. "Quickly!"

The soldiers brushed past the minister with barely a second glance, calling orders and commands to each other. Ju-Hai looked back toward the Batu household, hoping to catch a glimpse of Wu taking advantage of his ruse. Not even the hint of a shadow slipped out of the gate.

Returning his attention to the alley, Ju-Hai patiently waited while the guards rushed about, banging gates and searching doorways. Though he wanted to leave, Ju-Hai knew that his sudden departure would make the guards suspicious.

Ten minutes later, a drizzle began to fall. The rain was warm, almost hot, and did nothing to relieve the stickiness of the night. Ju-Hai did not care. It provided him with an excuse to leave the search.

"I have no desire to stand in the rain while you let the spy escape," he said to the sergeant. "If you are lucky enough to find the infiltrator, take him to Minister Ting. Ask her to notify me at once."

The sergeant bowed. "Of course, Minister."

Ju-Hai returned the bow with a cursory nod, then started down the street with his own bodyguard in tow. Instead of going home, however, he turned toward Ting's. His unexpected arrival at her house would provide another distraction for Wu. He might even learn something himself.

As he and his guards drifted through the dark streets, Ju-Hai occasionally stopped to listen for Wu. He did not see even the faintest suggestion of a trailing silhouette, and the only sound he heard was the squeak of his own guards' wet armor. The only hint of Wu's presence was a feeling of disquiet that raised the hair on the back of the minister's neck.

When he approached Ting's house, Ju-Hai stationed his bodyguard at the entrance of the alley that ran along the back wall of her compound, then went down the dark lane alone. If he were to use the front gate, by tomorrow morning, the summer palace would be filled with gossip of their "liaison." As he had no desire to make himself the subject of such gossip, he intended to use the back entrance.

Just before Ju-Hai reached Ting's back gate, the wooden doors opened. A figure dressed in a dark *samfu* slipped out of the archway and paused in the light of the single gate lamp. It was Ting Mei Wan, Minister of State Security. She carried a dark scarf and a polished ebony tube, such as one might use to store a paper scroll. The scabbard of a twelve-inch dagger hung from her belt.

She paused a moment to tie the scarf around her face. In that instant, Ju-Hai knew that Wu was right. Ting, the very person charged with ensuring the empire's security, was preparing to meet the enemy's courier even now. There could be no other reason for her nefarious dress. The ebony tube, the minister guessed, contained evidence of her betrayal, probably a report of how the emperor had taken the nobles' defeat.

Stomach knotted with sorrow and his heart pounding with rage, Ju-Hai decided he would not allow the traitor to deliver her message. He considered calling his bodyguard, then realized that so near Ting's house, they were sure to be outnumbered by the traitor's men. The Minister of State could not take the tube by force.

Still unaware of Ju-Hai's presence, Ting glanced up at the drizzle, then slipped the ebony tube inside her *samfu*. She turned away and started down the alley.

"Did someone tell you I was coming?" Ju-Hai called, his tone forcibly jocular.

Ting spun around, squinting into the darkness. "Who's there?" Her face was pale with shock.

Ju-Hai did not respond. Instead, he simply took another echoing step forward.

"Answer!" Ting commanded, drawing her dagger.

"It's just an old friend," Ju-Hai responded, stepping into the light of her gate lamp. "Why so frightened?"

"Minister!" Ting sighed, pulling the scarf off her face. "What are you doing here on a night like this?"

"Coming to see you. Where are *you* going on a night like this, dressed like that?" he asked, pointing at her *samfu*.

Ting glanced at her dark clothing, then frowned at Ju-Hai. She seemed at a loss for words and clenched her dagger hilt so tightly that her knuckles went white. For a moment, Ju-Hai feared she would attack him. Finally, she sheathed her weapon. "To a rendezvous," she said. "With whom is none of your business."

Ju-Hai tapped the tube beneath her shirt. "I'd give a thousand silver coins to know what present you're taking him."

Ting shifted the tube out of his reach. "Is there something you want?"

"Yes," Ju-Hai said. He did not elaborate, for he had intended to call on Ting under the pretext of a social visit. Having caught her as she was leaving, he needed a better excuse to detain her. He had not yet thought of one.

"What is it? I'm late as it is."

Ju-Hai glanced down the alley, hoping that Wu was somewhere in the dark watching the exchange. "Unless your rendezvous is with the emperor, this is more important. We'd better go inside."

Ting's irritation disappeared instantly. "Of course, if it's as serious as you say," she said, opening the gate.

"It is, I assure you." Ju-Hai stepped through the entrance into a small kiosk. To the Minister of State's surprise, it was empty. "No guard?" he asked.

"I had him sent away for a few minutes," Ting responded.

"Discretion begins at home."

She led Ju-Hai through the black, winding paths of her park. Though he knew Ting kept a man to care for her garden, it seemed overgrown and ominous in the darkness. All sorts of mosses and vines dangled from tree limbs overhanging the paths, and the shrubbery was feral and imposing in both size and shape. Ju-Hai felt as though a band of murderous thieves might leap from the brush at any moment. It was just the sort of place he imagined Ting would find enjoyable.

A few moments later, they reached the main hall. Ting showed Ju-Hai to a couch and summoned a servant to pour tea, then excused herself to change. A few minutes later, she returned wearing a white robe brocaded with the pattern of the mythical phoenix. Though the loosely fastened robe reached clear to the floor, it was cut to make the most of Ting's enticing form. It also revealed that she no longer had the ebony tube with her.

She sat on the couch opposite Ju-Hai and crossed one sculpted leg over the other. "So, Minister, what is more important than the diversion I had planned?"

Ju-Hai glanced at the servant uncomfortably, as if reluctant to speak. He was buying time. Though he had developed several excuses for calling Ting away from her rendezvous, none seemed particularly convincing.

The seductive mandarin dismissed the servant, then turned back to Ju-Hai. Her expression was openly curious. "Well?"

Ju-Hai looked away and sipped his tea. "I don't know how to begin," he said.

Ting raised an eyebrow. "Begin at the beginning, Minister."

Ju-Hai hesitated, asking himself if enough time had passed for Wu to find the ebony tube. Next, he wondered whether or not the nobleman's daughter had been in the alley and knew what to look for. Finally, he began to worry that he had misjudged her. It would not be unlikely that her concern for her children would prevent her from risking the emperor's wrath, even to expose a spy.

The minister forced the last thought from his mind. It would do him no good to doubt his plan now. His only course was to proceed as if Wu had followed him and was even now searching Ting's house. The more time he bought, the better would be Wu's chance of success.

"This isn't easy for me," Ju-Hai began, setting his tea cup aside and glancing at Ting's willowy legs.

An expression of comprehension crossed the Minister of State Security's face. "Say no more," she said. "I understand."

"You do?"

"I think so."

Ting rose and stepped around the table. She took Ju-Hai by the wrists and pulled him to his feet, guiding his hands inside her robe. "Even if my rendezvous had been with the emperor," she said, "I wouldn't have missed this."

Ju-Hai kissed her. It was a cold, dispassionate kiss, the kind to which he imagined the seductress was accustomed.

Ting returned the kiss with a warmth and vigor that surprised the Minister of State, then turned to lead the way into her sleeping hall.

Two hours later, Ju-Hai was exhausted. Ting pulled him toward her yet again, but he slipped out of the bed and said, "Enough! I'm an old man. I must conserve my energy."

"Nonsense!" she replied, pulling him back. "Let me rejuv—"

A wall panel slid open, interrupting Ting. The sergeant of her guard rushed into the room. "Minister, there's been an intruder."

The sergeant noticed Ju-Hai's naked form, then flushed with embarrassment and bowed.

Ting leaped out of bed and grabbed her robe. "Intruder?" she repeated, immodestly dressing right before the guard's eyes. "Where?"

"The alley entrance," the sergeant reported.

Ting immediately started for the door. Ju-Hai quickly donned his own clothes and followed, catching up to Ting in the garden. She was firing questions at the sergeant, who could tell her only that the sentry posted at the gate had been found dead.

At the kiosk, several guards holding lamps stood around their fallen companion. As Ting and Ju-Hai approached, they backed away. The dead sentry lay sprawled on his back, his *chiang-chun* at his side. The polearm's blade was bloody.

"This is how we found him," the sergeant reported.

Ting kneeled and examined the body. When she found no wounds on the chest or head, she angrily rolled the corpse over and examined its back.

"There are no wounds on this body," she snapped, returning to her feet.

"Then this is the intruder's blood," the sergeant concluded, picking up the dead man's *chiang-chun*.

"Yes," Ting replied, taking the polearm and examining the red blade. "Tomorrow, we shall find the intruder and finish the job."

She glanced at Ju-Hai, then asked, "I wonder why he picked tonight to come?"

"It is a moonless night," Ju-Hai answered. He focused his eyes upon the dead guard, but was thinking of Wu. If she were wounded, she would need help and, come morning, protection. He had to leave Ting's house and assign a contingent of the emperor's guard to protect the Batu household. He stepped toward the gate. "I should return home," he said. "My presence here tonight will generate quite a scandal."

Ting signaled her guards to block the gate. "I won't hear of it," she said, eyeing Ju-Hai with an emotionless, calculating gaze. "Whoever killed this guard is still free, and for all we know he was after you. You aren't leaving the safety of my house."

"I really must return—"

Ting lifted her hand. "I insist," she said. Holding her jaw set firmly, she studied her mentor with narrow, menacing eyes. "You will go nowhere until I find the intruder."

- 11 -
Yenching

On the Shengti River, as in the summer palace, the night was humid and black. Despite the warm drizzle, the General of the Northern Marches remained on deck with his ship's first mate. The wiry riverman hung over the gunwale with a lamp in his hand, watching the dark waters for any hint of trouble. The man's shirtless torso glistened with what might have been rainwater, but was more likely a nervous sweat. Periodically, he called out an instruction that another boatman promptly relayed to the helmsman.

The hull bumped something pulpy, and Batu inhaled sharply. "What is it?"

When the mate did not answer promptly, Batu feared they had hit a sandbar. The summer flood season had ended two weeks ago, and the river had since returned to normal, exposing hazards that had not previously troubled the general's fleet. Already tonight, a dozen ships had run aground. Batu was beginning to regret his decision to continue upriver in darkness.

"What did we hit?" Batu repeated, laying a hand on the mate's bare back.

The man did not look up. "I don't know, General, but there's no cause for worry. If it was anything dangerous, it would have slowed us down."

The mate's reassurance did little to make Batu breathe easier. The moonless night was stifling and ominous, silencing even the owls that lived along the riverbanks. Only the

soldiers, they had kept their boats moving twenty-four hours a day. Thanks to their skill and tireless effort, the general was arriving at Yenching nearly a week ahead of schedule. When he returned to the summer palace, Batu decided, he would recommend to the Divine One that he consider recruiting commercial boatmen as officers in the imperial navy.

The merchant rivermen were far more superstitious than their military counterparts. The first mate still had not returned to his post. Instead, he was casting frightened glances over the side and tracing mystic symbols in the air.

"The bodies in the river are just corpses," Batu repeated. "They're not going to hurt you. On the other hand, if we hit a sandbar or rock . . ." The general touched his sword hilt meaningfully.

The gesture reminded the riverman of his duty. "Forgive me," he said, resuming his position as guide. Batu stood nearby, eyeing the weed bed with as much suspicion as the mate eyed the corpses.

As the boat continued forward, the bodies came into view with increasing frequency. After several minutes more, it seemed the river was choked with corpses. The smell of rotten flesh grew stronger. Even Batu, who considered himself to have a strong stomach, found each breath a sickening experience. Several *pengs* came topside under the mistaken impression that the air would be fresher. Soon, the junk was buzzing with subdued discussions of the terrible smell and speculations as to why so many bodies were in the river.

Though he did not tell any of his men, Batu knew the reason for the awful scene. His great grandfather had told him tales of Tuigan atrocities on unimaginable scales. Assuming those stories had been even partially true, the general had no doubt that the corpses belonged to the citizens of Yenching. In the face of the enemy's advance, the inhabitants had no doubt retreated into their city, thinking they would be safe inside its walls. After Yenching fell, the Tuigan had probably punished the inhabitants with extermination, dumping the bodies into the Shengti.

Thirty minutes later, the general noticed a lamp shining through the drizzle ahead. The holder stood on the shore, swinging the light in a circle. Batu ordered the fleet to drop anchor. The circling light was a signal from his cavalry scouts indicating they had something to report. If, as the mate insisted, the fleet was within a few miles of Yenching, the message would be important.

Batu dispatched a *sampan* to fetch the officer of the scouts, then sent for his subcommanders. Next, he went below and awakened Pe, who it seemed could sleep through a battle. When the adjutant was dressed, the pair returned to the deck.

The provincial generals and the scouting officer were already waiting. Wasting no time with pleasantries, Batu looked directly to the cavalry officer. "What do you have to report?"

After a nervous glance at Batu's subordinates, the officer began. "Commanding General, Yenching is only five miles away. As you expected, it has been taken by the enemy." The young man paused and grimaced, clearly quite reluctant to continue.

"And?" Batu prodded.

"The enemy is still there," the scouting officer said.

"How many?" demanded Kei Bot Li, the stocky general from Hungtze.

"The entire army," the scout replied.

Batu frowned, thinking of his conversation with Tzu Hsuang just four days ago. His father-in-law had been expecting a major confrontation, and had not reported since. Batu could only guess at the reason. Hsuang might have been killed, the noble armies wiped out, or the mirror abandoned during retreat. Whatever the cause of the silence, however, Batu felt sure of one thing: the nobles had met a large force of Tuigan.

Addressing the scout, Batu said, "What you report is impossible."

The cavalryman inclined his head. "If that is what you say, General."

"Don't be so ready to change your report, young man," Kei Bot interrupted, stepping closer to the officer. "What makes you think the barbarians are still in Yenching?"

The officer glanced at Batu nervously, clearly afraid to contradict the commanding general of the greatest Shou army ever assembled. Batu nodded to the young man.

After receiving permission to speak, the officer said. "Horses. There are one hundred and fifty thousand or more outside the city."

"How certain are you of the numbers?" Batu asked, his mind reeling at the thought of so many horses.

The young cavalryman looked at the deck. "We can't be sure," he admitted. "We didn't dare approach their camps until dusk, and there were too many beasts to count in the short time we had. Still, I'm confident we haven't exaggerated. The beasts cover the plain like a blanket."

"What of the barbarians themselves?" asked Kei Bot.

"Yenching is well lit," the officer reported, glancing toward Kei Bot but addressing Batu. "It appears the enemy is taking shelter in the city."

"They're not sleeping with their horses?" Batu asked, frowning.

"No more than three hundred campfires burn outside the city," the scout said confidently. "Perhaps many of the barbarians are sleeping without fires, but then who is lighting the city?"

Pe pointed to the body-choked river. "Certainly not the citizens."

"This makes no sense," Batu said, leaning on the gunwale. "Why would there be so many barbarians in Yenching?"

"Evidently, the residents tried to hold Yenching," Kei Bot offered, nodding at the corpses. "Perhaps they didn't burn their grain before the city fell."

"The Tuigan must have taken the city weeks ago," objected one of the other generals. "Why would they remain here, consuming what must be a very limited supply of food? It would be wiser to eat their fill, then carry what they could and press forward."

"Our enemies are barbarians," Kei Bot snapped, turning on the man who had contradicted him. "After two months of starvation, they must now be content to feast and rest."

Batu stepped between Kei Bot and the other general. "Our enemies may be barbarians," he said, "but they are cunning and disciplined. Whatever their reason for remaining in Yenching, General Kei, it is not lethargy."

Batu deliberately delivered the comment with a scornful tone. Kei Bot received the censure with a bow and an apologetic expression, but Batu knew from experience that the reproach would have little permanent effect.

"The Tuigan must be ready for us," Pe said, addressing his commander. "Perhaps a spy learned of your plan, General."

All six commanders grimaced.

"That's impossible," Batu responded, shaking his head. "Only one person at the summer palace knows where we are, and she would never reveal the plan."

"The summer palace is far away," Kei Bot responded, looking toward the southeast. "Who can tell what is passing there."

Kei Bot's ominous comment sent an unaccustomed pang of concern through Batu's breast. He cast a disturbed glance toward the distant palace, wondering what his family was doing and if they were safe. The concern was a new emotion, for the general had always felt confident of his wife's ability to care for the family when he was gone. During their last two weeks together, however, Wu had seemed anything but assured or strong. Diplomacy had never been one of her gifts, and it had been clear that she felt insecure in the political atmosphere of the summer palace.

"Is something wrong, General?" Pe asked, daring to touch his master's sleeve.

Batu shook his head, forcing his family from his mind. This was no time to let such thoughts interfere with his duty. If familial concerns keep a soldier from focusing on the task at hand, Batu reminded himself sternly, he had no business having a wife and children. In war, there was too much at risk to let personal affairs take priority over military matters.

The general turned back to the cavalry officer. "What do you make of the horses and the lights in the city?" he asked.

The officer's eyes widened in shock. "Me, General?"

"Yes," Batu snapped. "You're the only one who has seen the enemy camp. Do they appear prepared for battle?"

The young cavalryman looked from one general to another, as if begging for mercy.

"Answer!" insisted Wak'an, the officer's direct commander.

The scout licked his lips nervously. Finally, he answered, "In truth, they aren't prepared for battle. They have established a wide perimeter of guardposts, of course. But the rain has made the ground muddy. Their patrols move slowly and do not range far. They have displayed a surprising lack of concern about the river—"

"They don't realize it's a means of transport," Kei Bot observed, a condescending smirk on his face. "The barbarians are not boatmen."

"No doubt," Batu agreed. He turned back to the cavalry officer. "Continue."

"There's little more to report. By moving only at night, our scouts have engaged but one patrol, and we destroyed it to a man. We haven't made any blunders, and the enemy's lazy deployment suggests they don't suspect our presence. They look as though battle is the farthest thing from their minds."

"They sound more like a garrison than a battle-ready force," Pe observed, furrowing his brow.

"Perhaps you're right," Batu said. "They might be only a garrison."

"With a hundred and fifty thousand horses?" objected another general.

Batu nodded. "Yes. Even if the Tuigan don't know our plan, their spies have certainly reported the disappearance of our five armies. As he has demonstrated so far, the barbarian commander is no fool. The only bridge across the upper Shengti is at Yenching. Yamun Khahan knows as well as we do that if he loses that city, he will be cut off from his homeland and trapped in Shou Lung."

"So he would garrison the city," Kei Bot observed. A moment later, he frowned. "But not with a hundred and fifty thousand men. From your estimates of the enemy's strength, General Batu, that's three quarters of the barbarian army!"

The other generals muttered in agreement, but Batu shook his head thoughtfully. "The Tuigan are as rich in horses as Shou Lung is in people," the general said. "Each man leads an extra mount, sometimes two. There are probably no more than seventy-five thousand warriors in Yenching."

"Even so, seventy-five thousand men is no garrison," countered Kei Bot, meeting Batu's gaze with a critical expression. "Until we know why there are so many barbarians in Yenching, we must proceed with the utmost caution."

Batu suffered a sinking feeling. "As much as it pains me to admit it, your counsel is wise," he replied. The General of the Northern Marches looked over the gunwale toward the city. "What *can* they be doing with so many men in Yenching?" he demanded, his voice betraying more frustration than he cared to reveal to his subordinates.

After a long and anxious silence, it was the cavalry officer who dared to speak. "If I may, General, I can offer one possible answer." He inclined his head to show that he did not mean to be presumptuous.

"If you know the reason for the barbarian behavior, it is your obligation to report it!" Batu snapped, irritated that the man's timidity had kept him from fully discharging his duty. "Speak!"

The officer paled at his commander's tone, then quickly wet his lips and began. "I have only a few thousand horses in my command," he said, staring at Batu's feet. "Still, we have found it difficult to feed them, especially in the areas the peasants have burned. With a hundred times as many horses, the problem must be a hundred times as severe."

Batu nodded. "Go on."

The cavalryman dared to look up. "If I were the enemy

commander, I'd leave my extra horses and as much of my force as prudent at Yenching—especially if the granaries were full when the city fell."

"You're right," Batu declared, laying a commending hand on the scout's shoulder. "They aren't foot soldiers, so the Tuigan ignore the possibility of using the river for transport. We aren't cavalrymen, so we forget the difficulties of feeding the horses and don't recognize the obvious problems our enemy faces."

The other generals voiced their agreement with the cavalry officer's analysis. Presently, however, Kei Bot scowled. "What difference does this enlightenment make, General Batu? Your plan is spoiled. Even if we had the proper equipment, it would take weeks to siege Yenching. Before it falls, the rest of the barbarians would return to aid the garrison."

Batu meet the stocky general's scowl with narrowed eyes. "Then we must take the city by surprise," he said. "Tonight."

His subordinates gasped. The cavalry officer nearly choked with shock. "B-But that's impossible!"

"Nothing is impossible," Batu replied, a smile of anticipation creeping across his lips. The general loved nothing more than testing himself and his men in battle, and storming the city might well prove a challenge worthy of their talents.

Still, Batu harbored no hope that Yenching would be a truly magnificent combat. The circumstances were not right for the epic confrontation he coveted. There was nothing illustrious about taking an enemy by surprise, especially when the opponent was outnumbered and far away from the supervision of a brilliant commander.

There was no chance, Batu realized, that Yenching would be the illustrious battle of which he dreamed. On the other hand, there was no chance that it would prove boring, either.

After standing for several moments in dumfounded silence, the scout bowed deeply. "Please forgive me, General," the young officer said. "I didn't explain the situation clearly. The barbarians will see us coming. There is a guardpost two miles outside the city. They will see your boat lamps as soon as you round the next bend. That's why I stopped you here."

"The enemy is not as poorly prepared as you had hoped," Kei Bot said, a satisfied smirk creasing his lips. "There is no way to surprise the Tuigan. You have no choice but to siege the city."

"I repeat," Batu said flatly. "We'll take Yenching tonight. I have just the way to do it."

Ignoring his subordinates' open mouths, Batu turned to the cavalry officer. "Can you stampede the barbarian's mounts?"

A grin crossed the scout's lips. For the first time that night, he looked certain of himself. "It will be a simple matter. The animals may be tethered, but no rein in the world will hold a frightened horse—much less a hundred and fifty thousand of them."

"Good," Batu replied, giving his subordinates a confident smile. "Yenching will be ours by morning."

He outlined his plan, assigning each general the responsibility for coordinating one particular aspect. When he finished, he ordered the fleet commander to begin debarking the army on the river's northern shore.

Batu took a few minutes to help the *feng-li lang* and his assistants from the Rites Section kill a hunting falcon. The *feng-li lang* claimed the sacrifice would persuade the spirits to grant favorable weather for the coming battle. After the bird's body had been ritually burned in a bronze caldron, Batu turned his attention to the most crucial part of his plan. He had a hundred and fifty volunteers, armed with swords and torches, hidden deep within the bilges of two cargo junks. Next, he had the boats loaded with grain, taking care to make sure that his *pengs* could not be discovered easily.

Batu ordered the two junks to light all their lamps and sail upriver, then returned to his cabin to write his customary letter to Wu. No sooner had he set out the ink and writing brushes, however, than Pe came below.

"The *pengs* are debarked and formed into units," the adjutant said, standing in the tiny cabin's door. "The Most Magnificent Army of Shou Lung is ready to march."

"Good," Batu responded, dipping his brush into the ink well. "We'll begin as soon as I finish writing to Wu."

Pe looked concerned. "More than half the night has passed, General, and we have a long march ahead."

"I am aware of the hour and the distance to Yenching," Batu snapped, irritated by Pe's presumption. He felt sure the adjutant had meant to imply he was wrong to delay the army while attending to a personal matter.

The adjutant blanched. "Forgive me, General."

"Don't apologize," Batu replied, realizing that Pe was correct to criticize him. Every minute he delayed increased the likelihood of the sun rising on his army before it reached Yenching. If that happened, even the Ministry of Magic's *wu jens* could not keep such a vast number of men concealed.

Batu laid his writing brush aside and stood, fastening his *chia*. "Issue strict orders that no *peng* is to speak. Every man is to secure all loose equipment. We don't want enemy sentries hearing even the faintest voice or the most distant piece of clanging metal."

Pe did not turn to leave. Instead, still looking at the floor, the adjutant said, "But your letter, General. I didn't mean you should not finish it, only that it might be wise to send the army ahead."

Batu cast a regretful eye at the blank paper. "I must be with the army at all times, in case the enemy discovers us," he said. "Anyway, I can't send the letter to Wu. If the Tuigan captured the messenger, they would certainly learn our position. The risk is too great to take just to keep a personal promise."

He motioned Pe out of the doorway. The adjutant led the way up to the deck and into a waiting *sampan*. After the general and his aide reached shore, Pe issued the orders concerning talking and clanging equipment.

A few minutes later, the army began marching through the mud, the cavalry leading the way. Within half an hour, the drizzle stopped and a brisk wind blew out of the west.

Batu had no idea whether the change in weather was the spirits' doing or not, but he whispered a silent thanks to them anyway. The breeze would carry any sounds his army made away from the enemy.

At regular intervals, the scouts sent guides back to lead the infantry over the next section of ground. The guides took the army through a labyrinth of shallow valleys. Because of the absolute darkness, men were constantly stumbling and falling on the broken, muddy ground. For the largest part, they avoided cursing or calling out, but it was impossible to prevent loud thuds and clangs.

Twice, the army paused while the cavalry surrounded and attacked an enemy outpost. During these times, Batu could hardly restrain himself from riding forward to direct the small engagements personally. If one of the enemy sentries escaped, the Shou armies would lose the element of surprise. Fortunately, the cavalry proved up to the task and most of the Tuigan died with their weapons sheathed.

Three hours later, the armies were still struggling through the mud and the cavalry scouts had not yet called a halt. It was nearly morning, and the first gray streaks of false dawn were appearing in the eastern sky. Batu feared the barbarians would be awake by the time his army arrived at Yenching.

Just when he felt sure the scouts had lost the way, the cavalry commander returned. Pointing at a hulking silhouette that loomed ahead, the young man said, "Yenching is over that hill, General."

"Let us see what there is to see," Batu replied.

The general and the scout dismounted and crept to the hilltop, Pe following close behind. The three men were careful to stay low to the ground, lest they cast a silhouette against the false dawn.

Yenching lay in the shallow valley of a tributary to the Shengti. The streets were barely discernible from the buildings at this early hour. A dark band, which Batu took to be a wall, surrounded the city. Outside the wall, thousands of dark shapes that could only be horses milled through the valley. The cavalry officer had not exaggerated their huge number.

A canal had been dredged from the Shengti River to Yenching, entering the city through a fan-shaped gate designed to accommodate boat traffic. Batu could see little else, for the night remained dark and moonless.

Pe pointed at the Shengti. "There are the junks, General."

Two sets of lights were slowly moving up the river. As the three men watched, it became apparent that the barbarian sentries had also noticed the junks. The trio caught several glimpses of mounted silhouettes skulking along the shore behind the boats.

Within a few minutes, the junks reached the mouth of the canal and turned toward the city. To Batu's relief, the enemy did not stop the boats. It appeared the Tuigan were every bit as desperate for supplies as the cavalry officer had suggested. Assuming the craft to be ladened with cargo, the barbarians were not making any moves that might frighten the crews and send the junks back down the river. The horsewarriors would probably not seize the boats until they were inside the city, where fleeing would be impossible. Shortly afterward, torches in hand, the *pengs* hiding in the bilges would rush from the junks. They would set fire to everything they could, burning Yenching from the inside and forcing the barbarians to flee into the arms of the Shou armies waiting outside.

The boats' progress up the canal seemed painfully slow. False dawn faded, then reappeared a few minutes later as first light. Batu could barely stop himself from giving the order to stampede the horses. He was anxious to start the battle, and not just because he was looking forward to it.

The general from Chukei was relying upon at least partial darkness to keep the barbarians confused. Every minute closer to dawn reduced his chance of victory. At the same time, if he attacked too early, the enemy would smell a trap and close the river gate. The junks would remain outside Yenching, forcing a siege.

Finally, the boats reached the gate. Batu turned to the cavalry officer. "Prepare your men."

A broad grin spread across the young commander's face. "Yes, my General."

As the cavalryman turned to go, Batu spoke to Pe. "Order the generals to advance behind the cavalry. Position one thousand archers along the canal to prevent the enemy from swimming out of our trap. Return here after you are finished."

"Yes, General," Pe replied, creeping down the hillside to relay the orders to the messengers.

A few minutes later, the river gate closed behind the two junks. Behind Batu, the cavalry assembled just below the crest of the hill. The Shou riders numbered less than three thousand, but Batu thought they would suffice for what he wanted today.

A sliver of orange sun appeared on the horizon, casting reddish light on the eastern side of the hill. Fortunately, the western side remained plunged in shadows. Thanking the night spirits for this small favor, Batu stood and waved the cavalry forward. Immediately, the line advanced. As they passed the general, the mounts broke into a trot, then into a charge as they descended upon the valley.

The infantry followed a moment later, rushing forward at a disciplined double time. They paid less attention to formation than to speed, for their goal was to surround the city as quickly as possible. Nevertheless, the officers did their best to keep the men grouped into assigned units in order to avoid confusion during the battle.

On the western side of the hill, the light was still dim. Batu could not see how the enemy sentries were responding to the charge. Nevertheless, he heard guttural shouts of alarm being raised all around the valley.

Pe returned to the general's side and stared down the hill. "What now, my commander?"

"We wait," Batu said, keeping his eyes fixed on Yenching.

The adjutant nodded. "The battle is in the hands of the spirits."

Batu raised an eye to the sky. Without taking any credit

away from the spirits, who seemed to be on his side so far, the general had to disagree with his adjutant about who governed the outcome of the battle. "You are mistaken, Pe. Like us, the spirits have done their part." The general waved a hand at the valley. "The battle is now in the hands of something less predictable than spirits. It is in the hands of our *pengs.*"

As the general finished his observation, the cavalry began to shout and whistle. A muffled thunder built deep within the valley as the first Tuigan horses fled the Shou charge. A few hundred barbarians carrying torches rushed from the city.

Though the enemy was responding earlier than he expected, Batu was not concerned. The more barbarians who left the city, the better. Any horsewarriors trapped outside of Yenching would be unavailable to defend the city against the second part of his plan.

As the Shou cavalry rode deeper into the valley, terrified whinnies filled the air. Within moments, the ground began to tremble. The great barbarian herd was stampeding.

The sun cast a few long rays into the valley, and Batu could see more Tuigan pouring from the city. As often as not, the flood of frightened horses swept away the confused barbarians. At the same time, the first Shou armies reached crossbow range. They fired at enemy soldiers and horses indiscriminately, doing more damage by further panicking the herd than by directly inflicting injuries.

"Your plan is working, General," Pe observed.

Batu did not answer, for he was far from convinced that the battle was won. Clearly, the horsewarriors would be deprived of their mounts. A few thousand of the barbarians had already died attempting to leave the city. As of yet, however, the general saw no sign that the most important part of his plan was working. Chasing the horses away and surrounding the city would be of little use if the enemy remained holed up inside.

As the sun lit Yenching more brightly, the Shou cavalry drove the last of the enemy's horses away, easily overwhelming the few confused sentries on the far side of the valley. The five provincial armies moved into position around the city, training their weapons on its gates. As Batu had ordered, one thousand archers took up positions along the banks of the canal.

"Not even a rat will escape," Pe said, studying the deployment.

"I don't care about the rats, but I would be glad for a few escaping Tuigan," Batu replied, his heart sinking. "The most important part of our plan seems to have failed. Yenching is not burning."

Though it no longer mattered, Batu wondered what had gone wrong inside the city. The volunteers could have been discovered before the cavalry charge distracted the barbarians. Or perhaps Batu had been wrong to think that a handful of men could burn an entire city.

"The battle is not over yet, General," Pe said, pointing at a column of smoke rising from the center of the city.

"It is," Batu snapped, shaking his head in disgust. He was not upset at his adjutant, but at his own failure. "The enemy knows we're here. One small fire will not chase the Tuigan out of Yenching. They'll just put it out."

Pe furrowed his brow. Though he was looking at the same scene as his commander, he clearly did not see the same thing. "How can they fight fires and us at the same time?" he asked.

"What do you mean?" No sooner had he finished the question than the general understood exactly what his adjutant meant. Batu had never intended to storm the city, but the barbarians didn't know that. With a little prodding, the Shou commander could keep the Tuigan at the city walls, leaving the volunteers inside Yenching free to burn the city.

"Send the order quickly," the general said.

"What order?" Pe asked, uncomfortable with the vagaries of what amounted to mind-reading.

"To prepare for storming the city, of course," Batu answered. "A brilliant plan, Pe!"

"Thank you, General," Pe replied proudly.

"However, your plan needs one minor adjustment," Batu added, frowning in concentration as he studied the city. "We've got to convince the Tuigan our attack is real. Order General Kei Bot to storm the gates on his side of the city."

"He could be wiped out," Pe objected.

The general hesitated, remembering how Kwan Chan Sen had selected the Army of Chukei as a decoy. There was little difference between what Batu intended to do and what Kwan had done. Still, Batu could see no other way to hold the enemy's attention while the city burned.

"Issue the order," Batu said firmly. "Inform Kei Bot of the true nature of his mission. Tell him that I selected his army because I know his *pengs* will perform their duty honorably. We will withdraw the survivors as soon as possible."

A pained expression flashed across Pe's face as he, too, recalled the destruction of the Army of Chukei. Nevertheless, he simply bowed and turned to obey.

Kei Bot did not protest the order. Within minutes of receiving the message, his twenty thousand *pengs* charged Yenching's eastern gate. The other armies supported his attack by moving forward and lobbing tens of thousands of arrows into the city, both fire-tipped and normal.

As Batu had expected, the enemy held fast. There were simply too many Tuigan, and they were too good with their weapons to let the Shou breach the wall. Kei Bot's men fell by the thousands, a constant rain of barbarian shafts pouring down on them. The ground near the city wall took on a red tinge, though Batu could not tell whether the color was a result of the morning sun or the fallen *pengs'* blood.

Still, the feint was working. Although only Kei Bot's men were attacking a gate, the aggressive posture of the other four armies kept the barbarians at the city walls. Inside Yenching, the plumes of smoke grew more numerous and much heavier.

Unfortunately, the barbarians remained at their posts for the next thirty minutes. Kei Bot's losses mounted steadily, but the pudgy general continued to press the attack fiercely. The smoke from Yenching poured over the walls, covering the Army of Hungtze in a thick blanket of haze.

Finally, the archers that Batu had assigned to guard the canal running out of Yenching began to fire into the water. The young general instantly realized that the barbarians had reached their breaking point. They were attempting to escape the burning city by swimming under the river gate.

"Recall Kei Bot!" Batu ordered, pointing at the archers. "Warn the other generals to expect the enemy to sally."

Pe bowed and left to relay the commands. Aside from the instruction for Kei Bot to withdraw, the orders were unnecessary and tardy. Before the messengers could reach the valley floor, Yenching burst open like an agitated anthill. Heedless of the Shou armies awaiting them outside, the barbarians rushed from every gate in Yenching, madly firing their bows.

The Shou armies greeted the Tuigan with wall after wall of arrows. The men did not pause even an instant to give the barbarians a chance to surrender. The sight of Yenching's citizens choking the Shengti river with their bloated bodies was too fresh in the soldiers' minds.

For many minutes, the Tuigan poured out of the burning city in a steady flow. From seventy yards away, the Shou ranks met the barbarians with an equally steady stream of arrows. Soon, the bodies of horsewarriors lay piled in front of the gates in fan-shaped heaps. Still the barbarians came, scrambling over their dead and wounded fellows without regard. Billows of smoke rolled over the city, and great tongues of flame shot out of every opening in the wall.

Finally, the bell towers collapsed and disappeared into the city's ruins. The Tuigan rush dwindled away to nothing. The air reeked of burned flesh, and Batu knew that thousands of Tuigan had not escaped the fires inside Yenching. The largest part of the army, however, lay outside the walls, one or more bamboo shafts protruding from their bodies. The loud, steady hum of thousands of groaning men filled the valley.

The Shou ranks stared at the heaps of Tuigan bodies in dazed silence. After a few moments, a single soldier drew his *chien*. The man walked to a wounded horsewarrior, then quickly and efficiently beheaded the moaning barbarian with his sword. As if by command, the rest of the *pengs* drew their swords and followed the man's lead.

It did not cross Batu's mind to stop the slaughter.

– 12 –

The Ebony Tube

One thousand miles east of Yenching, Batu's wife lay half-awake, oblivious to the great victory her husband had already won that morning. It was well past dawn, and golden sunlight filled the sleeping hall. By now, Wu realized, Ji and Yo would be anxiously awaiting her presence at breakfast.

The general's wife tried to sit up, and her stomach filled with fire. Wu cried out, then collapsed back onto her pillows. She placed a hand over her stomach. A wet bandage swathed her midsection.

Qwo appeared out of a corner and dabbed a wet cloth on Wu's forehead. "Be still, mistress."

Wu withdrew her hand and stared at the blood on her palm. "What's this?" She was still struggling against her sleepy confusion.

"You know better than I," Qwo replied pointedly. She wiped the blood off her mistress's hand. "You came home in this state last night."

As Qwo turned away to rinse the cloth, the events of the previous night returned to Wu: following Ju-Hai to Ting Mei Wan's house, the hurried search that yielded only the ebony tube Ting had been carrying when the Minister of State arrived, meeting the unexpected guard on the way out of the house. The sentry had taken Wu by surprise, stepping out of a kiosk that had been empty when she had passed it earlier.

If the guard had challenged her before attacking, he

might still be alive. When she had felt the blade of his *chiang-chun* burning across her abdomen, however, Wu had reacted instantly. She had lashed at the bone in front of the man's ear with an eagle-beak finger strike. The sentry was dead before he dropped his weapon.

Doing her best to staunch the bleeding, Wu had rushed home without regard to silence or stealth. She had not dared to examine the laceration's severity. As soon as the stinging blade had slid across her abdomen, Wu had known that she was badly hurt. Inspecting the wound would have increased her chance of fainting before reaching help.

At her house, only the gate guards had returned from searching for Ju-Hai's mysterious spy. Even wounded and dizzy from the loss of blood, Wu had scaled the wall and slipped into her home in silence. The last thing she remembered was stepping into the courtyard, feeling her knees buckle, and calling for Qwo.

Qwo finished rinsing the cloth and turned back to her patient.

"The tube," Wu asked. "What was inside?"

Qwo sighed. "I didn't look. Spying is not a woman's business."

Gritting her teeth against the pain, Wu pulled herself into a half-seated position. "Bring it here."

Qwo fetched the tube from the night cabinet. When Wu moved to accept it, her hand was sticky with blood. "You'd better read it to me," she ordered.

Scowling with disapproval, the old servant opened the end cap and removed a piece of paper. She unrolled it and squinted at the writing. Speaking slowly, she read.

" 'Mighty One: Your humble servant begs forgiveness for her lengthy silence. The guards captured your messenger of three fortnights ago as he fled the summer palace. Though he died rather than reveal my identity, security within the grounds has been tightened. Illustrious Emperor of All Peoples, not even I can pass freely, though I have tried several times to reach your agents in the city.' "

Qwo paused to look at Wu. "Who is this 'Illustrious Emperor of All Peoples?' "

"The enemy commander," Wu said anxiously. "Read."

Qwo turned her eyes back to the paper. " 'I have much to report. The emperor has relieved General Kwan of responsibility for the war against your indestructible armies, and surprised the Mandarinate by placing a young general from Chukei, Batu Min Ho, in command of the war. Batu is highly regarded by the wisest men of this court, who are but candles next to your brilliance. It is whispered that Tuigan blood runs thick in his veins. If he is as cunning as they say, perhaps this is the reason.' "

The old servant paused, unable to suppress a smile at the flattering reference to her mistress's husband.

"Go on," Wu urged.

Qwo scowled at Wu's impatience, but did as instructed. " 'The emperor has given Batu one hundred and fifty thousand soldiers. These troops consist of five provincial armies numbering twenty thousand apiece. The balance comes from twenty-five small noble armies. You have already engaged and defeated the noble armies under the leadership of Tzu Hsuang Yu Po—' "

At the mention of Hsuang's defeat, a catch developed in Qwo's throat. She paused to clear it, then continued reading a moment later. " '—and news of the outcome was received quite sorrowfully by the court.

" 'I can tell you nothing of General Batu's armies. He has disappeared with his entire force, and no one knows how. I will attempt to discover where they have gone. In the meantime, I have taken advantage of his disappearance to start several rumors suggesting General Batu has deserted and joined the mighty forces of your irresistible horde.' "

"I'll choke her with her own eyes!" Wu spat. The fervor of her words sent a wave of pain through her abdomen. She could not stifle a groan.

"Not soon, you won't," Qwo observed.

"Keep reading," Wu instructed. "I must know what else this traitor has done to my family."

Qwo returned her eyes to the document. " 'I have only

one other item to report, Dispenser of Ultimate Justice. Emperor Kai Chin had nothing to do with the attempt on your life, and even now does not know of Shou Lung's involvement. Two of my fellow mandarins, Ministers Kwan Chan Sen and Ju-Hai Chou, were the ones who sent the *hu-hsien* assassin against you. After your ultimate victory, it will give me great pleasure as your Shou regent to dispense the final punishment to these murderous dogs. Until we meet, I remain your dedicated and faithful servant.' "

Qwo looked over the top of the paper. "Can this be true?" she asked. "Did it take only two men to start this war?"

"Perhaps," Wu said, astonished by this last revelation. "It doesn't matter. The war can't be stopped now, perhaps not even by one hundred thousand men. We must take this message to the emperor."

Rolling the scroll, Qwo said, "I'll fetch Xeng and have him take this to Minister Ju-Hai—"

"No!" Wu snapped, her abdomen once again filling with fire. "It must go directly to the emperor."

"But Xeng will never get an audience," Qwo protested.

"He must," Wu countered. She was simultaneously afraid to charge Xeng with such an important mission and resigned to the fact that she had no other choice. Clearly, she could not deliver the message herself.

"We can't trust Ju-Hai," Wu continued. "This letter accuses him of some terrible acts. He might not wish it to reach the hands of the Divine One."

The old servant frowned. "But your father trusts him."

"My father didn't know of the minister's involvement in starting this war," Wu said, "and my father didn't see him sharing a spy's bed."

"That can't be possible," Qwo objected. She raised the hand holding Ting's message as if warding off an evil spirit. "Your father's alliance with Ju-Hai goes back ten years. There must be an explanation for what you saw."

"Perhaps," Wu replied, "but I'm not willing to take that chance. Summon your son, then get a brush and paper. An explanatory letter might gain him a faster audience."

Qwo left the hall, then returned a few moments later with a brush and paper.

Wu dictated a message to the emperor. In it, she apologized for disobeying his command, then explained what she had discovered. As she signed the letter, she hoped the Divine One would not be offended by the blood that smeared off her hand onto the paper.

Xeng arrived just as his mother sealed both Wu's letter and Ting's message into the ebony tube. Wu quickly explained what she wanted, telling him twice to ask the emperor to send a contingent of his troops to replace Ting's.

After Wu finished, Qwo handed the ebony tube to Xeng, then kissed him on the brow. "Take care, my son," she said. "If Ting's troops see you leave, I doubt you'll reach the emperor alive."

Xeng placed a hand over the jade pendant hanging beneath his robes. "There is no need to worry, Mother," he said. As he spoke, his body and clothes changed colors to match the hues of the chamber walls. "I won't fail Lady Wu."

By the time Xeng finished speaking, Wu could no longer see him. Qwo's son was not so much invisible, she knew, as perfectly camouflaged. As her father's steward slid aside a wall panel and left, the one weakness of his magic medallion became apparent. When he moved, Wu saw a watery, man-shaped blur against the backdrop of the wall.

After Xeng left, Qwo peeled Wu's cover back to reveal a thick swath of crimson bandages. "You need a doctor," she said, her tone almost chastising.

Wu nodded. "After Xeng returns with help, but no earlier. Ting may not know who stole her message. Until the emperor arrests her, it's too dangerous to reveal my injury. A doctor could lead her right to us."

"We must hope Xeng reaches the emperor soon," the old maidservant said. She unfastened the bandage and changed the dressing. As Qwo finished, two sets of small feet sounded in the stone courtyard outside.

"The children!" Wu gasped, pushing her maidservant away. "Don't let them see me like this!"

Qwo threw the cover over Wu, then stepped to intercept Ji and Yo.

She could not move quickly enough. A wall panel slid aside, then Ji burst into the room, his sister in tow. "Mother!" he cried, pointing a slender finger toward the front of the house. "The emperor's wife is coming!"

Wu and Qwo looked at each other, confused and alarmed. "The Shining Empress?" Wu asked. "Are you certain?"

Ji nodded. "She has a whole bunch of soldiers!"

"How do you know it's the empress and not a consort, child?" asked Qwo, fixing her eyes on the boy.

"Because I saw her before," Ji responded, scowling at being doubted. "In the emperor's house—"

"You've never been in the Forbidden Halls," Wu objected.

"Yes we have!" Yo interrupted, stamping a foot. "You remember. I went to sleep!"

"We weren't in the Forbidden Halls," Wu explained. "We were in the Hall of—" She stopped in midsentence, realizing Ji and Yo were mistaken about more than the building they had been in. Aside from Wu, the only woman in the Hall of Supreme Harmony that night had been Ting Mei Wan.

"Qwo," she gasped, "they're talking about Ting!"

The old woman's face blanched. "What are we going to do?"

Wu threw her covers aside and tried to rise, but the effort hurt too much. Fleeing was out of the question. It would be a marvel if she made it out of the room.

"Meet them at the gate and then stall," Wu instructed her servant.

"Stall," Qwo repeated, half dazed. "I'll try." She scurried toward the front of the house.

Wu turned to Ji and Yo. They were both staring at her bandage with big, frightened eyes. A lump formed in Wu's chest and she almost began to cry. She was more frightened than she had ever been, but only for her children.

"Come here, little ones," Wu said, holding out her arms.

They obeyed, their eyes still fixed on their mother's wound. Tears came to both their eyes, and they began to sob.

"Shhh," Wu urged, embracing them closely. She could barely restrain her own tears. "Mother has been hurt, but you must be brave. Some bad people are coming."

"What should we do?" asked Ji, choking back his sobs and wiping his eyes.

Wu wished that she had an answer. She might be able to move long enough to help Ji and Yo climb over the exterior wall. Even if they escaped, though, the little ones would be lost and alone in the immensity of the summer palace. Her only choice was to hide her children and hope Xeng returned with help soon.

Releasing her son and daughter, Wu said, "Do you know a good place to hide?"

"Under the floor!" Yo said, pointing a stubby finger toward the center of the room. "When I hid there, Ji couldn't find me."

"You were cheating!" Ji objected, furrowing his smooth brow.

"That doesn't matter now," Wu said, laying a gentle hand on her son's shoulder. "These people will search for you much harder than you look when you play games. Are you sure this is a good place to hide?"

They glanced at each other uncertainly. Finally, Ji said, "It's very dark and small."

"Good. You must go there quickly. Don't come out until Xeng, Qwo, or I tell you it's safe."

Wu kissed each of her children, then sent them away.

They had barely left the hall before Qwo's voice echoed across the courtyard. "I insist, Minister Ting. Lady Wu is ill. She is not receiving visitors."

"All the more reason I must see her," Ting replied tersely. "Now stand aside."

"I refuse," Qwo replied.

"Guards!" Ting roared.

The sound of a short scuffle followed, then twenty boots clattered across the stone courtyard. Wu adjusted her cover so that it concealed her bloody bandage, then prepared to receive Ting.

She did not wait long. Within moments, a soldier grabbed a wall panel and thrust it roughly aside. Two green-armored guards stepped into the sleeping room, their weapons held at the ready. Ting came next, followed by an angry Qwo.

"What is the meaning of this?" Wu demanded, scowling at the mandarin. "Can't you see that I'm ill?"

"Please forgive this intrusion," Ting said curtly, obviously unconcerned with whether Wu forgave it or not. The minister turned to a guard. "Uncover her."

The soldier frowned at being asked to invade a noble-woman's privacy. Nevertheless, he did as ordered.

Ting pointed at the freshly changed bandage, which was already spotted with new blood. "So you *were* the one," she said. "How disappointing."

"What do mean?" Wu demanded.

"Last night, a spy broke into my house and stole an impor-tant state document," Ting said, stepping toward the bed. "This spy killed a guard on the way out, but not before being wounded. As we can see, you are wounded."

"This?" Wu asked, indicating her bandage. "Qwo and I were cutting some silk. Her knife slipped."

"Not likely," Ting replied. "Save me the trouble of search-ing your house. Return the document and no harm will come to you or your family."

Even if the ebony tube had been in her possession, Wu would not have returned it. She had already seen that Ting was an accomplished liar, and the minister could not afford to spare the life of anyone who knew the truth about her.

In response to Ting's demand, Wu simply shrugged her shoulders. "What document?" she asked.

She had decided to feign innocence, but not because she hoped to fool Ting. If Ting's guards were not part of the mandarin's plot, and Wu suspected that they were not, Ting would have to go through the pretense of firmly establish-ing Wu's guilt before causing the noblewoman any harm. That would take time, and the longer Wu could stall, the better the chance that Xeng would return with help.

Xeng was not having much success, however. He stood at the gateway to the Square of Heavenly Delight, in the center of which rose the Hall of Supreme Harmony. His medallion remained activated and he was still perfectly camouflaged. Unfortunately, the pendant's magic only worked for a certain amount of time and it would soon fade. He would not be able to reactivate it for at least a day.

The emperor's guards stood shoulder-to-shoulder around the Hall of Supreme Harmony, their weapons drawn. The great square surrounding the tower was filled with the green-armored guards of the Ministry of State Security. Xeng did not doubt that Ting had arranged the tight security measures, probably by claiming to have discovered a plot against the Divine One's life. Still, considering the evidence he carried in the ebony tube, Xeng thought he would attain an audience—providing he could reach the chamberlain.

To do that, however, the steward had to slip past Ting's guards. Xeng had no doubt their orders were to detain or kill anyone attempting to see the Son of Heaven. Still, he had to try, for Wu's life clearly depended upon his success.

There had been a time when the steward would not have cared about Wu's safety. At the age of fifteen, a friend had remarked on his uncanny resemblance to Tzu Hsuang, and Xeng had finally realized why the lord took so much interest in his well-being. Instead of being thankful for Hsuang's attention and love, though, Xeng had grown resentful and bitter because his true lineage would never be acknowledged. Nevertheless, Wu had treated him with nothing but respect and kindness, tolerating his snide remarks with an easy-going grace that only infuriated him further.

Xeng had remained hostile for nearly five years, until his own mother finally grew so tired of his attitude that she asked him to leave the Hsuang castle. It had been Wu, the object of so much of his enmity, who had interceded on his behalf and asked Qwo to reconsider. Though Wu had not said as much, it had been clear that she realized their relationship and did not want to see harm come to her half-brother. After that, Xeng's attitude had reversed itself. Wu had subtly acknowledged his lineage and hereditary rights even more than his own mother. As a result, he was not about to allow any harm to come to his half-sister now.

Xeng stepped forward, moving slowly to take maximum advantage of his magic camouflage. Though he often used his dragon medallion to spy upon his father's enemies, the steward had never before attempted to sneak past so many armed men.

In the next minute, he advanced thirty steps and came to the fringe of Ting's troops. They stood at attention in small units of ten, each formation turned to face a different section of the park and separated by ten feet. Xeng selected the two groups closest to him. He slipped forward ever so slowly, carefully watching his footing so he did not trip or disturb a loose stone. Though his heart beat like a hammer and his panicked lungs craved air, he forced himself to breathe in small, even breaths.

Nevertheless, on several occasions a sentry squinted or shook his head as Xeng moved. Each time, the steward froze and did not move again until the guard looked away.

Finally, disaster struck. Two guards noticed him simultaneously.

As the one on the left rubbed his eyes, the one on the right asked, "Did you see something?"

"A blur," the other responded.

Xeng knew he was in trouble. He turned and, heedless of how easy it would be to see him, rushed toward the gate. The two guards shouted an alarm, then ran after his hazy form.

Well-practiced in escaping pursuit while camouflaged, Xeng did not panic. He suddenly stopped and dropped to his belly. A moment later, he slowly crawled a short distance back toward the Hall of Supreme Harmony and did not move. The soldiers began yelling in confusion, issuing contradictory reports of his whereabouts.

Xeng remained on his stomach for several moments, considering his next move. Ting's troops clearly wanted to capture him, for over a hundred of them ran about the square, wildly swinging their polearms at the air. As the steward studied his pursuers, it became clear that they were more concerned with preventing him from reaching the Hall of Supreme Harmony than with catching him. The largest number moved to form a wall between him and his objective. Behind Ting's guards, the emperor's troops watched the square with interest, but did not budge from their assigned posts.

Two units began moving toward the gate, trying to cut off Xeng's escape route. Realizing he had no chance of reaching the emperor alive, the steward reluctantly decided to flee.

Xeng stood and ran along the wall, away from the gate. When the troops noticed him, he dropped to his belly again, then slowly crawled toward the gate. He had failed in his mission, he thought, but all was not lost. He still had the ebony tube, and Wu would be able to develop another plan for delivering it to the Divine One.

But Wu was in desperate need of the emperor's help at that very moment. She lay crumpled on the floor, where Ting's troops had dumped her when they began searching for the stolen document. Qwo sat beside her mistress, and Wu's head now rested in the old servant's lap.

In the space of a few minutes, Wu's house had been reduced to a shambles. Even with a hundred men searching the compound, the troops from the Ministry of State Security had found nothing, not even Ji and Yo. Ting Mei Wan angrily paced back and forth, forcing her personal escort of twenty soldiers to stand crowded together at the edge of the chamber.

"Where is it?" Ting demanded for perhaps the hundredth time.

"I have no idea what you want," Wu gasped, also for perhaps the hundredth time.

"Liar!" Ting responded. "My patience is at an end." She turned to two guards, then pointed at Qwo. "Take her."

Wu forced herself to sit up. "No!"

Two guards seized Qwo by the arms and dragged her to

Ting's side.

"She knows nothing!" Wu said.

Ting studied Wu with narrowed eyes. "Tell me who does," she countered.

Qwo spat in the minister's face. "Tell this traitor nothing!"

A soldier quickly took a cloth off Wu's night cabinet, then gave it to Ting. Staring at the old maidservant, the mandarin slowly wiped the spittle off her brow. In a calm voice, she said, "Kill this woman."

The guards blanched, but one dutifully drew a ten-inch *pi shou*. The dagger glinted ominously in the morning sunlight.

"Wait!" Wu yelled. She was barely able to force the words from her throat. Qwo's entreaty and the guards' reluctance had given her one last idea.

Addressing the soldiers, Wu said, "We're not the traitors; Ting is." Her voice quivered with stress and fatigue. "The document she's looking for is evidence of her treachery."

A veteran with a missing ear frowned and looked to Ting. The mandarin appeared momentarily stunned and confused, but she recovered quickly. "If what you say is true," the minister said, "produce the document."

"Don't!" Qwo urged, feebly trying to pull free of her captors. "My life is worth nothing."

Ting and the soldiers turned to Wu expectantly. The noblewoman considered revealing where Xeng had gone. If the treacherous minister realized she was defeated, perhaps she would see no use in harming an old woman. Unfortunately, Ting did not seem like the type of woman who gave up easily.

Wu shook her head.

"Kill the servant," Ting ordered. As she spoke, she did not take her eyes off Wu.

The guard holding the *pi shou* obeyed without hesitation. Qwo let out a terrible, woeful scream, then quivered as the last traces of life fled her body. The guard twisted the dagger and plunged it farther in to finish the job. Finally, he withdrew the *pi shou* and allowed the old woman's body to slump to the floor.

Ting turned back to Wu. "Now, will you—"

She was interrupted by sobbing children. "Where is that coming from?" the minister demanded of nobody in particular.

A guard kneeled and put his ear to the floor. "From beneath the house."

Ting pointed at the floor. "Get them!" she ordered. "Perhaps they'll persuade this traitor to confess."

Several guards rushed outside, and several more used their weapons to begin prying up floorboards.

"They're just children!" Wu pleaded. "Leave them alone!"

"Nothing would please me more," Ting replied. "I have no wish to injure a child. Their fate, however, is in your hands."

Wu crawled into a kneeling position, ignoring the agony in her midsection. "I won't allow you to hurt Ji or Yo," she warned.

"Then tell me where you've hidden my paper!" Ting shouted.

They stared at each for several moments, Wu breathing slowly and evenly, gathering her remaining energy to defend her children. Several guards moved into defensive positions to either side of Ting.

Wu knew now that the minister intended to kill her whether or not she gave up the document. She could accept her fate because she had no other choice. The noblewoman was not ready to sacrifice her children's lives, however, not even for the sake of the empire. Fortunately, she could think of two ways to save them. Only one involved giving Ting what she wanted.

After prying up the fifth plank, a guard said, "Here they are."

He reached below the floor and extracted Yo. She was curled into a stout little ball, covered with dirt and sobbing loudly. The soldier passed her to the veteran with the missing ear, then reached into the opening a second time. He screamed and cursed loudly.

"He bit me!" the guard snapped, holding his hand.

"What do you expect?" asked the veteran. He set Yo aside, then stuck his head and shoulders below the floor. "Come here, little tiger!"

Yo took advantage of the opportunity to scurry over to her mother. Without looking away from Ting, Wu guided her daughter to her side. She continued to breathe evenly and steadily, focusing her mind on what she intended to do.

The guard emerged with Ji a moment later. Tears and dirt streaked the boy's face, but his expression remained determined and angry. He reached out and raked at his captor's face with his fingers, but his arms were too short to reach.

Ting looked away from Wu, settling her gaze on Ji. "Which shall it be?" she asked. "Your son—or the document?"

"Neither, traitor!" Wu yelled, releasing the store of energy she had been building.

The noblewoman's wound reopened as she sprang forward, but she felt no pain. Her thoughts, her spirit, and her body were focused only on one thing: reaching Ting.

Wu moved so quickly that she took all but three guards by surprise. The first stepped in front of her, his polearm held across his body like a staff. Wu stiffened her index and middle fingers into the secret sword position, then drove them into the man's throat. His larynx popped, and he collapsed, dropping his weapon and gasping for breath.

The next guard swung his *chiang-chun* at Wu's knees. She leaped into the air, catching the soldier simultaneously with a camel kick to the groin and a ram's fist to the nose. As he finished the swing, he collapsed into a twisting mass of groaning flesh.

Wu was not so lucky with the third guard. When she descended from her jump, he stepped forward and jabbed, using his weapon like a lance. Wu tried to knock the blade aside with a crane's wing block, but the guard was a strong man and held the shaft in place. The blade slipped between the noblewoman's ribs and punctured her lung.

Having seen the fate of his two fellows, the guard took no chances with Wu. The blade felt icy and painful in the noblewoman's lung, and the strength to continue fighting escaped with her final scream. The guard's thrust carried her a full two feet. She landed on her back with the polearm protruding from her chest. The guard still held the other end.

Ting had not moved. The minister stared at her attacker with a look of uncomprehending shock, hardly registering that she had come within a breath of dying.

Wu lay on the floor for what seemed to her like an eternity of silence, struggling to breathe through the cold agony in her lungs. The only thing she could see, the only thing she was aware of, was the guard at the other end of the polearm. He was a young man, no older than Batu had been when she had first met him. The youthful soldier looked deathly afraid.

Ji and Yo screamed and rushed toward their mother's side. The earless veteran caught and restrained them before they arrived.

Recovering from her shock, Ting stepped to Wu's feet and pushed the frightened young guard aside. The anger had drained from her face. It had been replaced by something between incredulity and sadness. "Why?" she asked. "Why such a foolish attack?"

"For . . . children," Wu gasped. Each word made her lungs ache as though she were breathing ice instead of air. An agonized half-scream escaped her lips.

Ting looked at the veteran holding the children. "They don't need to see this! Get them away from here!" She waved her arms at the other guards. "Get away from here, all of you!"

The veteran obediently took the children and left the hall. The rest of the guards retreated to the edge of the room.

Ting returned her attention to Wu. "Where is the ebony tube?" she asked, kneeling at the wounded woman's side. "It doesn't matter now. Tell me."

Wu shook her head. "Children are safe."

"What do you mean? Why are they safe?" the mandarin asked as she leaned close.

"No good to kill—if I'm dead," Wu said.

"Is that what you think?" Ting sighed, her voice breaking with regret and guilt. "They must die anyway."

Wu lifted her head. "Why?" Though she had intended to yell, a hiss was all that escaped her lips.

Ting could no longer meet Wu's gaze. "Because they might know."

"No!" Wu's arm shot up from her side, and she clasped Ting's throat. Her fingers closed into the dragon's claw choke, but the last breath left her lungs before she could crush the mandarin's larynx.

– 13 –

Besieged

Hsuang Yu Po had never thought the odor of roasting meat would make him so miserable. The smell was rich and sweet, for the meat had been basted with honey. A desperate longing stirred in his stomach, and his mouth watered with a hunger that he knew would not be satisfied.

"Knaves," commented Cheng Han. The *tzu's* powder-stained face was drawn with starvation. His good eye bulged from its sunken socket, but the useless one had receded even farther into his haggard skull. His breath stank from the internal effects of starvation, and his *k'ai* hung off his frame as though his body were an armor stand.

With the other commanders of the noble armies, the two men stood in the highest room of Shou Kuan's bell tower. Save for a rough-hewn table, several benches lining the walls, and a window overlooking the city's main gate, the room was barren. Even the plastered walls had never been painted.

The window looked over the gate to the dusty road running from Shou Kuan to Tai Tung, the location of the emperor's summer palace. Although the road ran eastward, it entered Shou Kuan from the south, as was customary. If the main gate had been on any wall but the southern, it was commonly believed, evil spirits would have found it easy to enter the city.

Before turning eastward, the road ran seventy yards south and climbed to the top of a knoll. On top of the knoll stood two hundred shirtless Tuigan. From the bell tower's window, Hsuang could barely make out their long braids of hair and the shaven circles on the tops of their heads.

The half-dressed barbarians were tending fifty large, smoky fires. Over each fire, huge slabs of meat were roasting. As the enemy clearly intended, the morning breeze was carrying the smell directly to Hsuang and the others.

Hsuang tore his eyes away from the tormenting sight. To the right and left of the bell tower, the city walls were manned by soldiers of the Twenty-Five Armies. Like Tzu Cheng and the other commanders, the soldiers appeared gaunt and haggard. To a man, their glassy eyes were fixed on the smoky fires outside the city. Although the men's appearance and obvious hunger concerned Hsuang, he was far from shocked or surprised. In the three weeks since the battle at Shihfang, nobody had eaten more than a few handfuls of grain.

After the battle, the Twenty-Five Armies had retreated under cover of darkness. The Tuigan had followed close behind, preparing to attack. Fortunately, the peasants had obeyed Hsuang's messengers and burned their lands that very night. As the noble armies retreated down the road, their flanks had been protected by blazing fields. Only a small rearguard had been required to keep the Tuigan from overtaking them. Most of survivors had reached the safety of Shou Kuan's walls shortly before dawn.

Up to that point, everything had gone according to Batu's plan, and Hsuang had remained confident that his son-in-law would overcome the barbarians. However, the noble's confidence had deteriorated when his subordinates reported the city's condition. Upon hearing of the noble armies' defeat, the efficient citizens of Shou Kuan had obeyed the directive Hsuang had sent before the battle. They had burned their food stores and fled, leaving the city deserted and barren.

Hsuang had begun each of the twenty-one days since by cursing himself for not sending a special messenger to the city prefect. Of course, his self-derision had done nothing to alleviate his mistake, and now he was in danger of failing Batu. The troops of the Twenty-Five Armies were starving. It would not be long before they lacked the strength to keep the barbarians from the city. Already, men were dying of hunger, and illness was on the rise.

Hsuang wondered where his son-in-law was. Two days ago, the *tzu* had promised his subordinates that help would arrive soon, but he knew they placed no faith in that vague reassurance. Unfortunately, without the Mirror of Shao, he could not contact Batu to ask when the provincial armies would arrive. Nebulous promises were all he had available to keep up his men's morale.

Hsuang was the not only one concerned with the army's morale. Pointing at the dusty knoll outside the gates, Cheng Han said, "Those cooking fires are within archery range. Let the men occupy themselves by making the enemy pay for his fun."

Hsuang considered the request, but finally decided against it. "No. We'll need the arrows when help arrives."

"Of course," Cheng said, bowing modestly. "What could I have been thinking?" There was a barely concealed look of mockery in his eyes, but he made no further protest.

Hsuang did not blame the man for his doubt. The gray-haired noble still had not told his subcommanders that Batu intended to surprise the Tuigan at Shou Kuan. If the enemy stormed the city and happened to capture one of the nobles, Hsuang did not want his son-in-law's plan revealed.

The old lord was beginning to doubt the wisdom of this decision. Shou nobles did not fear death nearly as much as they feared dying like cowards. Yesterday, one young lord had actually suggested mounting a suicidal charge before the *pengs* grew too weak to fight. To Hsuang's alarm, several wiser nobles had voiced support for the young man's idea. The commander wondered how long it would be before the rest of the lords urged him to choose battle over starvation.

Considering their restlessness, Hsuang decided it would be wise to allow his men some fun at the barbarians' expense —providing it didn't cost too many arrows. Turning to his subordinates, he said, "On further thought, I think Tzu Cheng is right: we should make the Tuigan pay for our misery. Each of you may select ten archers. Give each archer four arrows. We will see which of our armies kills the most barbarians."

The nobles all smiled and voiced their approval. Within seconds, each lord was laying wagers that his archers would kill more barbarians than those of any other army.

Cheng approached Hsuang. "A wise decision," said the scar-eyed lord. "By tomorrow, our men may be too weak to pull their bows."

"Let us hope they remain strong a few days longer than that," Hsuang countered, catching the *tzu's* eyes with a meaningful gaze. "I am confident that help will arrive soon."

Before Cheng could respond, a sentry knocked on the stairway door. "My lords, it is most urgent!" he called.

Hsuang cast an eye out the tower window to see if the enemy had moved. The fires on the knoll were smoking more than previously, but the Tuigan appeared no closer to attack than they had been at dawn.

"A messenger from Tai Tung has passed through the enemy lines!" the sentry added.

An incredulous murmur rustled through the room. Hsuang called, "Bring him in."

The door opened and the guard escorted an exhausted man wearing a purple, dust-covered *waitao* into the room. Though he had more flesh on his bones than the soldiers of the noble armies, the man looked every bit as drained. His face was pale and weary. Blood seeped down his brow from beneath a fresh bandage on his head.

Hsuang stepped forward to greet the messenger, but Tzu Cheng held out a restraining arm. "For all we know, this man is a barbarian assassin."

The old noble gently pushed Cheng's arm aside. "This is no barbarian," he said. "This is my steward."

The sentry's eyes widened in shock. Glancing at the wound over Xeng's brow, the soldier bowed. "Forgive me, Tzu Hsuang. Your steward knocked at my gate, but when we opened it, there was nothing there. We saw a blur entering the city, and thought he was an enemy spy!"

"It is only a cut, and there is nothing to apologize for," Xeng said to the soldier. He turned to his father. "It was my fault, Tzu Hsuang. I should have identified myself."

Though he did not feel as magnanimous as his steward, Hsuang dismissed the guard without punishment. He turned to Xeng, forgetting himself and holding out his arms to embrace his son. Fortunately, the younger man suffered no such lapse of decorum and simply bowed to the lord.

Flushing at his slip, Hsuang returned the gesture of courtesy. "I am both happy and sad that you have come, Xeng," the old noble said. "Seeing you again gives me joy, but I regret that you now share our danger."

"There is nothing to regret, Tzu Hsuang," responded Xeng, using his dusty sleeve to wipe a trickle of blood from his brow. "When I left the summer palace, I knew your circumstances. It was my choice to join you."

As the steward spoke, his knees began to wobble and he looked as if he might collapse.

"Perhaps you should sit," Hsuang said, directing his son to one of the benches along the room's stark walls. After Xeng was seated, Hsuang asked, "What are you doing here? Why aren't you watching over your mother and Wu?"

Xeng looked away. "I failed," he said. "They're dead."

Hsuang studied his son for a long moment, unable to comprehend what he was hearing. "Who? Who's dead?"

"Everyone," the steward replied, still unable to meet his father's gaze. "Ting Mei Wan killed them all."

The old lord backed away as if withdrawing from a leper's presence. "What are you saying?"

"I couldn't save them," Xeng said, his voice weak with grief.

Hsuang finally grasped what his son had come to tell him. His eyes grew vacant and glassy, as if his spirit had fled his body. "Ji and Yo?" he asked hopefully.

"I have heard that your grandchildren did not suffer. Ting had that much mercy."

Hsuang's knees buckled. He would have fallen had Cheng not caught him and helped him to the bench. Though the pained *tzu* found the strength to keep from crying out or sobbing, he could do nothing else but stare into empty space. Finally, the old noble asked, "Why?"

Xeng turned to face his father. "Before she was killed, Lady Wu asked me to deliver this to the emperor." He withdrew an ebony tube from his robe and gave it to his father.

Hsuang took it, then removed two papers from inside. The first was Wu's letter to the emperor. It explained how she had come by the second paper, which was Ting Mei Wan's report to the "Illustrious Emperor of All Peoples."

When he finished reading, Hsuang looked up. In a quivering voice, he told the other nobles what the letters contained. After the murmur of astonishment died away, the old lord asked his son, "Why did you bring these to Shou Kuan?" Though he did not intend it to, his voice held a note of reproach.

Xeng's lips dropped into a mortified frown. "I didn't know what else to do. Minister Ting's soldiers had surrounded the emperor, and she was searching for me in every corner of the summer palace."

"You could have hidden anywhere in Shou Lung!" Hsuang yelled, his grief finally overcoming his self-control. "What good do you expect these letters to do here?"

At Hsuang's outburst, the other nobles uncomfortably shifted their glances to the wall and stood motionless.

Xeng looked at the floor. "I failed you."

The old noble regarded Xeng for many moments, sorry that he had taken his anguish out on his son. Finally, Hsuang rolled the papers and returned them to the tube.

"No," the old noble said, grasping Xeng's shoulder. "You haven't failed me, but you will return these letters to the summer palace. See that they reach the emperor. Ting Mei Wan must pay for her crimes."

"He's wounded!" Tzu Cheng objected. "He won't last a day!"

Hsuang looked at his son with demanding eyes. "My steward is a strong man," he said.

"Tzu Hsuang," Cheng said, daring to meet his commander's severe gaze, "in your grief, you are asking too much of your servant. It is a wonder he reached us at all. That he could pass back through the enemy lines wounded is unthinkable."

Xeng returned to his feet. "I will try, if that is what my lord wishes."

Hsuang gave the ebony tube to his son. "That is what I wish," he said. The old noble was not being callous or cruel. Hsuang could not bear the thought of his son being in Shou Kuan if the city happened to fall before Batu arrived.

"Unless you wish your servant to flee during battle, it may not be possible to fulfill your wish, Tzu Hsuang," said one of the young *nans*. He was looking out the tower window.

"What do you mean?" Hsuang asked, stepping to the *nan*'s side.

There was no need for the *nan* to answer. On top of the knoll, two thousand barbarians sat astride their horses. A stiff wind was carrying the smoke from the cooking fires directly over the city wall, partially obscuring Hsuang's view. However, he could see well enough to know that the horse-warriors wore armor and held bows in their hands.

Beyond the knoll, at a distance of three hundred yards, a dark band encircled the city. Hsuang had no doubt that he was looking at the rest of the barbarian army. As the lord studied the enemy, a short man carrying a white truce flag separated from the group on the hill.

The messenger spurred his horse forward, stopping within thirty yards of the bell tower. Though the rider wore a fine suit of barbarian armor, his features were slender, with smoothly rounded cheekbones. The messenger had shaven his head in the fashion of a monk, and he was thinly built. The man's appearance was clearly not that of a Tuigan, and Hsuang guessed he might be Khazari.

Without preamble, the rider called, "The mighty khahan has grown weary of waiting for you to come out and do battle." He spoke the Shou language with a Khazari accent. "He sends me to accept your surrender, and offers a meal as proof that he will treat his prisoners kindly."

Hsuang did not believe the envoy, and would not have considered surrender even if he had. The old noble had lost his daughter and grandchildren, but he had not lost his honor. He had promised to hold Shou Kuan until Batu arrived, and he would do it or die trying.

"Your khahan underestimates our number," Hsuang yelled back. "He cannot hope to feed all our armies with so little food."

The rider smiled broadly and without sincerity. "We have been hunting for many days," he returned. "More than two thousand dressed beasts await you in our camp."

A murmur ran down the wall as the men repeated the rider's words. Even the nobles seemed to be discussing the idea of surrender.

Hsuang turned to his subordinates, completely ignoring the rider for the moment. "He's lying. They're trying to trick us."

"How do you know?" asked a young *nan*.

Hsuang pointed out the window. "Do the barbarians look like they expect us to surrender? They'll attack the instant we leave the city."

"Then we must fight," another noble replied.

"We are not leaving Shou Kuan!" Hsuang snapped. "That is my command!"

Many of the nobles met the *tzu's* gaze directly, indicating their disagreement with his decision.

"The emperor placed General Batu in command of our armies," Hsuang said, looking at the nobles who dared to oppose him. "Batu gave me command of your armies. To defy my word is to defy the emperor's. Are you prepared to do that?"

It was Cheng Han who replied. "No one would dare defy you, Tzu Hsuang. Yet, our armies are too weak to last much longer. Soon, we will have no choice except to surrender or die of starvation. Perhaps it would be wise to consider fighting now, while the option is still viable."

Hsuang felt irritated by the words. Although Cheng had questioned him before, the scarred noble had always yielded when Hsuang invoked his authority. Despite the man's careful politeness, it appeared Cheng intended to do no such thing this time.

"I will tell you when we will fight," Hsuang responded through clenched teeth. "We will fight when the provincial armies arrive to help us, or when the barbarians storm the city walls. Until then, I will not throw away our armies by sallying against five-to-one odds."

"Staying in Shou Kuan to starve is the same as surrendering," Cheng countered. "If we sally, at least we will kill some barbarians."

"There is no use discussing the matter further," Hsuang declared. Though he normally would have handled Cheng with more tact, he was too upset by the news of Wu's death to deal patiently with the man's challenge.

Cheng, however, would not be put off. "We wish to die honorably in battle. It is our right as noblemen."

"It is your right to die when I tell you to," Hsuang snapped, stepping over to stand face-to-face with the scarred noble. "If you wish to do it honorably, you will wait until I say it is time to fight."

With his one good eye, Cheng met Hsuang's angry gaze and did not flinch. "Your grief is interfering with your judgment, Tzu Hsuang. Otherwise, I would do as you ask."

A rage boiled up from Hsuang's stomach. As if it belonged to somebody else, he watched his arm rise and saw his hand lash out. He struck Cheng's face with an open palm, leaving a red print on the man's cheek.

"Apologize!" Hsuang ordered.

The nobles stood in awkward and dumfounded silence, Cheng staring at his commander with an expression of disbelief. Finally, the scarred noble said, "It is understandable that you are upset by the news of your daughter's death, Tzu Hsuang. Nevertheless, we must look at our options with a clear head." Cheng turned to address the other nobles. "We must attack now or surrender."

The other lords turned away from Hsuang and gathered around Cheng Han. Casting nervous glances at their legitimate commander, they discussed the two options Cheng had proposed.

Slapping the scarred noble had been a mistake, Hsuang realized. The other lords had interpreted the action as a loss of self-control, and he had to admit they were correct. Otherwise, he would have handled Cheng's challenge to his authority with much more tact. He certainly would never have struck the man.

Nevertheless, he could not allow the nobles to abandon the city before Batu arrived. "Tzu Cheng," Hsuang said, pushing his way into the circle surrounding his rebellious subordinate. "Even if what you say is true, I am still in command of this army. There are no choices except those I present."

Cheng met his superior's gaze with steady eyes. "That might be true under normal circumstances," he said, his voice betraying no trace of anger or indignation. "But it is clear your judgment has been impaired by your loss. Otherwise, you would realize that we stand to gain nothing by delaying our final battle. With every hour, we only grow weaker."

Many nobles murmured their agreement.

Reassured by the show of support, Cheng added, "I am sorry, Tzu Hsuang. Your orders don't make sense."

Several nobles echoed their reluctant agreement. In their eyes, Hsuang saw apology and sympathy, but no sign of support. Like Cheng, they all believed their commander's grief had overcome his logic.

As far as Hsuang could see, he had only one hope of retaining command. "You're committing treason," he said to Cheng, taking care to appear as rational as possible.

The accusation did not daze the scarred noble. "If the emperor or your own son-in-law were here, they would agree with our decision. At such a critical time, it's not in Shou Lung's interest to leave a grieving man in command."

The deft counter overcame any last doubts the nobles retained about disobeying Hsuang. The group voiced their approval of Cheng's reasoning, clearly shifting command of the Twenty-Five Armies away from Hsuang.

The old noble studied his mutinous subordinates for several moments. Finally, he turned toward the tower door, motioning for Xeng to follow. Before descending the stairs, however, he paused and addressed Cheng. "If I may ask, Tzu Cheng, what do you plan to do?"

Cheng lifted his chin. "Fight." As an afterthought, the scarred noble added, "Of course, you and your troops are welcome to join us."

Hsuang shook his head angrily. "I have better uses for my army," he said. With that, he left the room and abandoned his fellow nobles to their planning. Though he knew it was impossible to hold the entire city with only his *pengs*, he intended to keep his promise to Batu. Somewhere deep within the city, he would find a compound that a small force could defend.

As Hsuang and his son descended the stairs, Xeng walked one step behind his father. Halfway down, the steward stumbled and almost fell. The old noble stopped and grasped his son's shoulder. The steward's face looked pale.

"How is your wound, Xeng?" Hsuang asked. "Should I summon help?"

Xeng shook his head. "I'm a little light-headed, but it's nothing to worry about."

Hsuang scowled. "Somehow, I doubt that. We'll find someplace safe for you to recover."

"You don't wish me to leave?" Xeng asked.

Hsuang shook his head. "It would be pointless until those fools have had their battle, would it not?" He continued down the stairs, supporting his son by the arm.

When he opened the door and stepped into the street, Hsuang was surprised to hear the *pengs* on the walls calling to each other in alarm. The noble looked up. The soldiers were cocking their crossbows and staring at the knoll in front of the gate. From the streets, Hsuang could not see what had alarmed them, so he ran back up the stairs.

Xeng followed several steps behind, moving more slowly because of his wound. "What's wrong?" the steward called.

"The enemy must be attacking!" Hsuang answered, glancing over his shoulder at his son's bandaged head. "Don't strain yourself. I'll meet you up here."

The gray-haired noble reached the top of the tower a few seconds later. The other lords barely noticed as he entered the room. They were too busy overwhelming Cheng Han with contradictory advice. Hsuang slipped over to the window, peered out, then swore a vile curse in the name of the Celestial Dragon.

The Tuigan had resorted to magic. A single barbarian stood in front of the two thousand horsemen gathered on top of the smoky knoll. The man was dressed in a long silk robe covered with mystic symbols. In his hand, he held a scepter capped with a human skull. The barbarian's arms were lifted skyward and his eyes were fixed on one of the fires.

The shaman had magically braided the smoke from all fifty cooking fires together. The smoke columns now formed a wide gray ribbon that stretched from the hilltop all the way to Shou Kuan. The smoky bridge crossed the city wall directly over the gate, just a few yards to the right of the bell tower.

As Hsuang watched, the first horsewarriors spurred their mounts toward the hazy bridge. The frightened animals reared and tried to shy away. The determined riders kicked the beasts and lashed them with their reins, guiding the horses onto the gray ribbon as if it were solid rock. When their hooves found solid purchase on the smoke, the horses calmed and began galloping forward. The riders dropped their reins, then pulled their bows from their holsters and began to nock arrows.

Hsuang turned to his fellow nobles. "Get to your armies!" he yelled. "The Tuigan are topping the wall!"

The nobles stopped arguing and stared at him with varied expressions of incomprehension.

"What do you mean?" Cheng Han demanded. "They don't

have siege equipment."

"They don't need it," Hsuang replied, pointing toward the knoll. "Look!"

When the *tzu* looked out the window again, sheets of arrows were sailing back and forth between the smoke bridge and the city walls. The horsewarriors were already so close that Hsuang could lock eyes with the lead rider. The barbarian was a ferocious-looking man with a hungry smile that appeared at once jubilant and brutal. He had a drooping black mustache, a flat nose with flaring nostrils, and dark slit-like eyes that sat over broad cheekbones. The rider wore a filthy, greasy hauberk and a conical skullcap trimmed with matted fur. He guided his horse with his knees so that both hands were free to use his bow.

With a sinking heart, Hsuang realized that the Tuigan had tricked him. The barbarians had never expected the Twenty-Five Armies to leave the city. The roasting meat and the offer to accept a surrender had been ruses designed to mask the preparation of the shaman's smoke bridge.

The plan had worked all too well.

Turning his thoughts to countering the Tuigan plan, Hsuang looked back to the other nobles. "Send for your best archers," he ordered, automatically slipping back into his role as the group's commander. "We've got to kill that shaman—"

Something buzzed through the window and struck Hsuang's ribs like a hammer blow. His armor clinked once, then a painful vise clamped down on his chest. He looked out the window and saw that the lead rider was already passing the bell tower. In preparation for leaping onto Shou Kuan's ramparts, the warrior was holstering his bow and drawing his sword.

Hsuang grasped at the arrow lodged in his chest, then collapsed to the floor. As darkness filled his sight, the *tzu* heard the clatter of hooves on stone outside the tower, then the chime of sword meeting sword told him that the barbarians were inside the city.

– 14 –
Shou Kuan

Batu and a subordinate, General Kei Bot Li, lay on their stomachs at the crest of a hill. The mordant smell of burned grass filled their nostrils, and the dry acrid taste of soot coated their tongues. Normally, they would have avoided lying face down in a field of ash, but the best place for watching Shou Kuan happened to be this scorched hilltop.

The three miles of rolling terrain between them and the city was as black and as barren as the hill. Before fleeing, the citizens of Shou Kuan had set fire to most of the land surrounding the city. The barbarians had overgrazed the few fields the peasants had left untouched, turning them into bleak patches of ground.

The over-grazed land is a good sign, thought the general from Chukei. By forcing the enemy to siege Shou Kuan, Tzu Hsuang had greatly complicated the already difficult task of feeding so many horses and men. The Tuigan would be anxious to complete the siege and move on to better lands.

From what Batu could see, Yamun Khahan had already reached the end of his patience. Even now, the barbarians were preparing to attack. At this distance, the walls of Shou Kuan looked like no more than a ridge of clay surrounding an anthill. However, a dark band that could only be an enemy battle formation encircled the city. Batu guessed that there were over one hundred thousand riders in the dark ring.

More telling than the riders was the smoke in front of the

main gate. From three miles away, the smoke appeared to be nothing more than a band of haze, but Batu knew that only a large fire could create so much fume.

Pointing at the smoke, Batu asked, "What do you make of that, Kei Bot?"

The stocky general squinted at the gray column and watched it intently, as if he could magnify the image through obstinate study. It was a gesture typical of the general, Batu was learning. More than anything, it seemed to symbolize the headstrong determination that was the heart of Kei Bot's personality.

After the stocky general's assault on Yenching, Batu had made the ambitious man second in command. Though he had used the survivors from Kei Bot's army to garrison Yenching, it would have been an insult to leave the pudgy general with his troops after he had displayed so much bravery. Therefore, Batu had been forced to reward Kei Bot by promoting him.

It was an exigency the General of the Northern Marches regretted. In order to hold Kei Bot's dogged ambition in check, Batu kept the pudgy general with him at all times. Unfortunately, the two men did not enjoy each other's company.

Kei Bot finally finished his study of the smoke column. "I would guess that they're burning prisoners," he announced.

"To what purpose?" Batu asked, frowning at his subcommander.

"Intimidation," Kei Bot answered. "I've seen it before."

Batu shook his head. "They wouldn't hesitate to commit such butchery, but they don't take captives." He pointed at the riders encircling the city. "To me, it looks like they're preparing to attack. The smoke must have something to do with storming the city."

"If that's what you think," Kei Bot answered stiffly, miffed that his conclusion had not been accepted. "Shall I send the order to advance?"

"Not yet," Batu said, still watching the city.

"But we've been here for three hours!" Kei Bot objected.

"We'll wait a while longer." The young general faced the stocky commander. "If we move before the enemy is fully engaged, it will stop its attack and turn to meet us."

"From what we saw at Shihfang, the nobles are outnumbered five to one," Kei Bot countered. "The longer we wait, the greater the chance the enemy will sack Shou Kuan."

"I know," Batu replied, turning back to the city. "Still, we can't move until the barbarians are fully engaged."

Kei Bot's jaw dropped in open shock. "The nobles will be wiped out! They'll never hold against those numbers."

"Don't underestimate the nobles," Batu replied, "not while Tzu Hsuang still commands them."

At Shihfang, Batu had discovered the reason for his father-in-law's long silence following the battle: the Mirror of Shao had been shattered. He was sorry to lose the artifact, but not nearly as sorry as he would have been to lose Tzu Hsuang. Still, the mirror's destruction was a serious blow. Batu had been counting on it to coordinate the attack with the noble armies. Without the Mirror of Shao, the general had to rely on nothing but his best guess to time his attack.

More to reassure himself than Kei Bot, Batu said, "Tzu Hsuang will hold. His *pengs* have had three weeks of rest. Besides, even if the Tuigan breach the walls, they will find that city streets are poor places to fight from horseback."

"Don't you think you're risking Hsuang's armies without sufficient reason?" Kei Bot asked. "If the nobles collapse, the Tuigan will retreat into Shou Kuan when we attack."

"I won't lose the advantage of surprise," Batu replied sternly. He pointed at the ring encircling the city. "From what I can see, the barbarians still have over a hundred thousand riders. Our only chance of destroying them is to catch them completely unprepared."

Kei Bot would not be intimidated. "If you must run this risk, at least send word to make ready for battle."

Batu scowled, but realized that Kei Bot's suggestion had its merits. "I see no harm in doing as you ask," he snapped. Without taking his eyes off the pudgy general, he waved Pe forward.

The adjutant was waiting at the bottom of the hill, where he and Batu's fifty man escort would not be seen. It took Pe a few moments to crawl to the crest of the hill. Upon arriving, he removed his conical skullcap and scratched furiously at his matted hair. "Now I understand why the barbarians shave their heads," he said.

Like Batu and the other men in the provincial armies, Pe was dressed in Tuigan clothing. In addition to the fur-trimmed skullcap, he wore a greasy knee-length hauberk and wool trousers. The hauberk had an arrow hole and a bloodstain in the breast, and the trousers were so filthy that crawling through ash had done nothing to darken their color. In contrast to Batu, who felt strangely comfortable in the clothing, Pe looked awkward and clumsy.

The adjutant suddenly pulled his hand from his hair. Pinched between his thumb and forefinger was a white, squirming body the size of a rice grain. The youth squashed the louse, then wiped his hand on his pant leg. He renewed his scratching and commented, "Filthy beasts."

Batu was not sure whether Pe meant the lice or the barbarians. After the victory at Yenching, Batu had sent his cavalry to round up the enemy horses. In the meantime, he had instructed the remainder of the Most Magnificent Army of Shou Lung to clothe itself in Tuigan garb.

The order had not made the general a popular commander. The thought of wearing Tuigan clothing had turned the stomachs of the entire army, even the drunks and criminals. Nevertheless, Batu had insisted that his command be followed.

Two days later, the cavalry had collected more than eighty thousand barbarian horses. The number had been sufficient to mount the four armies that were still in battle condition. After a day of riding lessons, Batu had started for Shou Kuan with eighty thousand *pengs* disguised as Tuigan horse-warriors.

The General of the Northern Marches was wise enough to know that news of a large Shou army would quickly reach the ears of Yamun Khahan. That was why Batu had disguised his men as Tuigan. The presence of another barbarian force would not provoke nearly as much comment. Even if word of the army reached the khahan, Batu thought the reports would be less likely to alarm the Tuigan leader. It seemed possible that the khahan would dismiss the accounts as mere rumors or exaggerations. The last thing he would believe, Batu hoped, was that four Shou armies had disguised themselves as Tuigan in order to sneak up on him.

Unfortunately, in order to make the disguise believable, Batu's men had to act like barbarians. Several times, his scouts had given chase to frightened peasants. Once, they had even attacked and burned a Shou village the barbarians had overlooked. It was then, Batu realized, that he had begun to feel comfortable in barbarian clothes.

A few days after burning the village, Batu's outriders had begun to see signs of far-ranging enemy scouts. Since the khahan had left so many men in Yenching, Batu had hoped the Tuigan leader would feel secure and not bother to scout behind him. The general should have known better, for it was apparent that Yamun Khahan was a careful commander.

So, for the last three days, Batu's troops had moved only after sunset and under the heavy cloud cover summoned by the *wu jens*. The armies had traveled along streambeds and through secluded valleys, on routes selected by survey parties during daylight hours. Of course, the outriders had occasionally encountered smaller parties of Tuigan scouts. In most cases, the disguises had served the surveyors well. After a friendly wave, the enemy had simply ridden away.

Four times, however, enemy patrols had approached Shou scouting parties. In each instance, Batu's men had ambushed the Tuigan riders before the scouts realized they were impostors. Not a single enemy soldier had escaped such a meeting alive.

Last night, the provincial armies had finally reached an isolated valley in the hills southwest of Shou Kuan. Batu had stopped the advance five miles from city. At dawn, he had taken a party and rode forward to scout the enemy.

The army was still waiting in that valley. Even without being there, Batu felt certain his subordinates were all as impatient as Kei Bot. The general could hardly blame them. With every hour, the danger of discovery increased. Already he had received a report that an enemy scouting party had been destroyed because it had come too close to the Shou armies. If Tuigan patrols continued to disappear, Batu knew that the khahan would soon suspect something was amiss.

Still, with such a capable commander leading the enemy, Batu had to scout the horsewarriors carefully. Though the Shou armies were also mounted now, they would be no match for the barbarians in open combat. The Tuigan carried short bows ideal for fighting from horseback, and they were uncannily accurate with their weapons. Batu's soldiers, by contrast, were still equipped with clunky crossbows and were accustomed to fighting from rigid ranks. Only a fool would believe that because they now had horses, the Shou would be a match for the barbarians.

As the General of the Northern Marches had known all along, Shou Lung's best chance of victory lay in attacking while the enemy's attention was completely absorbed by something else. That was why Batu's original plan had called for the nobles to sally out of Shou Kuan as his forces attacked from the rear. However, with the Mirror of Shao destroyed, coordinating the two maneuvers had become an impossibility. Fortunately, it appeared the enemy was about to oblige Batu by occupying itself with an attack on Shou Kuan.

Batu directed his attention to Pe. "Tell the armies to prepare for the attack."

Pe smiled. "Then the war will be over soon."

A knot of excitement formed in Batu's stomach, and he answered, "One way or the other." With a little luck, he thought he would finally fight his illustrious battle.

"The enemy still does not know we're here," Pe said, his face betraying his absolute confidence. "We cannot lose."

"In battle, nothing is ever certain," Kei Bot warned.

Pe looked at the stocky commander with barely concealed contempt. The adjutant made no secret of his dislike for Batu's second in command. "Begging your pardon, General, but what you say is not true for this battle."

Placing a fatherly hand on his adjutant's shoulder, Batu said, "Pe, the only thing I am sure of today is that we shall fight a great battle." He reached beneath his hauberk to withdraw the letter he had written before dawn for Wu. Though he had not been able to send his customary letter at Yenching, today there was no reason to break his vow.

Batu gave the paper to Pe. "You know what to do with this."

"I'll send it to Lady Wu."

Kei Bot raised an eyebrow. "I had not thought you so sentimental, General."

The General of the Northern Marches flushed. He had repeatedly directed his subordinates to think of nothing but fighting until they destroyed the barbarians. Batu felt as if he had been caught in a lie.

"I'm not," he said sharply, looking from Kei Bot to Pe. "Send the order."

Pe crawled down the hill to the escort, and Batu turned back to Shou Kuan. The wind still carried the smoke over the city wall. The general from Chukei studied the hazy tendril for several moments. The more he watched, the more it seemed something was moving across the gray ribbon.

Batu wished that Minister Kwan's *wu jen* was with him, for the wizard would have found a way to show him more of the scene outside Shou Kuan. It was not the first time the general had wished for the wizard's company. After arriving at last night's campsite, Batu's first thought had been to establish some magical means of spying upon the enemy. Unfortunately, none of the *wu jens* supplied by the Ministry of Magic knew an appropriate spell, and the *feng-li lang* would not ask the spirits to perform such a mundane task. So the general had been forced to rely upon physical scouting.

Batu watched the scene for another ten minutes. Finally, Kei Bot pointed at the dark band of horsemen encircling Shou Kuan. "The enemy is moving! Shall I send the order to advance?"

"Not yet," Batu replied, laying a restraining hand on his subordinate's wrist. Although it did look as though the barbarian circle was tightening, Batu did not think they were charging.

"What are you waiting for?" Kei Bot asked. "As it is, it will take our armies thirty minutes to reach the battle."

"It won't take the enemy thirty minutes to know we're coming," Batu countered, pointing toward the valley where the Shou armies waited. "When eighty thousand horses gallop toward the city, they'll raise a dust cloud that will blot out the sun. If the Tuigan aren't fully engaged, they'll break off to meet us."

Kei Bot frowned and stared at Batu. "Your wife's father is in Shou Kuan. How can you allow the nobles to bear this attack alone?"

"I can do it because it increases our chances of winning the battle," Batu returned coldly. He looked back toward the besieged city.

Kei Bot stared at his commander with thinly veiled disgust. "You are a callous and cold man."

Without taking his eyes off the city, Batu calmly asked, "Could any other kind destroy the Tuigan?"

Kei Bot looked away, uncomfortable with both his own comment and Batu's easy reply.

A moment later, the barbarian circle stopped shrinking. Batu estimated the horsewarriors were within medium bow range of the city walls. Though he could not see them, the general knew that droves of arrows were flying between Shou Kuan's ramparts and the enemy lines.

"See?" Batu said, pointing at the circle. "The Tuigan would have seen us coming. It won't be long now."

The general could see that the Tuigan were pressing the battle hard. Volley after volley of Shou arrows opened holes in their ring, but instead of retreating to a safer range, the barbarians shifted to fill in the gaps. In front of the gate, the smoke still drifted over the city wall. It still seemed to Batu that something was moving along its spine, but he could not imagine what.

For several minutes, he and Kei Bot silently watched the battle. The longer they watched, the more convinced Batu grew that he had made the correct decision. The enemy maneuvered with such precision that he knew they would easily meet any obvious attack.

On the southern side of the city, the horsewarriors began to gather in a great mass. Within seconds, the throng was swarming toward the main gate.

"They're assaulting!" Kei Bot declared, pointing at the mob. "They've taken the gate!"

"Yes," Batu agreed, waving his adjutant up the hill. For the first time since the battle had begun, he was worried. The barbarians had breached Shou Kuan's defenses much faster than he had expected.

When Pe arrived, the general from Chukei addressed the youth immediately. "Send the order to attack," he said. "The Army of Wak'an is to secure the western perimeter and the Army of Hai Yuan the eastern, cutting off any avenue of enemy retreat. The Army of Kao Shan is to smash the throng at the gate, with the Army of Wang Kuo in close support."

"Yes, General," Pe said. He started back down the hill.

Batu grabbed his adjutant's shoulder. "Deliver these orders yourself. Remind the generals that no one is to attack from horseback. They are to dismount and fight in formation. After all, we must remember that we aren't true barbarians, mustn't we?"

Pe smiled. "Yes, General."

"Now, go," Batu said, turning back to the city.

After watching the assault for a few moments, the general from Chukei realized that something was terribly wrong inside the city. The Tuigan throng in front of the gate was decreasing in size at a steady rate.

Batu's heart sank. What he saw could only mean that the

barbarians were pouring into the city with little opposition. When his provincial armies sprang their trap, the enemy would simply take refuge inside the walls of Shou Kuan.

Rising to his feet, Batu said, "Come, General!"

Kei Bot also rose, saying, "Why such a hurry now?"

"You were right," Batu said, starting down the hill.

"Of course—"

"Now is not the time to offend me," Batu said sharply, halting. "It would be a pity to execute you while you can still serve the emperor."

The stocky general stopped in his tracks. "You wouldn't dare!"

"I would," Batu hissed. "At the moment, I have enough on my mind without your perfidy."

Kei Bot clenched his jaw and stared at Batu angrily. When the younger man's gaze did not falter, Kei Bot asked, "What do you want?"

Batu grasped his subordinate's shoulder and guided him down the hill, formulating a new plan as he walked. "We can prevent the barbarians from seizing Shou Kuan if we move quickly. We'll follow them straight into the city."

Batu spoke rapidly, his excitement growing with each breath. Although the nobles' collapse had caused him some serious problems, he was determined to overcome these troubles. After all, a battle could hardly be considered illustrious if a commander did not make a desperate decision or two.

"Here's my plan," Batu said, still gripping his subordinate's arm. "I'll meet the Armies of Kao Shan and Wang Kuo to change their orders. We'll mount a cavalry charge and follow the barbarians right into the city."

"To attack inside Shou Kuan?" Kei Bot gasped.

"Exactly," Batu confirmed. "The Tuigan are horsemen and nomads. City combat will be as foreign to them as fighting from horseback is to us. The odds should be even."

Kei Bot stared at the General of the Northern Marches as if he were mad. "What do you wish me to do?"

"We'll need all the strength we can gather inside the city,"

Batu explained. "You must meet the other two armies. Send the Army of Wak'an to support the charge. They must also remain mounted and follow on my heels, or the assault will lack the momentum to take the city."

Kei Bot nodded. "Wak'an is to follow you, and you will be with Wang Kuo."

"Good," Batu said. "You must take the last army and encircle the city at one hundred and twenty yards. Use your horses' mobility to make sure that no stragglers escape our trap."

"As you wish," Kei Bot answered, unable to hide his skepticism.

They reached the bottom of the hill. Batu turned to face Kei Bot straight on. "One other thing," he said. "If I fall, you will take command."

At first, Kei Bot's expression seemed puzzled, for Batu was merely stating standard military procedure. Slowly, however, he realized the full implication of his commander's words. "You expect to be in the thick of the fighting?" Kei Bot asked. There was an ambitious glimmer in his eye.

"I'll be in the cavalry charge," Batu answered, hardly able to suppress a grin. "Once inside the city, our armies will need me." Though this logic seemed valid enough, the general from Chukei had a deeper reason for joining the charge. He simply did not want to miss the best part of the battle.

For a long moment, Kei Bot studied Batu with an unreadable expression. Finally, he asked, "Anything else?"

"Only this: whether I was right or wrong to hold the attack, our best chance of victory now lies in the streets of Shou Kuan. I hope you agree."

"Whether I agree or not is unimportant," Kei Bot said, turning away to mount his horse. "I have my orders."

Batu mounted his own horse, wondering if the stocky general could be trusted. There was something in the man's manner that made the general from Chukei uneasy, but there was no time to worry about it now. Batu spurred his horse, leading Kei Bot and the remaining escorts in a mad gallop toward his armies.

Batu and the others rode down into a dale. Even sitting astride his horse, the general from Chukei could feel the ground trembling. Behind the blackened ridge on the valley's far side, an immense dust cloud eclipsed the horizon. Realizing that his army's approach army was responsible for what he saw and felt, Batu reined his mount to a stop.

A line of riders nearly a mile long appeared atop the far ridge and started into the valley. Within seconds, the slope was covered with horsemen wearing filthy hauberks and fur-trimmed skullcaps. Most had scarves or shreds of cloth wrapped around their noses and mouths. Though the swarm was riding at only a canter, their mounts' hooves churned up so much dirt that an impenetrable curtain of dust hid the largest part of the army.

The throng was roughly divided into four groups. One hundred men from each group held Tuigan standards that the Shou had substituted for their own banners.

Batu pointed at one of the standard-bearers. "There is Wak'an, General. Do not fail me." He could barely make himself heard above the rumble of the approaching army.

Kei Bot galloped off without another word. Batu remained a moment longer, searching for the golden yak tail that now served as Wang Kuo's banner. Finally, he found the standard he sought and spurred his horse forward.

As soon as Batu wheeled his horse into line, dust and ash coated his throat so thickly he could hardly swallow. Filthy as it was, he pulled the collar of his Tuigan tunic over his face. He found Wang Kuo's lanky commander as the army started up the other side of the valley. Shouting to make himself heard, he explained the change in plans. A messenger was then sent to the Army of Kao Shan with the new orders.

Finally, the Shou armies crested the ridge. The twenty thousand *pengs* from Kao Shan were in the lead, followed by Batu and the Army of Wang Kuo. The general from Chukei could no longer see the armies of Wak'an and Hai Yuan, but he assumed they were close behind.

A quarter mile ahead, ten thousand mounted Tuigan sat in a double line at the base of the ridge. They had turned to face Batu's army and held their bows in their laps. Beyond their lines rose a dusty knoll with fifty smoky fires burning on top of it. Several hundred men stood on the hill, still tending the fires. Past the hillock stood Shou Kuan's bell tower. The main gates hung wide open, and the streets beyond were filled with thousands of soldiers.

A flat arc of smoke nearly twenty yards wide ran from the hilltop over the city walls. Though nothing moved on the smoke bridge now, several dead horses and men lay strewn along its length. Batu felt sick as he realized how easy it must have been for the barbarians to charge over the bridge and secure the main gate.

The general turned his attention back to the first obstacle between him and retaking the gate: the ten thousand barbarians at the base of the ridge. As the Shou army started down the slope, the Tuigan signal drummers beat a slow, steady cadence. The other horsewarriors remained impassive and motionless, not even lifting their bows. Finally, a scowling officer rode out and angrily waved his arms at the advancing army, ordering it to halt.

A wave of euphoria coursed through Batu's veins. The Tuigan don't know that they're being attacked, he realized. Obviously, the barbarians were puzzled by the huge army's sudden appearance behind them, but they clearly did not suspect that it was not their own.

Wang Kuo turned to Batu, grinning. "What are your orders, General?"

The question was rhetorical. Even as Batu yelled "Charge!" the men leading the assault drew their weapons and broke into a full gallop. Instead of the curved blades of Tuigan warriors, they held the straight *chiens* of Shou infantrymen. Upon seeing the double-edged swords, the enemy officer realized his mistake. He hurriedly returned to his own ranks. Once combat was closed, Batu knew, the difference in weapons would be the only means of telling friend from foe.

As the Army of Kao Shan roared its battle cry, a deafening clamor filled the general's ears. Batu's heart started to pound harder. His horse snorted with excitement, and the ground rushed past its hooves at a dizzying rate.

At the bottom of the slope, the Tuigan raised their bows and fired. The volley seemed to hang in the air like a black fog. The wall of arrows didn't seem to fly at the attacking Shou; they seemed to ride into it. Thousands of men and beasts fell to the dusty ground, and the charge faltered for just an instant.

Then it continued faster than ever. Sweat rolled down Batu's body in constant, tickling rivulets. At the bottom of the hill, he saw the Tuigan holster their bows and draw their sabers. Batu found his palm gripping his weapon's hilt, and he did something he had not done in many, many battles: he drew his sword.

The Army of Kao Shan met the barbarians, and Batu felt a thunderous crash in the pit of his stomach. Ahead of him, thousands of Tuigan tumbled from their saddles as the heavy Shou *chiens* struck them down. An instant later, the Tuigan sabers flashed, cutting down a like number of Shou. Frightened cries and agonized screams filled the air. Batu's horse galloped even faster, drawn onward, it seemed, by the scent of blood and death.

As he rode toward the mayhem ahead, Batu realized he had become an ordinary soldier. His escorts had disappeared into the mad mob, as had the commander of Wang Kuo. To the general's left rode a rugged veteran with unkempt hair who would not have looked out of place holding a Tuigan saber. To Batu's right rode a helmetless man with the silky topknot of a Shou officer.

Batu no longer saw the barbarian ranks, for he had reached the bottom of the slope and did not have a good view. Directly ahead, all he could see were the backs of his own men. Beyond them rose the knoll with the smoke bridge. Thousands of his *pengs* were already riding up the small hill. Hundreds sat slumped in their saddles, wounded or dead, carried along only by the momentum of the charge. On top of the hill, a lone Tuigan wearing the robes of shaman gestured madly at the smoke bridge. The priest's escorts were fleeing in all directions.

Batu's horse began swerving and leaping, compelling him to pay attention to his riding. He had reached the Tuigan ranks, though little remained of the enemy lines now. The ground was littered with dead and wounded, forcing the general's mount to dodge wildly to keep from tripping.

As the general flashed through the area, a barbarian rose and fumbled at his arrow quiver. Batu swung his sword. The general was surprised at how good it felt to slay an enemy, for it had been many years since he had fought in the ranks. He did not get to see the Tuigan fall, however, for his mount had already carried him onward.

Batu's horse started up the knoll, and its gait slowed. He took advantage of the curbed pace to peer over his shoulder, then cursed angrily. He had expected to see a third army behind the one with which he rode. Instead, Wak'an was moving toward the western perimeter and Hai Yuan toward the eastern. Clearly, Kei Bot had not informed the armies' commanders of the revised plan.

Batu briefly wondered whether Kei Bot had deliberately disobeyed his orders or had simply not found the other two generals in time. Whatever the reason, the blunder meant that Wang Kuo and Kao Shan would be outnumbered once they entered the city. There was nothing Batu could do. Stopping the assault was out of the question, as was trying to break a messenger free of the charging mob.

Batu did not panic. Once he entered the city, he could send a messenger to fetch Wak'an. As long as his forces held the gate, the delay wouldn't cause him much trouble.

The general reached the hilltop. His horse dodged left to avoid a smoky fire over which hung a blackened side of lamb. To Batu, the knoll seemed a strange place to set up a cookfire, but he gave the matter no more thought.

Ahead, the smoke bridge collapsed, spilling dozens of bodies onto the *pengs* below. Men and horses tumbled in all directions, but the Army of Kao Shan did not slow. The lead ranks closed to within thirty yards of the gate. Barbarian arrows began to pour down from the bell tower and the city's ramparts. A column of Tuigan riders rushed away from the gate to meet the Shou charge head to head.

A moment later, Batu saw another group of horsewarriors —perhaps five thousand in all—ride *toward* the gate. This second group passed easily through the Tuigan rushing to meet the Shou charge. Immediately, he knew the retreating formation was the khahan's bodyguard, for they were uniformly dressed in fine black armor and rode white horses. Even the wealthiest emperor could only afford to outfit his best troops in such a manner.

Apparently, the general from Chukei realized, Yamun Khahan had still been outside Shou Kuan when the Shou attacked. The barbarian emperor had probably been waiting for his men to wipe out the last pockets of resistance before entering the city.

As Batu started down the hill, clanging steel and furious yells sounded from the base of the knoll. The Army of Kao Shan had met the enemy charge.

On the city walls, the Tuigan archers shifted their fire toward the charging Shou. Arrows began raining down around Batu. A scream sounded nearby, then the veteran to the general's left tumbled out of his saddle.

A black streak flashed past Batu's head, then something slapped the leather armor over his collarbone. He gasped in alarm, but felt no pain. Instinctively, he transferred his reins to his sword arm and felt for a wound with his free hand. He found a deep cut in the leather where an arrow had grazed his hauberk. As he realized how close he had come to perishing, the general's chest tightened.

In the next instant, he left the deadly shower of arrows and entered the melee in front of the gate. A rider leveled a saber at his head. The general dropped his reins and raised his *tao* in a desperate block. As the two swords met, a terrific jolt ran along his arm. The barbarian found himself holding the hilt of a broken sword. Batu countered with a slash and felt his blade cut through the man's leather armor.

Screaming, the Tuigan slid out of his saddle.

Batu grasped at his loose reins, but lost them. He was unsettled by the thought of having no control over his beast during the melee, but another barbarian slashed at him and the general gave up any hope of recovering the reins.

Batu turned the enemy blow aside, then slipped his blade along the Tuigan's shoulder and opened a wound in the enemy's throat. The barbarian gurgled and dropped his weapon, then kicked his horse onward. The melee became a whirl of flashing blades and dying men. Time after time, Batu blocked and countered, more often than not barely aware of whom he was fighting. Once, he barely ducked a blow from a soldier he had thought to be Shou until the man's curved blade sailed past his head. Twice, only the glimpse of a double-edged *chien* stopped him from slaying one of his own men.

As the general lifted his aching arm for what felt like the thousandth time, the deep reverberating rumble of Tuigan signal drums rolled from the city. Batu's opponent sliced at him with a wild cross-body swing, then wheeled his horse around and sprang away. The man was out of reach before the general could react.

To all sides, the Tuigan were following the lead of Batu's adversary and turning away from the battle. A few *pengs* reacted quickly, downing the fleeing horsewarriors with vicious hacks or beheading them with efficient slashes. More often, however, the stunned Shou found themselves swinging at empty air while their foes galloped toward the city gates.

An instant later, a spontaneous shout of triumph rose from the Shou *pengs*. Though Batu suspected otherwise, to his soldiers the sudden withdrawal seemed as though the enemy had been routed. Screaming their war cries, the Shou tried to pursue.

When they set their heels to their horses, however, the result was pandemonium. Like Batu, most of them had dropped their reins during the battle, so they had little control over the excited beasts. The horses bolted in all directions, crashing into each other or sprinting away from the throng altogether.

Anxious to avoid being carried away by the anarchy plaguing his ranks, Batu quickly recovered his own horse's reins. Once he felt in control of his mount, he turned his attention to Shou Kuan. The last of the Tuigan were slipping between the closing gates. There was no sign of Yamun Khahan or his bodyguard, and Batu realized that the enemy commander had reached the relative safety of the city.

The battle, for now, was over. Dead and wounded soldiers, both Tuigan and Shou, blanketed the ground between the knoll and the gate. Already, over a hundred *pengs* had dismounted and were efficiently dispatching the Tuigan wounded. It did not even cross their minds to take prisoners, save for the few officers who would prove useful for interrogation.

Atop the walls of Shou Kuan, thousands of Tuigan had gathered on the ramparts to watch the slaughter of their wounded comrades. Their faces betrayed no anger or shock, only cool detachment. Batu had no doubt that if the horsewarriors had been the ones outside the city, they would have done the same thing to the Shou survivors.

As the general scanned Shou Kuan's rampart, however, he was interested in more than Tuigan faces. He was searching the brick-lined walls for a weakness that he could use to bring a quick end to the coming siege.

As Batu studied the fortifications, the Tuigan on the ramparts raised their bows. An instant later, a rain of black-shafted arrows brought an end to his inspection. Amidst a chorus of anguished wails and cries, he wheeled his horse about and galloped away from the city gate.

– 15 –
A Caged Tiger

The morning sun touched the exterior of the tent, kindling an orange light inside. In his ire last night, Batu had driven away the engineers before they could stake the pavilion, so now its unsecured flaps slapped wildly in the late summer wind. The general's silk shirt was soaked with sweat, but he barely noticed. As he had been doing since before dawn, he stood motionless, staring out the tent's door.

The pavilion rested on a ridge overlooking Shou Kuan, giving Batu a clear view of the city's walls and towers. The general was trying to think of a way to bypass those fortifications, but he kept losing his thoughts. Over sixty thousand dead and wounded soldiers, both Shou and Tuigan, lay in front of the city. They had fallen in a triangular pattern that reminded Batu of an arrow pointing at the main gate.

A cloud of vultures and other carrion birds were already savoring the feast. Tuigan archers stood atop the bell tower, using tethered arrows to pick off the fattest birds. They were meeting with uncanny success, but the horsewarriors' accuracy did not surprise Batu. Yesterday, after the gate had closed on his unsuccessful bid to take the battle into the city, the enemy archers had killed ten thousand of his men in less than a minute. Given the precision of the barbarian bows, Batu counted himself lucky to be alive. He had dropped his sword as he fled, but that seemed a small price to pay for his life.

The other generals who had also ridden in the charge had

not been so fortunate, however. Wang Kuo's general lay outside, awaiting a proper cremation. Kao Shan's fate remained unknown, though it was hardly a mystery. If the general had still been alive, someone would have brought him to the pavilion by now. The commanders of the Armies of Wak'an and Hai Yuan had both survived, for they had not been involved in the charge. They were seated on the far side of the tent, waiting for their new orders.

Kei Bot was not present, but Batu doubted that his second-in-command had fallen in battle, for the general should have been nowhere near the heavy fighting. Batu suspected Kei Bot was intentionally avoiding him, fearing retribution for his part in yesterday's setback. The tactic irritated Batu almost as much as the failure itself, so the general from Chukei had sent his adjutant to find the missing commander.

The same suspicion kept returning to Batu's mind: Kei Bot had deliberately neglected to give Wak'an the new orders. If so, the stocky general from Hungtze had committed a terrible military crime. Worse, he had lost the fight for Shou Lung and robbed Batu of his illustrious battle.

The General of the Northern Marches turned away from the door. Across the room, both of his subordinate generals rose to their feet expectantly.

Addressing the commander from Wak'an, Batu asked, "What did Kei Bot tell you yesterday?"

The two first degree generals cast uneasy glances at each other. Wak'an asked, "When, my commander?"

"Before the battle!" Batu snapped, pointing at Shou Kuan. "When do you think?" Despite his lack of patience, the general understood the man's caution. When a plan went awry, Shou commanders often selected subordinates to serve as scapegoats, as Kwan had selected Batu himself after the battle of the sorghum field.

To reassure his subcommanders, Batu said, "Have no fear. The blame for this disaster rests on my shoulders alone, but I must know what went wrong."

Wak'an relaxed. "He said you were going to charge the city."

"And?" Batu prompted.

"He was to assume command until you returned."

Batu's stomach churned at the thought of Kei Bot commanding his armies. "Anything else?"

Wak'an shook his head.

As Batu started to ask his next question, he heard a small force of riders approach the pavilion and stop outside. A moment later, Pe entered the tent and bowed.

"General Kei," the adjutant announced.

The general from Hungtze bustled into the pavilion behind Pe. Kei Bot's bow was very shallow, and Batu did not bother to acknowledge it.

Instead, he turned back to the general from Wak'an. "Did General Kei tell you to follow me into the city?"

Before the man could answer, Kei Bot stepped forward and interrupted. "I did not."

When Batu turned toward him, the stocky general met his commander's gaze with a defiant stare. "I thought it best to hold both Wak'an and Hai Yuan in reserve," Kei Bot continued, sneering at Batu. "Your plan was foolhardy and suicidal."

"You cost us the battle," Batu countered. "If Wak'an had been behind the Army of Wang Kuo, we would have overwhelmed the barbarians and taken the gate."

Kei Bot ignored his commander and shifted his gaze to the other two generals. "When the barbarians massed for the attack, General Batu ignored my advice and refused to strike. Instead, he delayed until the city had all but fallen. Hoping to correct his mistake, our commander ordered a desperate charge. It was my duty to save what I could of our armies. At least the enemy is now trapped within Shou Kuan's walls."

"Until he chooses to leave," Pe retorted.

"Mind your place, young fellow!" Kei Bot snapped, barely sparing the adjutant a sidelong glance.

Batu did not immediately leap to Pe's defense, for he was pondering his subordinate's strategy. He had expected Kei Bot to make excuses or lie about his failure yesterday. Instead, the stocky commander seemed proud of his disobedience.

Without speaking, Batu stepped forward and stood face-to-face with his mutinous subordinate. In a quick, fluid motion, the General of the Northern Marches pulled Kei Bot's sword from its scabbard.

Staring at his sword's bejewelled hilt, Kei Bot gasped, "What is the meaning of this?"

"You have deliberately disobeyed my orders, and now you're fostering rebellion," Batu said, his voice cold and even. "That is treason."

"The emperor himself gave me command of the Army of Hungtze!" Kei Bot retorted, reaching for his weapon. "You wouldn't dare suspend my commission!"

Batu sidestepped the clumsy lunge, then brought the blade up and drew it across the stocky general's throat. "The penalty for treason is death," he said.

Kei Bot clasped a hand over the wound, his mouth open in astonishment. The surprised mutineer dropped to his knees, blood oozing from between his fingers. Finally, he collapsed and pitched forward onto the dirt floor.

"What have you done?" gasped Wak'an.

"Kei Bot disobeyed a direct order," Batu replied, nonchalantly cleaning the sword on the fallen man's *k'ai*. "He cost us the victory."

"Perhaps," countered Hai Yuan, "but to execute a general without a formal inquiry. . . ."

Batu shrugged, then sheathed Kei Bot's ornate sword in his own empty scabbard. "He admitted his crimes," the general said wearily. "I have chosen his punishment."

Killing Kei Bot had cleared Batu's mind, and he finally felt as if he could concentrate. "Pe, get me some brushes and paper," he said, walking over to an empty table. "From what the prisoners say, there are over a hundred thousand Tuigan inside the city. We'd better do some planning."

Batu's two subordinates simply stared at him, astounded by his indifference to the man he had just executed. When they did not follow their superior to the table, the general from Chukei said, "Gentlemen, your thoughts may prove valuable."

Both men shook their heads as if to clear them, then joined Batu. While Pe supervised the removal of Kei Bot's body, the three surviving generals fell into a discussion of logistics, debating the best type of shelters to build for the months ahead, where they could secure a steady food supply, how their soldiers would fuel cooking and, eventually, heating fires, and a hundred other details.

By the end of the week, the Shou were making considerable progress toward establishing a siege camp. A group of scouts found a bank of clay on the shore of a nearby river, so the Chief of Works built kilns to fire bricks. Without straw or something similar to add to the mix, the bricks would not hold together very long. That did not trouble Batu, for he needed them to last only a few months. Win or lose, the siege would be over by winter.

Just outside arrow range, under the guidance of the engineers, the Army of Hai Yuan was encircling the city with a trench that would eventually become a defensive fortification. The Master of Ample Supplies solved the fuel problem by developing a program to collect dried horse dung, reserving the small supply of wood within riding of distance of camp for firing the kilns.

Still, the Shou could not solve all their problems easily. Batu sent a messenger to the summer palace asking for artillery and reinforcements, but he knew it would be at least six weeks before any substantial aid arrived. Food was especially scarce, for the barbarians had been camped outside Shou Kuan for nearly a month. To procure even small amounts of provisions, the Shou foraging parties had to travel over one hundred miles. When the riders did find a village that might have some grain, the lookouts mistook the filthy *pengs* for barbarians and burned the communal food-stores.

Batu and his subordinates were in his tent discussing these problems when Pe entered. "Excuse me, General," the adjutant said, bowing low. "The Tuigan have dispatched a messenger and ten escorts under a flag of truce."

The two first degree generals raised their eyebrows. "One thing is for certain," said Wak'an. "The enemy isn't surrendering this soon."

"Not ever," Batu replied. From the stories of his great-grandfather, he knew that the Tuigan did not ask or grant mercy. That knowledge only made him more curious about what the envoy had to say. "Bring the messenger to my pavilion."

Pe bowed, then turned to execute the order.

While he waited for the messenger, Batu supervised the rearrangement of the pavilion. The barbarians, he knew, were careful observers, and he wanted the messenger to return to Yamun Khahan properly impressed. The General of the Northern Marches had his chair placed in the center of the room. His subordinates' chairs were placed to either side and slightly to the rear of his own. Finally, he had fifty senior officers summoned to the tent. After arranging them in a standing circle, he explained that no matter what he said or did, they were to remain solemn and perfectly quiet.

A few minutes later, Pe entered the tent. Bowing very low, the adjutant said, "With your permission, General, I present the Grand Historian of the Tuigan Empire, Koja the Lama."

Batu nodded, then Pe opened the tent flap. Koja was not the stocky, fierce figure Batu had expected. Instead, the lama was a small wiry man with a priest's shaven head. His bulky armor hung off his hunched shoulders like rags on a beggar. He moved forward at an overly confident pace, studying his environment with alert, intelligent eyes.

Behind Koja came ten Tuigan warriors. They all wore black *k'ai* armor and skullcaps trimmed in sable fur. Their swords remained in their scabbards.

Batu nodded to the messenger's escorts. "Who are they?"

"My bodyguard," the messenger replied in stilted Shou. "The khahan insisted. I am his *anda*, you see."

Because Batu spoke the Tuigan language, he knew that by *anda*, the messenger meant he was Yamun Khahan's brother in spirit. Koja was politely informing the general that killing him would anger the khahan. Batu found it interesting that the lama thought he should be concerned about the khahan's temper.

"Your bodyguards will wait outside," Batu responded, frowning at the messenger. "If I decide to kill you, a hundred times that many men will not save your life."

The lama studied Batu with a dubious expression. When the Shou commander's face remained fixed, Koja turned to the bodyguards and, speaking in Tuigan, told them to wait outside. The frowning warriors reluctantly obeyed.

As soon as the escort was gone, Batu addressed his adjutant. "Have the bodyguards killed."

Pe barely stopped short of gasping when Batu narrowed a warning eye at him. The other officers in the room showed no emotion, though Batu felt certain they were as shocked as his adjutant.

"We came under a flag of truce!" Koja sputtered.

The only response to the lama's objection was Pe leaving the room to execute the order.

"The khahan will—"

"You need no bodyguard in my camp, historian," Batu interrupted, resting his elbows on the arms of his chair. "The escort was an insult."

Batu did not truly find the bodyguard insulting. The general simply wanted to impress upon the khahan that he was not afraid to fight. Doing something so deliberately provocative would send that message.

Outside the tent, there were several screams and thuds. A Tuigan warrior stumbled into the pavilion, three crossbow bolts protruding from his back. Two Shou soldiers followed and cut him down with their *chiens*. The lama watched the display with an expression of revulsion and utter disbelief.

A moment later, the scuffle outside ended. Pe returned and bowed to indicate that he had executed the order. As two guards dragged the dead Tuigan from the tent, Batu said, "Now, *anda*-to-the-khahan, you may deliver your message."

Koja's face went white. Nevertheless, he looked Batu in

the eye. "On behalf of Yamun Khahan, Ruler of the World and Illustrious Emperor of All Peoples, I am here to accept your surrender."

Many of the Shou officers could not stop from snickering. Batu saw nothing funny about the khahan's message, for he was keenly aware that the Tuigan warriors outnumbered his *pengs* three-to-two. Nevertheless, he purposely turned up his lips in what he hoped would appear an amused and confident smile. A few moments later, he frowned as if remembering decorum. He scowled at his troops to quiet them.

After the pavilion returned to silence, Batu said, "Tell Yamun Khahan that we have no use for surrender. Our only interest is his death."

Koja grimaced at the words, obviously envisioning his master's fury when he delivered the Shou response.

Batu dismissed the lama with a wave of his hand, then looked to Pe. "Give Koja his bodyguard's heads to take to the khahan. We would not want Yamun Khahan to think that his men surrendered instead of fighting." Batu did not truly think that Yamun Khahan would doubt his guards' loyalty. He was just trying to make their deaths as striking as possible, thereby giving the Tuigan leader something to think about besides strategy.

The adjutant bowed. "As you wish, my commander." He moved forward to take the lama away.

As soon as Pe escorted the messenger from the room, Batu turned to his subcommanders. "Prepare for battle," he said. "Position the Armies of Wak'an and Hai Yuan in front of the gates."

A buzz filled the tent as the officers moved to obey.

"An ingenious plan," commented Hai Yuan, rising. "We can't storm the city, so you're provoking the enemy into leaving it."

"That is not my intention at all," Batu replied, taking the time to address both of his surviving subcommanders. "We must not forget that there are one hundred thousand Tuigan and only sixty thousand Shou. Sooner or later, the barbarians will get hungry and decide to leave. If we're going to win the battle that follows, we'll need time to ring them in with our fortifications."

"Then why insult the messenger?" Hai Yuan asked. "Provoking the enemy will only make him attack sooner."

"That is where you are mistaken," Batu replied, a wry smile on his lips. "Do you think he really expected us to surrender? He sent the messenger to spy upon our camps and to see whether I was confident or afraid. By insulting the messenger, I told the khahan I was confident, that I wanted to fight. If he believes I want him to attack, he will wait."

"How can you be sure?" asked Wak'an, furrowing his brow skeptically. "Is it not possible that he will see through your ruse?"

"It is," Batu admitted. "That is why we must be ready for battle."

The next week was a tense one. The barbarians kept a large force on the walls and fired at anyone careless enough to enter the archers' range. The Shou kept one army on watch at all times, while the others prepared the trench around the city to receive its fortifications. At the same time, the survivors from the Army of Kao Shan spent the daylight hours laboring in distant woods or at the kilns, making bricks and sharpening poles. They were careful to stockpile these materials behind ridges and hills where they could not be seen by the Tuigan.

Yamun Khahan would not be concerned by a trench, Batu knew, for the Tuigan horses could easily jump over or into a simple ditch. However, when the khahan realized the Shou were building a defensive wall, the barbarian commander would try to attack before the fortification could be completed. Batu intended to rob his counterpart of this opportunity. By preparing the wall's foundations in advance, the Shou general hoped to erect it in a single night.

Seven days later, the ditch was ready to receive its fortifications, and the survivors from the Army of Kao Shan had stockpiled enough sharpened poles to ring the city. Batu was inspecting the trench that evening, silently lamenting the fact that there was still a shortage of bricks, when the city gate opened.

The lama rode out, waving a white flag. This time, he was alone.

Before Koja could approach the trench, Batu took twenty guards and went to meet him. By riding into Tuigan archery range, he was taking a big risk, but he did not want the lama to see the preparations in the trench.

As the two men approached each other, the guards formed a ring around both of them. Koja ignored the soldiers and continued straight toward Batu, stopping only when their mounts stood nose to nose. The lama's horse looked haggard and hungry, its ribs visible beneath its hide. Across his saddle, the messenger carried two large bags. The general almost gagged as a rancid odor filled the air.

"What news do you bring from our city?" Batu asked, eyeing the lama appraisingly. Koja's cheeks were hollow and sunken, and there were deep circles beneath his eyes. Clearly, the messenger had not eaten much in the last week.

The little man's horse pawed at the dirt, then dropped its muzzle and began gnawing at the barren ground. Koja pulled on the reins, but the starving beast would not be denied its futile search for stray grass roots. After a moment, Koja gave up on the horse, then took one of the bags off his saddle and turned it over.

Five heads fell to the ground. Though they were in the early stages of decomposition, Batu could easily see that they had once belonged to Shou soldiers. Koja's starving horse nuzzled a head and decided it was no good to eat, then went back to pawing at the ground in search of food.

Before the general could say anything, the lama overturned the second bag. Another five heads fell out. This time, Batu recognized two of the heads. One belonged to his father-in-law, Hsuang Yu Po, and another to Xeng, the Hsuang family steward.

"The mighty Yamun Khahan, Ruler of the World and Illustrious Emperor of All Peoples, sends his greetings." Koja spoke as stiffly as he sat. "He wishes you to know that he meant no insult by sending an escort with his messenger. He repays the courtesy you showed him by returning his guards' heads, and sends to you the heads of ten Shou commanders who fell defending this insignificant town."

Batu barely paid the little man any attention. The general was staring at Tzu Hsuang. Though he had long ago accepted that his father-in-law had died in Shou Kuan, he could not help being shocked by the sight of the noble's gray-haired head.

A dozen contradictory emotions clouded the general's thoughts. He felt grief at the loss of a friend, and anger at the sight of a family member's mutilation. His thoughts turned to Wu and what he would to her say about her father's death. Would he reveal what he had seen? Perhaps it would be better to lie and say that Hsuang's body had never been recovered.

Koja's voice suddenly stopped droning. Batu realized that he had allowed his enemy to see his pain.

"Is something wrong, General?" Koja asked. The lama's face did not bear the smirk Batu had expected to see there. Instead, it showed a faint trace of surprise.

Batu shook his head, chastising himself for allowing familial feelings to interfere with his duty. "Nothing's wrong," he snapped, more harshly than he meant to. "Is this all your master sent you to deliver?"

"No," the lama responded. His horse moved forward to tug at a woody root. Koja jerked on the reins, then said, "These are the words of Yamun Khahan." He unconsciously straightened his back and sat high in his saddle. " 'I have killed a million of your people and laid waste to a million acres of your land.' " The lama's hand swept the horizon. " 'I have smashed six of your armies and killed two hundred thousand of your soldiers.' " The little messenger thumped his chest dramatically, as if he were actually the one who had done all these things. " 'I have captured two of your cities and plundered all that lies within their walls.' "

Koja paused, allowing ample opportunity for his audience to consider the words. Batu remained unimpressed.

The lama continued, " 'This I have done not out of greed, only to repay your treacherous attempt on my life. Now, I have learned that your emperor did not know of the attack on me. Two servants sent an assassin to my camp without his knowledge. Therefore, Shou Lung's punishment is complete. I will call an end to this war, keeping only the lands I have conquered.' "

Batu stared at Koja for several minutes, shocked by what the lama claimed. Though the general had no doubt that Shou Lung employed assassins as diplomatic instruments, he could not believe an imperial servant would take such a drastic step without the Divine One's knowledge.

Finally, seeing that Koja was again scrutinizing him, the general looked toward Shou Kuan and said, "Even if I believed this lie, it would not be worth a single foot of Shou territory." Batu pointed at Koja's starving horse. "Within two weeks, your horses will not be fit to ride. Tell Yamun Khahan that if I were him, I would attack soon."

The lama frowned, clearly puzzled. "You will not consider the khahan's offer?"

"There is nothing to consider," Batu replied. He turned his horse away, indicating the parlay was over.

The lama did not leave. "Please! The khahan is not lying about your assassin. You must agree or thousands of men will die needlessly."

Batu looked at Koja out of the corner of his eye. "If the khahan wishes his men to live, they may surrender and the emperor will take them as slaves."

Koja sighed, exasperated. "The Tuigan are not the only ones who will die."

"That does not matter," the Shou general replied coldly, regarding the priest with an icy stare. "My men are ready to die whenever I command it." Batu motioned to the guards. "Send him back to his master."

A soldier took Koja's reins. After the guard had led the messenger away, Pe and Batu's subordinate generals rode to his side. "What did he want?" asked the adjutant.

"There isn't time to repeat it," Batu replied. "We must erect our wall tonight. The barbarians will attack tomorrow. Go and tell the loggers to bring their poles forward, then meet me at my tent."

"As you order," Pe replied.

Batu quickly assigned supervisory duties to his subordinate generals, then rode to the kilns and asked for a report. The result was disappointing. There were only enough bricks to build a wall two feet high. Nevertheless, a two-foot barrier was better than none at all. If the wall was built on the far edge of the ditch, the men standing in the trench would have nearly four feet of cover. Batu ordered the officer in charge to prepare the bricks for transport.

After leaving the kilns, Batu turned toward his tent. By the time the general arrived, dusk was falling. He paused and looked down toward Shou Kuan. Already, thousands of torches were burning in the Shou trench.

The general went inside the pavilion and found Pe waiting. While Batu's soldiers labored at the wall, the general from Chukei reviewed each unit's condition, formulated his battle plan, and issued written orders. Even with his wall, Batu was far from certain of victory. He was determined that his chances would not be fouled this time by a lack of communication or a misunderstood order.

By the time dawn came, Batu and Pe had finished their plans. Though the adjutant could not keep from yawning, the general was far from tired. Anticipation of the coming battle invigorated him. He fastened his scabbard onto his belt, then led the way out of the tent.

"Dispatch the orders, Pe," the general said. "I'm going down to inspect our wall." He mounted his horse and rode down the hill.

As he had hoped, the wall had been completed in a single evening. The men had not had time to mortar the bricks into place, but the wall would stop arrows all the same. The sharpened poles had been placed at a forty-five-degree angle in front of the wall. They were spaced every two feet, close enough to impale any horse charging between them.

The commander of Hai Yuan's army rode close to Batu.

"The men did well, did they not?"

"Yes," Batu answered. "They are to be commended."

"Let us hope our soldiers fight as well as they build," the general said, nodding toward the city walls.

As Batu had expected, thousands of barbarians stood along the top of Shou Kuan's fortifications. They were dressed in their armor and carried their bows in plain sight. The remainder of the barbarians, Batu suspected, sat astride their horses in the streets behind the gate. When the gates opened, they would charge out in a long, seemingly endless column and the battle would begin.

Batu turned to a messenger. "Have the officers prepare their men for battle. We won't have to wait much longer."

The Tuigan, however, did not attack right away. An hour passed, then two. The barbarians remained on the wall, ready for battle, but the gates did not open.

The sun crept higher in the sky and the day grew warmer. Exhausted from the long night of labor, *pengs* began to nap behind the wall. Officers walked the line, yelling at their men and beating them to keep them awake. Even Batu, still expecting the barbarians to charge out at any moment, yawned and struggled to keep his eyes from closing.

Morning turned to afternoon, and afternoon to evening. Still, the Tuigan did not attack. Finally, as the dim purples of twilight began to creep across the rolling hills, the gate opened.

Instead of a mass of charging cavalry, however, all that issued from the city was the lama, Koja. He carried the same flag of truce he had carried yesterday. Batu was surprised the Tuigan leader had sent the messenger out again, but he was also curious as to what the khahan had to say now that the wall had been built. The general dispatched a dozen guards to escort the lama through the fortifications.

With Pe and his subcommanders following close behind, Batu met Koja as soon as he crossed the trench line. As the lama approached within speaking distance, he said, "I bring words of praise from Yamun Khahan. He says that the Shou build walls faster than any of the peoples he has fought."

"I did not build the wall to impress the khahan," Batu snapped. "I built it to keep him caged."

Koja ignored the terse response. "The khahan wishes you to know that he and his men eat well enough on the milk of their mares and the blood of their stallions. He says that when the horses grow too weak to fight, they will be slaughtered and used to feed his men."

The lama paused, looking to the generals of Hai Yuan and Wak'an in search of the apprehension he could not read on Batu's face. He did not find it. Both men were shrewd enough not to reveal their feelings to the enemy.

Koja continued, "The khahan says he will test the strength of your wall at his leisure. Perhaps he will attack tonight, while your men lie sound asleep, recovering from their many hours of labor. Perhaps he will attack many months from now, when the cold autumn rains come and your men grow ill from sleeping in the mud. Perhaps he will wait until the winter snows, when your men huddle with frozen hands and feet around burning dung, while his men eat and drink in the comfort of the city's warm houses."

"Tell the khahan that Shou can build houses as well as walls," Batu countered, resting his hand on the hilt of his sword. "The flesh of his horses will rot before we freeze. Tell him that whenever he wishes to fight, we will be ready."

Koja nodded, as if he had expected no other response. "Perhaps fighting will not be necessary," he said, reaching into his robes.

Pe, Hai Yuan, and Wak'an drew their swords and urged their mounts forward to shield Batu. "Please!" Koja said, slowly withdrawing an ebony tube. "There is nothing but paper inside. Let me show you."

The three men looked to their commander for instruction. Batu nodded his permission. To the lama, he said, "Open it."

Koja slowly opened the tube and withdrew two sheets of paper. "Read these," he said, handing them to Pe. "They prove that the khahan is telling the truth about the assassin."

Pe backed his horse several steps and handed the papers to Batu. In the fading light, it was difficult to make out the writing, so it took a few moments to read the first letter. It was addressed to Yamun Khahan and was from a spy in the summer palace. It reported Batu's appointment as General of the Northern Marches and his subsequent disappearance. The letter also named Kwan Chan Sen and Ju-Hai Chou as the two men who had sent the assassin after the khahan.

The general passed the letter to his subcommanders, then looked at the second paper. He immediately recognized Qwo's calligraphy. His heart pounded wildly. Forcing himself to remain composed, he read Wu's account of recovering the first letter and her identification of Ting Mei Wan as the spy who had written it. At the end of the account, Batu noted his wife's signature and the stain of dried blood next to it.

When he looked up, the general asked, "Where did you get these letters?"

"From a dead man," Koja replied simply. "As you can see, the khahan is telling the truth about the assassin."

"Perhaps, and perhaps not," scoffed the general from Wak'an. "This document could easily be a forgery."

"It isn't," Batu replied, passing the second sheet of paper to him. "I recognize the calligraphy."

Wak'an read the letter quickly, his face blanching with shock.

While his subordinates read the letter, Batu fought to conceal the distress it had caused him. His stomach ached with concern for his wife and children. He wanted nothing more than to take his horse and ride to Tai Tung to see what had happened to his family. Batu tried to put such thoughts out of his mind, for he was a soldier and knew better than to allow his feelings to interfere with his duty. Forcing himself to ignore the worry in his heart, Batu looked back to Koja.

"This is all very interesting, but it changes nothing," the general said, tightening his face to keep from showing his emotions. "Even if I had the right, I would not yield a single foot of Shou territory to your master."

Koja nodded in understanding. "That will not be necessary. In his infinite generosity and wisdom, the khahan will accept a different form of tribute. He will allow Shou Lung to retain the lands he has conquered, but you must give him the men who sent the assassin."

Batu studied the lama's face, considering Yamun Khahan's offer. The terms were not unreasonable: two lives in return for peace. Even if it meant sacrificing his friend Ju-Hai Chou, Batu could see the wisdom of accommodating the barbarian commander. Despite the attitude the general displayed whenever he met Koja, he was far from certain that the Shou could outlast the barbarians. With autumn coming and the surrounding land laid to waste, it would prove difficult to keep the army fed. Of course, he could bring supplies from other cities, but that would require the use of massive supply columns vulnerable to the muddy fall weather. In the end, it might be his own troops who starved to death, not Yamun Khahan's.

By not accepting the offer, he knew, he was risking his command. If the Tuigan sensed any weakness in his army, they would sally forth and wipe it out. In itself, such a risk did not trouble Batu, for soldiers had to be accustomed to danger and imminent death. However, if his army fell before the emperor could muster reinforcements, nothing would stand between the barbarians and Tai Tung. Shou Lung itself might fall, and that was a risk he did not dare take.

Koja shifted in his saddle. "There is no need to make your decision immediately," he said. "The khahan is prepared to receive your response in the morning."

"That won't be necessary," Batu replied, locking eyes with lama. "If the emperor will give me charge of Kwan Chan Sen and Ju-Hai Chou, I agree to the terms."

Koja breathed a loud sigh of relief. "The mighty khahan will be most pleased. There is only one other term: you will accompany myself and five thousand riders to retrieve the criminals."

"You're mad!" the commander from Wak'an exclaimed. "We'd be fools to let five thousand barbarians within a hundred miles of the emperor!"

"You must," Koja answered, meeting the general's gaze with a surprisingly stubborn frown. "We are not surrendering. Therefore, I am entitled to my bodyguard."

"You are entitled to nothing!" someone else snapped.

Batu silenced his subordinates with an angry scowl, then he addressed Koja. "You may have your bodyguard," he said. "But we aren't surrendering either, so I will also take five thousand men."

Even without looking at them, Batu knew his subcommanders did not agree with his decision. Nevertheless, he felt sure it was the correct one. Five thousand Tuigan did not concern him, so long as he had five thousand Shou to watch them. Besides, if the emperor rejected the peace proposal, he would make sure that Koja's bodyguard never returned to defend the walls of Shou Kuan.

The lama studied Batu for a moment, as if trying to read the thoughts of the Shou commander. Finally, the little historian said, "I am sure the khahan will agree to your request. When shall we leave?"

"At dawn," Batu replied.

Considering the exhausted condition of his men, one night was not much rest before beginning such a long ride. Nevertheless, now that he had decided to return to the summer palace, Batu was unwilling to postpone their departure for even an hour. Thoughts of Wu, Ji, and Yo were flashing through his mind so rapidly that he was burning up with anxiety for them.

With more than a little fear, the General of the Northern Marches wondered how much his concern for his family had influenced his decision. For if his emotions had played any part in his decision to accept the khahan's proposal, he was betraying his duty.

– 16 –

Renegade

As Ju-Hai Chou crossed the marble floor, he noted that he was the last minister to enter the Hall of Supreme Harmony. The other mandarins already sat in their seats, their breath rising from their noses in wispy plumes of steam. Except for Ting Mei Wan, who wore a cream-colored fur over a black *cheosong*, the ministers were dressed against the cold in heavy hemp *waitaos*.

Though it was a chilly autumn morning, the Hall of Supreme Harmony remained unheated. Because its venerable builders had intended the building for summer use only, they had made no provisions for warming even the emperor's seat. The Divine One sat in his throne wrapped in a colorless wool robe.

Keeping his own cloak wrapped tightly about his chest, Ju-Hai Chou bowed to the emperor, then took his chair. No one had told him the reason for this dawn meeting, but the minister felt sure it concerned the army of horsemen that had camped outside the city last night.

"I am glad we are finally assembled," the emperor said, glancing at Ju-Hai with visible annoyance.

In response to the Divine One's irritation, the minister simply bowed his head in apology and offered no excuses for his tardiness. He had come as soon as the chamberlain had summoned him, but no doubt the messenger had called upon him last. Thanks to Ting Mei Wan, Ju-Hai had grown accustomed to such treatment.

After destroying the Batu household, the beguiling Minister of State Security had mounted a propaganda campaign to convince the emperor that Wu had been a spy working for her traitorous husband. The cunning female mandarin had prevented Ju-Hai from contradicting her story by holding him prisoner at her house for several weeks. Ting had justified this unusual measure by claiming that Wu's death had unbalanced the Minister of State. She had further undermined Ju-Hai's influence by implying that the "spy" had become the minister's lover. By the time Ting had released the Minister of State, even his own servants had looked askance at him.

Fortunately, Ju-Hai had come across a way to restore a little of his credibility. A few days after his release, the minister had learned that Ting's subordinates were searching for the ebony tube Wu had taken the night before her death. Assuming the tube contained evidence of Ting's betrayal, Ju-Hai had quietly begun his own search. So far, neither he nor Ting had met with success. It seemed as though the tube had simply vanished.

Ju-Hai's reverie ended when the emperor spoke to Kwan Chan Sen. "What is our situation?"

The old man slowly rose to his feet and addressed the entire Mandarinate. "From what we saw last night, the barbarians have ten thousand men, twice the number of our defenders."

Ju-Hai stood and turned to the emperor. "Divine One, may I speak?"

The Son of Heaven studied the Minister of State with a look of strained patience, but finally nodded his head. "Please be brief. We have serious matters to consider."

"Thank you, Emperor," Ju-Hai responded, quickly bowing. "Shouldn't we consider what the messengers told us?"

Sighs of exasperation rustled around the room. In the last two weeks, two messengers had arrived from Shou Kuan. The first had come sixteen days ago. He had reported that Batu and the provincial armies had trapped the barbarians in Shou Kuan. The exhausted rider had presented a request for siege equipment, reinforcements, and food. The second messenger had arrived just four days ago, reporting that General Batu was riding to Tai Tung with a Tuigan delegation and a peace proposal.

Although they had carried the proper seals, the men had been greeted with nothing but suspicion. Both times, Kwan Chan Sen had suggested that Batu had sent the messengers to lay the groundwork for a traitorous trap. The emperor and the other mandarins had agreed, and the men had died at the hands of Ting's interrogators.

The other mandarins were no more inclined to listen to Ju-Hai Chou than they had been to believe the messengers were legitimate. Without exception, they greeted the Minister of State's suggestion with intolerant scowls and impatient moans.

Noting the reaction of the other mandarins, the emperor said, "Minister Ju-Hai, we have considered the words of the messengers and have all reached the same conclusion." The Divine One turned back to the Minister of War. "How do you plan to defend the city, General?"

The ancient mandarin answered immediately. "With the exception of your guard, I have placed all forces in Tai Tung under my personal command—"

"Take my guard as well," the emperor interrupted. "If the city falls, they will do me no good."

Kwan bowed his head. "Thank you, Divine One. They will prove most useful—"

The ancient Minister of War was interrupted again, this time by the chamberlain. "Excuse me, honored ones," he said, moving toward the center of the room. "I thought you would want to know that General Batu is at the city gate demanding entrance."

"He dares show his face personally?" The emperor asked, pushing himself to the edge of his throne.

The chamberlain nodded. "He is dressed like a barbarian, but several guards recognized him."

"To believe we would open the gate to ten thousand enemies, he must take us for imbeciles!" Kwan objected.

"The impudent knave!" Ting said, speaking for the first

time that morning. "Have an archer plant a feather in his breast!"

"No!" Ju-Hai shouted, rising to his feet. "Shouldn't we hear him out?"

Ting whirled on Ju-Hai, her eyes burning with anger. "The traitor will make no promises we can believe!"

A chorus of agreement ran through the Mandarinate and Ju-Hai realized that nothing he said would persuade his peers to listen to him. To gain entrance into Tai Tung for Batu, he would have to appeal directly to the Divine One. He was risking the little that remained of his prestige, for the emperor had already indicated his displeasure with Ju-Hai once that morning. Nevertheless, the Minister of State knew Batu was no traitor. The young general would not have returned to Tai Tung if he did not feel that doing so was in Shou Lung's best interests.

Ju-Hai turned to the emperor. "Divine One, what harm can come from admitting Batu into Tai Tung? Does anyone believe a lone man capable of defeating an entire city?"

"There is magic," Kwan countered. "With sorcery, one man can accomplish much."

"Batu is no *wu jen*," Ju-Hai returned.

"Neither are you," Ting said. "How do you know he does not carry some trinket to block the gate when we open it?"

"Then let him climb the wall!" Ju-Hai snapped, returning his eyes to the emperor. "The man has been accused of treason. Allow him to come and speak in his own defense. If his words do not convince us of his innocence, then at least we will have him in our grasp to punish!"

The Divine One studied Ju-Hai for several moments, his face, as usual, an unreadable mask. Finally, the emperor turned to the chamberlain. "Have the guards lower a rope to General Batu."

After the chamberlain left, Kwan outlined his plans for defending Tai Tung. The emperor asked a few questions, but it was clear that the court was more concerned with Batu's arrival than the Minister of War's report. Ting constantly fidgeted, rearranged her fur, crossed and recrossed her legs. Ju-Hai suspected she could hardly keep from rising to pace back and forth, for it was certainly possible that the general's return would expose her treachery.

Finally, the chamberlain returned with Batu. The two men were accompanied by a dozen imperial guards. As the small entourage advanced into the Hall of Supreme Harmony, a murmur of shocked disapproval rustled through the Mandarinate. The general wore a conical skullcap trimmed with oily fur, a filthy hauberk, grimy leather riding breeches, and mud-spattered boots rising to the top of his shins. If Ju-Hai had not seen Batu in civilized apparel before this, he would have sworn he was looking at a barbarian.

Batu and his escorts stopped in the middle of the hall. The general removed his skullcap and thrust it roughly at the chamberlain, revealing a mass of long unkempt hair. Batu dropped to his knees and touched his forehead to the floor three times.

"You may rise."

The emperor had barely spoken before Batu sprang to his feet. He held his jaw set firmly and his eyes burned with outrage. When he spoke, however, his words contained no trace of anger. "Thank you for seeing me, Divine One. I have much to report."

Kwan was quick to move in for the attack. "You mean to account for, traitor!"

Batu turned on the ancient mandarin with a stare so savage that Ju-Hai half-expected the general to fling a hidden dagger at the old man. Instead, Batu said, "As usual, you are mistaken, Minister Kwan. Was it at your order that I had to climb the city wall like a common thief?"

"No," the emperor interrupted. "It was at mine."

Batu looked back to the emperor, his expression finally betraying his injured feelings. "Why?"

The Divine One studied Batu with a scowl lost halfway between anger and puzzlement. "Why?" he snapped. "You lay siege to my summer home, then present yourself in the filthy rags of a barbarian, and you ask why you must climb the wall? General, you are more intelligent than that. Now say what you have come to say."

Batu's mouth dropped into a pained frown. "Didn't my messenger explain?"

"Your messenger explained," Ju-Hai interrupted, deciding it was best to let Batu know what he faced. "No one believed him. He was killed during interrogation."

"Killed?" Batu gasped. "But he was a Shou *peng!*"

"He was a traitor, like you and your family," Ting Mei Wan spat. She pointed a lacquered fingernail at the general. "Your messenger was put to death, the same as your wife and children!"

"What?" Batu shrieked. "What are you saying?"

"How long did you think the emperor would neglect your crimes?" Ting demanded. "Lady Wu was wounded while stealing secrets from my home. She died the next day, trying to escape. Your children were duly executed for her crimes, and yours, against the emperor."

"No!" Batu shouted. "It can't be!" He looked toward Ju-Hai, clearly hoping the Minister of State would report that Ting was lying.

Ju-Hai knew the cunning woman's purpose in telling Batu of his family's death. She was hoping to disorient him. Choked with grief, he might become irrational, violent, even self-destructive. In such a state, he would be easier to manipulate or to dismiss as demented if he revealed something that incriminated her.

Nevertheless, Ju-Hai could not lie about the deaths of Wu and the children. Even if the general believed him, someone else in the Mandarinate would confirm Ting's words, and the Minister of State would lose Batu's trust. His only choice was to tell the truth and hope the general could overcome his grief.

"She's telling the truth, Batu," Ju-Hai said, looking straight into the man's horrified eyes. "Your wife and children died at her orders."

For several moments, the minister and the general stared at each other. Batu's lower lip quivered, and his brow twisted into a shroud of grief. His eyes became red and puffy, then glassed over with unshed tears.

"General," Ju-Hai asked, "why did you return to Tai Tung?" The minister was hoping to help Batu refocus his thoughts. The general's only hope of escaping the same fate as his wife and children lay in performing his duty and proving his loyalty. The Minister of State did not imagine that Batu cared about living at the moment, but too much depended on the general to let him perish.

"Batu Min Ho," Ju-Hai repeated sternly, "your mission isn't finished yet. Stop feeling sorry for yourself and report!"

Suddenly Batu clenched his jaw and his eyes cleared. He looked away from Ju-Hai, then turned to the emperor. "Did you condone Ting's action?"

The emperor did not flinch. "You know the penalty for treason."

"Then you will find this most interesting," Batu said, reaching into his hauberk. Immediately his escorts leveled their *chiang-chuns* at him.

The general glared at the guards. "Do not mistake me for an assassin."

He withdrew his hand slowly. In it, he held a small ebony tube. It was the same tube that Ju-Hai had seen Ting Mei Wan holding on a dark, drizzly night many weeks past. It was the same tube for which Wu had died. Ju-Hai could not imagine how Batu had come to possess it, and he did not know what was inside. Yet, given Ting's frantic search over the past weeks, he was sure the tube's contents would condemn the beautiful mandarin to the death she deserved.

As if confirming Ju-Hai's suspicion, Ting grew pale and slumped in her chair.

Batu looked in the disheartened woman's direction and smiled grimly. He opened the tube and withdrew two sheets of paper, which he gave to the chamberlain. "These letters were meant for you, Divine One." Batu's voice was stiff and emotionless.

The chamberlain carried the letters to the emperor, who accepted them and began reading without a word. A few moments later, he looked up. "How did these come into your possession?"

"The barbarians sent them to me," Batu answered. "They took the letters off a body in Shou Kuan."

"Why would they give the letters to you?"

Batu glanced at Ju-Hai with a curiously apologetic expression, then said, "They want Ministers Kwan and Ju-Hai."

Ju-Hai felt as though someone had dropped a boulder on his chest. He knew without a doubt what the letters revealed. The barbarians could want him and Kwan for only one reason.

"Ridiculous!" Minister Kwan yelled.

"Perhaps, and perhaps not." The very calmness of Batu's voice seemed menacing. "In addition to identifying Minister Ting as a spy, the letters say that you were party to an attempt on Yamun Khahan's life. The barbarians claim that's why they started the war."

"I'd never do such a thing without your instruction!" Kwan shouted, looking to the emperor.

Batu turned back to the Divine One. "Those letters were sent as proof of the barbarian claim. I—" The general paused as the words caught in his throat, then continued. "I recognized Wu's signature, so I knew they were genuine."

"He's lying!" Kwan said. "He forged the letters!"

"Minister Kwan has a point," Ting added. "We have no way of confirming that the letters are genuine." Though she spoke in a calm voice and appeared relaxed, Ting's face was as pale as the fur on her shoulders. She glanced at Ju-Hai, her eyes carrying an unspoken suggestion.

The self-serving thing to do, Ju-Hai knew, was to join forces with Ting and Kwan. With three people calling Batu a liar, the emperor might take it on face value that the letters were forgeries. Even if the Divine One investigated further, the ploy would buy valuable time to maneuver. As unsavory as he found such a confederation, it was not something at which the minister balked. During his long career, he had made hundreds of unpleasant alliances and betrayed the trust of many friends on behalf of Shou Lung.

Ju-Hai realized that the eyes of the entire Mandarinate

were fixed on him, anxiously awaiting his acknowledgement or denial of the assassination attempt. Still, the minister was not ready to make his decision. He had to consider one more point.

The minister turned to Batu. "General, if we don't make peace with the barbarians, who will win the war?"

Several people seemed confused by the change of subject, but Batu answered immediately. "I can't say," he said, fixing a vacant stare on the minister. Continuing in an empty voice, he added, "The Tuigan are trapped in Shou Kuan, but they outnumber us and stand a good chance of winning when they sally. Even if they don't attack, we may not be able to starve them out, for I've heard they'll eat their horses and even each other. What's worse is that while the enemy sleeps beneath the roofs of Shou Kuan, our men are exposed to chill weather and autumn rains. The risk of epidemic is high."

The answer was not the one Ju-Hai had hoped to hear. It meant that much more was at stake than his life or Batu's.

The Minister of State bowed to the emperor, but did not dare to look him in the eye. "I beg your forgiveness, Divine One," he said. "The letters are genuine. When I learned of Yamun Khahan's success in uniting the horse tribes, I offered my help to his treacherous stepmother. At my request, Kwan sent an assassin to aid her."

A stunned silence fell over the Hall of Supreme Harmony, but only for a moment. Ting Mei Wan sprang to her feet as if to flee, but the emperor was not taken by surprise. "Minister Ting!" he boomed, pointing a long-nailed finger at her. "At the moment, you face only one death. If you flee, I will see to it that you die a thousand times!"

Ting looked from the emperor to the guards behind Batu. They still had not moved, and Ju-Hai thought his former protege stood a chance of escaping if she acted quickly enough. Then her gaze fell on Batu. The general's face was warped into a hateful scowl and his bitter eyes were locked on Ting's. Without looking away, the Minister of State Security collapsed back into her chair.

"A wise decision," Ju-Hai said. "There is no place you could run that General Batu would not find you."

The Divine One motioned to the guards behind Batu, "Lock her in the First Spire of Ultimate Despair. Ministers Kwan and Ju-Hai are confined to the palace grounds until further notice. Do not let them out of your sight."

"You wouldn't think of sending us to the barbarians!" Kwan protested.

Rising to leave the hall, the emperor said, "That will be decided after Ting's execution."

Kwan started to follow the Son of Heaven. "Divine One, let us explain!"

Ju-Hai rose. "There's nothing to explain, you fool." He knew that the emperor could reach only one conclusion: two lives were a small price to pay for ending a costly war that had little prospect of victory.

The Minister of State turned to the guards assigned to him. "I'd like to spend the day in my garden."

* * * * *

The sword fell and there was a hollow pop. Ting's head, covered by a silk hood, dropped into the waiting basket. The kneeling corpse remained perched on the executioner's block, its hands bound behind its back.

In the pale morning light, everything seemed gray except Ting's *cheosong*. It was her favorite scarlet dress, the one with the golden dragon that entwined her body. Now, clinging to a headless corpse, it was the dragon that looked full and alive.

Batu had expected to feel something when Ting died: vindication, relief, perhaps elation. Instead, his emotions remained as colorless as the morning. He could not seem to accept that the traitorous mandarin had killed his entire family.

Accompanied by Pe, the general had passed the night at the house where his wife and children had died, but he had not grieved. He had seen Wu's bloodstains in the sleeping hall. He had sat in the courtyard and tried to weep.

Throughout the night, he kept hearing their voices call to him. Once he had dozed off and awakened to the imagined touch of his children's hands upon his back.

The thought had occurred to him that his family's spirits might be trapped at the site of the murders. Though far from a superstitious man, the general had tried talking to them. When he had received no response, Batu had sent for a *shukenja*. The priest had found no wayward spirits, but had suggested that if Wu and the children were trapped in the house, their murderer's death would free them to begin the journey to the Land of Extreme Felicity.

So, at first light, the general and his adjutant had gone to the Square of Paramount Justice, where they had joined a small group gathered to witness Ting's execution. Although Pe had found ceremonial uniforms for both of them, Batu still wore his barbarian hauberk. The others who had been invited to witness the execution—the emperor, Ju-Hai, Kwan, and Koja—had raised their eyebrows at his attire, but Batu did not care. He could not bear to wear the uniform of the emperor who had turned a blind eye to the murder of his family. Feeling as he did, the general wondered how he could continue serving in the army of Shou Lung— or, for that matter, how he could continue living at all.

For the rest of his life, his mind and his heart would be at war. Though he knew rationally that Wu and the children were dead, he would never believe it in his heart. Batu's only hope of fully accepting their fates, viewing their lifeless bodies, had been taken away. His family had been cremated, their ashes scattered to the winds like those of common thieves. For that insult, especially, Batu had wanted Ting to suffer.

However, the traitorous mandarin had died with more dignity than she deserved. As the guards had led her into the Square of Paramount Justice, her knees had buckled, and she had looked pale and frightened. When the executioner had slipped the hood over her head, she had shamefully avoided the eyes of those gathered to witness her death.

Still, she had not begged for mercy, nor even cried out in despair, and Batu felt that his family had deserved at least that much retribution. If the general had administered the execution, she would have died shrieking in pain and pleading for mercy.

Unfortunately, the Divine One considered torture uncivilized, at least in his presence. He had only allowed Batu to watch an impersonal executioner exact the vengeance which belonged to the general.

"You must be very happy, General," Kwan Chan said, interrupting Batu's reverie. The old man stood between two guards. His hands were bound behind his back, as if there were a chance he would break free and totter away. As a badge of dishonor, Kwan wore a dingy *samfu* of undyed hemp instead of a mandarin's brocaded *waitao*.

When Batu did not answer the old man's comment, Pe took up the gauntlet. "Why should the general be happy, prisoner?" the youth demanded. He clearly enjoyed addressing his hated ex-superior with the derogatory term.

Kwan gave the adjutant a patronizing smile. "He has defeated his enemies."

"The khahan has not been defeated!" Koja snapped from a few feet away.

Though Batu knew the minister was not referring to the barbarians, the general had no wish to elevate either Kwan or Ting to the status of enemy. He always held at least a grudging respect for his opponents, and he felt nothing of the kind for either of the two mandarins. He added his own comment to Koja's assertion, "The Tuigan still hold Shou Kuan. I have not defeated any enemies."

"True," the emperor replied, speaking for the first time that morning. "But neither have the Tuigan defeated you. This war is over. I accept the barbarian terms."

Koja nodded politely, but before the barbarian's envoy could speak, Kwan interrupted. "No! I beg you to reconsider. Minister Ju-Hai and I had only your best interests at heart, Divine One. We do not deserve such a disgrace."

"There is no dishonor in dying on the empire's behalf," Ju-

Hai said. Like Kwan, he was wearing a hemp *samfu* as a badge of shame, but his hands remained unbound as a symbol of the emperor's continued faith in his integrity. "What is disgraceful is to beg for your life."

Kwan snorted. "I am hardly begging for my life, you fool. I have lived a hundred years, and I shall live a hundred more."

The emperor dismissed the old man's boast with a wave of his hand. "That will be for the barbarians to decide, Kwan Chan Sen. I will not change my decision. We will make peace with the Tuigan."

One day ago, Batu would have respected the emperor's decision, for Shou Lung had little to gain and everything to lose by continuing the war. With his family gone, however, the general no longer cared about the empire's security. Nothing remained to him except the love of war, and the less secure the empire was, the more battles he would fight.

Ignoring Koja's presence, Batu stepped toward the Divine One and said, "You mustn't make peace."

"You have a plan?" inquired Ju-Hai, a note of hope creeping into his voice.

By the vacant look in the general's eyes, it was apparent that he did not. "I will make one," Batu said.

The emperor cast a reassuring glance at the Tuigan messenger, then shook his head. "This war is over, General. I have every confidence in your ability to defeat the Tuigan, but Shou Lung is a nation that loves peace."

Batu knew that the Divine One was lying. Though the emperor undoubtedly intended to end the war, he was doing so out of practicality and not a love of peace. What the Son of Heaven left unsaid was that Shou Lung could not bring to bear enough force to destroy the barbarians. Reinforcing Shou Kuan would require stripping several armies away from the southern border. Such a desperate measure would ensure an attack from T'u Lung, Shou Lung's greedy neighbor to the south.

The difference between Batu's viewpoint and that of the emperor was that the general did not care if the rapacious kingdom attacked. After destroying the Tuigan, he would be more than happy to crush T'u Lung.

"Let me have just one more army," Batu pressed, "and I will reface the walls of Shou Kuan with Tuigan skulls."

Koja frowned, uneasy with Batu's sudden belligerence. "Your promise is easier made than kept."

"Have no fear," the emperor said to Koja. "General Batu will be too busy to make good on his threat. I have great need of him here."

"Here?" Batu echoed.

The emperor nodded. "I have three ministries without mandarins to lead them. As a reward for all you have done, you may have your choice of positions."

Batu stared at the emperor in uncomprehending shock. Never would he have dared aspire to a seat in the Mandarinate. Now that such an esteemed position had been offered to him, he wanted nothing in the world less. "I choose none of them."

The emperor frowned. "I don't understand."

"Yes, you do," Batu answered. "I'm no mandarin. I'm a soldier."

The emperor's mouth hung agape. "That is not your choice," he snapped indignantly. "The barbarian invasion has cost Shou Lung much. Need I remind you of this?"

"It has cost me more," Batu replied.

The Divine One's eyes softened. "I am sorry about your family, but many others have also lost their loved ones," he said. "Now, you must set aside your pain. I call and it is your duty to answer."

Batu shook his head. "No longer."

The emperor scowled at this defiance. Before the Son of Heaven could speak, Batu continued, "For twenty years, I have performed my duty to you and the empire without failure. If you had done the same for me, my wife and children would be alive."

"Watch what you say!" Ju-Hai cautioned, grasping Batu's wrist.

"Why?" Batu demanded, addressing the ex-minister. "What will the Son of Heaven do? He has already allowed my family to be murdered while under his protection." Batu jerked free of Ju-Hai's grasp, then turned to the emperor again. "Execute me if you will!" the general spat. "It will do no good. I am a soldier; I am already dead."

Kwan Chan chuckled malevolently. "Then you have no right to grieve. Dead men have no business with wives and children."

The words struck Batu like a sword, and rage spread over him like a sheet of fire. Kwan's words contained enough truth to pain the general, and he vented his anger by hitting the old man with his closed fist.

Kwan collapsed in a heap. Batu dropped on him, reaching for the ex-minister's feeble throat.

"That's enough, General!" the emperor snapped.

Ignoring the Divine One, Batu crossed his wrists in front of Kwan's throat. He grabbed the inside of the mandarin's collar and pulled, locking his arms against the old man's neck in a deadly choke. Kwan's face turned red instantly.

Six guards grasped Batu by the arms. It did not matter to the general. He tightened his grip, trying to crush Kwan's windpipe before they pulled him free.

"Stop!" Koja said, also grabbing Batu and tugging feebly. "The khahan won't accept a dead man as tribute!"

When Batu did not respond, Koja continued, "Leave him to the Tuigan. He'll suffer more than you can imagine."

These last words caught Batu's attention. Koja was right, he realized. Tuigan savagery was legendary, and falling into their hands alive was considered a fate worse than death. The general released Kwan and stood, saying, "It's a pity I won't be there to watch you suffer."

To Batu's amazement, the old man showed little sign of the abuse his throat had taken. At the least, most men would have been coughing and gasping for breath. Kwan, however, simply massaged his wrinkled neck and returned to his feet, staring spitefully at his attacker.

Several guards pressed the points of their *chiang-chuns* against Batu's body. The Divine One addressed him sternly. "General Batu, I understand the strain you are under. In consideration of your feelings, I have allowed you many latitudes today. Still, I will not tolerate such displays in my court."

Batu looked at the Divine One and snorted in contempt. "You don't understand, do you?"

The emperor frowned. "Understand what?"

"I am no longer your general," Batu said angrily. "You broke faith with me. I'm *ronin* now." The term he used came from the islands of Wa, but he was sure the Divine One knew its meaning. He had declared himself a renegade soldier, a mercenary for hire.

The pronouncement caused Koja to raise an eyebrow, but the lama said nothing.

The Divine One studied Batu for several moments. For once, his expression was readable. His lips were quivering in anger, and his dark eyes were narrow and menacing. Batu returned the stare with an empty gaze.

It was Ju-Hai who brought the stand-off to an end. "Divine One, General Batu has performed his duty well, but events have changed him. Even if you could make him stay, I doubt he would be the man we remember."

The emperor nodded, then looked at Ju-Hai. "Very well. Out of respect for your integrity and the service you once performed for the empire, I grant Batu Min Ho his life and liberty."

"As if that right were yours to grant," Batu scoffed.

"That's enough!" Ju-Hai snapped, turning to the rogue general. "You have what you want. Leave the matter be."

Pe stepped to his commander's side, then began to remove his uniform.

"What are you doing?" the emperor asked.

"Where my commander goes, I go," Pe responded.

Batu laid a hand on his adjutant's shoulder. "No. Your place is in the Army of Shou Lung."

"My place is at your side!"

"I doubt a *ronin* will have need of an adjutant," Batu responded. "Besides, I once ordered you to abandon a suit of armor. I would like to repay that debt."

"There is no debt," Pe protested. "I was wrong to question your order."

"That is for me to decide," Batu responded, speaking more loudly and stepping back so others could hear his words. "As Tzu Hsuang's sole heir, I grant you the rights to his lands and mine." He glanced at the emperor, then added, "If it is agreeable to the Divine One."

The emperor nodded.

Pe's eyes began to water. "Your gift is too great—"

Batu shrugged. "Who else can I give it to? Now take it— that is my last order, and it is your duty to obey it."

Pe bowed deeply. "If I have no other choice—"

"*You* don't," the emperor said. "I have granted Batu Min Ho permission to leave my service, not you." He looked at the guards surrounding Batu. "Take this man out of my sight. There is no place for a renegade within the summer palace."

As Batu turned to go, Pe began to speak. "Gener—"

Batu shook his head, then nodded at the emperor's frowning figure.

Pe glanced at the Divine One, then preceded his question with a title that would not offend the Son of Heaven. "My friend, where are you going?"

Batu shrugged. "Who knows?"

Escorted by six guards, the renegade walked toward the gate. As he left, the emperor turned away and fixed his gaze on the headless body still kneeling at the executioner's block. The two disgraced mandarins watched Batu leave, one with an expression of sad regret and the other with an expression of spiteful retribution. Pe raised a hand in farewell.

Koja bowed to the emperor. "I will leave tomorrow to inform the khahan of your decision."

Without waiting for a dismissal, the lama turned and scurried after Batu, catching the renegade just as he stepped out of the gate. "If you truly have no plans," Koja said, "I know someone who always has need of fighting men, someone who truly admires your skill."

– 17 –
Yamun Khahan

After an uneventful but rigorous five-day ride from the summer palace to Shou Kuan, Batu now stood in a courtyard that had once belonged to the besieged city's prefect. Along with Koja and Ju-Hai Chou, he was awaiting his turn to meet the khahan of the Tuigan.

Half an inch of autumn snow covered the stone pavement, and a chilly wind whipped over the brick-faced walls, but the prematurely bleak weather did not bother Batu's hosts. The khahan and his officers had dragged a dozen rolled rugs from the prefect's mansion and were using them as cushions. They now sat in a rough semicircle, exposed to the elements and drinking fermented mare's milk from gold and silver goblets.

The Tuigan wore grimy trousers and filthy silk tunics called *kalats*. Precious stones glittered from gold settings on their fingers, around their necks, and in their scabbards. The khahan's feet rested on an open chest filled with delicate jade figurines, endless strings of pearls, carved ivory, and other priceless treasures. The emperor of Shou Lung had sent the chest with Koja as a peace gift.

In the center of the barbarians' semicircle, Kwan Chan Sen lay spread-eagled on the ground, bound by his wrists and ankles to four heavy stones. For the last hour and a half, he had been screaming horribly. Considering what the Tuigan had put him through, it was no wonder. Two barbarians were still torturing him while the others watched. The khahan occasionally shouted advice or made wagers on how long the old man would survive.

Batu watched the scene with cool detachment. He felt no delight in watching his nemesis die so horribly, yet he experienced no pity. Kwan's agony seemed remote and unreal, as if the event were being reported by a messenger. Even considering the hatred between the two men, his lack of emotion did not surprise Batu. Nothing had stirred his feelings since the morning of Ting's execution. It was an emotional state well-suited to a renegade soldier.

The horrible sound coming from Kwan's throat changed into barely discernible words. "Cut my liver!" he gasped. "Please—I'm protected by magic. It's the only way I can die."

A swell of laughter surged through the ring of barbarians, and several began arguing as to how this revelation should affect their wagers.

Koja turned to Ju-Hai, his face a sickly shade of yellow. "For your sake," he said sympathetically, "I hope all Shou mandarins are not protected by such magic."

Ju-Hai shook his head. He was biting his lip, and his face was as pale as snow. Still, he was struggling to maintain his composure. Ripping his eyes away from Kwan, the ex-minister answered Koja. "No. I didn't even know Kwan had such protection. I have often wondered why such an old man seemed so hardy."

Batu had wondered the same thing many times, especially during the journey of the past week. With their horses well-fed and rested, the Tuigan army had ridden like the wind. Even for a man as battle-hardened as Batu, the pace had been strenuous, and the renegade general had often expected to find Kwan dead in the saddle. The old man had endured amazingly well, riding from dawn until past dusk, eating on the move and stopping to rest only when it grew so dark that the horses stumbled.

Covering up to a hundred miles a day, the Tuigan had quickly left their Shou escorts behind. The rapid pace had made Batu suspect treachery, but Koja had assured him that such travel rates were not unusual for the barbarians. They were simply rushing back to tell their commander the good news. The procession had stopped only once during daylight hours, when, on Koja's recommendation, Batu paused in a village to buy a personal gift for the khahan.

Finally, the small army had reached Shou Kuan. Batu and Ju-Hai had visited the general from Wak'an to deliver a letter from the emperor. The letter placed the astonished general in charge of all the provincial armies, and informed him of the emperor's acceptance of the peace terms. After an awkward farewell, Batu had accompanied the barbarians into the city.

That had been over two hours ago, and Batu still had not been formally introduced to Yamun Khahan. As soon as Koja had arrived and announced that the peace proposal had been accepted, the Tuigan ruler had ordered Kwan's death in celebration. Batu had not anticipated such a long wait, but he now guessed the khahan would be in good humor when Koja finally presented him.

As Batu watched the barbarians inflict yet more pain on Kwan, he realized that Koja's words in Tai Tung had been true. The Tuigan universally delighted in suffering, and Batu knew that even at his cruelest, he could never have matched the punishment the barbarians inflicted on the former Minister of War.

The contrast reminded the renegade Shou that though he shared some of their blood, he shared nothing of the horse-warriors' culture. He suddenly realized how alone he would be when Ju-Hai died. For a moment, he doubted the wisdom of his decision to leave Shou Lung, but the feeling passed as he tried to think of what remained for him there. With the Tuigan, at least, he would have his fill of fighting.

The two torturers finished their latest procedure and Kwan, protected by his magic, continued to beg for death. For several minutes, the Tuigan discussed new ways to amuse themselves with his pain. Finally, the khahan raised his hand to demand silence.

"We have had fun enough this day," he said in the thick, guttural language of the Tuigan. The khahan motioned to end the prisoner's misery.

One of Kwan's tormenters plunged a knife into the old man's liver. After the last scream died away, the khahan continued. "We have serious things to consider. The mares have stopped giving milk, and we have drank so much stallion blood that we should change our name to 'People of the Leech.'"

A chorus of raucous laughter rounded the circle of barbarians.

The khahan turned his golden goblet upside down. A few curdled drops of milk slid out of the cup. "This is the last of the *kumiss*," he said. "In another week, we will be reduced to drinking water and eating our friends."

Batu thought that Yamun was making another joke, but no one laughed.

The khahan looked toward Koja. "It is good, then, that Koja, my *anda*, returns from his mission successfully."

Koja bowed, then said, "It was the light of your wisdom and the fear of your wrath that persuaded the ruler of Shou Lung to accept our terms," he said. "I was only the humble vessel of your message."

"No doubt," the khahan replied. Looking in Batu's direction, he said, "I see you have brought a guest."

Taking Batu by the arm, Koja walked into the middle of the Tuigan circle. Remembering the elaborate security precautions surrounding his own emperor, Batu was surprised to see that no one took his sword.

Though the barbarians were seated outside, the air was ripe with the fetid smell of old sweat and fermented milk. Fortunately, Batu had grown accustomed to the odor of unbathed soldiers on the trail. He showed no outward sign of his disgust.

After guiding Batu into a kneeling position, Koja said, "Illustrious Emperor, I present Batu Min Ho, the commander of the Shou armies who opposed your mighty will."

The khahan leaned forward, staring at Batu with a fierce expression of displeasure. The ruler had the butter-colored skin and flat nose common to the Tuigan, but his features were so strong and sharp that they seemed chiseled in stone. The shape of his face was almost square, marked as it was by the hard lines of his jaw. A narrow mustache drooped over the corners of his tense-lipped mouth, and his strong cheekbones rode high on his face. His black and narrow eyes were set under a coal-colored brow.

The khahan looked back to Koja. "I did not ask for this man's life."

"I asked to see you," Batu said, daring to speak without permission.

Though clearly surprised that Batu spoke his language, the khahan did not seem offended at the Shou's boldness. "Why?"

"To present you with a personal gift," Batu said.

The khahan shifted his feet, purposely knocking a jade statue and an ivory talisman out of the chest. "Your emperor has sent me gifts," he said, curling his lips into a sneer.

"I am sure the Illustrious Emperor of All Peoples will find Batu's gift more to his liking," Koja interrupted. "Your guards are holding it outside the gate."

"Very well," the khahan responded suspiciously. "Bring it in."

An officer dutifully opened the gate, then one of the khahan's black-robed guards led in a horse bearing a small portion of Batu's gift.

The khahan's eyes lit up when he saw the two casks. "Wine?"

Batu nodded. "There are a hundred more casks, all from the finest plum orchards in Ching Tung."

"Wine from *plums*?" sneered one of the men seated with the khahan. He was a lean soldier with shifty eyes and a mistrustful expression.

"Wine is wine, Chanar," the khahan responded. "Tap a cask!"

Several Tuigan rose to obey, and the khahan watched them with a rapacious expression. After they had inserted the spigot, Yamun thrust his goblet at a quiverbearer to have it filled, then turned back to Batu. "Your gift is most welcome. We have done without wine since our second battle in this land." He paused and frowned. "Rather than leave a drop for our tongues, your peasants spilled it on the ground, the dogs!"

"On my orders," Batu revealed.

"That order cost many Shou lives," the khahan responded, grimacing at the remembrance of so many days without libation.

"It also slowed your advance," Batu replied, "and that cost many Tuigan lives."

The officer returned the khahan's goblet, but the Tuigan leader did not immediately drink. "You would do well to remember that you are in the enemy camp," Yamun warned.

Batu shrugged, not intimidated. "It is written that there are no rules in war."

The khahan's eyes narrowed and once again he regarded Batu suspiciously. "I have no use for reading," he replied, looking down his nose at the full goblet in his hand. A moment later, he handed the wine back to the quiverbearer. "I forget my manners," he said, staring into Batu's eyes. "Our guest has no cup. Let him drink from mine."

The other Tuigan, who had been waiting for the khahan to drink before lifting their own cups, nervously glanced at their own wine and wondered if the Shou had poisoned it.

The officer delivered the khahan's goblet to Batu, then stepped away.

"Go ahead," the khahan urged.

Batu raised his goblet to Yamun's companions, saying, "To the khahan's health."

The officers blanched, then lifted their vessels toward their lips. Even if the drink were poisoned, refusing to toast the khahan's health would have been an insult to their commander.

"No!" the khahan boomed, rising to his feet.

Sighing in relief, the officers stopped short of drinking.

"Our guest should drink the first cup alone," Yamun continued. "After all, he has had a long journey and we would not want him to find us lacking in courtesy."

Looking around the courtyard, Batu was glad the wine was not poisoned. Every officer held a full cup in one hand, and kept his other wrapped around his sword hilt. If the renegade general had refused to drink, he was sure he would have met a fate worse than Kwan's.

Batu rested his gaze on Yamun, then lifted the goblet in the powerful Tuigan's direction. "To *my* health, then!" He drained the wine in one long gulp.

The *ronin* wiped the spillage off his chin with his sleeve, as he was sure any Tuigan would have done. Still not taking his eyes off the khahan, Batu thrust the cup at the quiver-bearer, ordering, "Get me another."

The khahan smiled broadly, then called to the servant, "Not before you fetch me a fresh cup!"

As the youth scurried into the mansion in search of another goblet, the khahan returned to his seat and addressed Batu. "Your nerve amuses me, General, but war is no game. When it is over, opponents do not meet each other to brag about their victories over cups of wine—even if it is not poisoned. Why have you come to my camp?"

"I am a soldier in search of a war," Batu responded.

The khahan frowned, then twisted the end of his drooping mustache between his thumb and forefinger. "What do you mean?"

"I am *ronin*, a soldier without a country," he said. "I have an insatiable appetite for fighting and war, and Koja suggested I would find plenty of both with you."

"You *did* express your admiration for the enemy general's talents, Divine Master of the World," Koja interjected.

"That was before he knew the man would betray his own country," responded the lanky officer known as Chanar.

Batu turned on Chanar. "You are unaware of my reasons for leaving Shou Lung, so I will forgive your insult—once."

Scowling, Chanar reached for his sword, but Yamun raised a hand to stop him. "Chanar, you have just earned the right to stand in my sight again," the khahan said. "Are you so anxious to lose it?"

"You heard the dog!" Chanar objected.

Koja leaned toward Batu and whispered, "Him, you must watch. Were Chanar not an old friend of the khahan, his treachery would have been the end of him long ago. As it is, he only regained the right to stand within the Mighty One's sight by saving the khahan from capture."

Ignoring Chanar, Yamun asked Batu, "Why do you leave the emperor's service?"

"I am sorry, mighty khahan, but my reasons must remain my own," Batu responded, bowing his head to Yamun. He was not anxious to reveal the extent of his feelings for his family. He suspected that among dedicated soldiers like the Tuigan, such emotions would be regarded as a weakness.

The khahan frowned. "Nothing is yours that I wish to have."

The quiverbearer returned, saving Batu from the necessity of an immediate response. The young man gave a goblet of wine to the khahan, then another to Batu. The khahan lifted his cup, saying, "To *my* health, General!"

"To your health," Batu responded.

They each downed their wine in one long gulp. After they had given the goblets to the officer to refill, the khahan said, "A fine drink, though it is sweeter than wine I have had before." Without changing tone, the khahan returned to the subject of Batu's secret. "Few enemies have tricked me, and none have lived to brag about it, save you. Only a fool would let such an enemy go free, for that man will surely return to defeat him another day. So I have only two choices: take you into my *ordu*, or kill you."

When his words had no visible effect on Batu, the khahan continued, "If I am to accept you into my clan and my army, I must know why you left your own. A horse who throws one master may throw another."

Batu nodded. In similar circumstances, he would have had the same suspicions as the khahan. "There are not many horses in Shou Lung," Batu answered. "Perhaps that is because the masters do not protect the mares and foals while the stallion is away at war."

The khahan asked, "Am I to take it that one of your wives

and her children were killed while you fought us?"

"In Shou Lung, we have only one wife and but a few children, Mighty One," Batu replied. "They died under the protection of the Shou emperor."

"That is why you have renounced your duty to your master?" the khahan asked. "Because he allowed your household to die?"

Batu nodded, uneasy about revealing this weakness.

"That is no reason!" Chanar said. "An honorable soldier does not place his family above his commander!"

Chanar had barely finished the sentence before Batu stepped toward him, placing a hand on his sword hilt. As the Tuigan saw the Shou's intention, his jaw went slack and his eyes opened wide in surprise. He quickly rose to his feet and gripped the hilt of his own weapon.

"Apologize!" Batu hissed.

"I will not," Chanar responded, regaining his composure. "You must see that you'll be killed the instant you draw your weapon."

As if to emphasize the point, a dozen Tuigan stepped toward Batu.

The *ronin* paid them no attention. "Where or when I die does not matter," Batu said, stepping closer to the object of his wrath. "Apologize!"

Chanar looked to the khahan. "Let me kill this insolent mongrel," he said.

"Leave your blade in its sheath," the khahan replied, his voice perfectly calm. "Batu is a guest in my camp, and I will not be dishonored by having his blood spilled—especially when it is your own dull wit and sharp tongue that provoked him. Batu warned you not to insult his honor."

Chanar's face reddened, but he left his weapon in its sheath. Glaring at Batu, he said, "I meant no disrespect, renegade. I apologize."

"For now, that will do," Batu responded. He took his hand off his weapon. Chanar returned to his seat, staring at the Shou with undisguised hatred.

Yamun addressed Batu. "The next time you threaten one

of my officers, you had best be prepared to use your weapon."

"I *was* prepared," Batu responded, bowing to show that he meant no disrespect to the khahan.

The Tuigan's eyes narrowed. "Yes—I suppose you were."

Yamun took a long pull from his goblet, his brow furrowed in reflection. Finally, he lowered the cup and said, "I will consider your request, General Batu. Until I decide, you shall remain a welcome guest in my camp." He looked at his officers to be certain they had heard and understood his words, pausing for special emphasis at Chanar.

A moment later, the khahan turned his gaze back to Batu. "You have given me a gift and I must give you a better one. Is there anything in this camp you want?"

Batu studied the courtyard carefully. Though there was enough wealth in it to ransom a lord, Batu was not interested in gold. His eyes came to rest on Ju-Hai Chou, the one man in the government whom he had been justified in trusting.

"Great Khahan," Batu answered, "when a man goes too long without wine, it becomes more valuable than gold, does it not?"

The khahan scowled, but he said, "This is true. No man can drink gold."

"Then, in all of your camps, there is only one gift equal to the wine I brought," Batu replied, pointing at Ju-Hai. "Him."

Koja quickly grasped Batu's arm. "No!" the lama hissed. "He tried to kill the khahan, so he must die. If you try to save him, you will perish with him."

Batu shook the man off and pointed at Ju-Hai again. "Him," he repeated.

"What Koja says is true," the khahan warned. "Ju-Hai Chou must die."

Ju-Hai could not understand the Tuigan language, but he clearly knew he was being discussed. He looked at Batu with a hopeful expression, though his complexion remained pale.

"I know," Batu answered. "I merely ask for the privilege of

killing him."

The khahan smiled. "What you ask is a great gift, but I am a man of honor and will keep my word. Bring the prisoner forward."

Two officers rose and led Ju-Hai into the center of the circle. Batu drew his sword. "Minister Ju-Hai, please turn around," he said, speaking Shou.

"What are you going to do?" the ex-mandarin demanded, his voice trembling.

Ju-Hai had ridden all the way from Tai Tung to Shou Kuan with his head held high, but the renegade general did not blame him for being frightened now.

"Turn around," Batu repeated. "It will be quicker and less painful."

As he realized that his friend had not saved him, Ju-Hai began to shake. Nevertheless, he did as instructed. "I understand," he began. "My grat—"

Batu swung. The sword bit into the back of Ju-Hai's neck, killing him instantly and mercifully.

"What do you mean by that?" Chanar demanded. Even before Ju-Hai's body had hit the snowy cobblestones, the Tuigan had risen to his feet and pointed an angry finger at Batu.

"This man was a friend," Batu responded simply, cleaning his blade on Ju-Hai's *samfu*. "I did not want to see him die like an animal."

"You've insulted the khahan!" Chanar insisted.

"I will decide when I have been insulted," Yamun responded. "The prisoner's death was Batu's gift. If he wished to waste it, that is his privilege. Now sit down, Chanar, We have much to discuss."

After Chanar returned to his rug, the khahan turned to Batu. "Your loyalty to your friend is impressive, and I no longer doubt your motivations. If you are going to fight in my army, you must learn that I am the Illustrious Emperor of All Peoples. Obviously, this other emperor, the one who allowed your wife and children to die under his protection, must be an imposter. Is this not so?"

"Clearly, you are correct, Mighty One," Batu said, bowing. He could not help but compare the magnificence of the summer palace to the disorder of the khahan's besieged court, but he also knew there was more to being an emperor than the trappings of priceless and pointless luxury.

"You swear allegiance to me?" Yamun asked.

"For as long as you feed and pay me," Batu replied.

The khahan grinned. "Honestly spoken," he said. "Sit down." The khahan waved Batu to his side.

"I am honored," the Shou said, taking the seat to the khahan's right. "I look forward to fighting at your side."

After Batu was seated, the khahan began a general discussion about where his armies should attack next. Chanar favored breaking their word and riding on the Shou capitol. Another officer wanted to invade Tabot, the mountain kingdom on Shou Lung's southwestern border. One man, clearly a fool in Batu's opinion, even suggested capturing a fleet and sailing against the islands of Wa.

After listening patiently to each recommendation, the khahan turned to Batu. "You know this land better than any of us," he said. "Which option do you recommend?"

Batu did not even have to consider his answer. "None," he said. "You know less about sailing than Shou do about horsemanship, so I would not recommend attacking the Wa Islands. In the high mountains of Tabot, horses would prove more of a hindrance than an advantage, so attacking there would be bad judgment."

"And what about the Shou capitol?" the khahan asked, studying Batu with a raised eyebrow.

"You have made a peace agreement with Shou Lung," Batu responded, meeting Yamun's gaze with an intentionally blank expression.

"As you have said, in war, there are no rules," the khahan countered.

"True," the Shou replied cautiously. "In war, there are no rules. In personal conduct, however, there are. You have given your word, and I cannot recommend that you break it."

Batu paused, studying the khahan. The ruler's expression was unreadable, but he did not doubt the man was seriously considering riding against Shou Lung once more.

But to his surprise, the Tuigan ruler said, "What you say is wise, Batu. A man should keep his word." The khahan studied the faces of his officers for a moment, then returned to the Shou and asked, "So, where do we go?"

"If you cannot go east, north, or south, there is only one direction left," Batu answered. "West."

– 18 –
To the West

As Batu stepped into the khahan's *yurt*, the Illustrious Emperor of All Peoples asked, "Where are the kingdoms you promised?"

Accustomed to the khahan's impatience and no longer concerned by it, Batu did not respond immediately. Instead, he stamped the snow off his boots and waited for his eyes to adjust to the dim light. After the brilliance of the snow-covered wasteland outside, the interior of the *yurt* was as dark as a bear's den.

It also smelled like one. The air was heavy with the stringent scent of unwashed bodies, the acrid smell of burning dung, and the putrid sour-milk stench of *kumiss*. For over two months now, Batu had been traveling across the barren horse plains with the Tuigan. He was still astonished by the incredible filth of the horse nomads. They never cleaned themselves, or even changed clothes. The khahan himself still wore the same silk *kalat* in which he had been dressed when Batu met him. The renegade could not imagine why the grimy thing had not rotted away.

Batu removed his *del*, a heavy robe-like coat given to him by the khahan, and hung it from a hook on a support post. The khahan had installed the hook so that Batu would have a place to hang his *del*. The Tuigan required no such amenities, for they wore their coats inside as well as outside. In this and a hundred other things, the renegade Shou remained an outsider to the people of his ancestors.

When his eyes finally adjusted to the light, Batu faced his

commander and kneeled, his gaze taking in the near-empty *yurt*. Besides himself, the ever-present Kashik guards, and a slave, the only other person in the room was one of the khahan's wives. Batu did not know which one, for he no longer had any interest in women, at least in Tuigan women, and paid them no attention.

"I should have listened to Chanar," the khahan said testily, motioning Batu to rise. "Perhaps you *are* leading us into an empty wasteland to protect your home."

An angry knot formed in Batu's chest and he narrowed his eyes at the khahan. "My home is where I stand," he said sharply, repeating one of the Tuigan's favorite mottos. "If I am no longer trusted here, I will find a different place to stand." He stood and reached for his *del*.

"Leave your coat on the post," the khahan ordered. "Around Chanar and the others, it is fine to be arrogant. But I am the khahan, and your pride is nothing to me. If we cannot speak freely between ourselves, our friendship is worthless."

Batu returned his coat to the hook, unimpressed by the Yamun's profession of friendship. He and the khahan had developed a certain rapport, but the renegade would hardly have described it as friendship. He still felt like a visitor in the Tuigan camp.

The fault was his, he knew. Batu dutifully spent his evenings drinking sour *kumiss* with Yamun and the khans, but he made poor company. Though it had been close to three months since he had learned of his family's fate, he still had not accepted the loss. He could not shake the feeling that he was just on campaign, that he would soon return to his home in Chukei to find Wu waiting and his children an inch taller than when he had last seen them.

That could never happen, of course, but the realization did not change what his heart felt. On most nights he was so lonely he could only fall asleep by pretending that his family still lived, or by drinking so much *kumiss* that the slaves had to carry him back to his own *yurt*. It was a terrible circle: the more he thought of his family, the more he withdrew from his Tuigan companions. The more he withdrew from them, the more he thought of Wu and Ji and Yo.

The fighting to which Batu had hoped to dedicate himself, and which had been his reason for joining the Tuigan, had not materialized. Anxious to reach the kingdoms of the west, the khahan had led his army through the barren wastes of the horse plains. After passing the smoking peaks that marked the end of the territory known to the Tuigan, Yamun had turned the responsibility for guiding the army over to Batu.

Realizing that he had lost himself in his thoughts and was ignoring his commander, Batu turned his attention to the khahan. "You wished to see me?"

Yamun motioned to a nearby pillow. "Come and sit with me, or must I wait until Chanar's return for lively company?"

The Tuigan ruler was trying to use Chanar's rivalry with Batu to draw the Shou's thoughts away from his family. It was a trick the khahan had tried many times before. The tactic would never work, for Chanar's rivalry was one-sided. Batu did not care to play at politics with the lanky general. It was not a game he had enjoyed in Shou Lung, and he had no intention of concerning himself with it now.

Without responding to the khahan's barbed question, Batu took his place. As the renegade sat, the Tuigan ruler observed, "You are not the man I fought in Shou Lung."

"How do you mean?" Batu asked, adjusting his cushion.

"The man I fought in Shou Lung did not fear death," the khahan replied.

Batu absentmindedly accepted a cup of *kumiss* from a quiverbearer. "My contempt for death has not changed," the Shou responded. "I fear nothing."

"I know," the khahan said. "That is why Chanar is leading the scouts and you are here with me."

Batu scowled, for the khahan had touched upon a sore point. After two months of crossing the frozen deserts between Shou Lung and their present location, the Tuigan armies had reached a range of high mountains that seemed to block further progress. It had taken Batu's scouts several days to locate a narrow pass.

Yamun had sent five thousand men through the gap to reconnoiter the lands beyond. Batu had wanted to lead the expedition, but the khahan had sent Chanar instead.

That had been seven days ago, and the renegade had been quietly fuming about the decision ever since. Now that the khahan seemed willing to discuss the matter, Batu was determined to find out why he had been overlooked.

The renegade asked, "Why should my fearlessness disqualify me for command?"

"As you say, you no longer fear anything—including defeat."

"What?" Batu demanded. "How can you say such a thing?"

"It is true," the Tuigan ruler retorted, pointing a dirt-covered finger at the Shou. "Do not make the mistake of believing I am blind to the strife between Chanar and you. I have seen how you allow him to turn others against you, provided he is careful not to offend your honor."

The khahan picked a curd out of his cup and paused to chew it. Finally, he continued, "If that is how you want things to be, it is not my place to interfere. All I can say is that the general I fought in Shou Lung would not hide behind his memories, especially not from a petty rival like Chanar." The khahan spoke with a deliberately contemptuous tone.

"Do not think I will accept an insult lightly, even from you," Batu hissed. The Shou had no sooner uttered his threat than the Kashik guards drew their sabers and started forward.

Without taking his steely eyes off Batu, the khahan waved his guards away. "Of course, you should be killed for that," he said, "but that is what you want, is it not? I will not make dying so easy for you."

Yamun fell silent, then furrowed his brow as if recalling a distant memory. "When you came to me," he said, "you said it was because you had an appetite for war."

"That has not changed," Batu replied.

The khahan regarded the renegade Shou with a judgmental air. "Know this, then: if you wish to sate your appetite in my service, you must stop using your past to shield yourself from Chanar's rivalry."

Batu's first instinct was to be angry with Yamun. The khahan was clearly telling him to forget about his family, and that was something the Shou would never do. After Ting's execution, Batu had vowed to honor his dead family as long as he lived, and he had taken great care to make sure others knew that he would avenge even the slightest insult to their memories.

Still, the khahan's blunt order was not entirely misplaced and Batu knew it. As Yamun said, the renegade had been using his vow as a shield—not to protect himself from Chanar, but to protect himself from the truth.

Batu had often told his men that soldiers were dead men. As such, they had no business with families. Eventually, every soldier would perish on the battlefield, leaving behind lonely wives and children. It was a truth Batu had known all along, but he had always told himself that this axiom did not apply to him. If he fell, his family would not have suffered financially, so the general had always believed his death would be no more than an inconvenience. Now, he saw that he had been wrong. Wu's anguish and Ji's and Yo's grief would have been no easier for them to bear than his own sorrow was for him. It had been wrong to expect them to suffer such hardship on his behalf. Batu understood now that the day he had fallen in love was the day that he should have laid aside his weapons.

Yet, that had never been an option he would have chosen. The first time he had picked up a sword, Batu had decided to become a soldier. He had never known anything else, and had never wanted to. Instead of laying his weapons aside, Batu realized, it would have been better to harden his heart against love—as he hardened it against the death and agony of those who served under him.

As he reflected on his past blindness, Batu slowly realized that the time had come for him to command again. It was true that he had been wrong to take a family. Having taken one, it was equally true that he had been wrong to continue life as a soldier. But those were errors that he had made in the past. By refusing to face them now, he was shaming himself and minimizing the sacrifice that his family had made on his behalf. If Batu was to venerate his wife and children properly, he had to stop using their memories to shield him from his own guilty feelings. He had to start living again.

The renegade waved the quiverbearer to his side, then gave the servant his *kumiss* cup. "Take this away and get me some water."

The khahan raised an eyebrow. "Are you feeling ill?" he asked.

Batu shook his head. "No. It's time I started keeping a clear head."

The khahan smirked. "Don't get carried away. Chanar Ong Kho isn't that much of a rival."

Batu snorted. "I'm not worried about Chanar," he said. "I want to be ready for command when it's time to fight."

"Don't get ahead of yourself," the khahan warned. "You *will* have to deal with Chanar."

Yamun remained silent for several moments. Finally, he changed the subject and said, "Since you have decided to keep a clear head, let me make use of it and ask your advice."

"Certainly."

"I am thinking that if Chanar had found anything beyond the mountains, we would have heard about it by now." The khahan absentmindedly swirled the contents of his cup.

Batu did not hazard his own opinion. It was clear that the Mighty One's mood had shifted, but he did not know to where. Undoubtedly, Yamun was leading up to something.

"While we sit here, the snows only grow deeper and the men feel more restless," the khahan added, looking into his cup.

"This is true," Batu agreed. In the last week alone, more than ten thousand men had left camp, claiming the need to return to their clans, their *ordus*, to see that their families were fed through the winter. Although both Yamun and Batu knew that the real reason for the exodus was sheer boredom, the khahan had allowed them to go. He was a perceptive commander who knew that resentful men made poor warriors. Besides, once he sent word back to the plains that the battle had been joined, recruits would come streaming across the snowy waste by the thousands.

"I am thinking we should take the army and follow Chanar through the gap," Yamun said, still studying the contents of his cup.

"It is certainly possible that nothing lies beyond the mountains," Batu ventured. "But I would not want to gamble all my armies on it. After passing the gap, we could easily be cut off and destroyed."

"By what?" the khahan snapped, looking up from the study of his *kumiss*. "Since you advised me to leave Shou Lung, we have not seen a hundred men in one place, much less a kingdom that could field an army. The men are saying that I am lost or afraid."

"There is a great difference between fear and caution," Batu countered.

Yamun pointed at the renegade, then thumped his own chest. "You and I know this," he said. "But our soldiers do not. To them, inaction is cowardice."

Batu knew that the khahan spoke the truth. The men in most armies would have been elated to rest for a week, but not so with the Tuigan. They seemed born to ride and to fight, and were at their most miserable when not doing one or the other.

"Great Khahan," Batu said. "The courage of the Tuigan warrior is legend, but he is no less vulnerable to an ambush than any other soldier."

"Then you advise against following Chanar through the gap?"

Though he knew his answer would not please the khahan, Batu did not hesitate. "I do, though I appreciate your uneasiness at letting Chanar out of sight for so long."

The khahan allowed himself a wry smile at the remark,

then returned to the business at hand. "You have always been cautious, Batu. While you scheme and reconnoiter, I attack. That is why I drove all the way to Shou Kuan when I invaded your country."

Batu saw no purpose in telling the khahan that letting the Tuigan reach Shou Kuan had been part of his plan. He also saw no purpose in arguing, for Yamun had decided to move through the gap long before summoning his Shou general. By debating further, Batu stood to gain nothing. A better approach was to help the khahan develop a plan that allowed for the possibility of escape if trouble arose.

"Khahan," Batu said, "your wisdom is infinite, and if you think the time to move has come, I cannot argue—"

Batu was interrupted when a Kashik stepped through the *yurt's* entrance. "General Chanar returns," the guard reported.

The man who followed the Kashik hardly resembled the arrogant khan who had left camp seven days ago. Chanar's hat was missing, and the shaven circle atop his head was red and peeling from sunburn. His face was haggard and drawn, with a grayish complexion and deep circles beneath his eyes. The tattered remnants of a *del* were draped over his shoulders, and Batu saw a piece of yellow metal glittering through the ripped left pocket. The khan lacked several pieces of armor. What remained had been so severely beaten that it was full of gaping holes where metal plates had fallen off.

Chanar stepped forward and kneeled, filling the *yurt* with the unmistakable stench of sulfur and smoke. "I have returned, Khahan."

When he saw Yamun frown at the sorry sight, Batu dared to interject, "Barely, from all appearances."

Chanar's face reddened, but the khahan paid no attention to the affront. "Rise and report," the Tuigan ruler said, neglecting to offer his weary subordinate a seat or a cup of *kumiss*.

Casting a sinister glance in Batu's direction, Chanar returned to his feet. "There is a rich kingdom beyond the mountains," he began.

The khahan looked annoyed. "It took seven days to report this?"

Chanar grimaced and looked away for an instant. When he turned his gaze back to the khahan's, he said, "No, Great Khahan. I was *exploring* the kingdom in order to make a more complete report."

"Your orders were to scout and report," Yamun Khahan snapped, "not to *explore*. By your appearance, I would say your disobedience got you in trouble. What happened?"

Chanar immediately pointed at Batu. "It was his fault," the Tuigan said. "He sent us into a trap!"

The khahan raised an eyebrow. "What kind of trap?"

"Magic!" Chanar hissed. "It was everywhere—stinking clouds that choked man and beast, fire falling from the sky, wolves that walked and used swords like men. It was only through my great skill that I escaped with a *jagun*."

"A *jagun!*" the khahan roared, hurling his cup over the general's head. "I send you into the mountains with five thousand men and you return with a hundred!"

Chanar weathered the storm gracefully, and Batu realized the Tuigan had been expecting it. After the khahan stopped yelling, Chanar said, "As I said, the Shou sent us into a trap. We were ambushed as soon as we left the valley."

"On whom did you blame your failures before I joined the khahan's armies?" Batu countered.

"I didn't mean to offend you," Chanar responded smugly, barely sparing a glance for the Shou. "I only meant that you made a mistake and did not appreciate the position you were placing us in."

The renegade understood the khan's insidious plan. It had been Yamun, not Batu, who had sent the scouts into the pass. Nevertheless, Chanar was blaming the Shou, hoping to provide the khahan with a convenient scapegoat for what appeared to be a disastrous decision. In addition, he had constructed his arguments in such a way that Batu either looked like a traitor for sending the patrol into an ambush, or an idiot for not realizing that there might be one. At the same time, the Tuigan general had neatly sidestepped the central issue, which was that he and his men were the ones who were supposed to be searching out the ambushes.

Batu suspected that Yamun was as aware of Chanar's tactic as he himself. Nevertheless, bearing in mind the khahan's earlier comments about Chanar's rivalry, the renegade decided to turn the tables on the haggard khan. "General Chanar, you are a liar."

"How dare you!" Chanar responded. He turned to the khahan. "Must I continually endure this dog's abuse in your *yurt?*"

The khahan silenced the angry general with a gesture, then turned to Batu. "It is a terrible insult to call a man a liar to his face," he said. "Perhaps you wish to rethink your words?"

"No," Batu responded, staring straight at Chanar. "I can prove what I say, if you will ask Chanar to empty his pockets."

Chanar frowned. His hand drifted toward the left pocket of his *del* and he seemed worried. Batu knew he had caught his rival off-guard. The Tuigan had clearly not expected to be searched.

"Will you do this, Chanar?" the Mighty One asked.

Although the khahan phrased the request as a question, Chanar had no choice except to comply. Biting his lip, he reached into his pocket. He withdraw a handful of gold coins and a four-spoked golden wheel beset with rare gems—the crest of some religious or military order. Even from several yards away, Batu could see that the thing was worth a fortune.

"I brought these for you, Great Khahan," Chanar said, thinking on his feet. "They are but small samples of the wealth beyond the mountains."

"How did you come by them?" Yamun demanded, motioning Chanar forward.

"I took them off an enemy," the haggard man responded, giving his commander the golden wheel.

"Only a fool would take something so heavy and of such

value into battle," Batu declared.

Hefting the wheel, the khahan said, "So it would seem."

"You took it while looting," Batu continued, his eyes fixed on Chanar's snarling form. "No doubt, that is when you were really ambushed."

Chanar turned back to the khahan. "Nobody calls me a liar. I demand the right to avenge this insult!"

"Gladly," Batu responded, rising.

The khahan flung the golden wheel aside. "No!" he stormed. "I will not be dishonored by such behavior!" The Tuigan ruler stood. "We have been sitting too long. Our tempers have grown short with boredom, and we all long to feel the wind in our hair. It is clear that a strong enemy lies in our path, for five thousand Tuigan do not die easily, whether they are ambushed or not."

Yamun looked from Chanar to Batu, scowling at each man in turn. "Chanar is a Tuigan khan and a cunning leader. Batu has earned my respect on the battlefield, something no enemy has ever done. You are both my honored generals, yet you are more concerned with fighting each other than our enemies."

The khahan shook his head and walked away from the pair. "How should I choose between you?"

"I know," Batu said.

"How?" demanded Chanar.

Smiling confidently, Batu said, "I will take five *minghans*, the same number of troops as Chanar had, and blaze a trail through the mountains. If I and my five thousand troops fail, I will be Chanar's quiverbearer, honor-bound to follow his orders even though it means death."

"And if you succeed?" the khahan asked, turning around to face his quarreling subordinates.

"I will be Batu's quiverbearer," Chanar said, grinning confidently, "honor-bound to serve him even though it means death."

"Good," the khahan said. "I bear witness to your challenge and the wagers placed on it. Let all who question you know that this is done by the word of the khahan."

– 19 –

The Illustrious Battle

A tremendous crack sounded from the mountainside, and a bright light flared to Batu's right. Kicking free of his stirrups, he leaped out of the saddle just as a blinding flash struck the horse. A shockwave jolted the renegade so hard that his teeth snapped together. As he slammed to the ground, the breath fled his lungs and a deafening boom set the earth itself to trembling. The discordant smells of ozone and scorched horse-hide filled the air, then his mount's carcass collapsed across his lower body.

At first Batu thought that his legs had been crushed, then that he was blind, and finally that he was deaf. For several moments, he lay motionless and isolated, his only connection to the world the cold mud beneath his face and the dead weight of his horse across his thighs. Finally, the pressure on his legs eased, his ears started to ring, and the white before his eyes faded to shades of gray. A pair of hands grasped his shoulders and dragged him to his feet.

"Commander! Are you hurt?"

Though it seemed muffled and distant, Batu recognized the voice. It belonged to Jochibi, the grisled veteran whom Yamun had assigned to him as second-in-command. Jochibi's true task, the renegade knew, was to act as the khahan's spy and insure that Batu did not betray his Tuigan master. Fortunately, the task did not conflict with serving as an advisor and adjutant, and the two men had developed a respect for each other.

As Batu regained his feet, he said, "Nothing feels broken." His vision had returned to normal, and he could see his subordinate's face. Jochibi's braids were streaked with gray. On the Tuigan's cheeks were parallel, self-inflicted scars that prevented his beard from growing.

"Another near miss," Jochibi observed.

"Yes," the Shou replied. A hundred yards away, fifty of his bodyguard had already reached the base of the mountain and dismounted. They were alternately firing arrows and clambering up the steep slope in pursuit of Batu's attacker, one of the enemy's red-robed wizards.

The wizard was supported by a dozen of the huge dog-men that the prisoners called gnolls. Easily eight feet tall, the furry brutes stood on their hind legs and used their hands as men did. However, they had the ferocious faces of huge, heavy-snouted dogs, complete with wet black noses, pointed ears, and long, vicious teeth.

As Batu watched, the red-clad wizard left his hiding place and fled along the mountainside, leaving the gnolls to cover his retreat.

"I wish I knew how they were picking me out," Batu said. Though he was dressed exactly the same as his subordinates, it was the fifth time an enemy wizard had appeared behind the lines and tried to assassinate him.

"Magic," Jochibi responded. He grabbed a handful of earth, then kissed it in a superstitious attempt to neutralize the effects of the unnatural art. "The enemy has too much of it. It scares the men and makes them fight like women."

"They may be afraid of magic, but they're hardly fighting like women," Batu replied, pointing at the guards charging up the mountainside. The gnolls were raining arrows down on them, using bows so long and powerful that a normal man could not draw one. The deadly shower did not slow the Tuigan at all.

Jochibi observed the charge for a moment, then spat on the ground. "Tuigan can run faster."

"Perhaps," Batu responded, admiring his subordinate's spirit. "Get me another horse. I want to be at the front of the column when we break out of this deathtrap."

Jochibi bit his lip. "The khahan's orders were to bring you back alive."

"My orders are to get a horse!" Batu snapped.

Jochibi looked away.

"I don't want to miss the real fighting. Do it!"

The Tuigan officer flinched under the sharpness of Batu's command, then said, "By Teylas's breath, you don't have to get so angry. I don't want to miss the fun any more than you." He turned to obey.

While Batu waited for his officer to return, he studied the battlefield. He was in the same pass that Chanar had explored. The gap was sixty miles long and between five and fifteen miles wide. It had taken less than a day to ride through the first half of the canyon, but enemy ambushes had slowed their progress through the second half. It had taken more than two days to cover the last thirty miles.

The army was now within a half-mile of the gap's end. The scouts had reported that an enemy force twice as large as Batu's blocked the exit. As it was still early afternoon, the renegade intended to destroy the defending army before evening. By nightfall, he would be riding into the plains beyond.

Batu smiled at the audacity of his plan. If he had been commanding a Shou army, he would never have tried to do so much. When he had suggested his bold tactics to Jochibi, however, the horsewarrior had simply shrugged and asked why his commander thought there might be a problem.

Even allowing for their horses, the nomads were different from any *pengs* Batu had ever commanded. What other men considered impossible, the nomads took for granted, and what the Tuigan considered impossible did not exist. Batu was thrilled to command even a small force of such troops. He could hardly wait until he led them into the main battle.

Jochibi returned with an extra mount. It was a black stallion with fiery eyes and barding covering its shoulders and flanks. Patting the horse's armor, the scar-cheeked warrior said, "Judging from the attacks on you so far, your horse is going to need all the protection it can get when we reach the front lines."

"No doubt," Batu said, climbing into the beast's gilded saddle. "Where did you get this?"

"It belonged to one of the khahan's sons," Jochibi replied. "He won't be needing it."

"Dead?"

Jochibi nodded. "He was in the point *jagun.*"

Batu grimaced. That entire patrol had been wiped out by an enemy ambush. "You should of told me!" he snapped, anticipating the khahan's wrath.

Sensing Batu's thoughts, Jochibi shrugged. "There's no need for worry. Odelu died in battle," he said. "Besides, the khahan has many sons. If he blamed a general every time one fell in battle, there would be nobody left to command his armies."

Shaking his head, Batu said, "Let's see what's happening up front." He spurred Odelu's horse forward.

A few minutes later, Batu and his escorts reached the front line. There, the snow-covered valley floor was about ten miles wide. Four thousand Tuigan were stretched out across the entire distance, their line marked by a band of mud churned up by the horses' hooves. The riders were spaced fifteen to twenty feet apart, so the enemy's magical spells would not affect too many men at once. The horse-warriors rode back and forth in small circles, firing at the enemy from their saddles. The remainder of Batu's men, consisting of five fresh *jaguns* and five that he had used to flush out the ambushers, sat behind the lines as a ready reserve.

The enemy formation was much different. Though he could not see their entire line, Batu knew from scouting reports that there were at least ten thousand gnolls at the exit to the valley. Their line was roughly six hundred feet away, and they were gathered in tightly grouped companies of fifty. These companies were spaced every five hundred feet or so.

When the scouts had reported the enemy deployment, Batu had at first found it strange. After considering the long range of the gnoll archers, however, he had seen the wisdom of their plan. Each group was deployed within arrow range of the next one, so that they had interlocking fields of fire. When any one company was attacked, the two companies to either side could offer support. By clever positioning of his forces, the enemy had effectively tripled his firepower.

Batu considered concentrating his troops for a spearhead charge that would drive through the thin line, but quickly rejected the idea. By the time he gathered his forces, the enemy would see what was coming. They would allow him to charge, but the gnoll's flanks would close in behind the column and engulf it.

As he studied the situation, Batu occasionally saw orange fireballs or white bolts of lightning leap from the center of a gnoll company.

"More magic," Batu observed, pointing at one of the flashes.

Jochibi cringed. "It's enough to frighten a man."

"At least to test him," Batu replied, grinning. He had never before faced an enemy with so much magic, and he was relishing the challenge of countering it.

Jochibi frowned. "Magic is nothing to take pleasure in."

"Nor is it anything to fear," Batu answered, scowling at his adjutant's superstition. "Dead is dead. What difference does it make whether you're hit by an arrow or a lightning bolt?"

Jochibi seemed to relax. "I hadn't thought of it that way."

Batu returned his gaze to the battlefield. After a moment's study, he noted, "Their bows have more range than ours, so fighting from a distance like this is useless. We'll have to charge."

"Agreed," Jochibi responded. "What about their flying horses?"

"Flying horses?" Batu asked, astonished.

Jochibi pointed at the horizon, where a flock of specks was circling far behind enemy lines. "Perhaps they're not horses, I can't tell. They are definitely flying, though. I'd be concerned about them, if I were you."

Batu squinted at the specks, but could hardly identify them as flying cavalry. "They're just vultures waiting to pick the enemy's bones."

Jochibi frowned. "Since when do vultures fly in formation?" he asked. "Besides, they're too big to be vultures."

"You can see all that?" Batu asked.

Jochibi raised his brow. "Can't you?"

The Shou shook his head in amazement. "You're sure?"

"Of course," Jochibi responded. "I'd say there are about three hundred of them."

Several guards lent their support to Jochibi's contention, getting into a heated debate about whether the number was closer to two hundred or five hundred. Although he had always considered his vision perfect, Batu knew better than to doubt Tuigan eyesight. Over the past two months, their scouts had pointed out many distant landmarks and ridden down hundreds of deer that Batu had not seen.

"They must be holding the fliers in reserve," Batu said, a wave of excitement coursing through his body. The enemy commander, whoever he was, was good—perhaps even as good as himself. The coming battle promised to be one to remember.

"They're trying to lay another trap for us," Jochibi warned.

"A good plan," Batu observed. "If not for your sharp eyes, it would have worked."

The Shou returned his gaze to the battlefield, searching for a way to turn the enemy's cleverness against him. For the first time in months, his mind was completely absorbed in something other than his own feelings.

Finally, Batu's eyes lit on the steep walls of the valley. An idea occurred to him. "Send half the reserve to each side of the valley," he said. "They are to climb as far up the mountainsides as they can, taking their bows and all their arrows."

Jochibi raised an eyebrow. "What do you have in mind?"

"I've seen the khahan execute a false retreat," the Shou answered. "I assume this is a standard tactic?"

"It is."

"Good," Batu replied. He did a little quick math, then said, "We'll attack each gnoll company with two *arbans*."

Batu did not like the odds. An *arban* consisted of ten men, so that meant his troops would be outnumbered by a little more than two-to-one as they attacked. However, the khahan was fond of bragging that one of his warriors was a match for any four enemies. Now, the Tuigan would have a chance to prove it.

The renegade Shou continued explaining his plan. "After we've convinced the enemy of our sincerity, we'll feign a rout and disengage. Our retreat path will be along the canyon walls."

Jochibi smiled. "Beneath the arrow cover offered by our reserves."

"If this plan is to work, timing is everything," Batu continued. "We must begin the retreat at the center. You'll ride toward the northern side of the canyon, and I'll ride toward the southern. As we pass each group of soldiers, the drummers will signal for them to disengage. It will be important for us not to turn away from the gnoll line until we've collected the last of our troops from both flanks."

Batu paused to allow Jochibi to ask questions. When the Tuigan remained silent, the Shou finished explaining his plan. "The flying cavalry will almost certainly pursue, and we'll lead them beneath the arrows of our reserves, too."

Jochibi frowned and rubbed the back of his neck. Finally he said, "I don't like it. You're splitting the army. It's too risky."

"It is an intricate maneuver," Batu allowed, a note of eagerness creeping into his voice. "But the reward is worth it. As we ride in front of the enemy line, we'll shower them with arrows. By the time we reach the end, we'll have twenty archers for every target. Their flanks will be annihilated!"

"Only if every detail goes well," Jochibi objected. He met his superior's gaze with steady eyes. "I hesitate to send good men to their deaths on such a chancy plan."

"These men are soldiers!" Batu snapped. "I would not think a Tuigan needed to be reminded of this."

The adjutant scowled. "As you wish," he replied.

Jochibi turned and passed Batu's plan along to five messengers, being careful not to let his own doubts show. After the messengers rode off, Batu and the Tuigan officer waited in bitter silence. Finally, twenty minutes later, the messengers returned with confirmations from the commanders of the five *minghans* that made up the five-thousand-man army.

Batu drew his sword. Instead of the heavy *tao* he had taken from Kei Bot, he now carried the slightly curved saber of a Tuigan horseman. It felt warm and natural in his hand.

He turned to Jochibi, who was staring at the battle lines in stoic silence. "Can I rely on you?"

Jochibi drew his gleaming weapon, then kissed its golden quillon. "Your boldness frightens me, Shou. But the orders are issued. I'll do what I must to win the battle."

Batu remembered a similar assurance from Kei Bot. That assurance had turned into betrayal and cost him the victory at Shou Kuan. Jochibi was no Kei Bot, however. The Tuigan had always seemed a selfless and dedicated officer, so Batu thought he could believe the man's words.

"You are a good soldier, Jochibi," Batu said. "With your support, this plan will work—I promise."

"That's the emptiest promise anyone ever made to me," the Tuigan said, smiling grimly. "If your plan fails, who'll be left to punish you for breaking your word?"

"There's no place in the eighteen hells where I could hide from you, I'm sure," Batu replied.

With that, Batu spurred his horse forward. Screaming the Tuigan war cry, the hundred members of his bodyguard followed. As they passed through the forward line, the drummers sounded the advance. Within a minute thousands of barbarian warriors were galloping toward the enemy in a long thin line.

Almost immediately, crude arrows began to rain down on the Tuigan. Fortunately, the gnolls were not nearly as accurate with their weapons as the horsewarriors were with theirs. Out of the corner of his eyes, Batu saw only a few men falling, and it was a rare thing for a gray shaft to flash past his own face.

The Tuigan drums stirred a wild exhilaration in man and beast alike. Nevertheless, Batu did not feel carried away by his mount, as he had at Shou Kuan. Even with his bodyguard behind him, there were far fewer horses crowded into a small area, and the Tuigan were experts at controlling their mounts. The big black stallion simply kept pace with the other horses, advancing at a steady, rhythmic gait.

At one hundred yards, the Tuigan archers began to return the gnolls' fire, and to guide their horses toward companies of dog-men. Though the horsewarriors were firing on the move, many of their arrows found their marks. A few of the furry brutes began to drop, clawing furiously at feathered shafts protruding from their simple leather armor. To Batu's amazement, others simply broke off the shafts and nocked another arrow in their own bows. The archery of the wounded gnolls was weak and inaccurate, but Batu was impressed that they continued to fight at all.

As the Tuigan neared the enemy lines, Batu looked toward the flying specks Jochibi had pointed out. They had already moved closer, and the renegade could see that each one looked like a tiny "V." For him to see their wings from so far away, he realized, the creatures had to be much larger than any bird. They were flying toward the center of the battlefield, probably hoping to break the Tuigan line.

Batu smiled. They could not have picked a strategy better suited to his plan.

The sudden eruption of a fireball jarred him out of his elation. A glob of flame appeared to his left, engulfing four riders in its orange sphere. Batu's horse whinnied in fright and stumbled, but the Shou kicked its flanks and the beast recovered its footing.

A moment later, a dozen red streaks flared out of the closest gnoll company. They flashed past the Shou's head, each one striking a rider and leaving a burning hole in the man's chest. The magicians had started to do their work.

Batu glimpsed a red robe in the company directly ahead. He pointed at it. "The wizard!" he cried, screaming as loud as he could to make himself heard over the drums. "Shoot the wizard!"

No sooner had he screamed than a dozen Tuigan arrows flew directly at the figure. They smashed into an invisible barrier and fell to the ground. In the next instant, the wizard vanished.

It did not matter, for magic would not stop the charge now. The Tuigan were so close that the gnolls—at least the ones who still stood—were dropping their bows in favor of battle-axes and morning stars. Batu noted that his own troops were holstering their bows and drawing sabers. In another instant, the charging horsewarriors would smash into the gnoll companies and the melee would begin.

Batu used that instant to check the progress of the flying cavalry. The formation was so close that he could see the mounts did not resemble horses at all. Each beast had the head, wings, and forequarters of a giant eagle, while the tail and hindquarters were those of a huge lion. Although he had heard stories about such creatures and knew they were called griffins, he had always believed the animals to be little more than imaginary.

On each griffin's back rode a red-robed wizard and a rider armed with a lance and bow. Batu noted with pleasure that neither the rider nor his passenger wore armor, undoubtedly to avoid burdening the griffin with extra weight.

He had no more time to study the fliers. Batu's horse crashed into a gnoll company, and he was engulfed in a mass of gray fur. A pair of huge hairy hands reached for him from the left side. The dog-man's breath filled the air with the stench of carrion and half-digested meat. The beast was barking commands to another gnoll in a coarse, guttural language.

Batu slashed at the beast's hands. A huge fist fell to the

ground, leaving nothing but a bloody stump behind. The wounded gnoll growled and lunged for the Shou. The renegade pulled his foot from the stirrup and kicked the dogman square in the forehead. The blow would have felled a man, but the gnoll only snarled and knocked Batu's leg aside.

Batu slashed with his sword again, this time opening a gash in the beast's hairy throat. The gnoll roared, then slapped his good hand over the wound and backed away. The Shou turned to his right, just in time to see the flanged head of an iron morning star sailing at his face. Batu ducked, but knew his reflexes would be too slow.

A sword flashed past his ear, then connected with the morning star's chain. The deadly ball looped around the blade, a flange slicing Batu's cheek open. The rest of the weapon missed his face by less than an inch.

In the next instant, Jochibi wrenched the morning star from the hands of Batu's attacker, then urged his horse forward to trample the growling brute.

"Thanks, Jo—"

Before Batu completed his acknowledgement, a powerful hand seized his belt. Already unsteady from his narrow brush with the morning star, the Shou nearly lost his balance and slipped from his horse. Grasping the saddle's pommel, he jerked himself back into the seat, then kicked at his unseen attacker without removing his foot from the stirrup. His heel connected with an armored chest, then Batu swung around and ran his saber through the yellow-toothed gnoll's throat.

As he pulled his blade free, a shadow passed over the battle. Six golden balls of magical energy flashed out of the sky, killing six men. Batu looked up and saw a griffin swooping low overhead. The wizard atop the monster held his hand outstretched and pointed at the melee below him. The griffin's other rider allowed the beast to swoop safely past the battle, then wheeled it about for another pass.

At the same time, Batu saw a gnoll step toward him. He spurred his horse, and it pushed its way forward to where

Jochibi had just separated a beast's head from its shoulders. All around the Tuigan, the ground was carpeted with fallen gnolls. Nevertheless, their fellows pressed the attack, wildly swinging their maces and morning stars. Often, the dog-men had forsaken weapons altogether and were using bare hands to drag the Tuigan from their saddles.

They were meeting with entirely too much success. In Batu's group alone, nearly half the horses were riderless. Farther away, in the companies to either side of the renegade's, the story appeared to be much the same. He saw many empty horses and, fortunately, plenty of fallen gnolls. Near each group were three griffins bearing a wizard and a rider. While the riders guided the flying mounts, the mages flung various magical bolts, beams, and rays into the melee.

The gnoll that Batu had avoided earlier came up behind him. Just as the beast swung its morning star, the Shou turned his mount to meet the attack. The spiked ball bounced of the black horse's barding, then the stallion reared and thrashed the gnoll with its front hooves. When the horse dropped back to the ground, Batu finished the cringing dog-man with a swift chop to its collarbone.

"Time to leave!" Batu shouted, trying to make himself heard above the clamor of battle. When Jochibi showed no sign of hearing him, the Shou slapped is subordinate's leg with the flat of his blade. The grisled Tuigan twisted around, his guard raised. "I thought you were dead!"

"I am," Batu responded. "But the judges of the hells have allowed me time for a few battles more."

Another griffin swooped overhead, and a fireball erupted on the edge of the company. A half-dozen men, horses, and gnolls screamed in agony as the orange flames engulfed them.

"By now, the enemy should be convinced of our sincerity," Batu said.

"Agreed," Jochibi responded. "Let's go!"

Without waiting for Batu's command, the Tuigan spurred his horse and pushed his way out of the melee. An instant later, Batu turned his horse in the opposite direction and broke free of the fray. As the renegade and his adjutant bounded away, the nearest drummers silenced their instruments.

Within moments, the area was empty of Tuigan, and the Shou was riding past the next group of gnolls with more than twenty warriors at his back. As the drummer assigned to this melee saw Batu pass, he silenced his instrument. The horsewarriors disengaged and joined the retreat.

Batu could not help but admire the precision of the maneuver. As the time came, each man executed his orders flawlessly, regardless of what else was happening at the moment. Even in the heat of battle, there was none of the confusion common to Shou maneuvers. Batu continued past melee after melee collecting his troops with drill-field precision.

As expected, the retreat took the enemy by surprise. For several minutes the griffin riders did not pursue. By the time the airborne cavalry reorganized themselves and turned to the chase, Batu was only two miles from the valley walls. With him rode nearly five hundred warriors that he had collected from the melees along the line.

Even in retreat, his troops were dealing a serious blow to the gnolls. As their fellows disengaged and joined the retreating army, the Tuigan archers, accustomed to firing on the gallop, unleashed a volley of arrows. The deadly shafts rained down on the defenders like a hail storm. The massed fire was so accurate that barely a handful of gnolls escaped each time the archers fired on an enemy company.

As the Tuigan approached the next melee, it was the enemy who tried to disengage and run. Having seen what had happened when the mounted archers passed the last company, the gnoll officers had no wish to meet a similar fate. The Tuigan, however, were accustomed to battling fleeing adversaries and did not allow them to escape. As the gnolls turned their backs, the horsemen tarried long enough to cut them down, then joined the rest of their fellows.

The same thing happened as the riders approached the next three companies. Batu began to fear that the efficiency of his archers had alerted the flying cavalry to his plan. The Tuigan were only a mile and a half from the canyon walls, and the griffins still had not caught up.

With less than a mile to go before reaching the flank, two hundred griffins finally gathered into a formation behind the barbarians. Unfettered by the presence of their own troops, the wizards showered the Tuigan with horrible, destructive magic. Walls of fire and ice appeared in the middle of the Tuigan retreat. Struggling to avoid the obstacles at a full gallop, dozens of men and horses tumbled to the ground. Black clouds rained death down on small numbers of riders. Once, twenty horses drifted high into the air, then came crashing back down on their fellows.

Four hundred yards from the canyon wall, the Tuigan retreat turned into a genuine rout. Under the withering, airborne attacks, the barbarian horsemen could no longer ignore their fear of magic. The last few gnoll companies escaped intact, but Batu was not concerned. His troops had already dealt so much destruction that the enemy army was ruined for all practical purposes.

Besides, the rout would only serve to draw the griffin riders into his trap, and that was worth the lives of a few dozen gnolls. If his plans were to succeed, the enemy fliers had to be so caught up in pursuit that they did not notice their danger until it was too late.

The Tuigan and their pursuers reached the canyon wall. The retreating horsemen turned east along the base of the mountains, just as Batu had planned. Looking around, the Shou estimated that he had perhaps a thousand riders with him. Assuming that Jochibi had a similar number on the other side the of the valley, that meant he had lost two thousand men to the gnolls and the magic. The number was a large one, but he knew the figure would have been a lot higher if Jochibi's sharp eyes had not spotted the griffin formation before the battle began.

They continued along the base of the canyon for several more minutes, the enemy in close pursuit. Batu saw no sign of his reserves on the canyon walls, but he had too much faith in the Tuigan warriors to doubt that they were there. A few moments later, the sweet music of twanging bow-strings filled the air, and the Shou twisted around in his saddle to see what had happened.

He was greeted by the sight of chaos in the air. Over a hundred wounded or dead griffins were dropping to the ground. Their panicked riders were leaping free or trying in vain to pull the beasts back into the air. The Tuigan reserves stood along the mountainside, their shoulders and heads still white from the snow that had hidden them only moments before.

As the renegade watched, the reserves fired their second volley. Every arrow found its mark. Another forty griffins plunged to the earth, six arrows apiece protruding from their throats and flanks. Those that remained airborne, no more than a dozen, turned and flew away toward the west.

Batu screamed for joy.

He gradually pulled back on his horse's reins and signaled his men to reverse directions. Even without the griffins in pursuit, it required more than two minutes to bring the retreat under control. Eventually, however, the Shou sent his soldiers back to finish the few griffin riders who had survived the ambush.

As Batu watched the barbarians dispatch the survivors, his heart filled with a warm feeling. The attack on the gnolls was the finest maneuver he had ever executed. He had decimated a force twice as large as his own, and he had eliminated the enemy's greatest tactical advantage, its flying cavalry.

A sensation of elation came over him. He had not experienced such a feeling since earning his promotion to first-degree general and winning Wu's hand. A pang of sadness struck Batu as he thought of his wife and then his children, but he no longer felt empty or lonely. They would always be a cherished part of his life, but the sense of fulfillment that he now experienced left no room for doubt: his destiny had always been to make war.

Perhaps, in joining the Tuigan, Batu was returning to the

people of his destiny. Like the fierce Tuigan, he had always been an impatient and forceful man, and he had always lacked the grace and elegance of the Shou race. It was possible that his great grandfather's blood still ran in his veins, that he would find a more fitting home with the Tuigan than he had ever found in Shou Lung. Only time would tell, he knew, but for now the renegade was content to ride with the horsewarriors.

Epilogue

I
t was an hour after dawn. Batu and Jochibi stood atop a hill at the mouth of the canyon, ankle deep in sugary snow. The canyon walls blocked their sight to the north and south, but the view west was clear.

A light snow had fallen during the night, spreading a blanket of unsullied white over yesterday's battlefield. The only apparent sign of the combat was a ribbon of frosty mounds where thousands of dead lay under their cold veil. From atop the hill, these mounds could be seen only because the dim morning sunlight cast small shadows on their western sides. It seemed as though some snow spirit, sensing that neither side would cremate the casualties, had come to spread a funeral shroud over their bodies.

Beyond the battle line stretched a vast plain, ideal ground for the Tuigan cavalry. It was blanketed with the same sugary snow as the hill, and sparkled in the sunlight as though carpeted with diamonds. At the far edge of the plain, perhaps fifty miles away, there was a band of blue that could only be a lake. On the other side of the lake rose a handful of jagged, cloud-colored shapes identifiable as distant mountains.

It was not the mountains that Batu and Jochibi were watching. Dozens of gray lines were inching their way across the plain, moving toward the Tuigan position at the mouth of the valley. Though Batu's eyes were not sharp enough to pick out any details, he was experienced enough to know the lines were enemy columns. He estimated their distance to be less than fifteen miles. Their strength had to be several thousand apiece.

"I count eighty-two columns, commander," Jochibi said, pointing his finger at the last one. "We'll never fight through all that. It looks like Chanar wins the wager after all."

"Chanar wins nothing," Batu said, studying the columns with a predatory curl to his lip. "We're not going back."

"That's madness!"

"Glorious madness," Batu responded, grinning. The enemy would cut them to pieces, but the Shou did not care. Yesterday, he had fought his illustrious battle. All that remained now was to achieve the impossible victory.

"This time, we truly don't stand a chance," Jochibi objected. "Even if there are only two thousand men in each column, they have more than a hundred and sixty thousand warriors."

"To be precise, one hundred eighty-seven thousand, six hundred and seventy-nine soldiers," said a strange voice.

Both Batu and Jochibi drew their swords and spun around to face the speaker. They came face-to-face with a gaunt, balding man. His black hair and beard were streaked with gray, and his red-rimmed eyes were burning with spite and malevolence. He slouched as if he were seated in a comfortable chair, but appeared to be floating in midair. Behind the speaker stood four more figures, three males and a voluptuous, sinister woman. All four wore the red robes of enemy wizards. The mages stood with their arms linked and their eyes closed in concentration.

Without hesitating a moment, both Batu and Jochibi swung their weapons. Their blades passed through the speaker's body as though it were a mirage.

The stranger threw back his head and laughed. It was a stiff and artificial cackle. "Your audacity continues to amaze me."

Eyeing each other in wary astonishment, Batu and Jochibi stepped away from the red-robed stranger.

"Who are you?" Batu demanded.

"Szass Tam, zulkir of Thay," the gaunt figure responded,

his face growing serious and menacing. "I assume you are the chief of this band of savages."

"You assume incorrectly," Batu said, casually dropping his sword to a low guard. "That honor belongs to the mighty Yamun Khahan, Illustrious Emperor of All Peoples."

The zulkir looked toward the east and squinted, as if trying to see something very distant. "Yamun Khahan, you say? Who is that with him—the fool who led the first attack on our lands?"

Again, Batu and Jochibi glanced at each other in astonishment. "Does he mean Chanar?" Jochibi half-whispered.

"Chanar," Szass repeated.

No sooner had he spoken than two heavy thuds sounded next to Batu. A pair of Tuigan curses followed.

The Shou turned to his right and saw the bewildered khahan seated in the snow. His dark brow was wrinkled in anger, and his jaw hung slack in astonishment. Next to the khahan sat Chanar, equally confused and angry.

"Great Khahan!" Jochibi gasped. Sheathing his sword, the scar-faced warrior stepped around Batu, grabbed the khahan's shoulders, and pulled him to his feet.

Regaining his composure, Yamun motioned Jochibi away, then asked Batu, "How did I come to be here?"

"I brought you," replied Szass Tam.

"That will be your last mistake," Chanar growled. In one swift motion, the Tuigan khan drew his sword and leaped at the zulkir. Chanar's blade passed through Szass's body, then the khan followed. He fell face-first into the snow and lay there perplexed and cursing.

"Do all your subjects respond to strangers in this belligerent manner?" Szass asked, addressing Yamun.

"Yes," Yamun said simply. He turned to Batu. "What is your report?"

Szass Tam would not be ignored. "He has decimated an army of ten thousand gnolls, and completely wiped out the Griffin Legion," the wizard responded. "He is quite an impressive commander."

"I have many more like him," the khahan said, reluctantly

granting Szass his attention.

"I doubt it," countered the zulkir, pointing at Chanar's prone form. "At least if that greedy oaf is any example."

Yamun eyed Chanar with a spiteful sneer. "He isn't."

Noting the khahan's hostility, Chanar returned to his feet and sheathed his sword. He scowled at Batu as if the Shou had personally arranged this embarrassment.

Addressing Szass Tam, the khahan asked, "Did you bring me here to talk about my generals, or do you want something?"

"Look out there," the zulkir said, pointing at the plain to the west. The gray lines were still crawling over the snow. "Nearly one hundred and ninety thousand men are marching against you, and we can summon more at a moment's notice."

"Then do it," Batu said. "Twice that number would not concern us."

The zulkir scowled at the Shou, then turned his attention back to the khahan. "Do you allow your subordinates to speak for you?"

"When they speak the truth," Yamun replied with a steady gaze. "We have nothing to fear from your pitiful nineteen *tumens*."

Szass Tam raised an condescending eyebrow. "Is that so?"

"Yes. At the other end of the canyon, over three hundred and fifty thousand warriors await the order to attack," the khahan proudly lied.

The zulkir glanced to the east, then turned back to Yamun. "I count ninety-seven thousand, four hundred and thirty-two, exclusive of the two thousand, seven hundred and thirty-six here with the Shou commander—somewhat less than the three hundred and fifty thousand you claim."

Yamun grimaced, then snapped, "I have no use for your counting, or your sorcery. We are traveling through your land. If you stand aside, we will take only the food and wine we need to live. If you stand in our way, not an infant will be spared our swords."

Szass listened to the threat with a patient smile, then said,

"Perhaps I should show you something." The zulkir stared at the snowy plain. "This is what will be in a week's time."

Suddenly an image of the khahan's one hundred thousand Tuigan warriors appeared at the base of the hill. They were all fully armed and prepared for battle. As Batu and the others watched, a powerfully built figure in *t'ie cha* armor rode out in front of the army.

"Khahan!" gasped Chanar, looking from the figure back to his commander. "That's you!"

Batu shared his rival's astonishment. Even from this distance, the figure was clearly the khahan. That meant they were watching an illusion, the Shou knew, but it looked so real that he could hardly force himself to disbelieve it.

The illusory khahan lifted his sword and gave the signal to charge. Using one of the favorite Tuigan battle formations, the entire line started forward. There were two ranks of heavy, armored cavalry in front and three ranks of unarmored cavalry in the rear. The charge gained momentum, and soon the Tuigan were streaking across the plain unopposed.

All at once, the first rank of horses crashed to the ground, spilling armored men in every direction. Where no enemy had been standing, a line of pikemen appeared. They drew their swords and began hacking the unhorsed cavalry to pieces.

The second Tuigan rank charged forward. A wall of fire erupted in their path. Those that did not perish in its flames pulled up short. Moments later, several artillery legions appeared on the Tuigan flanks. Trebuchets and catapults began raining boulders down on the line.

The barbarians responded by rushing their light cavalry around to outflank the artillery. No sooner had they broken formation than several legions of gnoll longbowmen appeared on their wings. Clouds of arrows began sailing into the light cavalry.

"Enough!" the khahan growled. "This is not real!"

The illusion faded immediately. An instant later, all that remained below the hill was the snow-covered battlefield.

Batu admired the artistry that had gone into conceiving the plan. From what the Shou knew of Tuigan tactics, Szass Tam had foreseen every detail correctly. "I look forward to battling you, Zulkir," Batu said, bowing slightly. "Your plan seems bold and ingenious."

"And it will no longer work," the khahan observed gruffly.

"Yes," Jochibi agreed, a note of suspicion in his voice. "Why reveal your intentions to us?"

An icy smile creased the zulkir's thin lips. "Because I have better things to do with your army than destroy it."

"This is not *your* army to do anything with, stillborn kid of a sickly goat!" Chanar interjected.

"Only a fool would need to be reminded of that, Chanar!" the khahan snapped. "Now be silent. I wish to hear the zulkir's words."

"Your wisdom is as magnificent as your title, Illustrious Emperor of All Peoples," the zulkir responded, a mocking glint in his eye. "I have shown you what will be if we fight. Now, let me show you what *could* be."

Again, the Tuigan army appeared at the base of the hill. This time, it was spread out over a much larger area, practically the entire plain. The terrain seemed strange. There were dozens of villages scattered around a small, unwalled city. Most of the hamlets east of the city, and the city itself, were burning. The barbarians were riding toward a lake on the western side of the plain. As they traveled, they paused only long enough to loot and set fire to every settlement they crossed.

As the armies moved forward, the zulkir said, "You are looking at Rashemen, a land on our northern border. We have been trying to destroy its people for many years, but a great lake lies between us and them.

"When you appeared out of the wastelands," the zulkir proceeded, "I thought you were nothing more than an army of thieves. Now that I have seen the cunning of your generals and the might of your army, I know I was mistaken."

The zulkir motioned at the field below. "You will be destroyed if you invade my land, which we call Thay. Still, it will not be an easy task, and the battle will greatly weaken us."

As Szass spoke, the illusory Tuigan forces continued to ride toward the lake. They crossed ground and moved at such an incredible pace that Batu knew he was seeing in minutes what would take days to accomplish in reality.

"While I was pondering this unpleasant thought," Szass continued, "it came to me that you are the tool we need to destroy Rashemen."

"We are nobody's tool!" the khahan objected.

The zulkir rolled his eyes in impatience, but said, "Of course not. I only meant to imply that together we might succeed where neither of us could alone."

"You may continue," the khahan said after a pause. "I am listening."

The zulkir smiled confidently. "Good. My proposal is this: Thay will attack Rashemen's southern flank. In the meantime, you will ride north, then invade Rashemen from the east. With her forces occupied in the south, there will be nothing to oppose you."

The Tuigan army reached the great lake on Rashemen's western edge and began to regroup.

"What do you get out of this?" Jochibi asked.

Szass looked toward the scar-faced officer. "A wise question," the zulkir acknowledged. "The answer, I hope, is Rashemen. As you ride through, you will rip her entrails out, leaving nothing but devastation in your wake. It will be an easy matter for us to follow through and finish the job."

"A treacherous plan," the khahan said thoughtfully. He turned to Batu. "What do you think?"

The Shou did not hesitate to answer. "I will fight wherever the Tuigan travel," he said. "But I think the greatest battles lie in Thay—"

"Along with the surest defeats," interrupted the zulkir.

"What does that matter?" Batu answered, shrugging. "In the end, every soldier falls on the same battlefield."

The khahan nodded. "Wisely spoken." He turned to Jochibi next. "You?"

"Thay is a deathtrap," he said, glancing at Batu. "Yet, how can we trust the zulkir to keep his word? How do we know that what he shows us is real?"

"If it was not, would I show you this?" the zulkir countered, pointing at the illusion.

Batu returned his attention to the mirage. Most of the Tuigan army had regrouped. They were camped on the lakeshore in the winter, and the wooden skeletons of a fleet of ships were just beginning to take shape. A moment later, a mass of weary and ragged looking soldiers appeared on the Tuigan's southern flank. They charged, taking the camp by surprise and pinning the barbarians against the lake's icy waters.

"Who are they?" the khahan demanded. "What is the meaning of this?"

The zulkir shrugged. "They are exhausted soldiers from Rashemen. As for the meaning, I don't know. Perhaps they are a routed army fleeing before our advance. Perhaps Thay has lost the war, and the soldiers of Rashemen have rushed north to deal with your invasion. I cannot answer, for that area of the future is closed to my eyes."

"If this is to be our fate, there is no reason to aid you," Jochibi said. "Why trade death in one place for death in another?"

"Because you are capable warriors. Therefore, what you see in Rashemen is not certain death," Szass Tam countered. "On the other hand, what you saw in Thay . . ." He let the sentence trail off.

The khahan raised his hand for silence. "I have decided," he said. He allowed a moment to pass, then made his pronouncement. "You will pay us a tribute of ten thousand kegs of wine. For that price, we will invade this Rashemen and leave Thay to do as it will."

"It is an insult to ask tribute," the zulkir responded. Yet, for a man who had just been insulted, he seemed surprisingly calm. "You have not conquered us."

"I conquer everything I see," the khahan responded, fixing his gaze on the zulkir. "Besides, as you yourself have admitted, even if I fail, Thay will be greatly weakened. Perhaps Rashemen will conquer you, not the other way around."

The zulkir's eyes narrowed, and he regarded the khahan with hateful respect. "I proposed an alliance, not surrender terms."

The khahan shrugged, then glanced at Batu. "As my general has said, every soldier falls on the same battlefield. I see no reason ours should not be in Thay."

"A glorious choice," Batu said, allowing a grin of anticipation to creep across his lips. "The best fighting is here."

Szass Tam scowled at Batu's eagerness, then addressed the khahan, "I will not give you so much as a flask of wine in tribute, now or ever."

The khahan frowned. "Then we will let fate decide," he proclaimed.

"Wait," the zulkir responded, raising his hand as if to stop the khahan. "Here is what I *will* do." He motioned at the wizards behind him. "I will send these four mages with you as guides."

For the first time since they had appeared, the wizards showed some emotion. The woman opened her eyes, and the jaws of the three men dropped in astonishment. The zulkir's image immediately grew translucent and began to waver.

"Look!" Jochibi said, pointing at the illusion in the plain below.

Like the zulkir himself, the illusion had grown translucent and fuzzy. Yet, it remained clear enough to see that the four wizards were standing on the shore of the lake, and that they had somehow parted its waters. The khahan's army had mounted and was rushing through the watery canyon toward the other side of the lake, leaving Rashemen's haggard warriors behind them.

Batu turned back to the khahan. "I'd suggest we take the wizards," he said. "To me, it looks like they're worth much more than ten thousand kegs of wine."

"A wise recommendation," the zulkir commented, speaking to Yamun Khahan. "Do we have a bargain?"

"We do," Yamun replied, nodding grimly. He turned to the Shou, then pointed at Chanar. "Batu, send your quiver-bearer to your troops. They are to return to my camp."

Chanar started to object, but a sharp look from the kha-han silenced him. His face red with fury, he turned to obey Yamun's order without allowing Batu the pleasure of repeating it.

As Chanar descended the hill, the zulkir addressed Yamun again. "Before you leave, Khahan, there is the matter of compensation for the wizards I am sending with you."

"What compensation?" the khahan growled.

"I am loaning you my assistants," Szass said. "It is only fair that you give me someone of equal value." The zulkir shifted his glance to Batu. "Perhaps I could have the services of the Shou general?"

The khahan scowled. Before he could object, however, Batu said, "I'm not interested, Zulkir."

"Are you sure, General?" Szass asked. "Think of what you could accomplish with fifty thousand gnolls and a circle of fifty wizards."

"All the gnolls and wizards in Thay would not equal one hundred of the khahan's warriors in fighting spirit," Batu replied, looking toward Yamun. "No matter what you offer, I ride with the Tuigan."

FORGOTTEN REALMS
FANTASY ADVENTURE

EMPIRES TRILOGY

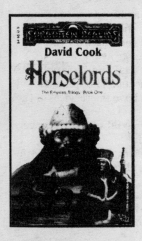

Horselords
David Cook

Between the western Realms and Kara-Tur lies a vast, unexplored domain. The "civilized" people of the Realms have given little notice to these nomadic barbarians. Now, a mighty leader has united these wild horsemen into an army powerful enough to challenge the world. First, they turn to Kara-Tur. Available now.

Crusade
James Lowder

The barbarian army has turned its sights on the western Realms. Only King Azoun has the strength to forge an army to challenge the horsemen. But Azoun had not reckoned that the price of saving the west might be the life of his beloved daughter. Available in January 1991.